I0645270

Down to the Soul

A Novel

Leslie Hayertz

Oregon, United States
SassyCrow Books @ Gmail.com
www.SassyCrow.com

A publication of Sassy Crow Books

Cover photo:
Dos niños saludan brazo en alto
ante un cartel de Franco en septiembre de 1939
Agencia EFE

ISBN: 978-0-999-7718-2-2

For Brian and Meg

Pueblo pequeño, infierno grande.

(Small town, big hell.)

Spanish proverb

Extremadura, Spain

A sudden wind rose from the land, as if in the late-afternoon heat the ancient plain had stretched its jaws in a yawn. Its breath coursed through the nearly deserted village, scouring the town with its own dust. Black dresses and black stockings flapped on clotheslines and, at the village's heart, the empty plaza hunkered down around a graceless fountain—bone-dry and bullet-pocked.

All at once the wind fell to earth. Dark clouds pressed together overhead and strained the slant of sunlight to a tallowy gold. The first drop of rain fell from the sky. It left a dark wound on the stone. A second followed. A third. Bruises all.

The clouds blackened and a deep rumbling rolled over the village. The rain poured then, roaring down, soaking even the narrow lines of dirt between the worn paving stones. Lightning ripped across the darkened sky. Its white light illuminated the plaza and the rivulets of pink running between the stones.

A woman in black stepped out of her doorway.

Others sat alone in dark rooms, gritting their teeth, feeling the thunder rattle their bones, but Reina was the only soul to venture into the storm. She alone staggered into the plaza.

She fell heavily onto her knees. She turned her crumpled face from the scent of wet stone and looked up to the wet heavens, breathed in the scent of electrically charged air.

She let the rain splatter against her upturned palms before she slid them across the slick stone, touched the blood the rain had raised from the dust in the cracks between the stones. Reina lifted her fingers to her face, fingers wet with rain and wet with traces of Justino's blood. The moment they touched her face, she began to sob.

Behind shuttered windows, people stared at their hands and tried not to hear. But not Rosario. She merely raised an eyebrow and shook her head.

In the plaza the rain drenched Reina's clothes and skin; it dripped from her hair, from the tip of her nose. The stone bit at her knees, tore through her black cotton stockings.

Would the day ever come when the plaza was washed clean?

Reina covered her face, but the torrent of rain carried away her tears, along with the relic of Justino's blood.

1

My mum was ailing, and my sister and brothers decided I would be the one to go home to take care of her. So, after 25 years away, I dragged myself back here to Fuentespina.

Ay, Fuentespina.

I found both of them, Mum and the village, shriveled to almost nothing. Hard to say which shocked more: my mum's hunched, boney frame and sunken, milky eyes; or the boarded-up stores, the eerie quiet in the streets and the chains looped through the church doors. Mum's spirit was still strong—feisty as ever. But Fuentespina? It was a pond that was drying up and too stubborn to see it—the fish singing the glories of mud while lying flat on the bottom to keep their gills covered.

> [Narda's got it wrong. Of course the village was in
> dire straits, but one has one's pride and if one drops
> all pretenses, goes about stooped in ragged clothes,
> there's no hope of coming back.]

I myself had leapt from the pond before it scummed over, pushed by my mum, I might add, when I was all of seventeen. I hadn't want to go, but took heart that I'd be back home in a year or two—surely it wouldn't take any longer than that to earn my fortune, after all, I was young and strong with all of four or five years of schooling under my belt. When I did come back, that was in '89—still no fortune and 43 years old—I certainly hadn't planned to stay in the village for good. I think I figured Mum would get better, because, mind you, I never wanted her to pass, not for a single moment. After all those years apart, the time we had together was a gift. But still, I kept telling myself I'd be back in England within a year, maybe two. Now, it's ten years later, Mum's gone, and here I am. That's the kind of boomerang fate beans you with when it thinks you're not looking.

Ay, Fuentespina, when did I stop thinking about leaving?

Here, like many a town, the plaza is the heart of the village. But ours is cramped and looks like a kid's connect-the-dots drawing. You're not going to find it on any postcard —its stones are worn and the fountain, never a beauty, has seen not only better days, but better centuries. Standing by the fountain, if you look west, you have the church on the shortest side of the plaza. Face north, and there's the big house taking up the whole length of the longest side—hard to miss. It's the only two-story building in town, and only the church is older. Between the two of them, we humans— with our comings and goings—are like gnats.

[Who needs a square plaza? So our stones are worn, and the fountain a bit homely. Beauty is skin deep. We have something finer, more noble: history, continuity, tradition. Why, the church of Nuestra Señora de Soledad was sanctified in the thirteenth century. More than 700 years of feet wearing down those stones in the plaza, more than 700 years of knees kneeling in the church in prayer.]

Like everything else in Fuentespina, the big house on the plaza, abandoned for decades, looked pretty forlorn.

Until the Fernán-Iñíquez family came back.

People blame Esmi for what happened later, but the real source of the trouble came that day eight years before when a convoy of work vans drew up to the plaza. That alone was nothing less than earth-shaking, and it quickly became part of village lore how a man armed with a clipboard hopped out in front of the big house and fiddled a key in the door.

"Do you remember, Narda" someone would say, "how, as if on cue, all the doors to the vans swung open and out swarmed those crews of workers?"

"And all of them wearing name tags," *Señora* Rosario might add.

That struck everyone as odd, since around here we know everybody and their dog's family tree back at least a hundred years.

"What must it be like," *Señora* Rosario scoffed, "to live in a place where you have to label yourself?"

Or for that matter, I thought, where you got to label yourself.

Everyone watched from the fringes of the plaza—everyone being a handful of old folks, mostly old women like my mum, clad in black. The removal van arrived and tried to pull into the plaza. That driver couldn't have got the lorry stuck any tighter if he'd been trying. Under the villagers' dour stares, his helper signaled and shouted and banged on the loading door until the driver—inching back and forth—worked himself and the van free.

All in all, no one had seen so much activity in years:

people actually bustling about. *Señora* Rosario appointed herself chief inquisitor and marched on the big house. In a breath we all knew the news. Our hitherto absentee lord of the manor was about to be very much present and accounted for: *Don* Manuel Felipe Fernán-Iñíquez de Muñoz y Sarmiento, in the flesh.

Some forty or fifty years had passed since anyone had seen the former occupant of the big house, *Don* Cayetano— grandfather to the current *Don* Manuel Felipe. It's hard to put a date to it because he'd been like an unfaithful husband who started spending more and more time with a mistress in the city; but who, now and again, just when you got used to him being gone, popped up: leaving his underwear on the floor and the toilet seat up, as well as demanding his dinner on the table and his conjugal rights afterward. That went on for years until one day the people of Fuentespina looked about and it dawned on them that they'd been properly and completely deserted.

[It was unsettling that *Don* Cayetano and his descendants turned their backs on us. The village languished in the family's absence and neglect.]

Not that we basked in milk and honey before.

I remember the old *don,* but just barely, and maybe mostly from stories, because to scare us into behaving ourselves, the grown-ups, in time-honored fashion, would terrorize us kids with all manner of monsters, demons and ghosts. The bogeyman *El Coco* was common currency, as was the wolf *Tío Juan.* But at our house—and ours wasn't the only one—the scariest threat was: *Don* Cayetano will get you if you don't watch out—if you don't go to sleep, if you skip catechism, if you take an orange from the neighbor's tree, if you don't do your chores... *Don* Cayetano would be lying in wait. *Don* Cayetano would sort you out but good.

My mates Mateo and Lolo swore that if you got close to the old man, you could smell the sulfur on him. I never got near enough—I was too scared—but I believed it. I still do.

The thing is, the grownups feared him even more than we did. When *Don* Cayetano paid starvation wages, and most of the time he did; then you went hungry, and so did your kids. If you spoke out, he might blacklist you, and since he owned Fuentespina, you had no choice but to leave the village—the only home you'd ever known. Or he could have you beat up—usually by his henchmen, but he had the Guardia Civil at his beck and call as well. Or he might send you to jail, which he did to more than a few townspeople, men and women both. And with the prisons rife with TB, typhoid and malnutrition; with mistreatment and forced labor; often as not, it proved to be a death sentence.

So *Don* Cayetano—may he rot in hell—was far scarier than any of the devils passed down by our great-, great-great-, and great-great-great-grandparents. I bet that to this day the children of Fuentespina—that is, if there were still any children living here—would wake up screaming from nightmares about old child-eating, sulfur-smelling *Don* Cayetano. Because if the hard-scrabble land around here is good for growing anything, it's long memories.

[Generations-long. Centuries-long.]

And now his grandson *Don* Manuel Felipe was on the scene.

[It was gratifying to have the family back. It brought back our pride. They were our hope for things to return to how they should be.]

"They must be here to stay," people said, all excited.
"After all, hasn't he brought his new wife with him?"
"Yes, *Doña* Pilar."
"And his son from his first marriage, don't forget that."
They convinced themselves that—presto change-o—the family would conjure up a future for the village.
Mum and me, we had reason to look a gift *don* in the mouth. Even so, I have to admit that for a time there, I got a tad bit hopeful too.

[Indeed, it lifted one's spirits to see the big house cared for again—the shutters freshly painted blue, the wrought iron of the balconies shining black and the brass door-knocker gleaming.]

And the Land Rover was there, adorning the plaza, tricking us into thinking we'd entered the twentieth century, and—good as a miracle—a grocery-mobile took to pulling up once every fifteen days by the fountain to do business for an hour or so.

Don Manuel Felipe and *Doña* Pilar took on a full staff

for the house, mostly from outside the village, but I hired on as cook—the wages were a godsend for Mum and me. And old Anselmo helped oversee the farm work for a time and brought his great-niece Chela from Badajoz to do the laundry.

As *dons* go, *Don* Manuel Felipe turned out to be a good sort. I got used to him coming into the kitchen and talking to me while I worked. He was tall and lanky, and he'd lean against the doorway drinking a cup of coffee that I'd top off with acorn liqueur. Or he'd sit at the table eating a thick slice of almond-carrot cake or a *buñuelo* and hot chocolate—he had a tremendous sweet tooth—and he'd tell me about the ancient history of the region and the early history of Fuentespina and of his family, and he'd explain about the architecture of the house and the antiques inside. It was a real education for me. I soaked it up like a brandy-drenched cake.

Of course I could have taught him a thing or two, too, but when he asked about the village, especially about his grandfather's time, I'd just shrug—a shrug to imply, what did I know? Hadn't I worked abroad until just a year or so before the family's return to Fuentespina?

As for his son, *Señorito* Roberto, when they arrived he was like any other little kid, maybe clingier than some, but in the end Fuentespina didn't suit him. He grew to be a cold fish of a boy— slow to meet one's gaze and given to clearing his throat. And sickly. I could only squeeze out a drop or two of patience for him by keeping in mind he was the *señor's* son.

Don Manuel Felipe had come to town keen to step into

his ready-made role as gentleman farmer. He assumed it was in his blood, but Fuentespina didn't suit him either. *Doña* Pilar, on the other hand, took to overseeing the estates like a sheep to pasture. She loved the land. I swear, like a lover she loved it. She was always out checking on the farms or handling business in Badajoz. But as far as I could see, she didn't give a pig's knuckle for the house, or the town either.

I suppose she was attractive in her way, polished looking, what with that pale, smooth skin, ash-blond hair and grey eyes. But then there were those cheek bones of hers, weren't there, like two little balled-up fists under the skin and those sharp little square teeth like a porcelain doll's. There's no accounting for taste—*Don* Manuel Felipe adored her. Downright enthralled, he was. That's why it was all the more surprising when one day the *señor* up and left. Just like that. I hadn't an inkling, and that was strange. As was his leaving the boy behind, but then men of that age...

[They say he's living in the south of France with his mistress. They say she's Danish and half his age. At least we have *Doña* Pilar taking care of business.]

To my surprise I missed the *señor* when he left.

Old Anselmo, one of the few people who remained steadfastly unimpressed by the Ice Queen, liked to speculate about where she'd buried the body, which gave me the shivers. I told him he didn't know what he was talking about. Didn't *Señorito* Roberto get a present delivered every year on the Day of the Magi Kings?

"And is there a letter, a card?"

"No, but who could it be from if not his father?"

After the *señor* left, everything went downhill. Before long his valet/butler followed. The governess was the next to jump ship. Then, one by one, *Doña* Pilar got rid of most of the others. Finally, Chela's little girl got very sick and she moved back to Badajoz, where there were doctors and clinics. That left me alone in the house with the boy, the Ice Queen and all the work.

My mum passed, and I moved into a servant's room off the kitchen in the big house. Each day became much like the next—flat as the horizon around here.

And then Esmi came to town.

2

April 1999

See that dirt track on the far side of the church? Follow it and after about three miles of dust and scrub you'll come to the highway. Of course, once you get to the highway, you're still nowhere, as Esmi was about to discover.

[We never liked the looks of that girl. You could tell
she was trouble.]

And that's where the driver eased the bus to the side of the road, the machine making the usual groans and hisses.

"*Señorita*, this is it," the driver called to her. He pointed off to the distance where the sun was dragging itself toward the horizon.

Esmi ached all over. Her eyelids felt heavy and gritty—the poor thing hadn't slept the night before. She'd taken a taxi to Madrid's Atocha Train Station before dawn, bought a ticket and darted for the restroom where she cowered in a stall, shaking like a leaf, until her train was due to leave. Then she'd spent all day traveling—two trains to get to that last town and its bus station, only to have the ticket agent tell her, "We don't go to Fuentespina."

Esmi, her hand on the silky red scarf knotted around her throat, had asked what bus company did.

The man shook his head. "Nobody goes there. Haven't for years."

It felt as if the tile floor were going soft beneath her feet —she'd convinced herself that all she had to do was get to Fuentespina, that once she was with her grandparents, she'd be safe.

"But I've got to get there." Her voice rasped and she winced behind her dark sunglasses. Then she pursed her small, full-lipped mouth and, finding her footing, she lied. "There's been a death."

The man sighed. "Look, talk to Charonte. That's the driver. He can let you off on the highway. He'll know where. After that, *señorita*, you're on your own."

So she'd bought a ticket to a town well past where she needed to go. At the door to the bus she'd handed it to the driver and asked him to let her off for Fuentespina. Charonte grumbled about unscheduled stops and regulations, but he jerked his head toward the bus for her to get on.

It wasn't until she'd sunk into the seat that it occurred to her that her grandfather might actually be dead, or her grandmother, or both. A lot can happen in thirteen years. A lot can end.

Now the door hissed open, and the driver called to her again, "*señorita*, Fuentespina."

Esmi roused herself. She'd been hit with a proper case of the collywobbles—getting off the bus would start the last leg of her journey. She saw the driver watch her in his rearview mirror as she hauled her suitcase down from the rack—one of those old ones covered in tweed cloth, practically an antique, with brass latches instead of zippers. It didn't fit with her city clothes: tight designer jeans, white camisole top, and what looked like a man's dark sport coat with the sleeves pushed up. The driver drummed his fingers on the wheel.

"I don't have all day," he said and muttered an obscenity.

Normally, as a matter of course and a point of honor, she would have flicked him a rude gesture impugning his wife's fidelity, but she didn't have it in her today. Her legs were all quivery, and she lowered herself from the bottom step to the uneven edge of the road as if she were wearing high heels instead of white trainers.

The driver scowled and yanked on the lever to close the doors.

The bus pulled away, raising a cloud of dust and exposing a dark, days-old spot of roadkill—grey fur and smashed innards. Esmi knit her broad eyebrows and turned her back, diesel fumes tingling in her nose, until the dust settled.

Esmi looked about her—the land stretched out flat in every direction. A tumbleweed skittered across the highway. On the other side of the road, a stork peered down at her from the top of a telephone pole, its nest looking like nothing more than a big jumble of twigs. The wind came sweeping across the plain again, whistling, nudging the tumbleweed further along, ruffling the bird's feathers, and whipping her thick dark hair about.

Esmi captured her hair, twisted it and clipped it in place. She set her sunglasses on top of her head and set out down the dirt road.

3

Meanwhile, back in Fuentespina, I heard the high heels of *Doña* Pilar's boots clacking and echoing on the floor tiles as she crossed the entry hall. She made a lot of racket for such a small woman—small and trim, she was.

That tap-tapping was the sound I'd been waiting for, and dreading; and I hustled from the kitchen—my worn-out flats slapping the floor—to catch her before she disappeared out the door.

She stopped just outside—the last rays of afternoon light, butter yellow, reflecting off her and shooting back to the eye as cool as moonlight. I pulled up short, huffing, with the stone threshold between us. She had sensitive eyes and she'd stopped, not because I was calling to her, but to adjust those mirrored sunglasses of hers.

Her chin tilted up towards the family coat of arms carved in stone above the door, but behind those glasses she could just as easily be looking down her nose at me, and most likely was.

"What now, Narda?" she said.

We lived in the same house, but I seldom had cause to be so close to her. I thrust my hands into my apron pockets, fingering the ring of house keys there for comfort.

"It's the *señorito*, madam," I said.

She was afloat in that French perfume of hers—very flowery but with something dark, very earthy, even metallic underneath. Esmi once told me that in a perfume that's called "complexity," and apparently for "complexity" you pay an arm and a couple legs. Personally I didn't care for it. It made my nose twitch.

As I said, she was short. Well, I'm short; she was petite. Anyway, we were pretty much eye to eye, except for those sunglasses masking her eyes, and for the fact that I was keeping my own eyes down, respectful-like. She wore her usual boss-lady outfit: silk blouse and tweed skirt suit; and my eyes alighted on the brass chain she always wore—that is, the small length of it not hidden under her jacket.

"Well?" she said.

I glanced up and saw myself cringing there in her mirrored sunglasses, so I stood straight and screwed up my courage.

"The *señorito*'s still not well, *señora*. I can't keep looking after him and get my work done."

Without deigning to utter a word, *Doña* Pilar turned and crossed to the shiny black Land Rover she kept parked in the plaza in front of the big house.

"I'm a housekeeper," I called from the doorway, "not a nurse." I'd decided that housekeeper was a better job title than dogsbody which is what I was.

Doña Pilar drove away without so much as a backward glance.

I clenched my fingers into fists in my pockets, muttering. It's like my mum used to say: With the very rich and the very old, much patience.

The light had dampened, the sun having just pulled below the horizon. I leaned against the door jamb and listened to the rumble of the Land Rover fade to nothing.

"Narda!" *Señorito* Roberto's voice came from upstairs.

I didn't move from the doorway. I liked how dusk made the empty plaza and its ugly old fountain look softer, gentler.

Señora Rosario, a widow dressed in black, moved stiffly along one side of the square, heading for her house. Seeing me in the doorway she came over, arranging her grey, crocheted shawl about her shoulders.

"Good evening, Nardita."

"Narda," *Señorito* Roberto called again, and the hair on the back of my neck rose.

I did not excuse myself to go see to him, and *Señora* Rosario looked at me through the thick glasses on her squarish face. She no doubt expected me to bound up the stairs two steps at a time, because she raised her eyebrows in disapproval.

"The boy keeping you busy?" she said.

"I never signed on to be a nursemaid."

"Of course not."

"Up, down, up, down. All day long."

"Still, the poor thing."

She expected me to agree, to say, 'Yes, poor thing,' but I didn't budge.

"Well, I'd best be going; I need to get dinner on for my brother," she said, as if the Pope himself had decreed it.

"How is *Señor* Valentín?"

"Fine, thank you. Good evening to you," she said, and looked pointedly upstairs before turning to leave.

Señora Rosario ambled towards her house. It faced the plaza, and I waited until she reached her door before I stepped outside. I peered into the deepening darkness. No sign, neither hide nor hair.

"Narda!" the boy called, a shadow of fear in his voice. "Narda, are you there?"

I took one more look before I went inside and closed the door behind me.

4

When *Señora* Rosario reached for the door handle, she noticed Reina, and so slipped into the side street by her house to keep an eye on her. She and Reina couldn't stand each other, and that's tricky in a small town. Neither wanted to turn a corner and run headlong into the other without warning, so they kept tabs on each other. That way they had the added satisfaction of glaring at each other from a distance. You'd never know that back in the Ice Age they were girls together, milk sisters, in fact.

So when I went into the house to check on the boy, *Señora* Rosario and Reina still lurked nearby in the shadows—two thick-waisted, droopy-breasted old ladies in black, each wondering what I thought I was looking for.

Señora Rosario was the thicker of the two and had more to droop. She home-permed her fluffy white hair, and powdered her soft skin, but its age spots showed through all the same. Reina was older and looked it—a wizened little thing with leathery skin, and her grey hair cut in the blunt bob of her youth. Of the two, she was by far the shabbier, as slight and skittish as *Señora* Rosario was big-boned and stolid.

They were dying to ask each other, "Did you see that? What does our Narda think she is looking for anyway? What might she be up to?" But God forbid they speak to each other.

Hanging about at opposite ends of the square, they were the ones who saw Esmi arrive.

Esmi had set off blindly down the dirt road. But then as she got farther from the highway and the sun hung lower and lower in the sky, she felt a hollow growing in her chest. What if the driver had let her off in the wrong place?

Finally the cutout wall of the church *campanario* with its three bells had come into sight, and her heart had leapt—she'd used it as her guidepost in the fading light. Now in the plaza, standing in front of Nuestra Señora de Soledad, she saw only a rather homely church, with patches of brown stone showing through in places where the plaster had slaked off.

I loved the old church, but seen through Esmi's eyes, I have to admit it wasn't much to look at. And it was as good as dead because some Church bigwig had ordered it desanctified. Church officials had come and locked it up tight, taken away the key, and for good measure, threaded a chain through the iron rings on the doors. But the iron cross still survived atop the *campanario,* not because the small delegation headed by *Señora* Rosario had begged that it be left in place, but because no one dared climb up there to remove it.

Esmi, relieved that she'd made it to the village before dark, footslogged over to the fountain to freshen up a bit. She didn't know the fountain was dry.

[In fact the fountain hadn't held water for decades, and one would think *Doña* Pilar would do something about fixing it. It would only be proper, since "fountain" is part of our name: Fuentespina.

Fuentespina de Vico when one wants to be formal. Father Ezequiel, the priest here when Narda was but a girl, used to protest that the shortened version should not be used, but the more beautiful and reverential original: *Fuente de la Sagrada Corona de Espinas de Nuestro Santísimo Señor de Vico*—Fountain of the Sacred Crown of Thorns of Our Most Holy Lord, Jurisdiction of the Marquis of Vico.]

Okay, so that's the village's official name, but who has time to stand around all day saying it. I bet before the herald who read the proclamation in 1236 had rolled up the parchment, we'd already shortened it to Fuentespina: Thorn Fountain.

Esmi sat on the rim of the fountain and lit a cigarette. The sky still held some light, but most of the plaza was in shadow, as if darkness grew upward. From where Reina and *Señora* Rosario were standing, I doubt they could see how her hand trembled.

Esmi blew the smoke skyward and let her eyes rest there. In Madrid, the sky is just an empty lot where the city dumps its used-up light, but out here the sky is pure and full of itself—it's a diva, the main attraction, even before she puts on her stars.

Esmi pulled deep breaths from the cigarette while she let her gaze wander about the empty plaza and absentmindedly ran her hand over the crack that snaked across the fountain's bowl.

Except for the freshness of her youth, Esmi didn't look

as out of place as she felt. She may have scorned provinciality, but she had the classic Spanish features of one of those mantilla-wearing *señoritas* on an old bullfight poster: dark hair, pale skin, almond eyes and a nose you could believe in—long, straight and not too narrow.

When she finished the cigarette, she stubbed it out in the dirt in the fountain and placed the butt in the pack of cigarettes. With no place to change into her skirt, she slapped the dust off the legs of her jeans and put on a pair of blue stiletto heels from her suitcase. Her stomach was full of warring butterflies, some anticipating her heart's desire, some flapping with foreboding. She put her hair clip in her jacket pocket, ran her fingers through her hair to fluff it out and put on fresh lipstick. Then she stood and smoothed her camisole and shrugged and tugged her jacket straight. She was as ready as she was ever going to be, and she headed out of the square.

Reina watched from the darkness, her very round, pale blue eyes widening as Esmi passed near her. There was something familiar in the girl's face, something beloved, and a little gasp hiccoughed from her body. The little sound coming from the murky shadows startled Esmi, and she hurried from the plaza.

The moment she'd gone, a man came walking along the front of the church—and not one of the old geezers in town either, but a young man, in city clothes. And if that weren't astonishing enough, *Señora* Rosario saw him continue on to the big house and slip inside.

Clutching her shawl tight, her chin set, *Señora* Rosario stepped from shadows on the other side of the plaza. Two strangers! Her head twitched, undecided as to which direction to stare. The girl was of whopping big interest, but that would sort itself out soon enough—something to look forward to finding out about the next day. But the other! What, she wondered, was I, Narda, up to? It was no contest; she fixed her unblinking attention on the big house. More precisely, she stared at the thick door and its wrought-iron fittings and willed it to spit out answers. Never taking her eye off the door, she slowly moved toward the center of the square.

On the other side of the plaza, Reina clutched the place where her neck rose from her collar bone. She stared after Esmi, stunned. Keeping her eye on the spot where the girl had disappeared from view, she moved backwards toward the center of the plaza.

Reina and *Señora* Rosario both came to a stop near the fountain, a body's length apart.

"*Dios mío*," *Señora* Rosario whispered to herself. "Did I really see that?" meaning a strange man entering the big house.

Reina nodded, meaning yes, she'd seen Esmi.

Each was so deep in her own thoughts that *Señora* Rosario was unaware of Reina responding to her question and Reina hadn't noticed who'd asked it, hadn't even noticed it was more than a voice in her head. Without seeing each other, like magnets you can't force together, they moved apart, in opposite directions, each toward her own house.

5

Nobody ever tells the whole story. I was a little kid when I figured this out, and it came to me all at once. Some men were loitering outside *Don* Fidencio's bar, the Bocanegra, just off the plaza.

[There were always men hanging about the Bocanegra.]

But on this particular day there were two I remember: *Don* Niceto—*Don* Cayetano's farm manager—and old Anselmo, who was a farmhand then and not at all old.

You can probably tell by looking at me, by my age, that I'm a child of the *Posguerra*, that grim, dressed-in-black time after The Civil War. The war itself ended on March 28, 1939 —at least you can say that for it, it had an end. But not the *Posguerra*. It dragged on year after year, then a decade, and then another, and another, as Franco lived on and on and on.

That day my playmates Mateo and Lolo tried to pull me into the plaza, but I was mesmerized by the cigarette dangling from *Don* Niceto's lower lip. The manager was doing all the talking, tooting his own horn about the good deed he was going to do for the Widow Ugalde. The two men didn't notice me gaping at them, or didn't care—I was that small.

Don Niceto said that he was going to take the widow's pigs to market for her, and he instructed old Anselmo, who was not yet old, to use the farm truck the next morning to fetch the animals.

Up to that moment I'd thought stories were for the telling and that truth was found out in the open. But the next second I knew I'd been wrong, because as I stared at the cigarette bucking on *Don* Niceto's lip, I realized that besides what the manager was saying, I was also hearing the words he wasn't saying—how he'd made her beg and cajole him, and something else I didn't understand then but certainly do now. And I knew he planned to cheat her, tell her the price the pigs sold for was less than it was, and so keep a hefty portion of the sale price for himself.

He pulled the cigarette from his mouth and dropped it on the cobblestones. His eyes met mine, and I saw a sneer on his face that wasn't there.

It was as if some childish veil had slipped from my brain.

I ran to my mum and found her sitting outside the kitchen with a chipped enamel bowl in her lap, paring a handful of undersized potatoes. I leaned against her leg and told her, as best I could, this amazing thing: people hushed up big pieces of a story, they even lied about them.

My mum shrugged her shoulders.

And sometimes, I told her, it wasn't just the pieces but whole stories that got twisted or kept secret.

"Why, Mum? Why?"

"Nardita," she sighed.

I thought she was going to tell me to quit plaguing her with questions, that she had supper to cook, such as it was. But she just picked up a misshapen potato and went back to her careful paring.

"But everybody leaves out big chunks of truth," I insisted. "All the time. Everybody."

I'd been scolded more than once for exaggerating—my aunt used to say that if the way I embroidered the truth were any indication, I was destined to be a great needlewoman, and my dad would agree and say I certainly hadn't gotten my imagination from his side of the family. But as my words hit the air—"all the time, everybody"—I knew they were fact, terrible fact. Yet there Mum sat, unruffled as always. So I struggled to find words to make her see, really see what grown-ups did to the truth, how they splintered it like kindling, locked it in a shed like a cat in heat, wrung its neck like a chicken.

"Enough, *mi amor*," she said. She looked at me with serious brown eyes. "What can I tell you? Maybe it's the way of the world. Maybe it's just us."

She dug an eye out of the potato cupped in her palm. She set the knife in the bowl and pulled my hand from my mouth—I was chewing on a cuticle. She held my fist for a moment and gave it two kisses, like two exclamation points, before picking up the knife again.

"We're not an open-hearted people, Nardita. Not in these times. We put blinders on our eyes, and on our hearts." She glanced at the patio wall and lowered her voice. "We've gotten so used to the censors on our backs that if we happen to glimpse something, because we can't help it, because it's right in front of our eyes; if we feel something, anger, hope, anything other than fear; then with no prompting, we'll take up the scissors ourselves and snip away at whatever we do see, do feel.

"Refusing to see becomes a habit, *m'ija*, a bad habit."

I could see she was speaking the truth. At least the surface of it, but there was a depth to it that she wasn't saying. She must have seen me, my eyes wide, listening hard, and wanted to distract me. "Like biting your nails..." she teased, and flicked a paper-thin peel at me.

I ducked, smiled, but closed my ragged fingernails into my fists.

She leaned over, picked up the peel and placed it back in the bowl. "...But," she said, "much, much worse than nail biting." Her voice, already solemn, became more so, became holy. "Because the blind spots become a blight on our souls."

I knew biting my nails was a nasty habit—I was trying hard to stop—but doing something that made your soul black was very different. That had to be a sin, or something even worse.

My face must have been a picture of horror and confusion.

"*Tranquila*, my love. It's nothing for you to worry about. It's normal."

That's when I started to cry, terrified of pointy scissors and black spots on my mum's soul, and absolutely everyone in the world keeping truths to themselves. Everyone as good as lying. And lying, I knew for a fact, was a sin, and wicked, too.

My mum put down her bent paring knife and put her arms around me. "Don't cry," she cooed. "For others, it's normal. But Nardita, you really do see the whole story, don't you?"

I nodded into her shoulder.

"Then for you it will be different." Her voice was both proud and sad. She held me away from her to look me in the eye and pushed strands of hair from my face with starchy fingers. "No blinders. It's a gift. A rare gift."

"It is?" I sniffled. My heart lifted. Wasn't a gift like a present?

The simple presents that I knew of—a pair of socks knit by one's mum; maybe a toy dog carved by one's grandfather; a sweet, or even two—didn't keep me from dreaming of toy cars of shiny metal with real wheels or dolls in frilly dresses in boxes with bows.

She nodded. "And a heavy one. You must pray to our Holy Mother, Nuestra Señora de la Soledad. Give thanks to her for trusting you with such a gift, and ask her for her help."

I didn't understand. How could I? But it seemed clear enough that there'd be no new plaything.

"Why help?"

"Because there will be times—like today—you'll know a story, a truth, and like a father confessor, you'll have to keep it to yourself. It won't be easy. Anybody can chase the truth out of a field, but to keep it harnessed to the plow, that's much trickier. Trust in Our Lady of Solitude. She'll help you."

And so it turned out. That and something else. You see, I'm not what you would call a friendly person. Warm and fuzzy, that's not me, and yet everybody talks to me, all kinds of people. Even if I don't want them to, and mostly I don't. But they talk anyway. They talk and I listen. I listen between the lines and fill in the blanks—it's second nature to me.

And I keep my mouth shut.

Even so, some call me a mindreader. Others claim I'm a witch. The latter are the few who don't come chatting at my door. Fine with me. I have work to do.

I'm no witch, and I'm no saint. And certainly no hero. Those blinders Mum warned me about, I've donned them myself now and then. Especially of late. Too much of late. Maybe it's been out of sheer tiredness or plain laziness. Maybe for reasons beyond my control. I'll never know for sure, only that, even as I grasped the truth of other people's lives, I refused to see the truth of my own, refused, and it blighted my soul.

May Nuestra Señora de la Soledad help me.

6

Another night was settling upon Fuentespina, and we all crawled into our respective hidey-holes and locked the doors, just as we'd been taught to do.

Except for Esmi.

She teetered down unnamed streets. As she wound her way out from the center of town, cobble gave way to dirt, and she wandered more slowly, more and more uncertain. She turned a corner and found yet another narrow street worming the length of another seamless wall of houses.

Then her breath caught.

There at the tail end of the street, like a familiar face in a crowd, she recognized her grandparents' house. It was, so to speak, precisely where she'd left it. She enjoyed one brief flash of relief, then had to fight back the urge to flee. Why not leave sleeping memories lie, she wondered.

You have to admit, it's a good question.

But the dark was deepening, and she knew she had nowhere else to go and no one else to turn to. So she pressed on toward the blank face of the house—one door, no windows.

The last time she'd been here, the house had presented an even, gleaming facade of freshly whitewashed walls—her grandmother had no use for people who didn't keep up the outside of their houses, and it went without saying that the inside should be spotless. But now, even in the dim light, Esmi could see the walls were mottled and discolored.

Her heart contracted. What if the house was empty? All she wanted was to feel her grandfather lightly pat the crown of her head with his cupped hand. And her grandmother, she longed to walk into her embrace and melt away. Holding tight to that thought, she slid on her sun glasses and knocked on the door.

Nothing happened.

Esmi was strung tighter than high C. So many uncertainties in the last 24 hours, and the grandaddy of them all, the ultimate cliff-hanger had been: would she live or die? Okay, she'd survived; she was still breathing, but she didn't seem to be breathing the same air as before. Everything had changed. Why else would she have run here, to Fuentespina?

She knocked again, louder.

It wasn't that Lourdes, puttering in the kitchen, hadn't heard the door, but years and years had gone by without a soul to come knocking. Why now? And at this time of night? A knock on the door after dark could never bode well—it could only be bad luck or bad news.

Maybe she should go get Adelfo. He sat in the patio in the back of the house, listening to the radio.

Now, the old bastard was the last person I would call in for reinforcements, but—*Bendita sea la Virgen!*—I wasn't married to him.

While she dithered, the second knocking came.

It's a simple knock on the door, she told herself. And she didn't want to disturb Adelfo. So she took her courage in both hands, well, in one hand because she needed the other to lift to her lips the wooden cross hanging around her neck.

The house was old and old-fashioned, with a tunnel-like corridor that ran the length of the house and separated its rooms left from right. Lourdes waded through long-held fears going down that hallway to get to the door. She opened it just a crack, squinting as she looked out.

What Lourdes saw confused her: a stranger to be sure, a young woman in her mid twenties, dressed in impossibly tight jeans, tarty shoes and, of all things, a poppy-red scarf. She wore her thick, dark hair in a frizzy, untidy style, and even though dusk was on its last gasps, the girl hid her eyes behind sunglasses.

Lourdes frowned. "What do you want?"

The frown on Lourdes face just about broke Esmi's heart. Nothing came out of her mouth. What did she want?

Lourdes, in her late sixties and at least ten years younger than Adelfo, had a gentle face under the scowl. Her smooth, fair skin was powdered, and she'd tucked her dove-grey hair —that Esmi remembered more as auburn—into a French roll. She wore a grey wool skirt she'd sewn herself; a white blouse buttoned to the neck with a bit of lace on the collar; a powder-blue cardigan with a crocheted shawl on top of it; and comfortable, brown leather shoes with low heels that her son, Ramón, had sent her from England. The scent of lilac was English as well.

I'd gotten to know Lourdes pretty well since I'd come back to town, in spite of Adelfo, who despised my mum and so had little use for me. Lourdes delivered eggs to the big house a couple times a week, and her son was married to my cousin; so if we had any news, we liked to share it. She also helped me with my hair. I liked to wear it short, so every few weeks, after she cut her husband's hair, she would show up at the kitchen door of the big house, snap her scissors in front of her face and say, "Snip, snip. It's time, Narda."

She was not, deep down, an unkind person.

Esmi and Lourdes peered at each other through the slit in the door. Esmi found herself staring at the familiar three-inch-long cross hanging around Lourdes' neck; Lourdes' eyes kept going to that bright-red scarf.

"Grandma?" Esmi finally croaked.

Lourdes gaped at her.

Esmi ducked her head and took a step back.

The stranger's identity started clicking into place. Why, was this unfortunately dressed young woman really her granddaughter, the one she'd last seen as a gawky thirteen-year-old?

"Esmeralda?" she ventured.

Esmi looked up. Lourdes couldn't see the girl's eyes, but everything else—the mouth, the chin, the nose—were her mother's. The coloring was different; but there was the way the girl stood, the yearning in the tilt of her face. Each detail, like a tumbler in a lock, fell into its precise and well-oiled slot in Lourdes' memory.

"Rosa Esmeralda!" she exclaimed and threw open the door.

Esmi took a tentative step forward to give her grandmother a peck on the cheek, but Lourdes pulled the girl inside and hugged her. She took Esmi's face between her hands and stared at her searchingly.

Esmi pulled away. She wiped tears that had escaped from behind her dark glasses and set down the suitcase she'd been holding the whole time. Lourdes looked at it and put a hand over her mouth. She crossed herself.

"Your mother's suitcase."

Esmi had called the porter at her block of flats the night before and asked her to pack a few things for her and send the bag over in a taxi. The woman had never bothered to hide her disapproval of Esmi and her goings on, but Esmi had no one else to call. The *portera* had overlooked her luggage and somehow—probably snooping—had found the old suitcase in the back of Esmi's bedroom closet. The case was small by modern standards, and heavy; it smelled musty inside, and had rust spots on the latches—Esmi only kept it because it had been her mother's.

Of course, it didn't really belong to her mother, but Esmi didn't know that. Teenagers back then, we didn't have our own suitcases. Not in Fuentespina. When I first left home to work in Badajoz, I took my things in a shopping bag. But the suitcase resting on the floor between grandmother and granddaughter was the one Teresa took when she ran away from home. Stole it, really, but I'm sure Teresa felt entitled. That's the way she was. And when she came back to visit, carrying her and Esmi's clothes in that bag, it was yet one more thing for her and Lourdes to bicker about. Adelfo didn't say much, which turned out to be worse.

"May she rest in peace," Lourdes said.

Esmi nodded vaguely.

Poor Lourdes. During Esmi and Teresa's last visit, there had been that big, final row. Esmi had been out of the house with Lourdes at the time, and good thing. Teresa held the old *hijo de puta* off with his own rifle, the old Mauser that stood next to the shotgun in the corner of the kitchen. Not surprising that they never made it up. Lourdes longed to, but old Adelfo wouldn't have it. Then Teresa died, killed in that bus accident.

Lourdes always figured Esmi never came back because Teresa had poisoned her against them, but the night Esmi and I holed up together (I'll tell you more about that later), she told me she hadn't stayed away on purpose, she'd just been busy, first studying, getting her degree at the Polytechnic, and then working—at first not feeling she could spare the money to make the trip, and then later, the time. Nor did she want to revisit her grief for her mother, make it all raw again by sharing it with her grandparents—they had not gone to Madrid for the funeral.

Esmi never knew why she and her mother had left Fuentespina in such a hurry. Apparently, whenever Esmi mentioned her grandparents, Teresa changed the subject. When she asked about going back for a visit, Teresa found excuses. You've got to hand it to her—it takes a lot of self-control to keep that kind of hurt and anger to yourself, to not poison your kid with it. Personally, I would have spoon-fed it to her.

[Before you think too highly of her, may she rest in peace, keep in mind that there are also selfish reasons to keep secrets, like wounded pride and shame.]

"I'm sorry to barge in like this," Esmi said.

"Barge in?" said Lourdes. "What nonsense!"

"I would have called, but I guess your number's unlisted."

"Unlisted? We don't have phones here." Lourdes flicked her hand in dismissal. "Anyway? Who would I talk to?"

"Me?" Esmi said in a forlorn little voice, but Lourdes didn't seem to hear.

"Take off those silly glasses so I can look at you properly," she said.

Esmi took off the glasses and stared at the floor. Lourdes bent her head and peeked up at her. The girl's eyes were bloodshot in an odd way, little pin pricks of red. Did that mean drugs? Was her granddaughter a drug addict? The only time she'd seen anything similar was when her little sister had whooping cough.

"Are you all right?" Lourdes asked. "Tell me the truth."

Esmi nodded and gave her a weak smile.

"Your grandfather will be so happy to see you," Lourdes said. "He's out back in the patio. Go. Surprise him."

Lourdes, bless her heart, really thought old Adelfo was going to be as happy as she was about Esmi's return.

Esmi remembered a grandfather who'd seemed formidable, but had nonetheless touched her hair and told her how beautiful she was and given her coins for sweets. I have a hard time picturing that, but according to *Señora* Rosario, the old fart could be charming when he chose to be. Personally, I've never seen it. Nor, I suspect, had his daughter.

"Wait," Lourdes said to Esmi. "First, why don't we take off that scarf?"

She reached for it, but Esmi pulled away, shaking her head.

Lourdes was about to insist, but Esmi would not meet her eyes. So, she swallowed the impulse. She was not going to drive the girl away by being overly critical as she knew she had been with Teresa. Besides, there was plenty more in the girl's appearance for Adelfo to take exception to. She shrugged and hoped for the best, that he would understand that times had changed and that the girl was subject to city fashions.

All smiles, Lourdes ushered Esmi to the back of the house and then stood behind her as Esmi peeked out the kitchen door.

It was just as Esmi remembered it. An adobe wall closed in the large patio with its packed dirt floor. The outhouse squatted in the far corner. The chicken coop, along with the combined tool and goat shed, hunched against the back wall. Closer to the house was the clothesline and the small garden plot. A wrought-iron window box by the kitchen door held two pots of red geraniums. Adelfo sat in a straight-backed chair, his back to the house, listening to a *zarzuela*—one of those old light operas with the corny plots—on a scratchy transistor radio.

He was tall, slender and for an old man, strong, with a vitality that ran deep—the air seemed to almost crackle with it. Everybody in town knew how many years he'd racked up—78—because at age 15 in 1936 he'd run off to join the army—it was part of village legend. He wore a white, collarless, button-down shirt; a black jacket; faded black trousers and a black beret. If you only saw him from his right side, you'd remark on his strong, handsome face, and that's the side he tried to keep toward you.

It was on that side that Esmi approached him. "Grandfather?" she said, but he didn't hear her because she spoke softly. He was also hard of hearing and he had the radio turned up. "Grandfather?" she repeated and touched his shoulder.

He turned to look at her then, and the sight of his face sent a shiver through her as it always had. He'd been wounded in the war and the left side of his face was heavily scarred from shrapnel, leaving him blind in that eye and missing part of his ear.

"What?" he said, startled. His gaze flew to the red scarf and the corners of his mouth pulled down.

Lourdes hurried over to them and put her arm around Esmi. "Look, *viejo*. We have a visitor. Turn off the radio."

He did so, his fingers long and pearly. Then he stood, straight in spite of his years.

"It's our little Rosa Esmeralda, all grown up," Lourdes said, beaming.

He turned his scarred face aside, moving his upper body to do so because his neck didn't have the mobility it should. He was well thought of in some circles and could easily have been mayor, back when the town still bothered with such things, but because of his face, he'd always refused and kept to himself.

He looked her up and down. A corner of his mouth raised half-heartedly. "Well, I'll be," he said finally. "Rosa

Esmeralda! You're a sight for tired old eyes. One tired old eye," he corrected.

The vanity that kept him closeted in his patio day after day, also required him to act as if it didn't matter in the least that half his face had been mutilated, left flat and rigid, shiny where it was not pitted with divots and crisscrossed with white, contracted scars.

Esmi kissed his good cheek.

"On second look," he said, "you must be an impostor. I demand you bring back that snot-nosed, skinny-legged kid I remember."

"Grandfather!"

"Seriously, child. You look a vision, a Moorish beauty, a captive princess from a storybook."

"And you are just as handsome as ever," Esmi said.

"From a certain angle, from a certain angle."

She didn't see how his eye narrowed when she looked away.

Caverns

Mists caressed the rolling hills, hushing the fields where, heads bowed, sheep drifted from one mouthful of grass to the next. And where, late in the afternoon, a little blue sports car came zooming up and down the green slopes, winding its way towards its destination.

Several years earlier the two teenage boys in the car had discovered the cave, and deep inside, a few primitive scratchings. They called the drawings "their find," and the cave "their cave." The prehistoric paintings at Altamira, not that far away, dated back at least 25,000 years. The boys told each other that because their drawings were simpler, they must be even older—maybe they would turn out to be the oldest in Spain, the oldest anywhere. They'd be famous, if they ever revealed their secret—which they wouldn't.

They parked in a field under an oak and tromped through the grass. The legs of their jeans became sodden. The fog filtered the twilight to a mustard yellow.

Iban's stepmother came forward from the cave to greet them, and Iban, uneasy, hung back to watch his friend's reaction. Manu had every right to be angry—they'd sworn never to tell a soul the location of the cave—but instead Manu could not hide his excitement, and to Iban that seemed a greater betrayal than his own.

She smiled and put her arm around Manu's shoulders in a way that might be motherly and said something close to his *ear. Manu looked back over his shoulder at Iban and grinned. Iban's fingers twitched and folded into fists.*

"I brought some refreshment," she said, and she led them into their own cave, where she'd placed a blanket, a hamper and a single candle. Manu, for all his lecherous remarks when he and Iban were alone, followed her with an expression of puppy-like devotion.

The older woman made sure she caught Iban's eye before she reached out and smoothed Manu's hair away from his forehead. She held Iban's gaze, a smirk on her lips—her lips, the ones that at night did not touch him when she came to his room, whispering unspeakable things in his ear: insults, promises, exhortations, her lips so close he swore he could feel them.

Now she laid her palm on Manu's cheek. A few months earlier, when Iban was still himself, he would have mused on the turn of phrase, "it made his blood boil," but as it was, he seethed, and hurt, and his blood roiled in his veins without reflection.

She had robbed the boy of his rationality, step by step, night by night; and finally this evening she would destroy the last of his scruples. Already he stood by, muscles tensed, watching her and Manu's every movement, bereft of all but clarified animal instinct—not the instinct for survival because nothing beyond this moment held any meaning for him. Iban was lust: undiluted, unmitigated, and soon, unleashed.

Since the eve of his seventeenth birthday three months earlier, she had appeared each and every night in his bedroom. Each time her presence took on a different shape:

a silhouette in the doorway, a shadow at the end of his bed, a pressure next to him on the blankets, a voice in his ear—her whispered words, her breath, that damning breath—an icy hand that burned on his forehead, on his neck, on his leg. Night after night, he tried but could not move. He could not speak. He could not touch her. No matter how firm his resolve beforehand, his body would not respond to his mind's commands. Every night he waited for her, sleepless, anticipating, dreading, longing, cursing her, mad to touch her and unable to reach out, humiliated by his lack of will, his obvious cowardice.

Some days, come morning, he managed to convince himself he'd dreamed it all—an evil, degenerate little bastard fantasizing about his father's wife. Other days he feared he was losing his mind. But more often he whispered to himself in horror, "It happened. It's real. I'm damned."

He burned with shame and desire, and sought relief in the confessional. He recited his penitences, but with less and less fervor, less and less hope of salvation because—be it dream or hallucination or reality—he could control none of it. At night, no matter how intently he beseeched God from within his trapped body, her breath on his skin wrenched all his good intentions out by the root. He kept going to church, but gave up on coherent prayer and confession and the blood and body of Christ. Instead, he sat in the back, gaunt and with rings like bruises beneath his eyes, and stared up at the vaulted emptiness. Shadows haunted his face and his thoughts circled and nibbled like caged mice.

The night before he and Manu drove to the cave, Iban had waited for her as usual, waited with agitation, with terror. But, she did not come. He expected to feel relief; but to his despair, he found her absence shattering. He lay in his bed in absolute loneliness and shuddered in misery.

Then he'd sensed her—she was the dark of the night. She was the air in the room, moving in and out of his lungs, scraping them, caressing them, and he'd found himself as totally paralyzed as before. He was sure that when she extracted her presence, his lungs would collapse, would stop expanding and contracting; and that in the vacuum of the night, without her, his heart would not beat.

He had not closed his eyes to sleep until, when the sun came up, she'd evaporated like the morning dew.

Now, in the cave, he reached out to grab her shoulders, and—triumph—his hands obeyed. The candle sputtered out and he was in the dark—with her. Impulse became movement. On the floor of the cave, he rolled on her like a dog on a dead thing; she, a sand dune turned to clay, an icy lake, a rag doll, flesh for his teeth.

Manu's dead body lay a foot away.

Her body was cool. Was she responsive? He didn't know. Didn't care. Total blackness, the smell of damp rock, the odd odor of her skin. Manu, the stillness emanating from his body. Her body—he was crazed—it was perfumed and oiled and soft on the outside, dry on the inside, dry like crackling leaves, like parchment. Manu. Manu didn't matter. What mattered was that Iban was inside her. He, she, a tangle of body. His eyes rolled back, blind in the dark of the cave, blind, in a sightless state, possessed, possessing. His skin burned where her cool hands touched him. He moved inside her. The intense sensation he had imagined and re-imagined took hold of him, kept him in her grip—white-hot pain—her teeth breaking his skin, her teeth sinking into his neck, and this pain, her inflicting this pain, melded with his release from the pain of his lust. The pain made their union more real to him, pain beyond dream or madness, nothing more real than teeth, than searing pain, her lips pulling on his neck. He clung to her all the more tightly.

The iron taste of his friend's blood in his mouth, the smear of blood caking on his face—these were his last sensations as he surrendered to utter darkness.

7

Have you ever noticed how going into someone's bedroom feels like you're putting on their clothes—the ones they just took off and are lying across the bed? Have you noticed how, even if the light is bright, the room seems dim and shuttered; how it sounds hushed even if they've left a radio on? It's as if in our sleep the room—the walls and furniture—absorbs our most private, secret self, and then when we're not there, it leaks it back into the air. You can feel the thickness of it at the threshold; you can smell it. And if there's a matrimonial bed in the room, well, that more than doubles the effect, doesn't it—him, her and it, that strange third being called marriage. It can make for quite a concoction, the air so dense that an outsider could hardly squeeze in, even if she wanted to. I've worked in a number of households over the years, for my sins, and one of my least favorite jobs was cleaning bedrooms. Give me a toilet to scrub any day.

As in any kitchen worth its salt, the air was heavy with the aroma of olive oil, bay, garlic and onion—for supper that night, Lourdes had fried up a pan of *repápalos*, savory fritters made from a batter of eggs and breadcrumbs. Esmi sat at the kitchen table and poked at the golden balls on her plate, while Lourdes popped up and down for this and that. Adelfo tore off a chunk of bread and dragged it across his plate. With his mouth full, he leaned back in his chair. The old bastard's brow furrowed as he eyed Esmi, who stared down at her plate and swirled her fork in the onion-garlic sauce.

"You're not eating, *hija*," Lourdes said.

Esmi's stomach was all topsy-turvy. "It's very good," she said feebly.

"Eat, then, *mi amor*. You look so peaked. Eat."

"Quit fussing, woman, and let the girl be," Adelfo said— up till then he hadn't said a word at the table.

Esmi looked up at him and grinned, but he did not smile back. He looked down at his plate and shoved it away.

After supper and cleaning up, Lourdes loaded a pile of white linen in Esmi's arms. Esmi's heart sank at the memory of the room she'd had to stay in when she was a kid. It had been her uncle's old room, and her grandmother kept it like some kind of shrine to young teenage-boyhood. On one wall hung the wooden rifles and pistols he'd carved as a boy, and on the others were pinned faded magazine photos, including one of the Pope and another of a radiant blonde in snowsuit and skis with mountains all around. A gruesome crucifix loomed over the bed, but that hadn't given Esmi the creeps as much as the framed picture of Jesus looking dolefully heavenward, that and Tío Ramón's decades-old clothes hanging in the wardrobe like mothballed ghosts. The room had so spooked her that every night as soon as the lights went out, she'd skedaddled straight to her mother's bed.

But Lourdes led her to her mother's old room, with its nearly blank walls and discreet, slender crucifix. Esmi felt a warm relief—it was just as she remembered, spare and stuffy, kept closed except for the occasional dusting.

Before Esmi could set down the sheets and before she could duck away, Lourdes pushed Esmi's hair back from her face and pressed down hard. When she took her hand away, the dark waves sprang back.

Lourdes shook her head. "*Hija*, why would you do that to your hair?"

"It's easy to take care of," Esmi said, "and I like it."

Esmi opened the wooden shutters and lace-curtained window to let some air in, and Lourdes pulled the blanket and pink, crocheted coverlet off the cot-like bed, exposing the bare mattress.

"Well, at least you don't have those awful bangs anymore."

"I was 13, Grandma. I've gone through a few hairstyles since then."

"You wore them so long. They hid your beautiful eyes."

They stood on either side of the bed and spread a sheet taut between them. Together they folded the edges of the bottom sheet under the mattress to make tight corners. They smoothed the cloth with their hands, and then spread the top sheet and tucked the corners in the same way. Esmi felt comfort in the familiar task—her grandmother made beds just like her mother.

"Rosa Esmeralda, why are your eyes red like that?" Lourdes asked. The wool blanket in place, she snapped the coverlet onto the bed, and Esmi pulled her side into place.

"Dust from the road, I suppose," Esmi said and looked away. She tucked the pillow under her chin and tugged on the pillowcase.

Lourdes sat on the bed and with one hand drummed her

fingers on it, inviting Esmi to sit down next to her. She took Esmi's hands in hers.

"Rosa Esmeralda, tell me. Are you...," Lourdes lowered her voice conspiratorially, "are you in trouble?"

Esmi flushed, her thoughts in a knot. How could she tell her?

"Because if you are... Well..."

Esmi glanced up at her grandmother. Lourdes looked determined, but impossibly embarrassed. All at once Esmi picked up on the unfamiliar code.

"Oh, you mean am I pregnant?" she exclaimed. "No! No, I'm not."

Lourdes' quick exhale of breath left her hunched. "*Ay, mi amor*, what a relief! I'm sorry."

"There's no reason to apologize, Grandma."

"It's just that it's been so long since you've visited, and now all of a sudden here you are. You make that long trip all by yourself—your grandfather and I, by the way, cannot approve of your traveling alone like that, no matter how pleased we are to see you. It's not safe and it's not proper."

"I wanted to see you," Esmi said.

"Sweetheart, we're so very happy you did."

And she was. She was floating on happiness. So much so that that evening she hadn't even been paying all that much attention to Adelfo. She hadn't been watching him as if he were a bloody barometer like she usually did.

Esmi calculated how much she should say, could say— she so wanted things to go well.

"And," she said finally, with chagrin, "I also needed to put some space between me and a boyfriend."

"A boyfriend?"

"Well," Esmi corrected herself, "ex-boyfriend."

Lourdes tsk-tsked. "Boyfriends are no good, Esmeralda. What you need is a husband." She reached out and placed her palm on Esmi's cheek.

Esmi jerked away, and Lourdes eyes widened.

"Sorry," Esmi said. "I'm not used to..."

Lourdes' voice went all soft, "You look so much like your mother."

I didn't see the resemblance myself. At least not right off. I remembered Teresa as small, scrappy, all bones and angles, with reddish hair and olive-toned skin. Esmi was taller, her build softer, her skin paler, and there was often a stillness in her that was unknown in Teresa. But she did have Teresa's tawny brown eyes, something uncannily the same about the chin and mouth, and the same facial expressions—neither were quick to smile.

When Lourdes said that about her looking like her mother, Esmi let out a sigh so big that it spilled out like a heaping cup of sadness.

This was the first time Esmi had been to her grandparents' without her mother, and it felt wrong. Back home it did too—her mother being gone. But there, because she came up against it every day, it was a familiar wrongness. There her heartache had grown calluses, but here the pain of her mother's absence was fresh and raw all over again. All evening she'd tiptoed around the subject of her mother and her death because she couldn't face her grandparents' grief or their asking questions that would make her relive that terrible time.

But they hadn't pestered her for details. In fact they hadn't even mentioned her mother's death. And the few times Teresa's name came up, it was as if she were a wayward daughter who neglected to write or visit—her grandfather making barbed comments and her grandmother's voice taking on a certain edge. She didn't know what to think.

Esmi—sitting next to her grandmother on Teresa's bed—ran her fingers over the lacy holes in the coverlet and scrutinized the pattern of crosses and circles.

"That's the first time you haven't sounded angry with her," Esmi said.

"Angry? What a thing to say." Lourdes stood and strode to the window. "Why would I be angry with her?"

Here you have a case in point of someone—that someone being Lourdes—who not only keeps the whole story from others, but from herself, too.

She pulled the double casement window shut that Esmi had opened, and then latched the inside wooden shutters over it. She turned back to her granddaughter and placed her hand on Esmi's head. Esmi froze, determined not to pull away from her again.

Lourdes traced the sign of the cross on Esmi's forehead. "*Que Dios te bendiga, mi amor.* Sleep with the angels."

Lourdes had been devastated when Ramón left home to go work in England—her only son in a godless, foreign country; and who knew for how long. But what could she do? What could any of them do? Ramón was a young man. He needed to make a living.

He wasn't the first to leave, and personally, Ramón had never been my favorite person; but being Fuentespina's fair-haired boy, he was sent off with much fanfare.

[Of course. Ramón Tena Donoso was a fine young man—unhappily sucked into the void beyond our shores (as were Narda and the others, for that matter), when by rights he should have been our standard-bearer into the future.]

Now Teresa's leaving, that was traumatic too, but only for Lourdes and Adelfo.

[And only because of the scandal.]

It was *Señora* Rosario who told Lourdes that she'd seen Teresa get on the bus.

[At that time the bus still came into town; it pulled up right by the fountain.]

You know how you blanch almonds—pouring boiling water over them to get rid of the tough skin—so that what you've got left is the nutmeat, all pale and exposed, and ready for chopping or grinding? Well, *Señora* Rosario's report was like the boiling water and Lourdes, the almond.

"I'm astonished," *Señora* Rosario continued, taking no small pleasure in Lourdes' distress, "absolutely astonished that *Don* Adelfo would allow Teresa to go to the city all by herself."

Lourdes tried to interrupt, but *Señora* Rosario was on a roll.

"Certainly no daughter of mine would be allowed on a bus unescorted. Make no doubt, *Señora* Lourdes, my husband would make sure that never happened."

"My family, *señora*," Lourdes stammered, "is none of your business."

"Well!" *Señora* Rosario huffed, and it looked as if all the blood that had drained from Lourdes' face had come to pool in *Señora* Rosario's.

Lourdes rushed home. There she discovered that Teresa's wardrobe had been emptied, as had the jar where Lourdes kept her egg money. The family suitcase was missing, too.

So it was true: Teresa had run away, and Lourdes had had to find out about it from that Rosario woman. Teresa—not quite sixteen years old—had trampled on the family honor, and she hadn't even left a note.

It still haunted Lourdes—Teresa leaving like that, and worse, without Lourdes blessing her. Clearly no good had come of it.

Not that long ago, she'd once again complained to me about Teresa's running away. "Some things are more important than cinemas and bright lights," she'd said.

I don't know why I was surprised that Lourdes had convinced herself that Teresa had run away from home purely in search of a more exciting life. After all, anyone who could live with Adelfo all those years must have had a flexible hold on the truth.

It was supposed to be a secret that Adelfo lost his temper with Teresa, but like most secrets in Fuentespina, everybody knew it—everybody knew the son of a bitch hit her. But I didn't say that to Lourdes. I just asked her how long she'd expected Teresa and Adelfo to live under the same roof.

"I don't know what you're talking about," she sniffed.

"Face it," I said. "If Teresa hadn't run off, it was only a matter of time before one of them ended up killing the other."

Lourdes shook her head fiercely. "You don't know what it's like raising teenagers, any teenager, much less one like Teresa."

Fine, Teresa had a mouth on her, I know that. And true, I don't have any children. But there were five of us kids at my house, and let me tell you, not one of us ever showed up at Mass with a black eye. I didn't say anything.

"She was always a restless child," Lourdes said.

That night, in spite of being dog-tired, Esmi couldn't sleep. The pain pills muffled the throbbing in her neck and throat, but they didn't stop it; and the bed may have looked inviting, but the old cotton mattress laid on wooden slats felt like it had been stuffed with lumpy rocks. Besides, she had a lot to chew over—what with her trip to Fuentespina and the reunion with her grandparents, not to mention the turn of events back home that had brought her here in the first place, both her mind and her stomach flipped and flopped.

And of course it was dead quiet—if there's one thing we have a lot of in Fuentespina, it's silence—which to Esmi was a thing unnatural, as was the darkness. In fact the dark was worse—the sheer blackness of it, not a shred of light to leak in around the curtains, impossible for her to make out the shape of a single thing in the room, not even the bed in which she lay.

It was that pitch blackness that bred the panic; making it hard to breathe, as if her lungs were threatening to close up on her. Arms stretched out in front of her, she inched her way to the window—she'd pulled open the shutters before getting into bed. When her fingers met the rough texture of the lace curtains, she fumbled with the latch and threw wide the double windows.

It was a relief to see the pinpoints of stars, so many and so bright, shimmering like silver sequins in the black sky. Their position up there, where they were supposed to be, gave her enough perspective to once again make up, up; and down, down, in the old familiar way. With one foot on the floor tiles and one on the raw wood of the sill, she sat in the window and leaned against the casement, taking deep, delicious breaths of air.

She was wearing only a tee shirt—the portera had packed nothing for her to sleep in—and she crossed her arms around herself for warmth. Sitting there, breathing with the stars, the rhythm of her breath became easy and normal. Fatigue washed over her. She pulled the iron bed frame closer to the open window so that she could see a corner of stars. It was enough—she fell asleep.

But she did not sleep well. In the dark of her dream a man grabbed her. She struggled to free her hands so she could fight him and push the suffocating weight of him away, but could not; and even though he did not have his hands on her throat pressing her windpipe shut, she could not scream for help. You never can in a nightmare, can you.

It's one of the clues that you're asleep—not being able to scream—but in a dream you never put two and two together. Sometimes, it's not so easy in waking life either.

Then she heard someone else shouting—the deep-voiced, guttural cries of somebody as doomed as she—and she woke up because they came from outside her sleep. The moon had risen, and in its light she saw where she was, and she recognized the voice. She jumped out of bed and ran down the hall.

"Grandfather!" she called.

She almost collided with Lourdes, who was pulling a pale-blue, quilted robe on over her long flannel nightgown as she came out of her and Adelfo's bedroom. Her hair, which Esmi had never seen free from its French roll, hung straight and fine past her shoulders. It made her look both girlish and witch-like at the same time.

"Heavens, child, you scared me half to death," Lourdes said.

Esmi looked past her to where Adelfo struggled to sit upright. The small lamp by the bed cast a circle of yellow light from beneath its shade.

"What's wrong?" Esmi asked her grandmother. "Is he all right?"

"Nothing to worry about," Lourdes snapped. "Just a nightmare."

In the first years of their marriage, Adelfo had been plagued by dreams so deep and so terrible that Lourdes had feared he might kill her in his sleep. And now, during the past few nights, they'd come back.

Esmi stepped back from her grandmother and her sharp tone.

Lourdes took one scandalized look at Esmi's long, bare

legs before she raised her gaze to the girl's throat. Her startled eyes met Esmi's.

"You'll catch your death of cold," Lourdes said. She whipped the crocheted afghan from the end of the bed. "Here," she said and wrapped it around Esmi, gathering the blanket tight at her neck. "Don't let your grandfather see you like that," she whispered.

Esmi took hold of the afghan and held it about her.

"I'm going to make some chamomile tea," Lourdes announced.

"I don't want tea, woman." Adelfo tried to sound his usual overbearing self, but his voice quaked. He coughed to bring it into line, and the throat-clearing turned into a series of hacks. "What I need is a shot of aguardiente."

Lourdes buttoned her robe, and left for the kitchen, her slippers slapping the floor.

The circle of lamp light lit only her grandfather's grey-stubbled chin, his chest in faded striped pajamas and his thin hands with the long, splayed fingers resting on top of the white coverlet.

His hand patted the bedcover. "Come keep an old man company," he said. He'd aimed for a light tone, but his voice cracked.

She had never entered this room before, partly because it had been off-limits, but mostly because the room hadn't seemed to want her in it. Esmi held the blanket tight around her and sat next to him on the bed. She slid one hand through the opening of the afghan Lourdes had wrapped around her and took his hand. In the weak lamp light, their hands were warmly lit and their faces dim to each other.

After a moment she said, "That must have been some nightmare."

He nodded, his face in shadow.

"Does it happen a lot?"

He shook his head. "In the years after the war. The strange thing is that during the fighting, whenever I got the chance to sleep, I slept like a baby, even after days of unspeakable..." He waved the thought away and did not finish the sentence. "That dreamless sleep, that was a gift from God. What we were doing—fighting for God and Spain—was the most important thing we would ever do in our lives, and we knew it. 'Spain: one, great and free!'"

One, great and free...? Even Esmi, with a total lack of interest in history or politics, recognized the fascist slogan.

And it sounds harmless enough, doesn't it. Except it's code. "One" meant fascism only, all other "ism"s to be exterminated, and of course Basque, Catalan and other languages, outlawed. While "free" meant freedom from the squalor of democracy, free to be Catholic, and if you want to idolize the *Generalísimo*, oh please, do feel free.

Under Franco, that motto was everywhere, but that was before Esmi's time. My poor mum, if she ever managed to get two coins to rub together, she could take no delight in it, what with that slogan on one side of every coin and Franco's ugly mug on the other.

Esmi's grandfather let go of her hand and raised his arm in the fascist salute. "*Arriba España!*" he said in a strong voice.

So that's where his sympathies lay. Esmi had never given it much thought, but she supposed it made sense that he'd been on the winning side. What took her aback was her grandfather's fervor. To her it seemed so long ago.

Adelfo dropped his arm and took Esmi's hand again. He closed his eyes. "'*Arriba España!*'" he repeated.

After a few moments, Lourdes returned carrying a tray with two cups of tea, a bottle of aguardiente and one small glass.

"Here we are," she announced, sweet as pie, as if they were to have a pleasant afternoon tea. She set the tray on her side of the bed, and Adelfo opened his good eye, but it was unfocused and his hand twitched in Esmi's. He pulled his hand free and groaned—it was a deep, hollow noise.

"Adelfo?" Lourdes said.

Esmi stood in alarm.

Lourdes came around the bed. "Adelfo," Lourdes said. She shook him by the shoulders.

Adelfo looked ahead, unseeing.

"He was fine a minute ago," Esmi said.

"Wake up, *viejo*," Lourdes said and shook him again.

Adelfo groaned and raised an accusing finger.

Esmi didn't know if the old man was awake or asleep or having some kind of attack.

"Wake up. You'll scare Esmi," Lourdes said.

The old bastard's eye suddenly came to life, became fierce. He fixed his stare on Lourdes and grabbed her wrists.

"Milú, it's back," he said to her. "It's been hiding all this time, waiting. Evil, Milú. God help us. It's back."

8

Esmi was clutching at the wrong straws when she came to Fuentespina—mistaking it for some kind of sanctuary. Peace and quiet in Fuentespina? Quiet we got plenty of. But peace? Even the dead aren't at peace here.

Truth be told, Fuentespina's sharp-edged and flinty. Its nature runs deep into the earth and deep in time. It'll flick a lone life off like a fly. Teresa could have warned her, but Teresa was gone, wasn't she.

That's where a healthy dose of history can stand you in good stead. Of course, like Esmi, most people aren't interested in History with a capital H. Kings, queens, battles: who cares, right? But then there's the real deal—the nitty-gritty low-down that can show the way and save your bacon—which has nothing to do with what they force-fed us in school way back when. Quite the fairy tale that was, a real humdinger of a morality play.

They told it pretty much this way. On the Iberian Peninsula, later to be called Spain, first there were pre-historic men painting masterpieces in caves (in other words, even our cavemen were geniuses). Then the Romans civilized the Peninsula, or rather by conquering us, we were able to civilize the empire—Seneca, Trajan, Hadrian, etc. All Spaniards. Next came the Visigoths. The bad news, they were barbarians; the good news, they were Christians. Yay!

Then comes the darkest of dark ages—711, the Moors overrun Spain, and Islam reigns, with virtuous Christian princesses captured as slaves and locked up in harems, etc., etc. Never mind the brilliance of the Caliphate of Córdoba, not to mention that of Toledo, Sevilla and Granada (in other words, even our infidels were geniuses). Then in 1096, our hero *El Cid Campeador* re-conquers Valencia from same said infidels.

Reconquest—the Peninsula is gained back inch by inch with the might of Saint James, who on at least one occasion came back in person, in armor and on horseback. Now that's a patron saint to reckon with: Saint James the Moor-killer (the meek shall inherit the earth, my foot). The Christians fought century after century after century until, hallelujah, by the grace of God (a little slow in coming, if you ask me), in 1492, the Catholic Monarchs, Queen Isabel and King Fernando, conquer Granada, the last Moorish city; expel the Jews; and in one fell swoop unite all of Spain as a Catholic country; and as an aside send Christopher Columbus off to start our empire.

[The glory of Spain! We, not Britannia, ruled the waves.]

There was Holy Roman Emperor Carlos V, and Felipe II, and the Golden Century—jam-packed with certifiable geniuses—and Spanish empire stretching from Europe to the New World to the Philippines, spreading civilization and saving pagan souls. Which was all pretty much hunky-dory until we ran out of empire in 1898, when we lost the last of our colonies to that upstart of a United States.

[Disgraceful! It should never have been allowed to happen.]

Following on the heels of this disaster, the Second Republic was set up in 1931. The decadent influence of democracy weakened us and Communism swooped in and consumed the country. They killed priests and raped nuns and corrupted our youth. But—Hip, Hip, Hurrah—God saved us in the form of *Generalissimo* Francisco Franco. He rose up in 1936, a knight on a Holy Crusade, to deliver us from the godless communists. Then he stayed on to rule as a stern but just father, for our own good, for almost forty years.

That's the kind of hogwash that gives history a bad name.

Real history, the kind we live here in Fuentespina, is nothing like that. The currents of time have brought peoples here in waves and then taken them away again, one after another, since before pretty much forever. There's no glory to it, no stardust, just regular old dirt, bodies, dust to dust.

And now the tide is out, it seems, for good. We're down to a few souls hanging on by a moth-eaten thread, having come to the end of a very long and not at all tidy history.

[We have our bones in deep dirt. One may appear to die, but one will rise again.]

Then again, this town is more than its people. To Fuentespina, the people are frosting, the people are window dressing.

[Teresa should have told her daughter. This is no place for outsiders.]

9

The same night that old Adelfo was carrying on about his nightmare, I had an odd vision of my own—odd only because I'd never before in my life dreamed of Teresa Tena.

I was sound asleep in my room, but I dreamed I was working in the kitchen scraping carrots at the basin. I was wearing my usual: navy-blue skirt, pale-blue top, flats worn down at the heel, and one of my mum's print smock aprons; and I was worrying about how much longer I could make my shoes last—they were shot, but I hated spending money and how was I going to get to the city to buy new ones anyway? I hated the city, surrounded by all those strangers, everything costing an arm and a leg. In other words, it was one of those dreams that doesn't feel like a dream. I was fully occupied—the knife blade going up and down and my mind making convoluted circles—when someone tapped me on the shoulder.

"Teresa, *Dios mío!*" I snapped. "You scared the living daylights out of me."

She was still a teenager, probably because I'd never seen her again after she left the village—the few times she came back to visit, I was away working—but I recognized her right away, as if the last time I'd seen her was the day before yesterday and not thirty-some years before. She slouched against the table, arms crossed, staring at me. The only thing missing was a cigarette, and that way she had of jabbing at her mouth with it.

"What do you want?" I said. "Can't you see I have work to do?"

She opened her mouth, but nothing came out; and mouth still open, she faded away.

I tried to scream, but nothing came out of my mouth either. I woke with a start, my heart pumping hard. And that's when I remembered, Teresa was dead. It felt like I'd seen a ghost. I reached up in the darkness, touched the crucifix over my bed and whispered a prayer. Even though it was just a dream, I remember feeling bad that I'd been so short with her.

Maybe it was at that very moment, at the Tena house on the edge of town, that Teresa's daughter climbed out the bedroom window. Maybe.

[If one's respectable, one has no cause to be out after dark.]

Because as I lay there waiting for my heart to slow to a trot, I listened to the ebb and flow of dogs barking, a relay of one dog after another, tracking the route of someone or something wandering the streets. At the time I figured it was a cat out for a stroll, taking pleasure in taunting the dogs tied up in patios.

Once her grandfather seemed recovered from his nightmare, Esmi had left him. She'd taken her tea back to her room and sat on her bed, cross-legged, and listened to her grandparents' muffled talk, their voices like mismatched music. After a while the talking stopped, and the snores started up. She longed to go back to sleep too, but when she closed her eyes, she sensed her own nightmare hovering there, lying in wait, and so she made herself stay awake. The room was moonlit now—it no longer closed in on her, but she still stared at the open window with a craving.

On top of everything else, she was dying for a smoke, but she only had a couple cigarettes left. She got out of bed and leaned against the window. She recalled Zambrano's, the dark little hole-in-the-wall of a store on the plaza with the single counter, where she'd gone as a child to buy cigarettes for her grandfather and candy for herself with the change.

Earlier that evening, when she'd asked her grandmother about it, she'd been told it had closed a long time ago.

"Where can I buy some cigarettes, then?"

Lourdes eyebrows arched in disapproval. "Nowhere," she said.

"What do people do?"

"Well, thanks to *Doña* Pilar, there's a grocery-mobile that comes to town. Very convenient. Things have picked up around here since she came to town. Did you notice how nice the big house on the plaza looks?"

When Esmi pressed her about the grocery-mobile, Lourdes admitted that it wasn't due again for more than a week.

A week! Esmi thought. She perched on the window sill. The house was the last on the street and her window faced out on the far-reaching skirt of scrubland surrounding Fuentespina.

Did she notice that the unvarnished wood of the window casement was worn smooth? Her mum's butt, may she rest in peace, did some of that polishing and her grandfather's before that. Yes, it had been the old goat's room when he was a boy, damn him, and any number of generations before him had also sat there admiring the stars or had crept over the edge in search of shady adventures. Esmi didn't know she was following family tradition, just that the walls were big sponges soaking up all the air in the room.

She pulled on her jeans and trainers, threw her jacket on over her tee shirt, dug into the pocket for her scarf and tied it around her neck.

Outside, Esmi found that, except for the wind hissing and lifting dust, nothing stirred in the narrow dirt lanes and cobblestone streets. No lamps glowed inside the houses and no streetlights dripped puddles of light on pavement, but the gibbous moon did its job well enough, and Esmi meandered through town to the barking of dogs. It grew quieter when she reached the plaza—no dogs lived there. No dogs lived there because *Doña* Pilar didn't like dogs.

Esmi saw the man the moment she stepped into the plaza. He stood next to the fountain, all nonchalant, as if he were waiting for a bus, or for her.

It was *Señor* Iban.

There's no getting around it, *Señor* Iban is one good-looking man: in his mid thirties, with that black hair and long nose, and eyes you wanted to go swimming in—wide and black under elegantly wide, arched eyebrows. Of course, there wasn't enough light for Esmi to fully appreciate all that, or the compelling, dark look—sad and weary—in those dark eyes. It made you wish you could touch his brow and tell him everything would be fine; made you think, rest with me awhile. I'll sing you to sleep and stand guard over your dreams. You may think I'm old enough to be his mother, but I'm not. Well, maybe I am, but just barely.

Señor Iban breathed in deeply from a cigarette and stared at the upstairs windows of the big house. When Esmi saw him she froze, then she stepped back into the protection of the moon shadows cast by the wall of houses lining the side street. She watched him with interest, noticing that he was well dressed, and expensively so—lots of Italian: shoes, sports jacket, tailored shirt.

Something about the way the moonlight fell on his upturned face made the hair on the back of her neck tingle, and when he turned and looked in her direction, his eyes dark and his features casting shadows on his face, her breath stopped. She told herself to stay calm, that there was no way he could see her.

But he did. He nodded to her.

"Good evening," he said, low and quiet and offhanded.

Her first instinct was to turn tail and run, but her pride balked. She stayed fixed to her spot.

"Please," *Señor* Iban said, and offered an open pack of cigarettes.

At that moment, a cigarette trumped chocolate or champagne or common sense. She found herself moving into the moonlight, into the open square. The circumstances she knew were not the wisest—alone in the middle of the night with a strange man—but she felt no danger from him. On the contrary, she felt intrigued and attracted, and nicotine had nothing to do with it.

[A hussy if ever there was one.]

She approached like a cat lured by a saucer of cream. She took a cigarette from the pack, and he produced a silver lighter. She leaned toward him a little for him to light the cigarette.

He smelled of tobacco, expensive cologne, sun-dried cloth and what she would come to recognize as himself. She inhaled the smoke with pleasure. After the strain of the day, and of the evening, a cigarette had never tasted so good.

They stood side by side, facing the big house, and did not speak. If people from town had happened on them, the two might have seemed like a fine pair of exotic birds, swooped in for a rest during a long migration.

But maybe not all that well-matched. Esmi had seen men like *Señor* Iban in Madrid—coming out of exclusive restaurants, and escorting long-legged beauties. Esmi, as a rule, did not worry about not being air-brush beautiful. Normally she was content with being desirable. She wore her simple clothes tight and well and had an air of independence and self-assurance that men seemed to find attractive. She liked men—she liked to sleep with men, she worked largely with men, her friends were men, at least what until recently had passed as friends.

On the train trip from Madrid, she'd realized there was not one woman of importance in her life. Women didn't, on the whole, seem to take to her. The middle-aged *portera* in her building made it clear she did not like Esmi; the secretary in her section at work was polite, but cool; the girlfriends and wives of the other programmers kept their distance; and acquaintances from school had fallen away. Up until that moment she hadn't cared. Staring out the window of the train at fields of olive trees, she'd made up her mind to do something about it. She'd had enough of men.

Or so she'd thought. It was ironic to find herself, in Fuentespina of all places, standing next to a man like this, whose direct gaze made her breath catch. Ironic and unfair. She felt like the dun female of another species: her hair was mussed from sleep, her red scarf clashed with her lime-green tee shirt, and instead of wearing her lucky blue heels with the cunning little bows on the instep, she was wearing dusty old trainers.

She kept her eyes averted to hide their redness from him and held her cigarette down by the side of her leg so he wouldn't see her fingers trembling. With her other hand she held on to her forearm. Her legs were shaky, so she sat down on the bench that circled the small fountain.

"May I, *señorita?*"

Esmi nodded, and he sat next to her.

"*Señorita,* allow me to introduce myself..."

All this *señorita*-ing was making her all the more nervous. It made her feel like a shop girl.

"Iban Velasco Ylla-Gual, at your service."

A lot of information can be tucked into a name. For one thing, she knew the given name "Iban" was a Basque name. His first family name, "Velasco," came from his father's side. It was not an uncommon name in Spain. His second family name, "Ylla-Gual," would be his mother's. She hadn't heard it before and guessed it might be Catalan, the language spoken in Barcelona, the Balearic Islands and along the east coast.

Esmi switched her cigarette to her left hand and extended her right, as if in a business meeting. "Esmi," she said. "Thanks for the cigarette." She hoped her voice sounded husky instead of raspy.

He took her hand, and the little hairs on the back of her neck stood at attention again. And when he turned her hand and kissed it, that tingling was echoed with more tingling in her stomach.

"Pleased to meet you, *Señorita* Esmi."

She looked about her theatrically and questioned his formality.

"It's a small town," he said, "and there are certain conventions."

"I'm not from here," she said. "I'm just visiting. From Madrid." She couldn't keep the edge of pride out of her voice.

"Ah," he said, with a small smile. "Just Esmi?"

She shrugged. "OK. Rosa Esmeralda Salvater Tena."

"*Encantado*, Rosa Esmeralda Salvater Tena."

Esmi wrinkled her nose, as if the length of her name were silly, but she liked the sound of it in his mouth. She noticed his accent was not Castilian and his s's carried more of a hiss than her own.

"So, how are your grandparents?" he asked.

She felt the first twinge of unease, and maybe a bit more than unease.

"Who said anything about my grandparents?"

"A surmise," he said.

Señor Iban tended to split his sentences apart when he spoke, leaving gaps between them.

"You said you were visiting. The median age here must be at least eighty. Don't be frightened."

"I'm not frightened."

"Maybe you should be."

Esmi stood. On an earlier occasion, she might have found this kind of banter amusing, but not tonight.

"I'm sorry," he said. "Forgive me. But truly, I am concerned for your well-being." He twitched a smile, and stood. "When people are accustomed to city life, a village may lull them into a false sense of security. Look at you, wandering about in the middle of the night talking to strange men."

She looked at her feet, and forced a smile. "Oh, you're not that strange."

"Thank you."

"What are you doing here?" She blurted, but she'd had enough of being on the defensive and did not backpedal. "I mean," she softened her voice, "look at you." She waved her cigarette up and down at him. "You're not from here either. Are you visiting grandparents?"

"Business."

"Business," she snorted. "What, cattle? Hogs? Sugar beets? I don't think so."

"Personal business."

"And private?"

"Very, I'm afraid. And I've been completely on my own here, so I'm delighted to meet someone I can finally talk to, someone charming and beautiful and..."

"Nosy?" she said.

"Inquisitive," he corrected, holding her gaze.

A shiver went through her, and he wasn't even touching her. She felt the need to break the spell.

"So, are you Basque, or what?"

"Do you have a problem with Basques?" he asked, cooly.

She shook her head. "Just curious." She sat down again, and he, next to her.

"I live in Barcelona, now," he said.

"I've never been."

"That's a crime," he said. "It's a beautiful city."

She put out her cigarette against the stone of the fountain and placed the stub in her pocket. *Señor* Iban produced the pack of cigarettes again.

She hesitated. "You do know there's no place to buy more cigarettes, don't you?" she asked.

"Help yourself. I can take them or leave them."

Once again he lit her cigarette. Then he dropped the one he was smoking and ground it under foot.

"Don't do that," she said quietly, pointing with her chin at the butt. He looked confused. She picked it up. "It was a pet peeve of my mother's," she said.

He took the dusty butt from her, and she flinched a little when he put it in the expensive pocket of his expensive wool and silk jacket, but smiled to herself.

Her mother used to say, "I'm just a cleaning lady." And Esmi would always groan, because humbleness didn't suit Teresa, and because she only said it when she was riding Esmi about her studies. "You're going to have to make your own future, *mi amor*. You get yourself a good career. Make money. Make a lot of money, or I'll have to come back to haunt you."

"You know," *Señor* Iban said, interrupting her thoughts, "there's something... The way you look at me, it's like you see right through to who I really am."

Esmi let the memory of her mother—bittersweet and fleeting—slip away. She aimed her most seductive smile at Iban.

"If you really believed that, I think maybe you wouldn't still be talking to me."

His eyes smiled back at her.

A cock crowed and *Señor* Iban looked up at the sky.

"It's almost dawn." he said. "I'm sure you know people get up early here. It wouldn't do for you to be seen with me like this."

"Protecting me again?"

"Meet me here again tomorrow night. Will you?"

Esmi didn't answer. Why at night, she wondered.

"I have business to tend to until late, but I have someplace I'd like to show you, someplace special to me."

"I don't think so," she said, but she very much wanted to.

He took her hand, and smiled that smile of his, the one that blooms out of the desert of his face, surfacing from a deep, deep melancholy.

"Esmi. Don't play the village girl playing at village games. It's very simple. I want to see you again. And you want to see me." He kissed her hand again. "I'll bring cigarettes," he coaxed. He raised and lowered his eyebrows twice, comically.

She smiled in spite of herself. That's the irritating thing

about *Señor* Iban, he makes you smile when you least expect to, and least want to.

"I have to go," he said. He kissed her on both cheeks so quickly that she didn't have time to pull away. "See you here. Midnight." And he was gone down the passageway along the side of the church.

The first footfall of the new day reached the plaza at the very moment she lost sight of him.

10

If it had been me that *Señor* Iban had just kissed, on the cheek or hand, or anywhere else, I wouldn't have heard or cared about the little footsteps behind me. But Esmi did. She looked over her shoulder. What she saw was a tiny scarecrow of a crone, all in black.

It's hard to say who was the more startled—Esmi, with her hand still hanging there in space where *Señor* Iban had left it, looking like a kid caught with her hand dipping into the cookie jar, or Reina, her pale eyes quickening with fear, willing herself invisible, half turning away and raising her forearm to her face. But Reina's jolt of panic passed and she dropped her arm; and head jutting forward, she stared at Esmi, straight on. You might think she was gripped with curiosity, but curiosity had no place in her life, did it. Curiosity was a frill, an indulgence stripped away long ago. No, if she was riveted, it was by recognition, by remembrance.

Esmi pulled her sunglasses from her jacket pocket and slipped them on as the old woman scuttled across to her and peered up into her face—Reina had never been a tall woman, and over time she'd shrunk like a little bird in a cold wind. She gave Esmi a creaky smile, as if she were the dearest sight she'd ever seen, and reached for her hand.

Esmi pulled her hand away. She felt cornered. The strange creature stood too close. Her clothes gave off a sour smell and the woman herself, a bitter odor.

[It was that awful ointment of rue she made for her rheumatism.]

"What do you want?" Esmi demanded.

"You don't know me," Reina said in a flutey whisper, "but I know you."

She reached out to touch Esmi's face. Esmi pulled away, and Reina flinched at the sudden movement. But she did not give ground.

"You are the spitting image of your great-uncle Justino."

"You must be mistaken," Esmi said. "I don't have any great-uncle Justino."

Esmi turned from Reina, but Reina grabbed Esmi's arm.

"Don't say that," Reina said, anguished. Then with as much fierceness as the poor thing could muster, she repeated, "Don't say that."

It was just then that I opened the door, broom in hand, to sweep in front of the house, as I do first thing every morning. I was more than a bit surprised to see a stranger in the square, and absolutely astonished to see her trying to shake off timid little Reina. As I stood there gaping, *Doña* Pilar drove up in her Land Rover.

She called sharply from the window, all high and mighty as was her wont, "Reina, who's that you're talking to?"

Reina stepped away from Esmi. She looked down at her feet and mumbled something.

Doña Pilar swung out of the car as if onto a stage. Her tweed jacket was unbuttoned and you could see that clunky gold and silver amulet she always wore on a three-stranded brass chain. It hung low over where her heart should be.

[It was said to contain water from the River Jordan.]

Sometimes *Señora* Rosario would ask me how old I thought *Doña* Pilar was, and I'd say the devil if I knew or cared. But between you and me, I suppose she was forty-something, though I never looked like that when I was forty, or something. Nor did anyone else around here. She was forty-something in a Hollywood sort of way.

[What would Narda know of Hollywood?]

When I worked in Badajoz, I went to the movies every chance I got, didn't I. In London, too, even though I couldn't understand a word.

Unlike *Doña* Pilar, I—à la Fuentespina—looked every one of my fifty-two years.

[Plus a few for good measure.]

But then I'd never been pampered like her—no face creams or manicures for me. Not that *Doña* Pilar didn't work, you have to give her that, she worked hard. Still, there's a difference between ordering people about and scrubbing floors.

Except for our height, she and I were a study in contrasts. She, the boss, me the servant; she, short and trim; me, short and not so trim—more chorizo-shaped, if you must know. That day by her car she looked taller, partly because of her boots, but mostly because she was indignant. She slammed the car door.

Don't go thinking she was concerned for Reina's well-being. Not a bit of it. She just didn't like strangers hanging about.

"You, girl, who are you?" *Doña* Pilar demanded of Esmi.

To *Doña* Pilar's way of thinking she had every right under heaven to know exactly who was in her town and why. But Esmi was not used to being talked to like that.

"What business is it of yours?" she said.

That made my ears perk up.

"She's Teresa's daughter," Reina croaked, and gave Esmi a little shove in *Doña* Pilar's direction. Esmi looked a bit startled, but she did not retreat, because that would be, well, retreating and she wasn't about to give an inch to whoever *Doña* Pilar was.

"Teresa's daughter!" I said. "Teresa Tena?" You can imagine my surprise, having just dreamt about her hours before. I added her mother's family name just to be sure. "Teresa Tena Donoso?"

Esmi glanced in my direction, and Reina nodded.

"Who's Teresa?" *Doña* Pilar asked in exasperation.

"*Doña*, this is *Señora* Lourdes' granddaughter, Esmi, from Madrid," I explained.

You should have seen the questioning look that flitted across Esmi's face—here she'd never seen me before in her life and I was talking like I knew all about her. Then, just as quickly, her mouth hardened. Her eyes may have been hidden behind sun glasses—suspiciously, I thought, so early in the morning—but I could feel her eyes narrow at me and flash, as if I'd betrayed her and given *Doña* Pilar the upper hand.

Doña Pilar did not look like the information pleased her, and Esmi looked unpleased right back at her.

"Esmi? What kind of name is that?"

"Rosa Esmeralda, *Doña* Pilar," I supplied and made no points with Esmi.

Esmi was the name Teresa wanted for her daughter, but back then by law you had to use a name from the Catholic Index, so she chose "Rosa" and told Esmi it was for the flower.

"Ah, named for Santa Rosa de Lima?"

Doña Pilar always made a show of being pious, like with that little simper at the mention of Santa Rosa's name. But she didn't practice her faith, did she. I never saw her say a rosary, and if she owned one, she kept it locked away from the likes of me. The only crucifix in the house was the one over my bed, and her taste in art ran to the archeological— Roman and pre-Roman—no Madonnas or martyrs.

[*Doña* Pilar knew that if something is to be done properly, it's done by the Church.]

Doña Pilar looked Esmi up and down. "Santa Rosa who shunned vanity?" she said pointedly.

"No. My name's Esmi." She spoke as if cradling her voice.

Even though Esmi had heard me call *Doña* Pilar by name, and even though she'd listened to her grandmother sing the woman's praises the night before, she pretended she didn't know who *Doña* Pilar was.

"And you are...?" she asked.

You would have thought Esmi had asked her how old she was or how much money she had in the bank. The Ice Queen paused before answering, a long pause to let Esmi know she'd decided to be generous and answer.

"*Doña* María del Pilar Sepúlveda-Villanova Bendiscana de Fernán-Iñíquez."

During *Doña* Pilar's recital Esmi, looking unimpressed behind her dark glasses, twisted her hair up and clipped it in place.

For a moment *Doña* Pilar seemed mesmerized—she actually faltered for a whole blink of an eye. I thought, my word, how interesting.

Then, almost as if to cover up her lapse, teensy though it was, she waved in my direction.

"This is María Bernarda."

Hah! An introduction! And María Bernarda, yet. I hid a smile—the great lady had never called me anything but Narda.

Esmi and I looked each other over, and I thought, so this is hotshot Teresa's hotshot daughter.

I was of the opinion that the girl hadn't done right by her grandmother, dropping out of sight like she had. The last word that Lourdes had had from her, right after Teresa's death, was that she was studying computers at the Politécnica, and Lourdes had worried that the girl's studies would interfere with her finding a husband.

Seeing the way she'd just treated Reina didn't impress me either. If she hadn't warmed my heart by speaking up to *Doña* Pilar like she had, I wouldn't have thought much of her. Not much at all.

Then, out of the blue, *Doña* Pilar said to Esmi, "I have a job for you."

I tell you, you've got to keep your eye on my boss because you never quite know what angle she's going to come at you from.

Esmi was taken aback. "I have a job," she said.

"How long will you be in Fuentespina?" *Doña* Pilar asked.

"I don't know yet."

I was hit with a sudden image of her standing alone on a broad street, shoulders hunched. It was night, but the clouds caught the city's glow, filling the sky with dirty light. The wet tarmac reflected the red tail lights of passing cars.

"Strange job, lets you come and go as you please."

Esmi did not respond.

"My stepson, Roberto, has been unwell, and he's missed a lot of school. He needs a tutor."

"I'm not a teacher and, as I said, I already have a job. In Madrid."

Doña Pilar and Esmi stared each other down as if they were faced off at twenty paces—high noon in a spaghetti western, showdown at the Tombstone Corral, USA. Even *Señora* Rosario entering the square didn't distract them.

"*Buenos días*," *Señora* Rosario muttered, and intrigued by what she saw, she lingered by the fountain, listening and watching.

"You may start this afternoon," *Doña* Pilar announced, turning on her heel and brushing past me into the house.

Esmi lowered her dark glasses, peeking over the tops to gape after her. "I have other plans," she called after her, but the great lady was long gone. Then Esmi turned to me. "She does know I said no, doesn't she?"

Señora Rosario came forward, and Esmi slid her glasses back over her eyes.

"Nobody says no to *Doña* Pilar, do they, Nardita?" *Señora* Rosario said.

"I just did," Esmi said.

She glanced up at the big house and, head high, strode from the plaza with all three of us staring after her. Reina scurried away, and before *Señora* Rosario could ask who the girl was, I said, "That was *Señora* Lourdes' granddaughter, Esmi."

Then I set to sweeping, raising enough dust so that *Señora* Rosario left, coughing in protest.

11

weep, sweep —I couldn't get the girl out of my mind. She'd turned those amber eyes on me and asked, "She does know I said no, doesn't she?" and something long-frozen puddled deep inside me.

It was as if she were saying, "You and I know what's what. You and I are on the same side." And the tone of her voice—amused and exasperated—so naive. It drew me in, in spite of myself. It made me, me of all people, want to protect her.

Sweep, sweep—And heavens, the sparks between her and *Doña* Pilar!

By the time I finished sweeping, Esmi was climbing back through the window at her grandparents' house. Lourdes had pushed the bed back to its usual position, and she perched on the one chair in the room, placed to face the window. She waited stony-faced, but her body hummed with outrage. How dare the girl behave this way.

As for Esmi, she was well aware that being caught climbing through a window was juvenile, to say the least. Absurd, really. And even as she assured herself that she had nothing to be ashamed of, Lourdes' grey face said otherwise.

She kissed Lourdes on the cheek—her skin felt like kneaded bread dough, her face powder smelled of gardenia and sandalwood.

"*Buenos días, abuela,*" Esmi's voice croaked.

Lourdes did not respond—she didn't trust herself to. The girl had no right putting her through this again.

Well, fine, Esmi thought. That's that. She'd made a hash of everything. Her suitcase waited next to the dresser. It would take her all of 30 seconds to pack and be out of there.

The problem was she didn't want to leave. She was scared. She'd hoped for someplace safe where she could lick her wounds in peace and come up with some kind of future for herself. A life that made sense, one with people who loved her. She wasn't much good at relationships; she knew that. But she had to start somewhere, and she'd convinced herself that that somewhere was Fuentespina.

[How dare she drag her sorry tail here amongst
decent people? Whatever sordid business she'd been
up to in Madrid, she should have faced up to it there
and left us out of it.]

She'd figured that she would start here and then build back to the outside world, but if she couldn't make it work with her grandparents, how could there be any hope for her?

"I went for a walk," Esmi said. It was the truth, but it didn't sound it, and the blood rushed to her face.

"Through the window?" Lourdes' voice was brittle.

"I didn't want to disturb you."

"Don't lie to me."

"I'm not."

"You sneaked out of this house," Lourdes said, her voice threatening to crack.

"I didn't sneak. I just couldn't get back to sleep after grandfather..."

"If you don't use the front door, it's sneaking. If no one knows where you are, it's sneaking." She glanced over her shoulder. "I won't have it, Rosa Esmeralda. Your grandfather..." She broke off and stomped into the kitchen.

She wanted to lash out at the girl—it was all too familiar. She grabbed the edge of the table and held tight as if it would fly out the door if she let go.

Teresa used to say hateful things to Lourdes. She'd blamed her for everything. Lourdes had tried to push aside self-recrimination as best she could, convinced as she was that she'd done her duty. She'd told herself that if Teresa refused to see that, then she had indeed failed.

But now Teresa was dead, and there was no chance of reconciliation. Not in this life. She could not lose Teresa's daughter, too. She refused to.

Esmi, left alone in her mother's bedroom, tried to come up with a white lie that would smooth things over, but for once she couldn't think of any. Her throat tightened and her eyes filled with tears. Her grandmother clearly did not want her here. She grabbed the suitcase and threw it on the bed; she would not wait around to be thrown out.

Lourdes went to the stove. The coffee pot was still warm and she quickly brought the saucepan of milk back to a boil. She returned to the bedroom, composed, carrying the cup of coffee. She saw the open suitcase.

"What are you doing?"she asked, horrified.

"I've got to get back to work," Esmi said cooly.

"But you just got here." She set the cup on the night table.

"We're in the middle of a big project. It was a stupid time to leave."

She opened a drawer in the wardrobe and took out the few clothes the portera had packed for her.

"Like mother like daughter," Lourdes accused, angry and hurt.

"You say that as if it were a bad thing," Esmi said, equally angry and equally hurt. She plopped the clothes into the suitcase and snapped the clasps shut. "I have to get back to work."

"'I have to get back to work.' You say that as if it were important. Family is what's important, Rosa Esmeralda." Lourdes stepped on her anger. Teresa had obviously coddled the girl. She must take more care how she spoke to her. She took a deep breath. "Esmita, *mi amor*," she coaxed, "don't go."

"What?"

Lourdes reached out and touched Esmi's arm. "Don't go like this. Sit. Please."

Esmi, brows knit and lips pursed, slumped next to the suitcase on the bed.

"Drink," Lourdes ordered, nodding toward the coffee, but Esmi just stared at it, her stomach roiling.

Lourdes pulled the chair closer to the bed—it scraped harshly against the tile floor. She sat down facing the girl, their knees almost touching.

"Your mother," her voice dropped and dripped with disapproval. "Your mother may have let you do whatever you felt like, but..."

"Grandmother," Esmi interrupted. She was in no mood to hear criticism of her mother.

Lourdes folded her hands in her lap and stared at them. "*Niña*, what I'm trying to say is, whether you want to hear it or not, some things are correct and proper, and other things are not." She glanced up at Esmi to see if the girl were going to bolt, and then looked back down at her hands. "This is a decent home." She fixed her gaze on Esmi. "And you, you are la *Señorita* Rosa Esmeralda Salvater Tena."

"*Ingeniera*," Esmi corrected. She couldn't help herself. "I graduated in computer science engineering, *abuela*. My title is *ingeniera*, not *señorita*."

"*Ingeniera*, how grand," Lourdes said with sarcasm before continuing in earnest. "It's your grandfather's name I'm concerned about. The name of Tena carries a great deal of weight in Fuentespina. Your grandfather may not have gone to La Universidad Politécnica de Madrid, but his conduct in the war not only redeemed the family name, it brought glory to it. Tena is a name to be proud of, a name to protect. It's up to you to uphold the honor of the family."

Naturally, Esmi had not considered any of this—to her it was so old-fashioned.

"It pains me to have to speak to you in this way," Lourdes said, "but it would be wrong to turn a blind eye. It would be shirking my responsibility to you." She threw her hands up. "Sneaking out like that! Galavanting about in the middle of the night! Alone. Defenseless. What were you thinking? It's improper—that goes without saying. It's also dangerous."

Lourdes' face wilted, all sternness gone, and she passed her hand across her eyes. "I'm too old for this." Her hands fell back into her lap. "You scared me, Esmi."

Esmi placed her hands on Lourdes'.

"I didn't mean to upset you, Grandmother," she said and felt truly contrite.

"What if something had happened to you out there? The least, the very least, I can do for your mother, may she rest in peace," Lourdes crossed herself, "is to try to keep you safe." She looked at the open window ruefully. "And keep you respectable, *ingeniera* or not."

"Let me stay," Esmi blurted.

"Let you? What a foolish thing to say. Of course you'll stay. This is your home."

At the time, Lourdes, poor fool, believed what she said.

"I'm sorry. I didn't think."

"No, you didn't." Lourdes beamed at her, her heart thoroughly warmed and soothed.

"Is Grandfather upset, too?"

"Your grandfather, thank Merciful God and the Blessed Virgin, doesn't know. And he mustn't, do you understand?"

Esmi didn't understand any of it—honor, name, impropriety—but there was no doubt her grandmother took it all very seriously, and she imagined so would her grandfather.

"It's good you're staying." Lourdes patted Esmi's knee. "Drink your coffee before it goes cold."

Esmi took a sip. The warmth in her mouth felt good, but it hurt to swallow. Lourdes saw her wince and said she would prepare some sage tea for her to gargle to sooth her throat.

"So," Lourdes said, "tell me what's going on."

Esmi looked confused.

Lourdes waggled her finger back and forth at the level of Esmi's neck. "Your neck, child. I saw it last night. What's happened to you?"

Esmi shook her head, meaning, nothing's wrong; meaning, I don't want to talk about it; meaning, delete from reality.

"Esmi, there's no doctor here," Lourdes worried.

"It's okay, *abuela*. A friend took me to the emergency room before I left the city." Esmi knew better than to try to explain a male flatmate. "And I'm fine."

"Are you sure?"

"Bit of pain. A sore throat. It will go away."

"Take that red scarf off," Lourdes ordered. "And your jacket. I'll be right back."

She left the room and returned with a tray she'd prepared earlier. She set it on the bed next to Esmi. One by one she pulled strips of cloth from a bowl and wrapped them gently around Esmi's neck. They were soaked in oil of thyme and would help with the bruising. Esmi found the odor strong, but not unpleasant.

"At least your mother's not alive to see this," Lourdes said as she worked.

Esmi held the bandages in place while Lourdes knotted one of her own cotton scarves around Esmi's neck to keep them in place.

"You don't want that silky thing to get stained," she said, when in point of fact, she intended to sneak the red rag into the trash first chance she got.

How to explain to Esmi that a red scarf roused memories of communism, that it was like waving a cape in front of a bull, and the old bull was Adelfo? Nor did Lourdes want to remember what, once upon a time, happened to women who had dared to wear red scarves, or even red lipstick. She looked at her beautiful, foolish granddaughter and shuddered thinking of it.

"And what about your eyes?" Lourdes asked. "Are you taking drugs? Painkillers maybe?" she prompted.

"No, Grandma. It's because of..." Esmi waved toward her neck. "It should go away in a few days."

"Did that ex-boyfriend do this to you?"

Esmi looked away.

"Boyfriends are no good, *niña*. You need a proper *novio*, someone who'll marry you."

Back in Madrid, after a long stint at the computer—when dawn and dusk would bleed one into the other, and she needed to shake free from work—Esmi would go in search of a dance floor. Tony, a workmate and later on her flatmate, told her he wondered what the others at work would say if they ever saw her wild-woman-of-the-dance-floor act. Not that she didn't dance well, she did, with abandon. They just wouldn't recognize her.

I, for one, would have liked to have seen that: Esmi dancing. Esmi carefree.

That's what Esmi was doing the night she met Lucho. Dancing at a discotheque. She was wearing her favorite little black dress, short and tight, with her favorite pair of blue stilettos. She'd draped a sheer, sky-blue Moroccan scarf over her shoulders—a partial veil to the low neckline. The black of the dress brought out the paleness of her skin, and the color of the scarf contrasted with her dark hair. Her hair was shorter then and her long silver earrings dangled almost to her shoulders, showing off her long neck.

She leaned into the bar, next to where Lucho sat, to order a drink. She'd noticed him right away. Like Esmi, he was in his twenties, but his hair was already thinning. He had a lean, muscular build that appealed to her. He wore glasses with designer frames and a white shirt, the sleeves rolled up just above his wrists, showing off a nice watch and nice forearms. His conservative tie was loosened and his suit jacket was folded carefully over his knee. The studied casualness of it all made her want to muss his hair and wad his jacket into a ball.

He cradled his hands on either side of his glass. Their eyes met and he smiled a sad little smile at her.

"You look like you're feeling sorry for yourself," Esmi said.

"You look like you're not."

"No time."

She let him pay for her Scotch on the rocks, and nodded toward the opposite side of the room. He followed her to a table near one of the dance floors, but she dragged him out to dance before he could sit down. Later in the evening, she learned that he was an ambitious young banker. Ambition was something she understood. He had also just had a final row with his parents, and since he lived with them, he was homeless.

He spent a few token nights on her sofa. Then he moved into the bedroom.

At first it was all, in her word, brilliant, and it continued on long enough—seven months—for Esmi to come to the conclusion that her long string of bad luck with men had come to an end.

That's when she came home to find a note from Lucho explaining that he had sorted things out with his family and was engaged to the girl they'd always expected him to marry. And, P.S., he would always love her.

El muy cabrón.

It caught Esmi blind-sided. Not that there hadn't been warning signs; there are always warning signs. She could see that, now. She had not, as he'd claimed, imagined the strange shifts in his moods or the way he'd been treating her—in the flat, in public, in bed.

She wandered from room to room, finding little pockets of empty air: in the closet where his suits had hung, in the refrigerator bare of juice bottles, next to the sofa where the barbells were not there to be tripped over, in the bed where...

She'd been sucker-punched, damn him. It left her a little crazy and a lot vindictive.

As far as Lourdes was concerned, Esmi could stare off in space on her own time. Lourdes had business with her.

"Tell me," Lourdes said, "this *sinvergüenza*, he isn't going to show up here looking for you, is he?" Her thoughts drifted to the guns standing in the corner of the kitchen nearest the back door.

Esmi shook her head. "Nobody knows I'm here."

"Nobody?"

Esmi shook her head.

She'd left a message at work that a family emergency

was taking her to Almería—the port city on the Mediterranean was a good 300 miles away from Fuentespina—and she'd told Tony she was going there as well.

"I just couldn't face... I don't know. Everything suddenly seemed changed. I needed to get away."

In fact, it was as if the oxygen in the atmosphere had altered from one day to the next, and the strength of gravity, and the direction rivers ran. And all because someone she'd loved, had slept with, bickered with, laughed with, someone she'd shared her life with had reached out and stopped the air from entering her lungs. Guns and knifes were scary, to be sure, but this... There was nothing to hide behind, nothing to duck; and just like in all those horrible dreams, she couldn't scream because there was no air to carry it. He'd just reached out.

Lourdes shook her head. "Rosa Esmeralda, this is what comes of living in Madrid all alone. A young lady should have family looking after her."

She allowed Esmi a quick cat nap, then she gave her a crockery mug of coffee to take to Adelfo. He was sitting in his usual place in the patio. There was grey stubble on his face, but his white shirt was crisp and he sat stiffly erect. He seemed at once jagged and hollowed out. She greeted him with a kiss on his good cheek, and sat next to him. He nodded and took the cup from her.

He regarded her in the clear morning light, and from the shadow of his nightmare. The harshness in his one functioning eye took her breath away.

"What is it, Grandfather?"

He shook his head and looked away.

"You had a rough night," she said.

He dismissed her with a wave of the hand.

Last night she had held that hand. According to her grandmother, he knew nothing of her "indiscretion." So why was he acting so cold to her?

The old bastard slurped his coffee and still did not look at her. She wavered, but rose and went back to the kitchen.

Sarmizegetusa, Dacia
The Priestess

C*ries and screams gusted through the city like the wind, but it was the blood that set her to trembling—her blood-smeared legs. It caused a shaking deep in her marrow, a rift that quaked her entire body. The pain, fear, outrage were her own, but her blood was consecrated to the Great Goddess, Bendis the Huntress. Trajan's ignorant mercenaries may not fear Her—bare-chested savages, desecrating the priestess, desecrating the innermost circle of Her sanctuary—but they would be made to pay. Nemesis, fearsome Daughter of the Night, would exact retribution.*

The priestess had scratched the first attacker. His flesh under her nails. He'd hit her in the face with his fist. Blood, in her throat from her nose, and on her face, her blood on his leathery skin.

These barbarians would know Her wrath. Nemesis the Implacable—bridle, scourge and sword. Nemesis, the Inescapable.

Blood bubbled up under her skin, pooling purple marks where they'd seized her arms to hold her, grabbed her breasts, her thighs. One gripped her stomach where there was little spare flesh to hold on to, but made good a hold anyway.

Blood dribbled from the wound along her jaw where one of the savages had lightly drawn the point of a dagger, the one who then loomed over her, eyes rolled back, mouth open, teeth bared, grunting and rutting, defiling Bendis, defiling her.

They all blasphemed on her body.
Bendis! Nemesis!

The hated Roman legionnaires, auxiliaries and barbarian allies were at work dismantling the wall around Dacia's fallen capital, the priestess's beloved and doomed Sarmizegetusa. She wrapped herself in a hooded cloak of dark wool, hiding herself within it—herself and the knife she used to slice the throat of goats, blood sacrifices offered up to Bendis. Let a Roman try to stop her, she told herself. But at the first sight of a foreign soldier—even at fifty paces and with his back to her—a trembling took hold of her and her grip grew slippery on the knife handle.

She gritted her teeth and muttered invocations to Bendis for strength. She changed direction, but not her destination. She was determined to seek out the vampire, and now that she'd recovered enough to walk the distance—according to her servant it would be five miles or more to reach his lair in the heart of the beech forest—nothing was going to stop her. Certainly not the servant's warnings: the vampire could attack as a wolf, a wildcat or a giant hawk.

The priestess slipped out of the city and stayed clear of the stone-paved road that led down the mountain. As she walked through the burned stubble that had been fields of barley and rye, she saw no living being, neither dog nor goat, farmer nor shepherd.

Then, as she had many times before, she was entering Bendis' domain, the beech forest with its high green canopy and grassy forest floor. Only this time it was daylight and she came alone, without devotees, without torches. Still she inhaled the sweet, crisp air and anticipated the embrace of the Goddess, expected to be enveloped again in the remarkable intensity of Her presence, waited for it to calm the convulsive shaking of her body.

What she felt instead was absence—cold, complete, desolate absence. She raised her arms to pray, but they dropped as dead weight at her side. She had been degraded, violated, her sanctity profaned; and Bendis had forsaken her.

She leaned against the smooth grey bark of an aged tree and sank to the earth. Bereft, enveloped in inner darkness, she laid her head in the grass and dirt and dried leaves.

Hours passed.

The sound of a man's footfall rousted her. She leapt to her feet and pulled her knife. But what she'd heard were only the man-like steps of a deer. The startled doe and her fawn sprang off in panicked flight. She could almost feel the mother animal's fear on her skin, the rapid vibration of her heart, beating even faster than her own.

She made a vow—since she could not be priestess to the Huntress, she herself would become huntress. She would be the wolf, not the deer. She walked on, determined.

The dusk-darkened woods had turned chill, and she shook all the more. Her body thrummed with pain. Her head jerked and darted like a robin's, and in the feeble light her eyes ached from trying to see what lurked behind each tree. The howl of wolves in the distance raised the hair on her neck.

Then she saw it: a solitary house with stone foundation, log walls and steep shingled roof.

An owl hooted somewhere behind her, and startled, she glanced over her shoulder. When she looked back at the house, a strange old man, tall and sticklike, stood in the doorway.

Balaurghiuchu, the vampire.

She called to him and approached. Facing him, this creature her servants deemed a monster, a calmness enfolded her, and her trembling stopped.

"Lord Balaurghiuchu, I have grave news. Sarmizegetusa has fallen to the Romans, and to escape dishonor, King Decebalus has slit his own throat."

The man said nothing, his face blank of emotion, empty of curiosity.

"I entreat you, sir. Help me wreak vengeance on our enemies." She found it hard to believe that this praying mantis of a man could be the fabled killer her servants whispered of, afraid of even saying his name. "If you are, as they say, a vampire."

He raised a thin, plucked eyebrow in response, and turned without a word.

She followed him into the dark house. In the twilight, near the door, she saw whitewashed walls dirtied with soot. He lit a tallow candle on the table. It smelled of grease and its flame sputtered and smoked.

"I have no enemies," he said in a voice barely louder than a whisper. "Only victims."

He closed the iron-braced door. The room shrunk to the limits of the smelly glow on the table.

"But I do have enemies, sir."

A gurgle rumbled in his throat, something like a chuckle, or a strangled bird, "I have no interest in revenge. I am a hunter. Like your Goddess." He held up a hand. "Oh yes, I've seen you in the wood, Priestess—hymns and chants, invocations, sacrifices. Making offerings to your deity. As I understand the way it works, you slaughter some animal, praise and plead, and then your great Goddess may answer your prayers, or She may not. The Gods are fickle that way. I, on the other hand, guarantee results. When I hunt, someone dies."

"Then hunt Romans. I will pay for your help. I have gold."

He shook his head once.

"I'm told, sir, that you weren't born a vampire. If that is true, then someone must have taught you your powers. I want you to teach me. I'm sure we can come to an agreement."

His mouth turned up, but it was no smile; his eyes remained cold. "This is a lonely life, Priestess." He circled, appraising her. "You might be attractive, once that swollen eye opens, that cut heals and the bruises fade. Would you pay the price of companionship?"

"If that is the price, yes. If we couple, will I then become a vampire?"

An amused grimace creased his gaunt face.

"Humans couple. Wolves, on the other hand, mate for life," he said.

For the first time her sense of well-being in his presence abandoned her, as if he'd snuffed a candle, and a shudder ran through her. His reaction was immediate, a dilating of the eyes, a slight twitch in the upper lip. She must conceal her reactions from him.

"And vampires," he continued, "vampires mate for death."

He watched for her reaction. She gave him none. He waved his hand impassively up and down, indicating her body, "Romans, I assume."

She suppressed a flare of rage before saying in an even voice, "I implore you, sir, let us not delay. We could begin our studies immediately, and then, later... Lord Balaurghiuchu, if you teach me, I am willing."

"Priestess, if there is willingness, it is I who will create it; I who will make and mold it. And if I should decide to do so, I will make you want me in a way most unbecoming to the High Priestess of Bendis."

"Sir, I no longer serve the Goddess. I desire to be a vampire. I want to kill Roman soldiers."

"Feeble nonsense," he snapped. "You desire! You refuse to understand. If I choose you, you will have me or die, because I will be the only one who can quench the thirst, fill the gaping emptiness that I will place in the deepest core of your being. You will beg, grovel, because, well... Priestess, you cannot imagine the anguish of need with which I will replace your soul."

She did not lower her gaze. She doubted this creature could ever dominate her. After all she was, or had been, High Priestess.

He sensed her skepticism and became more interested. Her very lack of wariness now aroused his predator blood.

"You've heard of souls, I'm sure," he said.

"The priests of Zalmoxis preach about an immortal soul. It's a strange idea."

He shrugged his bony shoulders. "You say you want to be a vampire, but your understanding is wanting."

He explained that each night a vampire is resurrected from his tomb, that he inhabits the night and feeds on the blood of humans to survive.

"A vampire is a superior being, with superior powers. He is indestructible."

But Balaurghiuchu kept certain crucial facts to himself, facts that the priestess learned only later on. He was not truly alive, nor truly dead. And there were dangers that could indeed put an end to his existence—sunlight, failure to return to his tomb before each sunrise, a stake through the heart and decapitation.

He told her that most humans served as sustenance and nothing more. After being attacked by a vampire, they simply died, or they might be kept alive for repeated feedings or to provide other services. But the end was the same; they died and did not become vampires. Only rarely did a vampire cultivate and initiate one of his victims. Then when the human died, he or she would become a vampire—vampire and consort to the ascendant vampire.

"Believe in it or not, Priestess, if I decide to keep you alive for a time, you will lose your soul. And once you are enthralled to me, I may have you do any number of—from your point of view—unspeakable things, but it is very unlikely that I shall transform you into one of us."

He slid behind her and lifted the cloak from her

shoulders. For an old man, she thought, he moved incredibly smoothly and quickly. Suddenly, he stood facing her. She was gripping the ceremonial knife in both hands over her stomach. He smiled in amusement.

"So, when the Romans relieved you of your virginity..."

Her fury flamed. She lifted the dagger. But smirking, he held her eyes. She lowered it.

"...When they savored your flesh, I'm sure you recall, Priestess, how it felt to lose all control of your body."

She tried hard to still her heart, to calm her stomach, to smooth the fear from her face, but her confidence wavered, and she quailed. That excited him, and she saw his excitement. If she reacted to his arousal with greater fear, the situation would soon spiral out of all control. She mustn't let that happen, not if she was going to get what she'd come for.

"If I decide to keep you," he whispered, "as I might decide to keep a stray cat, you'll have no more control over your body than when they raped you. Only, I'll control your mind as well, and as completely." He ran his finger along the painful cut on her jaw. The wound burned anew. "You want to run away now, don't you?" he said, "Not that you could."

He was wrong. She could certainly leave if she wanted. Two soldiers were not holding her down. And she held the knife, although she felt very relaxed listening to his whispery words, the threats feeling syrupy, her body finally at rest from the shaking, the dull ache subsiding, the sharp pangs quelled. A moment earlier she would not have been able to imagine this, a time when her body did not feel broken.

Balaurghiuchu moved behind her again. His odd,

metallic scent enveloped her. He placed one cool hand over her eyes and the other over her hands. The knife fell onto the packed clay floor. Had she let go of it? She felt his mouth, cold on her neck.

It was true she did not want to move, but it was not true she was incapable of movement and it was not true she wanted his touch. Her revulsion rose. He lifted his lips from her neck—she realized she must hide the strength of her will, the toughness of her need for vengeance. She feigned passivity, a compliance tinged with fear. It worked.

His teeth broke through the skin of her neck. It was nothing like the men's bites on her shoulder and breast. The vampire's smooth teeth sank deep into her flesh, and it burned hotter than when the soldiers entered her. She cried out, but did not scream. Calling on a lifetime of discipline as a priestess to the Huntress, she used her will to not pull away.

She felt the impulse to swoon, felt it come from him and let it happen. He carried her to his bed and she felt the odd and not unpleasant sensation of the blood being sucked from her neck. She let it go freely. It no longer belonged to Bendis. Bendis had discarded her. She felt odd fluttering thoughts as the blood was pulled from her and her neck burned and his mouth and face against her skin grew warmer.

She dared open her eyes, expecting to see the beastly apparition of stories told among servants, but instead, the vampire had the expression of a suckling babe, and she thought: oh, yes. I will get what I want. I will have my revenge against the Romans, and against this loathsome creature.

12

I'd just put the broom away in the kitchen when I heard a faint tapping, almost a scratching, at the door, a noise I well recognized.

I sighed because it was so early in the day, with all my morning chores yet to do, and I didn't know if *Doña* Pilar had settled into work yet at her desk. Once she did, I wouldn't see her till late afternoon, but at this hour she might still be flitting about. It's not that I was afraid of her exactly, but I felt more at ease when I knew where she was.

I opened the door, and there stood Reina, looking more stirred up than usual.

[That *loca*. She was simply called "Reina". What else? But was that good enough for Narda? No, she thought it was too plain, and tried to call her "*Señorita* Reina" and, heaven forbid, "*Doña* Reina." But Reina knew her place and thought Narda was making fun of her.]

Reina didn't like me calling her *señorita*, so as usual, I said, "Reina, *mi reina*," and she looked quietly pleased, as she always did when I greeted her that way.

Most people think our Reina's a scoop or two shy of a bushel, but let me tell you, she's as sane as you or me, considering. My kitchen table was one of the few places in town she was welcome. And I'm not talking charity—nasty thing, charity. She was welcome because I liked her. I would serve her some coffee and a bite to eat. When it was chilly, I would drape the table with a thick felt cloth that hung to the floor, cover that with a tablecloth and light the brasier underneath the table. Sometimes while she sat there, I would iron or peel potatoes and yak on and on, knowing that nothing I said would go any farther, and she'd have a pleased look on her face. Other times I would accompany her in silence at the table with a cup of coffee for myself, and her face showed she appreciated that, too. Given the fact she was strung tighter than a bow, being around her could be oddly restful.

When she wasn't sipping coffee, she'd make a tent of her hands over the cup as if protecting the steam. Sometimes she'd run her finger around the rim of the fine porcelain. That's right, I always served her coffee in *Doña* Pilar's china; it's the everyday set, which is still plenty fine by anybody's standards. I saved the crockery for *Señora* Rosario.

"I'd cook you up a couple eggs," I told her, "but *Señora* Lourdes"—as usual, Reina frowned at mention of the name—"hasn't brought the eggs this morning."

Then Reina smiled tenderly and said in a quiet voice, "Company."

I nodded. "Yes, *Señora* Lourdes must be on cloud nine. It's been a long time since she saw her granddaughter."

"Little girl, then. Very different."

"I bet," I said, thinking about the tight jeans and red scarf, and also noting that I'd seldom heard Reina put so many words together at one time.

Reina looked at me with longing, as if willing me to understand, to make whole the bits and pieces of her story.

She looked about the kitchen for witnesses, then touched my hand, tears in her eyes.

"My Justino," she whispered. "His eyes. His chin. The way he moved." She shook her head. "*La niña*, Nardita. She doesn't know him."

"But Reina, *mi reina*," I cooed. "How could she? Your Justino died over sixty years ago."

"It's not…right," she said, and stared into her coffee. After a moment she looked up. "The spitting image," she said and tapped her cheek beneath her right eye with her index finger.

Was she was confused, I wondered, using the gesture for emphasis instead of as the signal of warning, of "watch out?"

Later, I realized she'd known exactly what she was doing.

Esmi found it dim inside the chicken coop. Light sifted in between the rough wooden boards of the door—stripes thick with motes of dust—and through gaps between the adobe walls and the roof. Snatching the eggs toasty warm from the hens was not the game she remembered. The acrid stink overpowered her nose and went straight for the back of her throat, and the hens squawked and pecked at her hands.

From the patio the usual staticky litany of bad news sounded on the old transistor radio.

"Esmi!" her grandmother called from the kitchen door. "Esmi!"

"How do you expect me to hear the radio with all that racket?" the old bastard barked from his chair in the patio.

Esmi heard Lourdes make soothing noises to her grandfather as she crossed the patio to the hen house.

"*M'ija*, there you are," Lourdes said from the doorway. When she saw Esmi's face and one lone egg in the basket, she grinned. "Heavens, don't tell me you're afraid of my pretty girls."

She instructed Esmi on how to gather eggs, as she had when Esmi was a little girl.

"You used to be quicker, and you didn't take any of their guff," Lourdes said. "Narda will be waiting for these eggs. She's the housekeeper at the big house, you know," she said proudly.

That's how I got to know Lourdes as well as I did, her delivering the eggs, because otherwise she kept pretty much to herself. Not that she had much choice. When she first came to town as a young bride, the other women started out snubbing her, and it had become a habit. If you ask me, she'd done them all a favor by taking the old bastard off their hands, but she was an outsider and they resented her for snapping up one of the few eligible bachelors around.

Lourdes told Esmi that she expected her to deliver the eggs to the big house that day.

Esmi groaned. "Please, no, Grandma. I've already run into *Doña* Pilar once today, and once is plenty."

Lourdes' jaw dropped. "You met *Doña* Pilar?"

"Yes. From what you'd said about her, I expected some kind of saint. But that..." Esmi censored herself for her grandmother's sake, "...that woman is no saint."

"You met her? Like that?" Lourdes looked Esmi up and down in dismay and picked a chicken feather from the girl's hair.

Not only had she met her, Esmi told Lourdes, but the

woman had offered her a job tutoring her stepson. "She couldn't seem to get it through her head that I'd turned the job down. I wouldn't be surprised if she were waiting for me right now."

Lourdes face blanched whiter than the eggs in her basket. Oh, the shame of it. *Doña* Pilar had seen Esmi when she was out traipsing about... And yet, she'd offered the girl a job. And as a teacher! A granddaughter of hers, a teacher! Now that was something to be proud of... But had Esmi accepted the favor with modesty and gratitude? No! The pipsqueak of a girl had said no, and to *Doña* Pilar, of all people... *Doña* Pilar was a great lady. She lived in the big house, for heaven's sake. She owned most of the land for as far as you could see, and then some. The fate of Fuentespina and of everyone in it rested in her lap... Esmi's behavior was inconceivable. Lourdes couldn't bare to think...

These thoughts, all in a jumble, heated up her face, made it burn with disgrace, and not a little fear. If Lourdes were to open her mouth, it seemed she would only sputter. She would sound like her hens, all clucks and cackles. She pressed her lips tight.

"Grandma?" Esmi said. "Are you all right?"

"*Desgraciada*!"

Lourdes turned and stomped past Adelfo on her way back to the kitchen, muttering, "ingrate, ill-mannered..."

He showed no interest.

Esmi, bewildered, followed her into the kitchen. Lourdes closed the door, faced her wayward grandchild and placed her hands in prayer position under her chin, but there was no entreaty in her voice.

"You will go at once to the big house. You will apologize to *Doña* Pilar and you..."

"Apologize for what?" Esmi said.

"And you will beg *Doña*..."

"Beg?"

"Do not interrupt your elders, Rosa Esmeralda! You have shamed your family."

"How have I..."

"Shh!" Lourdes made the sound short and harsh.

It startled Esmi—she hadn't been shushed since primary school. She raised her hands as if in surrender, but she was no more surrendering than Lourdes was entreating.

"You will," Lourdes began again, "beg *Doña* Pilar to forgive your impudence. You will thank her for her kind offer of employment, and you will tell her you will be honored, do you hear me, honored to teach *Señorito* Roberto."

"But Grandma, it's absurd."

"Do you call good manners absurd? Do you call respect absurd? Holy Mother of God grant me patience!"

Face-offs and laying-down-the-laws and or-elses— Teresa had had her fill of them growing up, and look how well they'd worked on her. So she'd made a point of raising Esmi with a light hand. Now Esmi floundered. She didn't know how to stand up for herself against her grandmother—she didn't have the practice. But she was not well-versed in knuckling under either.

"I don't want to work for her," she said. "I don't like her."

"Honored, do you hear me?"

"Grandma, I have a job. In Madrid, remember?" She reached in her pocket for a cigarette before remembering that Lourdes did not approve and that she only had a couple left anyway.

"You little idiot. Do you understand nothing? If you don't accept *Doña* Pilar's offer, if you don't obtain her forgiveness, how can we face her? You are in Fuentespina now. Your grandfather and I live here, in Fuentespina. *Doña* Pilar is Fuentespina."

"You're afraid of her," Esmi said.

She was finally getting the picture.

["It's not a matter of fear, it's a matter of respect."]

Esmi thought the whole thing was medieval, but fear she understood. "Grandma," she said, gently now, "I'm not a people person. I'm a computer programmer. I write code, alone, in a cubicle. I'm not a teacher. I don't know anything about it."

"Nonsense, look at all the schooling you've had. More than anyone in the family, more than all of us put together."

"That doesn't mean I can teach. I don't know a thing about kids. I have no patience. And I don't want to. You're shaking your head, Grandma, but if I'm not a good teacher, won't that embarrass you? And in a few days, when I quit to go back home..."

"A few days! Surely after coming all this way you'll stay longer than that."

Esmi wanted to plead with her that she was tired, that she needed to rest.

"Esmi, you're not a little girl anymore. You have responsibilities."

"But Grandma..."

It was no use; the fear that she'd seen on her grandmother's face undid her. She was caving, and they both knew it.

Lourdes gave her a gentle smile. "Look at it this way, that clothing store you talked about last night that you want to begin..."

"Not a store, Grandma. A start-up, my own software company."

"Well, this company you dream about, *Doña* Pilar is a very successful businesswoman, an important person with connections, influence. Who knows?"

"I can't quite see *Doña* Pilar as my fairy godmother," Esmi said.

After Esmi, at Lourdes' prompting, had made herself reasonably presentable, Lourdes handed her the basket of eggs.

"Now go," she said, patting Esmi on the cheek. She made the sign of the cross on Esmi's forehead, "*Que Dios te bendiga, hija!*"

13

Reina had left and I was making up the tray for *Señorito* Roberto's breakfast when I heard the firm rat-a-tat-tat on the kitchen door that could only be *Señora* Rosario. I groaned.

Rat-a-tat-tat, it came again, more insistent than ever.

Señora Rosario used to walk right in, until one early morning, not finding me in the kitchen, she walked on through into the main part of the house and came face to face with *Doña* Pilar, who'd come looking for me to complain about Lord-knows-what. I heard a commotion—any noise in this house constitutes a commotion. *Doña* Pilar hissing something about flogging and *Señora* Rosario stammering apologies. As I came into the room, a very pale *Señora* Rosario rushed past me in a blind beeline for the kitchen door, her not inconsiderable pride shredded and flapping in the wind.

That was the last time *Señora* Rosario helped herself to the welcome mat; and it gave me a breather for a number of weeks, the weeks then working themselves into months before she came back—so many, in fact, that I'd started to miss her. She told me, not then but much later and not giving up any details, that she'd never in her life been so insulted, *nunca jamás*, and certainly not by anyone in the big house. I thought, then she hadn't been around the big house much.

"Taking insults is stock and trade in service," my mum used to say. "Never answer back, that's rule one. Just say, 'as you wish, ma'am,' or some such nonsense. Otherwise keep your mouth shut. That way you won't swallow the insults whole. Let them roll off you like water off oilcloth. Whatever you do, don't be cowed, but be sure to keep your pride to yourself, keep it deep inside where it's safe and they can't see it."

Mum knew what she was talking about—she'd spent two years in prison. She always told me there was nothing to be ashamed of in that, that she'd been in the best of company there.

"And remember, little girl, Our Lord was imprisoned, and any apostle worth his salt. And look at all the saints, hundreds of them, maybe thousands. Don't you ever hang your head on my account."

But still, it hurts. I can't help it. It gives me a twinge of shame to say it out loud: my mother, the jailbird.

At the time, two years was an uncommon sentence— light to say the least. I don't think they quite knew what to make of her. Mum was nothing if not original: a card-carrying anarchist and a devout Catholic.

[It was an act of patriotism to denounce enemies of the state. In fact it was a crime not to. Before '41, denouncements didn't have to be signed, so there's no official record of who informed on Marigraviela. Not that any is needed.]

Mum was a particular fan of the anarchist leader Federica Montseny, and she'd kept a pamphlet from before the war, from the time of the Republic when Montseny was

Minister of Health and Social Services—the first woman minister of anything ever in Spain.

[*El Generalísimo*—may God keep him in His glory—put an end to that kind of nonsense. A woman's place is in the home as a wife and mother.]

So someone informed on her and Mum was convicted under the Law of Political Responsibilities. She'd been in the same prison as Reina, only Reina was in fourteen years and a day. Her crime: she was heartbroken and wouldn't shut up about it, that's what Mum said. They both came back mouths shut, but Mum still held her head high.

Reina and Justino.

Reina had been in love with Justino her whole life. They'd made a childhood pact when she was just eight and Justino was ten, and from that day on she'd looked forward to their getting married. He started openly courting her when she turned 16, and they made their engagement official in 1935. She'd always thought her real life would really start on their wedding day. Then one week before the ceremony, Justino was killed.

A week later, a measly week, and he would have been Reina's legal husband. The poor thing still would have gone to prison, and she still wouldn't have a hole to drop dead in —Justino's house would probably have been confiscated. But still, one week later and she would have seen her life begin, if only briefly. One week and it would have been the official loss of an official husband—she'd have an official paper to prove that half her soul had been amputated. It might have made all the difference.

Look at me, imagining a meager week's difference for Reina, *mi reina*. If I'm going to fantasize, why don't I dream up an escape to another country, a long life without fear and as many children as she wanted? What can I say? We're taught to think small here.

Now *Señora* Rosario's family was *nacionalista* all the way. (The exception in the family was her brother—*Señor* Valentín never bothered himself about politics more than was absolutely necessary.) To this day a picture of Franco hangs in the Salgado sitting room. So *Señora* Rosario never understood what it was like for Mum and Reina. No constable or *guardia civil* ever stopped her in the street, and she didn't know what it was like to work for *Don* Cayetano, or for anyone else either. Some might blame her for a lack of feeling, but I chalk it up to a lack of imagination. And can you fault her for believing—hook, line and sinker, or as some would say: crook, liar and stinker—everything the priest, her father and her husband told her? She's not a bad sort. It's just that sometimes you've got to dig a bit deeper to get to where she's not a bad sort.

Rat-a-tat.

I answered *Señora* Rosario's knock at the door.

"*Buenos días*, Nardita," she said as she peered past me. She looked disappointed to find me alone. I guessed she'd been hoping to run into Lourdes here. Even though *Señora* Rosario wouldn't go out of her way to say hello to her, in fact quite the opposite, that wouldn't keep her from leaping at the chance to pump her about Esmi.

"*Señora* Lourdes is late with the eggs," I said.

"And why would I care about that?"

"No reason. Coffee?" I asked, calculating what chore I would have to let slip until the next day.

She turned me down, but didn't show any sign of leaving. It seemed there was a second item on her agenda.

"Narda, have you seen that handsome young man around town?" she asked pointedly.

Damn! I'd warned *Señor* Iban that he wasn't being careful enough.

I laughed. "A young man in Fuentespina?"

I turned away from *Señora* Rosario and checked on the water for *Señorito* Roberto's tea to escape her scrutiny.

"And handsome to boot? I think I'd notice," I said, peering under the lid to the tea kettle.

"I could swear I saw him enter the big house last night."

I removed the kettle from the stove. "A man in this house?" I snorted. "What were you drinking, *Señora* Rosario?"

"Narda!"

"Sounds like a hallucination to me. Or a mirage," I said. "Remind me, what does a young man look like? If they don't have grey hair, what color is it, purple?"

"You're being silly."

"Not purple?"

"Nardita!"

"Seriously, this place is a graveyard in the offing. I should get me to Madrid, or at least Badajoz."

Señora Rosario would not be put off. "Who is he, Narda?" She squinted at me through her thick glasses.

"How would I know?" I said. "He's your delusion, not mine. Excuse me, *Señora* Rosario. I have to get this tray up to the *señorito*." I nodded toward the tray with my hands in my apron pockets and waited.

She raised her eyebrows at me with a sigh before she trundled out. I closed the door behind her and leaned against it.

You may have noticed that, besides complaining about the stairs, I haven't said all that much about the *señorito*. Well, there was something not right there, and I didn't like to think about it. He was one of the three people who had blank spaces about them, black holes where stories should be. *Señor* Iban was one and *Doña* Pilar was the biggest, blankest story of all. As for the *Señorito,* I reciprocated with a big blank spot in my heart where I should have felt something for him; I should have felt something other than off-balance and uneasy around him. I think I understand now what was going on, but at the time I figured it was just my yawning lack of maternal feelings.

After all, the poor mite had lost his mother when he was tiny and he had Dragon Lady for a stepmother; if nothing else, that should have squeezed a drop or two of pity out of me. If *Don* Manuel Felipe had met and married *Doña* Pilar first, they might have had a son who wasn't so puny, a son with a little blood in him. He was too thin, pale blond with dusty-looking skin overlaid with a pallor of sickness. He was nothing to write home about in the brains department either. School was no picnic for him. But he was dogged about it, you have to give him that. He nagged me to nag *Doña* Pilar —as if she would listen to me—to get him a tutor. He was worried, and rightly so, about being able to catch up after missing so much school.

On top of that, the poor kid was a cold fish—without a spark of charm to offset his dull wit—and to make things worse he was at that awkward age that only a mother can love, when there's nothing left of a little boy's charm and no sign yet of any grace of manliness. But *Señorito* Roberto had no mother. Just the Ice Queen.

[*Doña* Pilar was very conscientious about the boy, a fine example of duty and Christian charity—many women in her position would have done far less.]

The *señorito* was in bed when I entered his room with the tray. He looked the same as usual, and said little, as usual. I set the tray down on the table, adjusted his pillows for him to sit up and brought him the tray. I gave him the news that *Doña* Pilar was looking for a tutor for him.

His face brightened. "She didn't say."

I saw a glimmer of how lonely this boy was, lonely to the nth degree. I felt bad for raising false hopes. "But don't hold your breath, *señorito*. I don't think she's having much luck."

He slumped into his pillows.

"But Narda, I want to be prepared for when I go back to school."

"Well, don't look at me, *señorito*."

He looked askance. "I didn't mean you."

You could do worse, I thought. Even though in my day schooling was pretty limited for girls: reading, sums, religious instruction, sewing and calisthenics plus a lot of hogwash about the mission of the *Generalísimo* and our sacred duties as future Spanish wives and mothers. I still know a thing or two. But then again, maybe nothing that would help him pass a test.

I laid out clothes. "In case you decide to get dressed today," I said, and collected yesterday's nightclothes.

"Surely my stepmother could find someone in the city who would come here. They could live in. Like you."

Now there's a carrot, I thought, and more work for me.

He pushed away the tray—he'd taken only a nibble or two—and closed his eyes. I removed the teacup from the tray and set it on the table next to the bed, and with his clothes balled under my arm, left with the tray.

The big house had a front-door knocker, but *Doña* Pilar never had any visitors, did she. Sometimes I thought it existed solely to give me one more thing to polish. It was a bronze hand, life-size, that hung like dead weight from a bronze cuff in the center of the door—the cold fingertips gently grasping a small bronze apple that you rapped against a little metal disk on the wood.

As I came down the stairs, I heard its unexpected bang-bang-bang.

14

No matter how curious I was, I couldn't very well open the front door—not with a wad of clothes under my arm and a tray of half-eaten food. So I dropped my load off in the kitchen first, expecting to hear another round of knocking or two, but I didn't hear a thing.

When I hurried back and opened the door, I didn't see Esmi right off. She was sitting on the paving stones to the side of the door—sullen as a schoolgirl and leaning against the wall smoking a cigarette. She wore dark glasses, but unlike earlier that morning, her hair was tidier and she wore lipstick. She had on those same tight jeans, but instead of the mold-green tee shirt, she wore a white camisole shirt under the man's sports coat. Plus a cotton kerchief at her neck instead of red silk, and blue high heels instead of tennis shoes. Despite the get-up, my first impression was of a child who's suffered no small insult.

What flashed in my mind was the image of myself after Mrs. Pinniger fired me—me waiting on that London bus-stop bench. I hadn't wanted the fool woman's husband pawing me, and let me tell you, she would have been a lot better off keeping me and getting rid of him. Anyway there I'd sat, all afternoon and into the evening, with a plastic shopping bag stuffed with my few clothes and belongings, letting bus after bus go by because I couldn't bring myself to face my brother and I had no place else to go.

That's how miserable Esmi looked.

But my first impression of "poor thing" quickly gave way to irritation. I'm not as stodgy as some people around here. In fact, I may very well be the least stodgy of any of them, but still, sitting like that, on *Doña* Pilar's doorstep! Is that any way to behave? I shoved my hands in my pockets and scowled down at her.

"I brought the eggs," she said and nodded toward the basket next to her on the paving stones.

I held out my hand for the basket—I wasn't about to lean over and collect it myself. She handed it up to me.

"You don't have any cigarettes, do you?" she asked.

I shook my head and she carefully stubbed out the one she was smoking on a paving stone and placed it in between the cellophane and the paper of the squashed pack in her pocket. Then she stood and played a tattoo on her derriere to wipe off the dust. Quite unnecessary, I thought, and insulting, because everyone knew I kept my doorstep clean. Hadn't I just swept it that morning?

"So, Narda, right?" she asked.

No title of address, mind you, no "ma'am" or "by you leave," just plain "Narda," hardtack dry.

[They say such bluntness is the norm now in cities, but mercifully one need not be exposed to such poor manners here.]

"But your boss called you something different. María Bernarda, wasn't it?" She held out her hand. "I guess we're shirttail relatives."

Maybe that was why she was being so familiar—my

cousin married to her uncle. I waited a moment before taking her hand, wanted to make sure she felt my hesitation. She leaned forward and kissed me on both cheeks. It took be by surprise. Her skin was soft and her hair damp from washing. She must have used some fancy shampoo, because her hair smelled better than most perfumes.

"Call me Narda," I stammered. "Everyone does, including Miss High-and-Mighty."

"I have to talk to her," she said.

I snapped back, "I can count your money out for you just fine."

She looked surprised. "I don't care about the eggs." she said.

I backpedaled—I'm told I can be a bit prickly. "I wouldn't let your grandmother hear you say that."

She sighed, and I thought, still one leg over my high horse, this girl better not be exasperated with me. I was the one around here with exclusive rights to exasperation.

"Would you tell *Doña* Pilar I'm here," she said, just like that—no "please," no "ma'am," no "cousin" even.

"She can't be disturbed," I said, and I wasn't lying.

I expected some snooty demands on Esmi's part, but instead she looked relieved, unburdened even. She may have stood up to *Doña* Pilar that morning, but that was before she had an inkling of who she was standing up to. Someone had clued her in, or tried to. In a flash I saw her argument with Lourdes.

"*Doña* Pilar stays closed up in her office until late afternoon," I said. "Your grandmother won't expect you to wait."

She looked doubtful.

"You can tell her I told you not to. Come into the kitchen. I'll pay you and return your basket. But next time come to the kitchen door."

"Fine with me," she said, wrinkling her nose at the door knocker.

Stepping inside the entryway, she stared up through her sunglasses at the heavy, wrought-iron chandelier—seventeenth-century—hanging from between the dark wood vigas high above our heads. Then her eyes turned to the simple seventh-century-BC Tartessian urn on the nineteenth-century parquetry table. I told her about it and pointed out the Roman mosaic under our feet.

"It was removed from ruins not far from here. Some of the artifacts from there date back to the second century, but this is probably fourth century."

"So, you know a lot about history," she said.

I beamed. "I learned a lot from the *señor*. *Don* Manuel Felipe was very proud of his heritage and of this house. He used to tell anybody who would listen, and I liked to listen. Many of these items are museum pieces."

Esmi shook her head. "It's like living in a mausoleum."

I didn't mind that she snubbed the house. I could see her point.

"Up there," I pointed to the stone stairs, "are *Doña* Pilar's private rooms and *Señorito* Roberto's bedroom."

She nodded without interest.

I thought about how she'd stood up to *Doña* Pilar, and yet she'd looked so lost sitting by the door. "How about a cup of chocolate?" I invited.

In the kitchen Esmi slouched in a chair at the table. "I promised my grandmother I would take *Doña* Pilar's job."

"Ah," I said, as if I hadn't already figured that out, as if I couldn't see the conversation between her and Lourdes.

I placed the demitasse cups on the table—the chocolate so thick you could stand a spoon up in it—and a plate of cookies. Then the stranger-on-a-bus syndrome struck again—you know, when the passenger next you, who you don't know from Adam, tells you their life story, tells you things they wouldn't even tell their priest. Well, one sip of chocolate, and Esmi let loose about her and Lourdes.

Looking at her more closely now, I could see she looked a lot like Teresa, and for a moment that put me off. But Teresa would never be sitting with me in the big house prepared to do the very thing she loathed just to make things easier on Lourdes. Never.

"Whatever she says or does, I'm sure your grandmother," I avoided any mention of old Adelfo, "is in seventh heaven having you back."

"But this thing with *Doña* Pilar," she grimaced. She took off her sunglasses. Her eyes were a honeyed brown, but the whites were rusty with tiny pinpricks of red. She noticed me squinting at her, and started to reach for her glasses but stopped. "Allergies," she said, by way of explanation.

I'd never seen allergies do that to your eyes, but I didn't say so. Instead I said, "Look, *Doña* Pilar is expecting you this afternoon at 5:00, she already gave me instructions."

"But," she sputtered, "why would she...?"

"The point is, you don't have to say a word to her about taking the job. As far as she's concerned, you already have."

"But I said no."

I shook my head. "No one says no to *Doña* Pilar."

Esmi ran her spoon around and around the small cup, long empty of chocolate.

"Would you like to meet the *Señorito* Roberto now?"

"Not really," she said.

She looked so defeated. There was that shadow I'd sensed before that made me think she was nursing a fresh wound.

"You look tired," I said.

She shrugged.

"Tell you what. I'll tell *Doña* Pilar that today you are regrettably indisposed. Then you can, with a clear conscience, tell your grandmother that *Doña* Pilar expects you tomorrow."

I thought I'd have to convince her to tell the white lie, but she needed no convincing. It seemed Esmi was not above twisting the facts when it suited her.

15

I showed Esmi to the kitchen door and the narrow path along the side wall that led to the plaza. Out came the sunglasses again. The way was uneven, and so narrow that except at high noon it lay cloaked in shadows. I looked up at the sliver of brilliant blue overhead and down at the dark at her feet and warned her not to trip.

At the edge of town, Lourdes stood planted near Adelfo in the patio, hands on her hips, inspecting the same old workaday blue sky, as if it held signs of something other than another dry, cloudless day.

"We should whitewash the house, *viejo*," she said. "It's been ages."

"The walls are the same as they were yesterday," Adelfo said. "There's no need to go fussing about just because that girl's here."

"Why do you say things like that? That girl is our granddaughter."

He waved her complaint away.

"Besides, Esmi has nothing to do with it," she said.

But of course she did. It was having Esmi here, seeing things through her eyes, that made the difference. And it wasn't just the whitewash. There were the dingy walls in the dining room and the knob missing on the sideboard, the broken window pane covered with cardboard in the kitchen and the cracked floor tile in front of the basin, the wire holding the legs on Adelfo's chair in place, and the outhouse. It smelled more than it should; they hadn't been adding lime, and really they should dig a new hole.

"The house," Lourdes said, "is an embarrassment in and of itself."

"There was a time you thanked God for this house."

She stood behind his chair and rested her hands on his shoulders. "Not the house, old man, you."

She patted the hair at the nape of his neck. It was time to get the scissors out again. Adelfo slapped at her hand.

"Well, the house came with me, didn't it? Didn't it?" he insisted. "There was a time you were damn happy to have a roof over your head."

"Don't, Adelfo."

She sat down near him on a low milking stool, and smoothed her apron over her lap.

"If you feel the need to whitewash, then whitewash," he said.

Lourdes sighed. What had she expected? That he would help? At his age, and with women's work? The thought of the job was overwhelming. It had been so long—how many coats would it take? Then there was the nasty smell of the lime, the big, clumsy rubber gloves that made her hands sweat, the dipping of the coarse brush with the long handle in the whitewash and hauling it overhead, swabbing of the walls with it, back and forth, the ache in her back and shoulders.

"But if there's not a bag of lime in the goat shed," he added, "I don't know where you're going to get any."

She nodded. She would check later. She reached out and

touched his knee. It felt bony even through the thick wool of his trousers.

"She's a pretty girl, isn't she? A good girl."

He didn't answer. Had he heard her?

"What was all that about earlier?" he said.

"All what?"

"You went flying by here with the girl on your tail."

"Oh, that. A little misunderstanding."

"Misunderstanding! I told you last night. The girl is trouble. Maybe more than trouble."

"How can you say that? Wait till you hear. I was going to let Esmi tell you herself when she got back, but I want to tell you, so you can see how wrong you are about her."

"Then tell me already."

"*Doña* Pilar has asked Esmi to teach *Señor*ito Roberto while he's sick." She slapped his knee. "She's hired Esmi. Our Esmi. Isn't that wonderful news?"

He shook his head. "I don't know," he said.

As Esmi crossed the plaza after leaving the big house, she felt her back tingle as if a pair of eyes were trained on her—maybe the boy was watching her from an upstairs window, or maybe it was *Doña* Pilar. But Esmi told herself she was being silly. She did not turn around—backs could not know they were being looked at. Still, the urge to glance back was demanding of her attention, and as she reached the edge of the plaza the tingling grew stronger and the impulse to check behind her was throwing a full-fledged temper tantrum. So even though Esmi was not looking over her shoulder, she wasn't quite seeing what was in front of her either, much less to the side.

A hand grabbed at her arm.

Esmi gasped with her whole body. She jerked her arm away, but Reina's hand had latched on tight.

"Let go of me!" Esmi shrieked, adrenalin rushing every which way through her veins.

Reina looked up at her and held on. "They pretend he never existed," she said in a quiet voice.

The beseeching look in the old woman's eyes gave Esmi pause, and she forced herself to calm down, embarrassed now at being frightened by this tiny old lady.

"Because if he never existed," Reina whispered, "then he was never betrayed."

Yes, she was talking about Justino again, the love of her youth, the love of her old age and of all the long years in between. Who else was on her mind, was ever on her mind? She'd been on the same track, a closed loop, since August 1936.

Meanwhile, Esmi's thoughts ping-ponged all over the board. So far that morning she'd taken on *Doña* Pilar and wrangled, unsuccessfully, with her grandmother. She had little red wounds and bruises raising on her hands from the chickens pecking her, not to mention the marks hidden under the kerchief—and in all the fuss she'd forgotten to take her pain killers and was very much feeling the lack of them. She'd also found, unexpectedly, a confidant in a dowdy old housekeeper—me! She'd yet to find anyone who would share their memories of her mother with her, and what was going on with her grandfather? Then there was the man last night, *Señor* Iban, who would be waiting for her right here in the plaza at midnight. The prospect made her throat throb and little white moths dance in her stomach. And this little creature here, she could hardly ignore her, seeing as she was clutching her arm and probably raising even more bruises.

"You're talking about what's-his-name again? Julio?"

"Justino," Reina hissed her correction with some vexation. She looked over her shoulder before repeating in a whisper, "Justino. They killed him."

"*Señora*, please." Esmi tried to remove Reina's hand from her arm.

"Reina. I'm just Reina."

"Look, I..."

"Oh!" Reina shook her head in wonder. "That nose, that brow, the same expression about the mouth, dear mouth, and the eyes. Please, let me see your eyes."

She reached for Esmi's glasses with her free hand. Esmi pulled back.

"Please, let me see his eyes."

Esmi thought it might be the quickest way to get rid of her, so she took off her sunglasses.

"The very same color," Reina said, looking at Esmi with adoration. "The very same." Then, with an odd expression of dismay, terror even, as if she wanted to look away but could not, the old woman fell back. "No love. His eyes, but no spark of love there, no love for me." She pressed her fingers hard against her mouth and squeezed her eyes shut.

Even though Esmi was finally free from Reina's grip, she did not make a run for it. She thought of the thousands of people she passed in Madrid each day, thousands who never noticed her, never really looked at her, certainly not like this old lady did.

"Are you all right?" she asked Reina.

Reina opened her eyes and let her fingers slip down her chin and come to rest on her breast. She was calmer, calmer for her, anyway; and she ventured a sad little smile.

"Your mother, her likeness to my Justino was strong; but you, dear child, only a twin sister could be more like him."

"But, *señora*, there's no Justino in my family, I swear."

"Daughter of Teresa. Granddaughter of..." She tapped her forefinger under her eye. "Watch out for that one." Her voice raised almost to normal volume. "He won't like having you around, not with that face, that precious face."

That's when *Señora* Rosario entered the plaza. She flapped her hands at Reina, *mi reina*, shooing her away like a begging dog. Reina moved a few feet away, but no further.

"For heavens sake," *Señora* Rosario said. "Leave the poor girl alone."

"Beware, Rosa Esmeralda Salvater Tena," Reina said. "Beware."

Señora Rosario stamped her foot and Reina slunk off with many backward glances.

Esmi was not unhappy to be rid of the old woman, but was shocked at how crudely *Señora* Rosario had driven her off.

"Don't mind Reina," *Señora* Rosario said. She circled her finger by her ear.

"If you'll remember, we spoke this morning, but we weren't properly introduced. I'm Rosario Salgado Sánchez, widow of Chaves." She tilted her head rather nobly. "At your service."

Esmi opened her mouth to excuse herself and get away from this woman, but *Señora* Rosario cut her off.

"And you, child, you don't need to introduce yourself. Why, I knew your mother when she was in diapers." She crossed herself slowly and with deliberation. "May she rest in peace."

It had taken Esmi no more than an instant to take a dislike to *Señora* Rosario.

"I know all about you, too," she added with an annoyingly knowing look.

As I said, you have to dig a little sometimes to get a glimpse at the decent, generous soul beneath, and Esmi had no inclination to dig, not with all the other things she had on her mind. Besides her neck ached, and she had a headache from not sleeping.

"It was most distressing when Teresa ran off," *Señora* Rosario said. "And then later the divorce!"

Señora Rosario can be just as tenacious as Reina, only she grabs with words instead of hands.

"Well, it was terrible about her death, just terrible. *Que en paz descanse*!" She crossed herself again, less precisely this time, a bit slapdash even. "And so young. My condolences, *hija*."

Esmi thanked her cooly, and tried to slip away, but *Señora* Rosario wasn't going to let her go that easily.

"So, Rosa Esmeralda, lucky you, working in the big house. It's beautiful, don't you think? Wouldn't you love to live in a place like that, surrounded by all those beautiful things, "

"Chipped mosaics and old dented urns? No thank you."

Señora Rosario was scandalized—it's one of her talents, her great leaps of scandalization. "But all that history and tradition..."

"I'm not interested in any of that. It's now I care about, and the future."

Señora Rosario harrumphed.

Esmi went on, "Everyone around here, you're all looking backward all the time. If you ask me, it's not healthy."

"And, young lady, if you are walking alone in the night and you hear footsteps behind you, do you not think it prudent to look over your shoulder?"

Esmi looked at her askance and *Señora* Rosario saw her askance and raised it.

"Fine. Don't listen," she said. "I'm just an old woman. I drag my past with me everywhere I go. I can't help it, can't do anything about it. I hear it thud thud thud on the stones every time I cross the plaza. But you, you're different, aren't you? You're young, the future stretches before you like a field of new snow, fresh and clean, with nary a footprint in sight, right?" She harrumphed again as only she can. "A life without nostalgia, without regrets. Must be nice. Enjoy it while you can, *niña*. It won't last."

How dare she, Esmi thought. Did this woman really think she had no regrets, no sorrows? After all, hadn't she just offered Esmi condolences on her mother's death? She tried to take her leave again, but *Señora* Rosario plucked her back once more.

"One moment, *hija*. It was terribly early when I saw you this morning. In fact, so early, one might call it night. Being from the city, perhaps you don't realize the dangers. You must be careful, my dear."

"Of what?"

"Beasts," she whispered. "Wild beasts."

"You're kidding."

"You're not in the city anymore. Have you ever seen the carcass of a fully grown stag brought down by a bobcat? The throat ripped apart? Or a whole deer left uneaten, killed out of pure blood lust? They do that, you know."

"Good thing I'm not a deer."

"Go ahead, make jokes. See where it gets you. Then there's *El Otro*."

"*El Otro*? What other?"

"You know, *El Otro, Tío Juan*," she said, her voice low and a bit exasperated.

Esmi still looked confused.

Señora Rosario dropped her voice lower. "Wolves," she whispered.

[One never says that word aloud. One says *El Otro, Tío Juan or El Amigo,* because saying that animal's name is the same as calling it. And if you call it, it will come.]

Señora Rosario's raised her voice back to normal. "Even in the city, people must know *El Amigo* kills."

"That's an old wife's tale."

"Suit yourself, but when it gets dark, wise girls stay home behind closed doors."

Esmi smirked. "I really have to go."

"Fine, don't listen; it's no skin off my nose. But think of your grandfather. *Don* Adelfo would be most upset if he knew you were out at such hours."

16

Have you ever roasted meat on a spit? You turn it gentle and slow, very slow, so that the meat cooks evenly. The fat drips into the fire and sizzles, and the flesh changes from pink to brown and crusty, and the aroma from sickly sweet to mouth-watering. It's a slow job, tedious.

Well, for the rest of the day and evening, that poor lamb on a spit was Esmi, always one side hot and the other cold. There was her grandmother, the wrinkles at the side of her eyes deep with smiles, her mouth pursed tight, smiling in a way that looked more painful than proud as she bustled about the kitchen, thrilled to have someone to cook for—it had been years since Adelfo showed signs of a true appetite. But then there was old Adelfo, the dark side of Lourdes' moon, not moving from his chair, heavily present but silent.

Esmi thought she could feel his stare on her back—her back had never been this sensitive in Madrid— and when she'd turn, she'd find his eye trained on her. He'd look away, but not before she saw his mouth set in a firm, straight line and a coldness of expression in his eye that made her stomach lurch.

At 2:00, they sat down to quite a spread, with Lourdes bemoaning the limited ingredients she'd had to work with. She'd gotten so little when the grocery mobile had come, and now it wasn't due back for another week. Lourdes encouraged Adelfo to go hunting the next morning so she could make Esmi a partridge hotpot or rabbit with rosemary.

"You're letting that old shotgun get rusty, *viejo*." He could at least get them a lizard—she could make *lagarto con tomate*; but she'd have to use canned tomatoes. Oh, or a pheasant! They hadn't had a pheasant in a month of Sundays.

Old Adelfo only grumbled.

So she switched gears, wondering aloud if Narda could arrange it with *Doña* Pilar, to sell them a lamb. And some soft, creamy sheep cheese that she knew Esmi would love...

"No!" the old *hijo de puta* decreed. "I don't want you talking to her."

"To Narda?" Esmi asked.

"And how am I to sell her eggs if I don't talk to her? Heavens, she's about the only one in town who will talk to me."

"Don't exaggerate," Adelfo said.

"What do you mean they don't talk to you?" Esmi asked.

"Of course they talk to me when you're with me," Lourdes said to Adelfo. "But how often does that happen? When's the last time you left the house? When I'm by myself, it's a different story. "

"Why, Grandma?"

"This doesn't concern you, little girl," Adelfo said.

"Adelfo!" Lourdes admonished.

"Sell her the damn eggs, if you have to."

"The eggs are for *Doña* Pilar."

"Fine. But you don't have to be all chummy with that Narda. And don't go asking her for any favors. Lamb!" He shook his head at the absurdity of it.

"Then, old man, you better bag me some partridges, hadn't you?"

Even though Esmi didn't have a clue what was going on,

she decided not to press her questions. Patience might not be her best attribute, but if ever there was a place to learn it, she told herself, it would be here in Fuentespina.

For the rest of the day, time yo-yo-ed, up and down, in and out. Cleaning up after lunch seemed slow and drawn out, until Esmi checked the clock—she'd finished in no time flat. She took a much-needed siesta, but woke up with hours stretching ahead of her, flat and endless as the steppes and scrubland outside.

It was dark out before the house seemed to rouse itself again, filling with the aroma of bacon, green pepper and garlic frying in bacon fat and olive oil as Lourdes put together *migas* for a light dinner. It was chilly, so she asked Esmi to light the brasier under the table for her. She pointed out the coal scuttle and handed her matches, newspaper and a piece of cardboard to fan the flames.

Esmi reported her success and came to stand close to Lourdes at the stove, looking over her shoulder, but Lourdes shoved a bottle of wine into Esmi's hand and shooed her back to the table to take her place. Esmi's legs and feet grew toasty under the heavy tablecloth, but above the table her nose stayed icy. Lourdes called to old Adelfo—dinner was almost ready.

When the old man sat down across from Esmi, Lourdes was still at the stove finishing off the *migas*. She'd fried thin pieces of salted bread in the hot oil and broken them up with a slotted spoon and was now stirring in the other ingredients—she wanted to serve them good and hot.

Old Adelfo looked at Lourdes' back, at his hands resting on either side of his plate, at anything that wasn't Esmi.

"Grandfather, is something wrong?"

He grunted.

"Are you angry at me?"

He looked at her then, but there was no twinkle in his eye.

Personally, I can't imagine that rheumy old eye with a bloody twinkle in it, but Esmi had remembered it, counted on it, and now she missed it. Was it only the night before that he had welcomed her—with affection, she'd thought—and she'd felt she was home and safe?

"Why? What did you do?" he said.

"Nothing," Esmi said, and this time she was the one to look away.

After dinner Adelfo did not go back out to the patio. He stayed at the table with its warmth, and his radio filled the house with its tinny sounds and grating static. The harsh smell of burnt coal and her grandfather's cigarette smoke clotted in the already thick air of the house, air suddenly heavy with the stale odor of salt cod from lunch as well as the fried garlic from dinner. Esmi longed to get outside.

She took up her grandfather's post in the dark of the patio, the only light coming from the kitchen window. She lit the cigarette butt she'd put out earlier and leaned back. Cradling her right elbow, she blew smoke up towards the stars. Her thoughts drifted with it.

Of all the things she had to mull over, from Fuentespina to Madrid and everything in between, what do you think she kept coming back to?

Señor Iban.

And why not?

She thought about how forlorn he'd looked sitting alone at the fountain, and the fine, graceful way his clothes had hung on him. Why did she think of water slipping down a falls? His sad, slightly down-turned eyes had looked right into her, and had seemed pleased to do so, had seen her even in the dark. It was unnerving. And his voice. As much as hearing the tone of his voice, she had felt it—quiet, deep, caressing. She could feel it even now. But she would not be meeting him at midnight. For one thing, he was a stranger, and what could there possibly be of interest in Fuentespina for him to show her? It was crazy. And for another, if Lourdes found out, she'd kill her.

As if reading her thoughts, there stood Lourdes framed in the kitchen doorway, fussing at her to come inside—she'd catch her death, it was late, she couldn't sit there in the dark all night.

Later in her mother's bed, Esmi lay awake for a long time listening to her grandparents' snores rasping in harmony—her grandfather's sawing over Lourdes' rhythmic rumble. Then she heard choking snorts—old Adelfo's sounds pulling away from Lourdes'—and murmurs and bed creaking. She found herself holding her breath, waiting for her grandfather's shouts, for his nightmare to return. But it got quiet again and she lay there, the dark tucked in about her, smothering her.

She threw back the covers, stumbled to the window, pulled it open and leaned out. The air was cool but still laced with a leathery smell—that would be the gum rockrose—and hints of sage and wild lavender, heather and grasses. The rhythm of her breathing smoothed; and all the sensible reasons for staying away from *Señor* Iban relaxed as well, slipping into the night and fading into nothing. She could stay in her room, feeling trapped, or she could get out and get some air, take a walk. And, if she took a walk, why not to the fountain? Why not at midnight? She could meet a handsome, wealthy man with sad eyes. Why not? Besides, he had cigarettes, not to mention a way of seeing into her that made her feel like she might have a soul.

Her grandfather's mutterings started up again. Sleep would be impossible.

She dressed with more care than the night before, or with as much care as possible without light or noise to alert her grandparents. She wrapped the red silk scarf around her neck and pulled on her tight jeans, changed the tee shirt she slept in for the camisole top with thin straps and put on her tailored jacket over it. Last, she slipped on her favorite blue heels. She put on lipstick, brushed her hair in the dark, fluffed it with her fingers and climbed out the window.

With her feet on the earth, her shoulders relaxed and her lungs filled with air. As she walked away from the house, she felt it behind her, tethered in place like a huddled beast, dark and growling and licking its wounds. She marveled at this; she was normally such a straight-line thinker, literal and logical all the way, but she'd had such odd thoughts since coming to Fuentespina.

The Dream

He senses the absence of Lourdes' weight next to him in bed.

That's how the dream starts, with something not quite right and without his knowing it's a dream.

He listens for her noises in the dark room— a sigh, a creak of the wooden shutter as she peaks out, a shuffling across the floor. Nothing. He listens for her noises coming from elsewhere in the house—a clink of a drinking glass against the tile in the kitchen, slippered steps returning from the outhouse or from checking on the chickens, the clank of the shotgun being returned to its corner by the back door—but it is silent.

He gets up, and doesn't notice how easily his joints and muscles lift him from the bed. He calls to her, and does not hear the youth in his voice.

"Old woman," he calls, "what are you up to?" and then, "Old woman, where are you?"

He wanders through the house, seeing perfectly well in the dark. The door to the kitchen is closed. He pauses in front of it—a faint uneasiness makes him rub his thumbs back and forth across the tips of his fingers. What if she's collapsed? What if her body is blocking the door so he cannot open it?

No, he tells himself, she's fine—healthy, and much younger than he is. But, you never know about women. And death, hijo de puta, ni hablar—*always too soon, or too late.*

He turns the knob. The door swings open freely. She's not in the kitchen. He turns back, cursing her, muttering in irritation for causing him this... uneasiness. He calls to her again, but there is no answer.

He walks stealthily through his own house. Aside from Lourdes' being gone, something is wrong, profoundly wrong. He pauses in the parlor, the outer corner of his good eye twitching. He listens closely.

It's the house. It seems to breathe. Or it's some thing not human, something so massive and powerful that he feels the walls of the house draw inward with each inhalation. Adelfo is convinced evil is breathing in his house. His fists clench.

Turning, he catches sight of himself in the mirror and gives a start. He is furious with himself for flinching, and furious at this thing for making him show that he is afraid.

He thinks, if I look in the mirror straight on, I will see it behind me. After all these years. I will see evil face to face.

He steels himself and looks at his reflection. He's a young man, and the flesh around his wounded eye is pink-red, as when it first tried to heal. It sickens him. Then he sees that his good eye matches it. He cries out in horror. He is blind.

The evil in the house has done this to him. He feels the pressure of its breath now against his own chest, a compression and release, working against the rhythm of his lungs. He is breathing in its exhalation; it is pulling at his breath.

He must get out.

The number of rooms in the house has doubled, tripled.

He rushes through them, opening and closing doors, searching for a way out. It does not seem odd to him that he can see with no eyes. He finds the door and bolts from the house. He must find Lourdes and alert the village, but like his house, the narrow streets of the town have become a maze. Each time he turns a corner, he runs into a dead end. Each time he retraces his steps, he encounters a different corner that wasn't there a moment before. He must get to the church. He must ring the bells to warn the town.

At last, he stumbles into the plaza. He pounds on the church door, but to no avail. He turns to the big house. The shutters are all closed. He beats on the door. No answer. Out of breath, his old-man's heart groaning, he sinks onto the fountain bench. The demon will find him soon. If he can't save himself, he won't be able to save Lourdes or Fuentespina.

A vapor lifts from the stones in the plaza with a sizzling sound like escaping steam. It forms a brown mist that swirls near the earth. Adelfo pulls his feet up on the bench as if that could save him, as if he were avoiding nothing more than mice scurrying about underfoot.

The evil vapor grows thicker and rises higher.

He cowers, abject with humiliation and fear. He hears himself whimper. He waves his arms as he would to disperse smoke, but it engulfs him. It swallows up the fountain. It blots out the roof of the big house, the campanario *of the church, the night sky.*

In a corner of the plaza, swirls of the vapor drift and twist into a shape. Adelfo detects a narrow breadth of shoulder, a flow of cloth, a feminine curve of hip. Like everything else—the rooms of his house, the streets of his town—the figure is unfamiliar, and yet known.

He struggles to scream, but where his scream should come from, where his throat should be, feels like an old wound, once sutured and now closed in a useless, puckered scar.

The figure expands and arcs. It swoops toward him.

He begs his heart to stop beating.

17

The moment Esmi hit the night air, she bloomed like a moon flower.

Personally, I did not share her craving for open air or her newfound longing to be out under the stars. Things of the night—an owl hooting, a fox shrieking, the vastness of a black sky stuffed with stars—they all gave me the willies. As did highways. And train tracks that went on forever. You can have them all and you're welcome to them. People gossiped that I had a Gypsy father. Hah! Some Gypsy I'd make.

No, give me my kitchen anytime. Or my hideaway of a bedroom. I just wish the ceiling weren't so high—it disappears into darkness once the sun sets, well out of reach of my bedside lamp. For all anyone knows, there could be loathsome creatures perched up in the corners, watching.

But that wasn't why I was lying there staring into the dark. I was fretting about *Señora* Rosario having seen *Señor* Iban.

It was high time our business arrangement came to an end, and that's what it was, business, cut and dried. One evening *Señor* Iban had showed up at the house and introduced himself as *Señorito* Roberto's uncle. He'd wanted to visit the boy, but he hadn't wanted *Doña* Pilar to know because, due to no fault of his own, she had deemed him persona non grata. At the time I figured more power to him. Any persona non grata of the great lady's was persona very grata to me.

Besides, truth be told, I felt bad for *Señorito* Roberto, all alone with just grumpy me for company—not that he wanted my company. An ignorant old servant, that's all I was to him.

The last playmate of any kind he had in the village was Chela's little girl, Meche. Chela was our washerwoman at the big house, and her Meche, just three years old, was as roly-poly and round-cheeked a moppet as her mother was small-boned and stringy. *Señorito* Roberto doted on that little girl and while Chela worked in the service patio, he would play with the little one in the garden patio, which was not as grand as it sounds. Except for a lemon tree and an almond, it was a third-rate oasis at best—the gardener long gone, the fountain drained and the grass and flowers dried and withered. On Chela's days off the *señorito* would sneak off to her house and play with little Meche. *Doña* Pilar didn't like that one bit, but the *señorito* did it anyway—it was the only gumption I've ever seen him show.

Chela was the last young person in the village, so it was no great surprise when she picked up and left.

[They all leave, all the young—our life's blood draining away.]

But she didn't leave for the usual reasons, did she. Her Meche had fallen ill—limp and listless she was and not getting better—so they moved to Badajoz where the little girl could go to the doctor. We haven't seen hide nor hair of them since.

Anyway, I thought a visit from *Señor* Iban would be a treat for the boy, and a one-time deal. But then the next night

Señor Iban was back, and the next. And the next. There'd be hell to pay once *Doña* Pilar found out, but since I was still breathing, she obviously didn't know. Not yet, anyway.

Earlier that night, I'd handed *Señor* Iban the basket that he'd asked for—bread, wine, cheese, ham, plus a few extras that I threw in on my own. He slipped me some bills, as he did every evening, as if to a maitre d', shaking my hand—I was gathering a nice little wad of mad money from his nightly tips.

This time I held on tight and cupped my free hand over his—I wanted his full attention—but then I dropped my hand and looked away. Just looking into his eyes made me feel funny, like my stomach was bubbling with cava.

"*Señor* Iban. Please. *Doña* Pilar is going to find out."

"But, Narda. No one knows I'm here but you."

"Hogwash!" I looked up at him and saw his dark eyebrows arched high. "*Perdone, señor*, but the question is not if someone tells *Doña* Pilar, but when—that is if she doesn't trip over you herself."

He stared at me a moment. There was a sneer there I hadn't seen before, and it made him seem less handsome, less charming. But he closed his eyes, and I studied his face. He took a deep breath and relaxed his expression. He opened his eyes, and the way he looked at me, all intense, made me feel giddy, made me look away again.

"I promised his mother I'd keep an eye on him."

"But *señor*..."

He pulled his hand away. "I'll see you tomorrow. You will let me in, won't you?"

I looked down at the Roman mosaic under our feet,

feeling like I was standing over a trap door. "How much longer, *Señor* Iban?"

"Trust me, Nardita. You have nothing to worry about."

18

Esmi headed for the plaza, one dog after another raising the alarm as she click-clicked by in those blue stilettos of hers. No one bothered to rush out into the street to see the cause of the racket—the dogs barked the same whether the intruder was a homicidal maniac or a cat, and the odds were in favor of a cat.

[Or a fox. It could even be *El Otro*.]

"Up to no good," they barked. "Worth the watching. Watch. Watch."

I'd finally fallen asleep and only woke up long enough to turn over and curse every dog in town and its owner.

On the edge of town, Lourdes lay awake listening until she was sure that whatever it was was not advancing on her henhouse. And old Adelfo, he slept through it all, if you can call what he was doing sleeping. He jerked and grumbled and snored, all of which kept Lourdes from falling back to sleep.

He quieted a moment and she dozed off. But then his body shuddered and startled her awake. He was making strangled croaks and whimpers.

She touched his shoulder. "Adelfo," she whispered.

He didn't hear her. He was too deep in his own personal torment—and well-deserved, I might add.

She nudged him. "Adelfo."

No response. He was submerged in his dream up to his eyeball. He was murmuring now, too, but she couldn't make out the words.

"Old man," she said.

She nudged him harder and pinched him, but he would not wake up. It was like he was possessed—he was moaning and his hands twitched. Was he in some netherworld battling unseen enemies, and losing, while she watched, helpless?

She often worried that he would die before her—after all, he was twelve years older than her—but she'd never known of anyone succumbing to a nightmare. She took hold of both his shoulders. "Fito, wake up!" The pouches under her eyes were tight with fear. She shook him, harder. "Wake up!"

"No!" He lifted his head and yelled, not at her but at someone or something invisible. "No!"

That was clear enough. He seemed to be trying to break through from someplace deep. He grabbed Lourdes with both hands.

"You're here, Fito, with me. You're safe."

He struggled against her but she dragged his consciousness back to her.

"It's me, *viejo*. It's all right."

His eye finally came to focus—moonlight sifting through the lace curtain revealed first Lourdes' face looming over him, and then the familiar trappings of his bedroom. He let go of her and fell back on his pillow, exhausted.

She was breathing hard herself, her heart pounding.

After a moment she said, "*Viejo*, that was some nightmare."

He said nothing—his good eye stared into the night and the tight line of his lips quivered. He dragged his hand over his face.

Lourdes, to calm herself properly, needed the busyness of hands and the shelter of her kitchen. She made to stand. "I'll get you some tea, *mi amor*."

"No, Milú" he said. "Stay." He looked at her, his tone beseeching. "Stay."

Now that he was back amongst the awake and the living, irritation crept up on her. Why had he scared her so—clinging like that so stubbornly to his nightmare? And raising her from a sound sleep three nights in a row!

She switched on the bedside lamp. His face was unnaturally pale.

"Milú," he cooed, and grabbed her hand.

"Fine, I'll stay. I've stayed for forty-nine years, haven't I?"

He gripped her hand, and a few moments passed in silence. With her free hand, she smoothed the bed covers—she was not one for sitting still.

"You were such a child," he said.

"You always say that. Seventeen is not a child."

"A child," he insisted, "and I was an old, battered soldier."

"Twenty-nine is no more old than..."

"Old and crippled."

Her voice softened, "You were a war hero."

They were silent again. A wave of barks started up again somewhere near the center of town and moved away to the far edge.

"The dogs have been sleeping as poorly as you lately," Lourdes said.

"No coincidence, that," Adelfo said gravely.

"What do you mean?"

"They know evil. They can smell it. They know it's back."

"Again with the evil? Taking midnight strolls through the streets of Fuentespina?"

First the nightmare and now this crazy talk. It worried her.

"It's no joke, woman. It's come out of hiding. It longs for the bad times."

She knew he meant the war. But she'd been a small child then, a mere six-year-old when the fighting ended. For her the bad times came later, with the *Posguerra*—that endless Sahara of a time, that desert of misery dotted with prisons and concentration camps. And executions—a hundred thousand or more. And disease. She doubted if anyone even counted how many died of disease.

"And which bad times are those?" she snapped.

He knew where she was heading, and it wasn't a subject he wanted to hear about.

"Bad times!" she scoffed.

She remembered the hunger. Hunger and hunger and hunger. Around here, after the war, malnutrition and disease took half the babies. Half. Lourdes' family had worse luck: two baby brothers and they both died. Bad times indeed.

"Which bad times, Adelfo. Which ones? When my family lost our farm?" Her voice quavered. "For no reason, Adelfo. No reason."

If her family hadn't lost their house and land, they might have scraped by. But Franco, as far as she could see, had as good as killed her baby brothers. Why would he do that? She rhythmically grasped the bed clothes and let go of them, grasped and let go.

This is when Adelfo would lose patience with her, and this time, too, he said what he always said, with no thought to comforting her, "Your grandfather was a Red. What did you expect?"

"He was dead!"

"And just as well. If he hadn't been dead, he would have gone to jail. Or worse."

Usually, this is when Lourdes would get a grip, nod and get on with the housework. But it was the middle of the night, his crazy dreams had upset her, and there was Esmi—a new spirit in the house—a fresh face. but at the same time Teresa all over again. It stirred up all the old guilt and doubts and recriminations.

"Yes. He died. He died in his bed before the war ever started. They declared a corpse Red, confiscated a corpse's property."

Lourdes got out of bed and pulled a crocheted shawl around her.

"Milú, where are you going? Come to bed."

"He wasn't, Adelfo. He was never a communist." Then she added something she seldom said because it was logical to her but damning as far as Adelfo was concerned. "He supported the Republic because it was the government, Adelfo, the elected government, and my grandfather was a law-abiding man."

"Corrupt laws, laws inspired by Marx and the devil," Adelfo grumbled.

She came around the bed to face him, surprising herself as much as Adelfo. "He died in his bed, Adelfo. What did they care what a dead man believed or didn't believe?"

"Lourdes, not now." There was no sharpness in his voice.

She saw his gaunt face and her anger deserted her. "Why, Adelfo? Why did my father have to lose our farm? Why did my little brothers have to die?" She really wanted an answer, one she could believe.

Adelfo pulled her down to sit on the bed. She faced away from him.

"Stop it, now," he coaxed. "You're acting like a sentimental old woman."

She leaned back, her shoulder against him, sensing new edges between them. Marriage seemed to her a shape-shifting thing, slippery at times. Yet marriage was a sacrament. How could a sacrament be changeable? She was sitting off balance, suspecting her shoulder was digging into his chest, and feeling the hardness of his ribs against her flesh.

"So you lost your childhood home," he said after a moment. "So what?" His tone turned indignant, offended. "You're my wife now. I've given you a home. This is your home."

She looked down at her hand that clutched the shawl. "But was it your home to give?" She wasn't even aware of having said it out loud.

His arm snapped up, a strangle hold on her neck.

Lourdes gasped before his hold tightened. She grabbed at his arm, pulled on it.

"Adelfo. Please," she struggled to say against the pressure on her neck. "I'm sorry."

He let go of her, his forearm sliding down the front of her body to lay limp in her lap. She forced herself to remain still. After awhile she took his hand. It was trembling. She patted it and kept on patting it, afraid to look into his face, thinking he must feel terrible for hurting her.

Personally, I wonder if regret is what she would have seen on the old maggot's face.

"I didn't mean it, *mi amor*," she said. "I don't know why I said it; I don't even think it." She knew that last bit was a mistake—it wasn't wise to call attention to the fact that she had her own thoughts and that he might not know what they were. "You rescued me," she added hurriedly.

He tried to pull his hand away, but she held tight.

"I'm an old woman, like you said. All this talk about evil, about the war, I guess it upset me more than I..." She stopped short. "Blessed Mother! We must have wakened Esmi." And off she hurried to Teresa's old room, as if Esmi were a little child in need of comfort.

Adelfo called after her but she paid no heed. In the few steps it took to reach the door, she knew the girl was not in the house—she could feel her absence. Still, touching the skin of her throat, she took a moment to say a silent prayer to the contrary and listen at the door.

Quietly she opened it and faced the emptiness inside. She felt shaky and dropped onto the hardback chair sitting next to the door. She gaped at the empty bed with dismay and the open window with anger. She rubbed her neck and gathered tight her emotions.

When she returned to their bedroom, Adelfo was lying on his back, eyes closed, perfectly still and, Lourdes could tell, perfectly awake. She got into bed and he turned onto his side, his back to her. Did he turn away out of anger or shame? At the moment she didn't care—glad that she wouldn't have to lie to him, wouldn't have to say Esmi was sleeping undisturbed, like a babe lost to the world in sweet dreams.

19

The wind hummed across the moonlit grasses like it does around here—there aren't many trees or anything else to slow it down. *Señor* Iban clambered up a low mound of rubble. He'd just left the trail—an all but unused track, narrow and hard to make out, awash in white light, and slashed by their knife-sharp moon shadows. Yup, their shadows. It was the middle of the night and there was our Miss Esmi, trudging after him—well, as close to trudging as you can get in high heels.

She'd entered the plaza around midnight, eagerness setting off rockets in her stomach at the thought of finding him there, remembering how he'd looked the night before, in a halo of smoke by the fountain, all cool and composed. This time she'd hoped to spot a hint of impatience as he waited for her.

But, the plaza was empty.

"Great," she thought, "Stood up in Fuentespina."

She sat on the edge of the fountain and breathed in the night air with disappointment, and argued with herself about smoking one of the two cigarettes she had left.

Then, there he was, standing before her. She just about jumped out of her skin. She hadn't seen him slip silently from the shadows of the church. It made her mad, him scaring her like that.

"I thought maybe you'd been caught in traffic," she said, mocking herself more than him.

A wee bit of a smile, the offer of a cigarette, and she was somewhat mollified. After all, it wasn't his fault she was on edge. They sat side by side on the fountain, a basket at his feet—a picnic, he said. He lit a cigarette for her. Holding her elbow and hugging it close to her body, she drew the smoke in deeply.

"It's spooky how quiet it is around here," Esmi said.

"I'm afraid Fuentespina de Vico doesn't have much to offer in the way of nightlife." As always, *Señor* Iban measured his words and spaced them with pauses like caves.

He pointed to *Don* Fidencio's old place, the Bocanegra. "I suppose at one time that hole in the wall there was it. Some kind of gin joint."

The Bocanegra had never seen anything as high-class as gin. *Don* Fidencio himself had been a strange, mole-like little man, and in those days only men crossed the gloomy threshold.

[A decent woman's reputation could be tarnished just
by walking by that place.]

Now the door was missing and the opening yawned like a toothless old man. The dense darkness within looked bottomless to Esmi.

"You said you had someplace you wanted to show me. I hope that's not it."

Señor Iban smiled just a little. "Come with me."

"Where?"

"Fuentespina's one attraction."

She felt a nibbling of anticipation even though she

doubted any attraction around here, so-called, could live up to its billing.

They left the plaza behind, and then the town. When he cut off the road, she asked again where they were going.

"You'll see," he said with that slight smile of his.

If the villagers had seen them, they would have said with village common sense and ill humor, "Someday a lost shepherd will stumble across her bones."

[It would be no more than she deserves.]

And *Señora* Rosario would have added, "The girl doesn't have a lick of sense."

So, was Esmi foolhardy?

Well, I myself came face to face with *Señor* Iban on a daily basis, and I can tell you this, he stirred up a lot of feelings, but never your garden-variety fear. You might dread laying bare his contempt—it seemed to lie pretty close to the surface—and there was the fear of letting him down, of his turning away; misgivings about going too far on his behalf. I used to ask myself what it was that made you want to go out of your way to believe him.

After leaving the road, they'd followed a pathway, walking single file, with Esmi wishing she'd worn her trainers. The moon that night was waxing gibbous. Not full, Esmi noted, and yet its frosty light was enough to leach the world of color. It left everything looking cold and drained of life. Not exactly romantic, she thought.

Then *Señor* Iban had climbed atop that little knoll and set the basket down. It seemed to her as if they were trapped in a massive disco strobe light, the music frozen between beats. He turned and stretched his hand out to her.

She hesitated, thinking, I didn't sign up for a fucking hike, and doesn't this damned wind ever stop?

As if hearing her thoughts, he said, "We'll be out of the wind soon. We're almost there."

She brushed her hair back from her face. "Where?"

He gave her the slimmest of smiles in response.

It wouldn't have been enough for most of us, that is the most of us who marry the boy next door, live down the street from our parents, and settle down to a life of cranking out children. But God has a different plan for a certain number of us—at least that's my theory. He puts into some of us a yearning for the distant, the unknown, the mysterious. He carves that longing right into the stone of our natures. It's a biological thing. It keeps the gene pool mixed up—like war, but I prefer not to think that's any of God's doing.

Esmi looked up at *Señor* Iban's outstretched hand and then into those sad eyes of his. She saw the suffering that was always there. It was intriguing, that, good as bait—a lure tied by God or *Señor* Iban, maybe by both.

[Or the Devil.]

She took his hand.

A tingle went through her, but she still gave him a challenge of a look that said, you better make this hike worth my while.

He helped her up the little mound. She—looking at the ground, carefully picking her footholds—was surprised when he took her by the shoulders. She looked up and into his eyes so dangerously close to her own. She stopped breathing.

Guiding her shoulders, he changed her direction. "Look," he said.

She wobbled, found her balance and looked in the direction he'd aimed her. This was their destination? The earth was lumpy with hummocks and grasses grew weedy around stone debris.

"The remains of Ulpia Victrix," he explained. "Roman, of course. The city was named in honor of the emperor Trajan's victory in Dacia."

She shrugged, meaning she didn't know what he was talking about, also meaning she didn't much care; but he didn't seem to pick up on that because he kept on.

"The Dacian Wars ended in 106 AD, and this city was settled by veterans of the campaign, as a reward."

Looking out over the ruins, the wind still whipping her hair into her face, he detailed more particulars: more Trajan, more Dacia, more conquest. She nodded a couple times without enthusiasm.

"Trajan was Spanish, you know. A general as well as emperor. Born in Italica."

Her larynx felt broken, her neck throbbed, and now her legs and feet ached.

"Have you been to Italica? The excavated ruins near Seville?" he said.

She shook her head.

He took her hand and led her through the debris until they came to the edge of a slope. At its foot, she saw that one fluted column—quite thick and still in one piece—remained upright. Near it, several broken pillars stood like burned-down candles and others lay in pieces on the earth, like chunks of chopped carrot.

He sighed in appreciation. "This was the amphitheater,"

Esmi saw nothing as grand as an amphitheater. She saw damaged columns, a few steps still in place, and here and there a short curved section of what had been steep tiers of stone seats—a laundry list of bits and pieces that to her added up to nothing.

He took her by the elbow and they made their way down until they were sheltered from the wind. Then he led her along what remained of one of the rows and stopped where the stone was smooth and flat. They sat shoulder to shoulder, close but not touching. He opened the bottle of wine I'd given him from *Doña* Pilar's *bodega* and poured the wine into two stemless wine glasses from *Doña* Pilar's everyday crystal. If I'd known why he wanted a spare glass! In the moonlight the blood-ruby color of the wine looked black.

She took a sip—it hurt to swallow. She took another—maybe more alcohol would dull the pain.

Resting his forearms on his knees, he held his glass in both hands and gazed down at the ruin of a stage as if it were a thing of beauty.

Gloomy is what Esmi thought of it.

"And you come here because...?" she asked.

Señor Iban shook his head. He took a sip of wine, and as if commenting on the quality of it, he said, "You don't feel it."

Feel it? She mulled that over a moment—she'd already

fallen into the rhythm of his talk with all its lulls and empty spots. Feel what? She came up with nothing. Zilch.

She shrugged. "It's a bit..." creepy was the first word that came to mind, but she put it aside and said, "desolate."

He looked down into his glass of inky wine, silent; and she felt she'd fallen short, as if she'd failed some kind of pop quiz. Her hand drifted to her scarf where she fingered the knot at her throat. When Iban looked at her, she forced her hand down and feigned a sudden interest in the rubble of the stage. She pretended not to notice him studying her—an appraising gaze, cool and not particularly kind.

When he'd turned his attention back to the stage, she said, "I give up. Tell me. What's the 'it' I don't feel?"

He didn't answer immediately. She could feel him deciding something—it was physical, this deciding, his mind seesawing and his whole body sending out waves of tension. Crazy imaginings on her part, she told herself, and yet she knew the instant he'd come to a decision, could almost hear it click into place. And sure enough, a split second later, he opened his mouth.

"It's 1999. As you know, there's all this doomsday talk about the end of the millennium..."

This was the last thing she'd expected him to say. She glanced at him warily. When he didn't go on, she said, "Ripping a page from the calendar isn't going to bring the world to an end."

"No, and the point is it's not the end of *the* millennium, but of *a* millennium—one of many. We inhabit this one but that does not give it more substance than previous ones. Close to two millennia ago, this theatre would have been filled to capacity, packed to the rafters." He looked up at rafters that had never existed.

She looked up as well. Even in bright moonlight, more stars splayed across the sky than she'd ever seen in Madrid. It made her shiver.

"Can you picture it?" He looked to her for an answer, but she said nothing. "I come here and I see it all, imagine it all: the smells, the sounds, the faces of the people, how it must have felt to be one of the audience, a proud Roman citizen in a faraway colony."

"Why?" was the question on Esmi's lips, but she kept quiet. What *Señor* Enigma had just said was about the most personal piece of information he'd let slip so far. She didn't want him to pull back into his well-appointed shell, so she sat very still, as if he were a feral cat she were trying to befriend, a stag she did not want to startle, any one of a whole menagerie of elusive beasts to put her on tiptoe.

"It's more than idle curiosity," he added quickly, once again answering a question she had not said aloud. Then his words clogged again, plopped out in dribs and drabs, "Because of circumstances and, admittedly, inclination, I generally find myself a recluse, a perpetual outsider." His rueful smile edged into a grimace, and then was gone.

In the pause that followed, Esmi held her breath. He weighed his words, still taking her measure—she was sure of it. When he continued, she felt his voice as much as heard it, and her heart started beating again.

"But not here. Here in Ulpia Victrix there's a vibrancy, an aliveness," he looked into the distance. "It crosses time. I feel a connection with the people who lived here."

She couldn't fathom what he was feeling—why go out of your way to romanticize a bunch of dead people? As her mom would have said, "People are people—anytime, anywhere—and that's nothing to be proud of."

"You don't feel it?" he said and flashed a foolish grin. "Not at all?"

She wanted to reach out and grab that smile, pull it back to her—with it gone, the night seemed darker. She strung her words together slowly, feeling her way.

"I suppose I'm not what you would call particularly sensitive, at least not to that sort of thing. And, I just don't see the point. I'm sorry. Perhaps I'm not very imaginative."

She expected him to say something gallant, like, of course you are; you're the most sensitive, perceptive, intelligent and disarming woman I've ever met. But he didn't. She looked heavenward. The sky loomed immense and weighty.

"If anything, I feel insignificant." And, she thought, alone.

"You see? The power of this place does affect you."

She shook her head, irritated. "All I see is rubble, Iban. There's nothing here that has anything to do with me. You probably think that's superficial, that I'm superficial." Always alert to condescension and snobbery, a variety of oaths and expletives tickled the tip of her tongue, but unlike her mother who'd been quick to boil, Esmi was more of a simmerer. So now she pulled her punches. "If that's what you think, fine," she said.

"I'm not judging you, Esmi," he said carefully.

"Aren't you?"

"No. And I didn't bring you here to offend you."

"Then, why did you?"

He looked fixedly into his glass. "Ever since I saw you by the fountain..." Again, he stopped mid thought.

Esmi reckoned in a straight line, a very straight line, and *Señor* Iban kept playing havoc with that: jumping tracks, stopping short, leaving her dangling. She kept waiting for the logical next step. Here, for example, was the perfect opportunity for a bit of flattery. She wouldn't have trusted it, but all the same she wouldn't have minded hearing it.

Another zigzag. "You have me at a disadvantage," he said, but did not explain. Instead he picked up her hand as if he'd just found a pretty shell on the beach. He examined it, turning its cupped form this way and that as if mesmerized. She found herself staring at her own hand as if she'd never seen it before. He straightened its fingers, laying open the palm, smoothing it flat, examining her hand like a doctor making a diagnosis. Esmi watched fascinated. Then he stroked the length of her stretched-out hand a few times as if putting it to bed, smoothing it to calm, done. He might as well have been working out the kinks in her cramped heart—it unknotted, warm honey pumping through it.

"If we were in Barcelona now..." he said. He folded her hand into a fist and imprisoned it between his two hands.

She looked up at him. She'd been doing a slow burn a moment ago. Why was that?

"...I would take you to an excellent Argentine restaurant I know. Very fashionable these days—dark and romantic."

"I think I'd like that."

He rewarded her with a slight smile. "Then we could go to a club, listen to some jazz..."

She wrinkled her nose.

"Or go to a disco, near the beach?"

She nodded. "I like to dance."

"But," he shrugged in a rather French way. "We're not in Barcelona."

She shrugged back. "*C'est la vie.*"

"Yes. Exactly."

"It's good to get out of the village, though," Esmi said. "My mom always said that hell would be ending up as a ghost rattling her chains in the dust of Fuentespina. I thought she was being melodramatic; now I'm not so sure."

"Your mother's dead?"

Esmi nodded.

"So, you think your mother's spirit's in Fuentespina?"

"God, no. But I have been thinking about her a lot here. I mean it's where she grew up. The people there knew her when she was a girl. But no, of course not. My mother didn't really believe in any of that. No, when you're dead, you're dead. That's it."

"Hmm. You'd have fit right in here in Ulpia Victrix. Except for the odd Christian here and there, and a veteran or two who'd picked up a belief in the immortal soul from the Dacians, they would have agreed with you."

"I never said I had nothing in common with them."

"But they're dead and gone, and you're not."

He was needling her. Why?

"And your mother? Dead and gone like my moldy old Romans?"

It felt like she'd gulped down icy water. She pulled her hand from his and stood to leave, but *Señor* Iban grabbed her hand back and stopped her.

"Forgive me. I'm rusty at..." His pointed finger waggled between himself and Esmi.

She raised her eyebrows. Could it be true he was uncomfortable with women, inexperienced even? No, she doubted that very much.

"I spend too much time alone. Please, stay."

Esmi freed her hand, but sat down again, gingerly, perched as if to flee.

"The fact is," he said, "I wish I could believe as you, that when we're dead, we're dead."

She felt a chill. "You're not about to tell me I'm going to hell, are you?" Her stomach pulled into a knot. "Please tell me you're not trying to convert me." A worse thought came to her. "Oh God, you're Opus Dei, aren't you?"

She'd first run into the lay order at the Politécnica, where they'd kept trying to recruit her, but her real beef with Opus Dei was Lucho. She blamed his leaving her on his ultra religious upbringing in the cult, and if you ask me, Catholic or not, that's what it is, a cult.

"No, no. Don't worry," *Señor* Iban said. "I'm as lapsed a Catholic as they come—I've not confessed or taken communion since I was seventeen."

"But you were raised Opus Dei, right?" She knew she was sounding paranoid, but she couldn't help it.

Señor Iban shook his head no, shrugging his shoulders.

Nice shoulders, she thought. "Are you sure?" she said.

"I swear."

"OK." She extended her hand. "Truce."

He took her hand, kissed it, held on to it. She felt a little flutter in her stomach.

"My mother is dead too," he said. She started to say she was sorry, but he interrupted her. "It was years ago. I was sixteen."

The nice shoulder was now touching hers. She leaned into it.

"I've never been to Barcelona," she said.

"You'd like it. And we have Roman ruins there, too." He flashed a grin. "Even older than these. Would you like to see them?"

"I bet you live in the Barrio Gótico," she teased. She knew the Gothic Quarter was the historical heart of the city—medieval and picturesque.

"Barri Gótic," he corrected, using the Catalan name.

"Probably in some old mausoleum of a building, like the big house in Fuentespina." She mock shuddered and felt his shoulder go rigid. Maybe she shouldn't tease him.

"Actually I have a flat, very modernized."

"Modernized?"

"The building is eighteenth century," he conceded.

"Hah!"

"Why do you mention the big house? Have you been in it?" he said.

She nodded without enthusiasm.

"So you've met *Doña* Pilar?"

She groaned a yes. "There I go again," she sighed, "breaching the village's code of conduct. I'm told I'm ungrateful, disrespectful and tactless." She did not wait for him to contradict her. "My grandmother blames it on my mother and my being raised in the city.

"What about you? Do you know the venerable *Doña* Pilar?" she asked.

He shook his head no.

"Wish I could say the same," she said. "She acts like you should be curtsying to her and offering up your first-born. She..." Esmi stopped. "I'll never get the hang of this small-town discretion."

"Go ahead. Talk freely. I'm an outsider, too, remember. Maybe that's why we're drawn to each other—we're both trying to make our way in enemy territory."

"Oh, is that why?" she said, her voice full of irony, her eyes full of warmth. "Well, if you figure out the password and secret handshake, let me know, will you? I'm scrambling to keep up."

He rested the hand holding hers on his leg.

"Doña Pilar's already sucked me in," she said.

He seemed to think about that a moment. "What do you mean?"

"She wants me to tutor her stepson—I guess he's missed a lot of school."

"Ah, you're a teacher."

"No, I'm not. I keep telling everyone that, but no one will listen. I already have a job in Madrid, but apparently *Doña* Pilar gets what she wants."

Iban nodded solemnly. "So you've agreed?"

"To keep the peace at home." She liked the taste of the word "home" in her mouth. "You know who I like though? Pilar's housekeeper. She's kind of cranky—who wouldn't be, working for *Doña* Pilar? But somehow she's really easy to talk to. And she was a childhood friend of my mom's."

"Is that what you two talk about? Your mother?"

"No. Whatever pops into my head—I don't feel I have to watch what I say around her." She didn't know how to explain to him the novelty of having a woman friend. "Anyway," she sighed, "as of tomorrow, I'm stuck."

There were those cold eyes again. "I think the boy... What's his name?" *Señor* Iban asked.

"Roberto."

"I think Roberto is a lucky little boy."

Esmi pulled a face.

"But we can talk about something else, if you like."

She nodded. "Please."

He poured more wine into Esmi's glass. It had been a balm to her throat and she was feeling a cozy glow inside—a pleasing contrast to the cold night air on her face.

She raised her glass and clinked it on his, "*Salud.*"

"*Salud,*" he repeated, and then added the usual refrain, "*Amor y pesetas.*"

"Euros, soon," she said.

"OK. Health, love... " He bowed his head to her. "...and euros."

She smiled at his correction and responded, "And time to enjoy them."

"Yes, time," he said.

"How long are you going to be in Fuentespina?" She decided it was her turn to play inquisitor.

"I'm not sure."

"So, what are you doing here?"

He didn't answer.

"And how is it that everyone in town knows every step I take and every word I say, but no one seems to even know you're here?"

"I keep my distance from the townspeople."

"What, are you in hiding?" she said, half joking.

"You have nothing to fear from me," he said. He lifted one end of her red scarf.

"You're going to be all mysterious, aren't you, and not tell me anything."

He smiled ever so slightly and moved in closer. He fingered the scarf closer to where it knotted at her throat.

"There's mystery in your beauty."

Outright flattery, and when she least expected it. She felt the heat in her face. Thank goodness for moonlight, she thought, I've only changed to a deeper shade of grey.

"I thought that truth was beauty," she bantered.

"Not in my experience," he said.

He leaned in to kiss her. She could feel the pressure and aliveness of the empty air between them. She closed her eyes, ready to drift into the kiss. His hand moved to her throat, to the knot in her scarf, barely touching it.

Suddenly, she couldn't breathe. She pulled back, eyes wide. She lurched to her feet.

He reached for her, grabbed her wrist, but she pulled away and stumbled along the terraced row.

"Esmi!"

She scrambled her way to the top. Embarrassment took the place of panic, but she kept going.

20

Esmi plodded towards Fuentespina, and of course she turned Señor Iban over in her mind—over and over, up, down and sideways.

But what with all that space to cross and all that time to fill, her mind insisted on returning again and again to that damned phone call. She winced at the thought of it—winced, cringed and shuddered. It threw her off her stride, and she stumbled. It had been a stupid, stupid thing to do—she knew that now. She'd never been a stranger to white lies, even some grey ones, but she'd never before lied with intent to do harm. With that idiotic phone call, she'd crossed some invisible line and everything had changed. If only Tony had stayed home when she'd asked him to. Wasn't that what friends were for?

She righted herself, reached down and touched the smooth leather of her shoe. Hard to believe it was only three days ago. If not for that call, she'd never have had reason to cut and run to Fuentespina in the first place, would never have run into *Señor* Iban at the fountain and wouldn't be out here alone trudging back towards town in the middle of the night. The stars, vast and insistent, crowded the sky above; and below, the pungent scent of sage and the sawing of cicadas choked the night air. She wiggled her foot and resettled it in her shoe.

She recalled a time, soon after she'd met Lucho, when she and her programmer friend, Tony, were sharing a drink at a favorite haunt after work. The memory of it was like a snapshot, dog-eared and creased from carrying it around in her pocket: the thick smoke in the bar, the three-sided aluminum ashtrays full of cigarette butts, the marble-topped tables on the black and white tile floor, and Tony, wry and pleased with himself, as usual, and bragging about his plans for the evening. He'd just begun a new love affair, although love had little to do with it.

She'd heard it all from him any number of times before and wasn't really listening. She was keen to get home to Lucho. But there sat Tony—as if Lucho hadn't changed everything—looking to her to pick up her end of the conversation.

He raised his hand to call the waiter.

Esmi said, "Not for me."

"My date's not for ages yet."

"That's not my problem."

"It's not my problem either. I'm just saying, I've got time."

She took a last puff on her cigarette and stubbed it out in the metal ashtray. It had a rather military look to it, like it had been pounded out of an old airplane part.

"So," Tony said, "he's still at your place?"

"Who?"

Tony raised his eyebrows.

Esmi gave up being coy and nodded, trying not to smile. "He followed me home. What was I to do?"

"God, Esmi. Not you, too."

"Not me, what?"

"Another friend lost to the jaws of domesticity."

She grinned in answer.

"It won't last, you know." Lucho, he assured her, like the woman Tony was seeing that evening, would go the way of all the rest, and if she thought otherwise, she was fooling herself.

Esmi paid him no mind—he didn't know what he was talking about. Lucho was drunk with his newfound freedom and crazy about her, his delivering angel. That's what he called her, and a man wasn't likely to turn his back on his *ángel liberador*, now was he?

Of course everything changes. Esmi knew that. As the months passed, things between her and Lucho creaked, shifted, and then kept shifting. She wasn't overly concerned; relationships, like code, she supposed, progressed one line at a time. He'd stopped railing against his family. She saw that as positive—he was no longer dwelling in the past. He'd become more critical of his *ángel*. That was healthy too— she'd felt a little tottery up on that pedestal.

But then, out of the blue, the name of the girl his family had wanted him to marry popped up: Encarnación. And once it popped, it kept popping—Encarnación was sweet; Encarnación would have been a stone around his neck; Encarnación would know this; Encarnación would not know that; Encarnación's eyes were not as bewitching as Esmi's; her mouth wider, her lips thinner; Encarnación was a virgin; it was Encarnación's opinion that one should have children young, but there was more to life than raising brats, wasn't there? Encarnación wanted this for him; she didn't think he should do that; Encarnación was naïve; and had he mentioned that Encarnación was a virgin? Encarnación...

Esmi limped through the night, feeling the stones on the road through the thin leather soles of her shoes. She found herself chanting: En-car-na-ción,-En-car-na-ción,-En-car-na-ción. She told herself to shut up.

The wind had picked up again. She fished her hair clip from her jacket pocket and twisted her hair up and out of reach of the wind.

Another snapshot came to mind, this one crumpled into a ball—another drink many months later with Tony at the same bar. She was complaining about Lucho, and tossing words about like unpredictable, condescending, distant.

Tony listened, his face like the hard-ridged plastic of one of those hologram postcards—his expression changing, back and forth, from smug to sympathetic.

"And he keeps talking about the virtuous Encarnación," she said, avoiding looking at Tony. She motioned to the waiter to bring another round.

"You're jealous!" Tony sniggered.

"Of course not."

He raised his eyebrows at her.

"I'm not jealous. She's a child."

Esmi had never known jealousy before, and it had caught her unawares. It had ambushed her, taken her hostage—she was staggered by how bitter and gnawing it was.

"It's not funny, Tony."

"Oh, I don't know."

Lobbing a few obscenities at him, she grabbed her coat and shoulder bag, and left him to pay for the drinks she'd ordered.

It was only a few weeks later that she'd opened the door

to the flat and felt a strange chill, as if someone had left a window open. Her stomach turned—she could see right off that things were missing. Someone must have broken in and robbed them. They lived on the fourteenth floor, but she'd heard of thieves lowering themselves from rooftops. She rushed to the phone. Should she call the police first, or the *portera*?

Then she saw it. The note from Lucho that said he'd gone back to the family, to Encarnación, and to God.

She didn't quite take it in. This and robbed too? Dazed, note in hand, she wandered through the flat noticing what was missing—nothing of hers. It took her a while to sort out that there was just the one problem: the misery of Lucho having left her. She slid to the floor and huddled against the door. Somehow she still felt like she'd been robbed—not burgled but mugged, punched in the stomach. How could he have gone back to his old life, the one he said he despised?

She called Tony. He said he didn't know why she was so surprised. It seemed obvious from what she'd been saying.

But it hadn't been obvious to her.

"You should have told me," she said.

"I thought you knew. Next time I'll spell it out for you."

Next time! She hung up on him, hammering the phone with the receiver, over and over again, until the phone upended and slid with a bang and rattle onto the floor. She cradled the receiver and cried.

Months passed. She continued to stew and smolder. Tony's sublet ran out and he moved in to help with rent. He wasn't at the flat much, but when he was he refused to listen to her moan about Lucho doing her wrong.

One evening—as it happened, the anniversary of her meeting Lucho—she was feeling especially low, and she asked Tony to break his date and stay in. She didn't want to be alone.

Tony hit the roof. "Go to a bar if you don't want to be alone. You know you should get help because this whole thing has made you a bit crazy."

She knew that—a bit crazy, and a lot vindictive.

"Stay anyway," she said.

He slammed the door on his way out.

She cursed him and kicked the gym bag he'd left by the sofa—it was unzipped and his dirty workout clothes spilled from it, sending a rank smell into the air. She wrinkled her nose and groaned. He was right about one thing, damn him. She couldn't sit eating her heart out any longer. She had to do something.

She paced the flat.

For the past several weeks an impulse had plagued her waking hours. Now she decided to give in to it: she would telephone Lucho's fiancée. She gripped the phone and dialed. She was nervous about being able to control her voice, but she felt strangely calm about what she intended to say.

The ringing stopped. "*Diga,*" answered a very young female voice. Esmi looked for something to dislike in it, an arrogance, a nasal twang, squeakiness, anything, but it was soft and pleasant.

"Encarnación?"

"Yes?"

"This is Rosa Esmeralda Salvater Tena."

She surprised herself—she always identified herself

simply as Esmi Salvater. She never used her first given name, Rosa, and never both *apellidos*—her father's family name, followed by her mother's. At least she hadn't started the litany off with her title, *Ingeniera*.

A thick silence waited on the other end of the line.

"We have a mutual..." Esmi started to explain.

"I know who you are," she said with wounded tones.

Her voice. It was so young. Not surprising—the girl was, Esmi calculated, barely eighteen. An innocent, just as Lucho had described her.

She realized that what she had intended to say—crude descriptions of just how well she knew Lucho, and of how well Lucho knew her—would be akin to child abuse. The hurt in the girl's voice also kept her from saying the planned "he still comes to me," or the "he's settling for you to keep peace in the family," and the "he'll always be thinking of me." It was Lucho she wanted to injure, not this impossible child. But she'd come this far. She couldn't just hang up. She opened her mouth and this is what came out: "Encarnación, I want you to be the first to know. I'm pregnant."

Silence.

"And Lucho is the father." Hang up, she told herself, hang up now. But she had a sudden inspiration. "I can't raise a child alone. I'm going to abort it." She scrambled to hang up. Hand trembling, she clattered the receiver in its cradle.

"I am going to hell," she said aloud, "Lucho was right. I'm going to hell."

Lucho had once said, "You do understand, *mi ángel*, I'm angry with my family, not with God?"

"No," she'd said, "I don't understand any of it."

Teresa had had her baptized—while Franco was alive you couldn't buy a Kleenex to sneeze into without a baptismal certificate—but neither mother nor daughter had much use for religion, or God either, for that matter. Esmi argued that point of view with Lucho.

Lucho kissed her on the nose and said with odd affection, "Esmita, I love you, but you're going to hell."

She laughed. He didn't.

Now as she paced the flat, she replayed that scene in her mind, and remembered his earnest expression.

Well, at that point there was nothing to be done about the phone call. It was out of her hands. Besides, it was Lucho who'd lied to the girl, to his parents, to her. He'd betrayed them all. It was all his fault.

Lucho called the next night. His voice stabbed. "Bitch!"

She hung up. Now she knew—she'd gotten his attention and thrown a monkey wrench into God's plan. Knowing this, however, did not ease her pain. Instead she felt worse, and she couldn't have imagined feeling worse.

He called right back and kept calling. She stopped picking up. Still it rang. She unplugged the phone.

It was late. Tomorrow. Tomorrow she'd call Encarnación. Straighten things out. Try to.

Unable to sleep, she kicked Tony's gym bag towards the door and curled up on the sofa. She flipped through a fashion magazine for a while, but was mostly staring into space when she heard the sound of the key in the door. Tony. No, too early for Tony.

It was Lucho—she'd never changed the locks; she'd never wanted to keep him out.

He had the stunned, raw look of someone who's learned his beloved has died. Yet, for just a second upon seeing her, his eyes softened and warmed—for just a second—and her heart lurched. She was instantly awash in regret.

He was angry and confused. His parents were threatening to disown him. Encarnación had broken off their engagement. She said he must be free to do the right thing: he must marry the mother of his child.

"I'm sorry," she said, and she was.

"Sorry?! How can you be pregnant?" he shouted.

She laughed at the innocence of the question.

His eyes flashed cold. In that moment he was feeling more emotions—she could see them dashing across his face—than she'd seen him experience in all their time together. The thought crossed her mind that if one more emotion elbowed in, he might short circuit like a robot in an old movie, smoke pouring from his ears.

Lucho glanced about. Tony was such a slob—signs of his maleness were scattered everywhere. His scent lingered in the air. And the gym bag spewing Tony's sweaty clothes lay on the floor at Lucho's feet. The shock of it—of jealousy on top of everything else—jolted Lucho.

"*Puta!*" he shouted, "It's not my child."

Lucho was the one who'd lied to her, gone off and gotten engaged, and he accused *her* of being unfaithful? The heat rose in her face, her anger matching his. He'd used her and discarded her for a child bride. It was humiliating.

"Oh, it's yours," she shouted back.

"Whore!" he swore again.

He kicked Tony's gym bag across the room. Clothes

went flying. A teeshirt landed on his foot. He kicked himself free of it.

"I don't believe you."

"You believe me all right, but don't worry," she said. "Your problem's solved."

"What?"

"You didn't want me. Well, I didn't want it. I got rid of it."

He was stunned.

"Atone for that," she said.

The pain she saw in his face went right to her heart. All at once she understood why the poor *pendejo* had left her. He may have loved her, but like it or not, he believed what his folks had taught him to believe, so he'd recast her, his angel, as temptress because you can turn your back on a temptress. You can abandon a seductress and never regret it. She finally got that he wasn't settling for a marriage arranged by his parents. He wanted it because the virginal Encarnación was the only future he understood. And thanks to Esmi, that future was now lost to him.

To her surprise, compassion swept through her. She reached out to lay a forgiving hand on his cheek, and that gesture—the true one, after all the lies—was what made the boy snap.

"I would have strangled you, too," Tony had told Esmi at the hospital.

Can you imagine saying something like that to a girl in an emergency room? And after all she'd been through?

Tony held his arm tenderly. They were waiting to have

an X-ray taken of his wrist. Esmi had already been examined, and now that he knew she would be fine, he was feeling annoyed and sorry for himself.

Earlier that night, home hours before time from a date gone sour, Tony had let himself into the flat. And not a minute too soon. It took only a second for him to realize what was happening. He shouted at Lucho and lunged at him. He tried to pull him off Esmi, but he wouldn't let go. Tony had to wrap his forearm around Lucho's own windpipe before he could break his hold on her neck. On the verge of losing consciousness, Esmi was sure it was her mother saving her. Lucho grabbed at Tony's arm. In the tussle Tony got his wrist hurt, and Lucho bolted for the door.

In the taxi on the way to the hospital, she whispered to Tony, "Where's my mother?" which really shook him—he knew full well that Esmi's mother was dead. Leaning against him, her eyes closed, she recalled Teresa's touch, her familiar scent—not from memories from before her death but from just then in the flat. More than anything, she wanted to feel her mother's arms around her, hear her murmuring to her, "You're going to be fine, Esmita. Everything will be fine. I won't let anything happen to you ever again, *mi amor*."

Later in the hospital, Tony grumbled under the bright lights, "How am I supposed to work with one hand?" He'd been bellyaching for hours by then.

Because of her bruised voice box, Esmi said nothing, but she scrunched her face up at him.

"What were you thinking?" Tony accused.

He should talk, she thought. She bet there were plenty of

women out there who wanted to strangle him. Lucky for him, women didn't usually go in for that kind of thing, but he should watch out for knives and guns. And poison. When it didn't hurt so much to talk, she'd tell him so.

Before Lucho came into her life, she and Tony had always called themselves romance magpies, attracted to shiny new lovers. Neither of them had the knack for relationships; neither knew how or in whom to invest time and affection and loyalty. They were not, they'd joked, relationship literate.

It didn't seem funny now.

She listened to Tony grouse, her head feeling leaden and her throat throbbing. With her feet on the edge of her chair and her knees pulled to her chest, she rested her head on them to blot out the fluorescent lighting. She wanted to tell Tony to shut up—she already felt stupid enough, and guilty enough, as it was. And worried. She imagined emergency rooms had to report things like strangle bruises on someone's neck. She didn't want to cause Lucho any more trouble. She'd whispered to Tony to say it was a stranger who'd attacked her, that it was dark and he couldn't describe him. But if the police questioned him, could she trust him to stay quiet?

Even more than worried, she was scared. When she recalled Lucho's hands choking her, his face twisted in hate, her stomach heaved. Would he come back to finish the job?

Fear, shame: I've been on a first name basis with them since before I can remember. But not Esmi, not really. She felt them now, though—it was why she was being so easy on Lucho. And now Lucho would have entered a whole new world of fear and shame as well. Even if he escaped going to prison and somehow made it up with his girl and his family, in quiet moments he would always be able to feel his hands crushing Esmi's neck, would always fear the rage he now knew was a part of him. He was a murderer—a failed one to be sure, but if he was worth his salt, he'd forever lost his trust in himself as a decent man. I think that would be very hard for him to live with. At least I hope so.

21

I wouldn't have slept a wink if I'd known Esmi was out there all alone in the middle of the night, much less walking all the way home from the ruins. If it were me out there, apart from the usual terrors of the night, I would have felt, well, untethered, and on edge, as if each step would be the one to take me tumbling off the edge of the earth.

The air felt colder against Esmi's skin. She turned up the collar of her jacket.

The moon had slipped below the horizon. And with the moonlight switched off, the stars scurried back into the night like so many cockroaches glittering fiercely in the black sky. She cursed herself for bolting from the ruins without so much as a flashlight and plodded on, much more slowly in the thick darkness. The dirt road was a different shade of black than the land around it and also pretty much straight as a broomstick, which helped Esmi follow it. She told herself that the even darker lump on the landscape ahead had to be Fuentespina. She hoped she was right.

In spite of all the upsets of the last days, everything feeling jumbled and topsy turvy, Esmi tackled the trek as she would her work: focused, head down, one step at a time. In a way it felt good, satisfying, normal. Still, she couldn't help but wonder why *Señor* Iban hadn't followed her. Was he that tactful, or that insulted? Or did he just not care enough to rescue her? "Rescue me from what?" she said aloud. "A stubbed toe?"

She heard a motor in the distance behind her. Maybe *Señor* Iban had a car stashed somewhere and he'd come looking for her after all. If so, he'd certainly taken his own sweet time; she was almost home. She turned to look. She saw no headlights, but the sound of the motor grew louder.

Of course it might not be *Señor* Iban. Her spirits plummeted at the thought because the only person around here she knew of who had any kind of car was *Doña* Pilar—and Esmi was in no mood for that woman.

And what if *Doña* Pilar ratted on her to her grandparents that she'd been out here in the middle of the night? They would be shamed, and she guessed no explanation she concocted, no matter how believable, would ever make things right.

She looked about; there were no dark shapes nearby—nothing to hide behind—and besides, if she strayed too far from the road she was likely to twist an ankle, if not break it. And she might have a hard time finding her way back to the road.

The motor sounded nearer. But still no lights. Who would be driving without lights on such a dark, moonless night? Whoever it might be, she figured she'd better get out of their way. She took a few paces away from the narrow dirt road and waited, still facing towards Fuentespina so her back would be to the car and the dust it would raise, and also hiding her face from the driver. She hoped, almost to the point of praying, that without headlights to catch her, she wouldn't be seen at all.

She glanced over her shoulder. A dark shape was approaching fast, motor humming.

The pitch of the motor dropped. It was slowing! So much for her being invisible. The car braked next to where she stood. She couldn't very well pretend it wasn't there, so she turned and saw, worse luck, that it was a black Land Rover, and inside, *Doña* Pilar. Her broad forehead and cheeks glowed white in the reflected lights of the dashboard; her deep-set eyes and small mouth remained shadowed.

Esmi told herself she should act as if this were the most natural situation in the world. She should step forward, thank *Doña* Pilar for stopping and ask for a ride. Instead she stood frozen like a pint-size critter caught in headlights or a burglar caught in the act.

As for *Doña* Pilar, her head turned just a tad in Esmi's direction, hardly noticeable except Esmi could see her eyes now. They were fixed on her with a strange look of, well, foreboding was the word that came to mind. Foreboding and questioning. The pale sheen of her face turned a dead white. The small mouth opened, then snapped shut. She faced forward, and hit the gas.

Esmi smelled car exhaust and felt the dust the car raised sting her eyes and face.

What was that about, she asked herself. And how much trouble was she in? Would *Doña* Pilar tell her grandparents that she'd seen her wandering about in the night?

Well, if they asked her about it, she'd deny it. They'd have to take her word over *Doña* Pilar's, wouldn't they?

Or would *Doña* Pilar keep this to herself, but demand an explanation when Esmi showed up to tutor the next afternoon?

Well, again, she'd deny it. After all, there were no

streetlights, no moon, no headlights. "*Señora*," she would say, "You must be mistaken. What would I be doing out there in the middle of the night?"

She stared after *Doña* Pilar, making out nothing in the dark, but listening to the engine fade away. She saw the headlights turn on.

When Esmi finally climbed back over the wooden window sill into her mother's old room, it was like stepping into a big hot bath of relief. All that vastness and darkness out there, the tangle of unfriendly stars glutting the night sky, her fiasco with *Señor* Iban, and that strange encounter with *Doña* Pilar—she was glad to leave it all behind and crawl into her mother's small, simple bed. The cotton mattress was hard and misshapen, but welcome—the hollow in it had been made by her mother's body.

Her eyes drifted shut, but the stuffiness of the room—and the blackness, with no up or down or depth or air—pressed in to torture her. She got up and pushed the bed next to the window, and kneeling on the bed, she opened the window wide. Esmi sucked in the night air and used the cloudy starlight of the Milky Way to fix herself and the familiar room in time and place.

Still, she did not fall asleep. Sore feet and achey legs, her throbbing neck, the murky mess that was her feelings for Fuentespina—it all kept her awake. I can sympathize. I've spent many a sleepless night myself, and for the same reasons, except the pain in my neck was the hellcat who paid me my wages, and meager they were, too.

All in all she had much to mull over. Maybe she should clear out in the morning before *Doña* Pilar could say anything to her grandparents. But her grandmother wasn't likely to let her go without a fuss—at least not before *Doña* Pilar ratted her out. Esmi would have to have a good excuse ready for leaving. Maybe she should hike out to the highway right now before anyone was up and flag the first bus that passed. Would one pass? Would it stop? What about lorries? Should she hitchhike? And, for that matter, where would she go?

There was Almería on the Costa del Sol. Her father was there, but he was practically a stranger, a stranger with a new wife and a tiny flat—the woman's teenage son slept on the couch.

Madrid?

Madrid certainly wouldn't be my choice. Can you imagine, five million souls at each other's mercy? At history's mercy? Most of us in Fuentespina saw the capital as an overwhelming behemoth—shapeless, writhing, hungry for new blood, sending out tentacles that snatched away our town's young people.

But to Esmi, Madrid was her flat in Carabanchel, a district in the southern part of the city. It was the familiar tradespeople between her block and the metro station; the rainbow of Vespas and *motos* lined up in front of her office building; her cubicle, and Tony's; the café-bar she went to for morning break and the very correct elderly waiter who always waited on her; her favorite club for dancing, where the bartender bared his muscular arms and his shaven head. But if she pushed her thoughts beyond her usual bailiwick to, say, the long green corridors of the hospital or the black tunnels of the metro, or to the hollow echo in the train station or the endless blocks of flats the train passed before reaching open countryside, then the capital didn't feel so much like home.

More to the point, what if Lucho were waiting for her?

She felt her neck gingerly. She got up, felt around in her handbag for the little prescription bottle and swallowed a pain pill. Even if she were safe from another attack, what if one day she turned a corner and there he was, Lucho, alone, or with a wife, his wife and baby? Because surely that fiancée of his would take him back in the end. It couldn't be that she'd really separated Lucho from his childhood sweetheart and his family forever.

And Tony was in Madrid. Esmi imagined turning the key to her flat. There would be his clothes strewn all over the place and the flat reeking of his hyper-masculine-scented soap and shampoo and cologne. She grimaced. She couldn't face it—not Tony and not his grousing and not his cynicism.

For that matter, how could she go back to her airless little cubicle at work and fall in again with the people there? She'd thought they were friends, but when she was in the hospital, waiting while they put a cast on Tony's wrist, she realized that there was not one of them she could or would call. They were all strangers, strangers with familiar faces who happened to work on the same floor as she, in a row of cubicles much like the row of *motos* parked side by side downstairs. She tossed in the bed and shoved against the ridge in the mattress left by her mother's body. Resentment slithered into a corner of her heart. Her mom had kept her distance from her family without, it seemed, any thought to Esmi. It hadn't been fair, because when Teresa died, Esmi had been left all alone, stranded and isolated in her grief.

But her grandmother and grandfather were alive. Esmi was here with them now, and they were family. She didn't know what to do about *Doña* Pilar, but she couldn't leave. Not yet.

And let's not forget to throw *Señor* Iban into the mix. *Señor* Iban running hot and cold, and tantalizing her with both temperatures—hot, oh the possibilities; cold, oh the questions, the challenge of it.

The pain pill started to soothe her. Maybe *Doña* Pilar wouldn't say anything to her grandparents, and if she did, maybe Esmi would just dig in and deal with it, because Fuentespina mattered. Here was her mother's bed. Here her actual grandparents. Here was me, Narda—an unexpected confident who'd known her mother. And here, here was *Señor* Iban: Iban of the Sad Countenance.

Her eyes closed. She remembered the texture of the air between their lips—hers and *Señor* Iban's—before she'd pulled away from him. As she drifted to sleep, she felt how his hand had tugged on the scarf, only now it was all right. In her dream she could breathe just fine. She felt his lips on hers and she did not pull away.

Nemesis

The heavy drapes in her room blot out the light, but she does not have to see the sky to know the rising sun will soon graze the roofs of the houses. She paces until the weakness grows, weakness like the lethargy of a lizard or a snake caught in dropping temperatures, exposed and helpless to any hawk circling overhead. She lies down on the bed.

She places one hand over the cool metal of the amulet she wears around her neck and slides the fingers of the other hand slowly over the satin coverlet. At least she no longer has to lie each day in the moldy earth of her tomb. She soon learned to free herself from that prison, and by carrying dirt from her grave with her, she's traveled far from Sarmizegethusa. Being freed from her grave makes her less vulnerable to discovery and attack, but it does not relieve the daily terror of sleep.

She's called it sleep since her transformation—this daily death.

She pulls at the smooth, cool fabric to crumple it in her hand, but lacks the strength. She must close her eyes now while she still can. In her mind she clenches her fist, but in truth her fingers lie limp.

It had been hard to accustom herself to this sleep, to close her eyes and cease to be—straightforward as snuffing out a candle. Absolute blackness, absolute absence of consciousness, death.

Those first months nearly broke her. In the woods behind the old vampire's house, under a low lean-to camouflaged by brush, she would crawl into the shallow pit after Balaurghiuchu and lie down on the whitish brown dirt. She would stare at the planks near her face and fight to keep her eyes open. Her body would ache from violent trembling. Then, it would lose the flexibility to shake and her eyelids would freeze, open or closed.

Then as now, the oblivion is complete.

As a girl she had frightening dreams, silly dreams and dreams in which her mind sorted out a shopping list of the day's happenings. As priestess, she'd been trained to be mindful of her dreams and heed them—they were gifts of the Great Bendis. Now in this sleep there are no dreams, neither trifling nor meaningful. Those other worlds within her being had died with her.

She had died. But Balaurghiuchu had transformed her, and she'd sloughed off mortality along with human sleep and dreams. And while it's true she can be destroyed, it's most unlikely—she's as good as immortal.

Today, in the instant between closing her eyes and sleep, an apprehension shakes her with the strength of the dread of those first months: she fears the dream. But why now? It hasn't come for years. She calls it a dream, but she knows it's no more a dream than her sleep is sleep. It's a visitation.

Sleep overtakes her. Time does not exist for her, and she does not exist in time.

In the absolute nothingness, the visitation announces itself in its usual way, creating a ripple in the void. She feels a flutter of wings near her temples, over her heart, on the palms of her hands. She is in her sleep and yet cognizant. She is on her feet gazing up at the night sky: immense, moonless, glittery with stars.

That's when she sees Her: Silent Nyx, Goddess of the Night, swooping from the sky in Her black robes. In each arm She cradles an infant: Sleep and Death. She looms overhead, suspended, expanding until She replaces the entirety of the heavens. The priestess's eyes cannot take Her in. The Goddess is simply, completely primordial Night. The priestess's heart swells with awe and reverence—ancient emotions from before her transformation.

Oh heart-stopping Nyx, Daughter of Air and Darkness.

Then, exactly as the priestess has dreaded, Nyx's Daughter, Stony-Eyed Nemesis, steps from the folds of Night's robes. The fearsome Daughter appears in the guise the priestess knows best, identical to the Greek-carved statue brought into the mountains of Dacia from the coast and placed in the sacred precinct of Sarmizegethusa. She knew the stone features well—a young woman's face, heavy-lidded, with low broad eyebrows and a small full-lipped mouth. The priestess had always wanted to reach out and touch the sculpted hair—reminiscent as it was of flames, of waves, of snakes writhing—upswept and coiled on top of Her head. When she was High Priestess of Bendis she passed the statue every day, and each time she would mutter a prayer to Nemesis to keep the Goddess at bay—a prayer of praise, and of fear not keenly felt.

Now She—Indignant Outrage and Humbler of Kings— steps forward from the embrace of glorious Night, and the priestess's heart is worm-eaten with dread. Strong-necked Nemesis, as unfeeling as her statue of white stone. Her blank, merciless eyes bore into her, eyes petrified like dark amber.

Nemesis, Scourge of Vanity, steps forward, a small, ceremonial step. The priestess hears herself moan, feels hot tears run down her face.

Another step, small and measured.

The priestess tries to flee but finds herself frozen in place.

The priestess's victims emerge from Night's skirts to form an arc behind Nemesis. Each carries a blazing torch. Closest to Nemesis, she recognizes Balaurghiuchu and the soldiers who raped her. Near them stands her own Roman centurion, the one who rescued her from the ruins of occupied Dacia and took her with him to a new life in Iberia. At the far ends of the crescent, hover more recent prey, their faces indistinct, unrecognized. Over the centuries, with each subsequent visitation from Nemesis, the arc has grown broader and more crowded.

The torches are many, blinding. Her victims push forward, jostle each other. For the first time the arc breaks apart. They form a mob behind Nemesis. They shout, plead, demand divine retribution.

Righteous Vengeance raises Her sword and they fall quiet. She takes another solemn step. An odd rustling sound is created—bodies brushing against each other as they surge forward, then pull back in respectful distance from the Goddess.

The priestess knows there is no weapon to wield against

Pitiless Nemesis. There is no hiding from her. Nor does contrition move Her.

No matter, the priestess has none to offer.

Her eyes fly open. A gasp is trapped in her lungs, waiting for release. She is stiff, the blood still and pooled in her veins. She feels tears on her face, but weeping belongs to the time before her transformation. When she can move her hand, she reaches up and brushes her fingertips along her cheek. She looks at them. There is blood on each one.

22

The next day, as *Señora* Rosario crossed the plaza on her way to visit me in the big house, she saw an unusual sight: *Don* Adelfo Luis Tena Prieto, in all his glory. The old phantom tended to keep to himself, didn't he, not often deigning to visit us common folk. And yet there he was in the flesh, entering the plaza and heading straight for *Señora* Rosario.

She automatically and efficiently took inventory. She begrudged granting Lourdes any credit, but she noted in particular the white shirt, starched and pressed; the black trousers, soft and faded from washing but not worn or frayed; and the heavy leather work shoes, well-oiled.

She approved of proper shoes—she hated seeing a grown man in trainers. Just look at old Anselmo. He still wore a dark, v-neck pullover as was the wont of men his age, but he'd given up his humble but respectable cloth and jute *alpargatas* for a pair of cheap, white athletic shoes. Ridiculous! The old fool was seventy-eight years old if he was a day! It's not like he was going to sprint around the plaza or pole vault over the fountain. Next he'd be giving up his flat tweed cap for a cowboy hat. She'd given her brother Valentín notice that if he ever put on trainers or bluejeans, from that day on he could do his own cooking and cleaning, because she would disown him.

None of that nonsense for *Don* Adelfo, she noted. He wore a black wool jacket and, as always, a dignified, black felt beret—a *boina*—instead of a tweed cap. She did observe, with perverse satisfaction, that he was looking very thin and pale—Lourdes must not be much of a cook—and grey stubble stippled his face. Her husband, may he rest in peace, would never have shamed her by leaving the house unshaven. All this went through her mind in the blink of an eye, hard and fast judgements being her specialty.

The old *hijo de puta* strode toward her with purpose, albeit distracted and, she realized, unseeing. Too late for her to step aside—not being so nimble in her old age—*Señora* Rosario held out a hand, stopping him before he walked straight into her.

"Good morning, *Don* Adelfo," she said, smiling. "What a pleasure to see you out and about."

Startled to see her standing in front of him, he focused on the hand that lay on his chest. Blushing, she pulled her hand away and stuffed it behind her back.

He seemed dazed, lost.

"Why not come and sit a minute, *Don* Adelfo."

She took him by the arm to maneuver him over to the fountain, but he shook her off. He moved toward it on his own, and she walked next to him as if ready to catch him, and then oversaw his sitting down on the bench formed by the broad edge of the fountain's basin.

He ran his hand over the stone. "I came to see the fountain," he muttered. "I needed to see it. I had a dream..."

She told me later that he looked like death warmed over.

"I think I'll just fetch you a glass of water, *Don* Adelfo. All right?"

He didn't reply.

"You wait right here. I'll be right back."

I don't know why she was so worried about him. As far as I could tell, the old goat was invincible.

He suddenly snapped out of whatever haze he'd been in. "Wait," he said, grabbing her arm. *"Señora Rosario,* isn't it?"

She told me this, insulted, "As if he didn't know me!" But to him she just nodded. "Yes, *Don* Adelfo."

"Do you hear it?"

"What?" she asked.

"The sounds that are no longer here. The plaza—people coming and going, calling to one another. Old man Belarmino's little store doing a lively trade. Right there. It's like an echo in my mind. When we were kids, remember?"

"Of course," she said. "And we kids playing and shouting." A sad smile crossed her face. "We thought life was waiting to shower us with rose petals."

He nodded. "Life showered us with something, but it didn't smell as good as all that," he chuckled, unconsciously stroking the scar at the corner of his bad eye.

"You did your duty, *Don* Adelfo. We're proud of you. Fuentespina's proud of you."

He raised a hand and shrugged, as if the old bastard had an ounce of humility in him.

"Señora Rosario," he said, "please sit down. Here." He gestured next to him.

Señora Rosario hesitated.

"Come, come. You have nothing to fear from an old ruin like me."

"Of course I'm not afraid. And what are you talking

about? You're as fit as any man half your age. ...But people still talk out of turn."

"Everyone gone but the gossips, eh? Well, if you don't sit, I'll have to stand. Can't have the gossipmongers impugning my manners."

So *Señora* Rosario sat down. After all, they'd known each other their whole lives. They'd been children together, and until he left for the war, there'd been no distance between them.

As if thinking along the same lines, he said, "What was it all for, Charo?"

"What's that, *Don* Adelfo?"

"We rooted out every last trace of the enemy, at least that's what we thought, godless demons that they were."

She glanced at him sideways.

"The April 1st proclamation, remember that day? 'The war has ended,' Franco said."

She nodded, smiling. "Sixty years ago! Can you imagine, Fito? Sixty years plus a few days."

"We weren't naive. The military war was over, but we knew the task ahead would take decades, decades..."

"Yes," she said. "The Postwar called for sacrifices as well."

"What was it all for? Look at the Socialists now in Madrid, lording it over the government. Socialists, hah! Reds, that's what they are."

Señora Rosario patted his hand. "They're out of power now, Fito. Six years now."

"Bah! Mark my words, they're waiting in the wings. Reds. *Políticos*. Damn them all to hell. They all snub the

Church. Divorce, decadence, depravity. The three D's of democracy, the three D's, *Señora* Rosario."

"Things are different, now, *Don* Adelfo. Times change, and peace is a blessing."

He turned on her. "You accept the way things are? You applaud what's happening in Madrid?"

She back-peddled. "No, of course not, Fito. Have you forgotten who you are talking to? Have you forgotten who my husband was, may he rest in peace?" She crossed herself. "And my father, God grant him peace?" She crossed herself again.

"*Claro, claro.* Forgive me." He sighed so deeply his chest shuddered. "How has all this happened?"

She gave his hand another pat and said, "Madrid is a long way away."

"Small comfort, Charo, small comfort," he muttered. "Look at us—me, you, we've all got one foot in the grave. Fuentespina, too, one foot in the grave."

Señora Rosario did not appreciate his shoving her into his grave, but she searched for something to raise his spirits. "We have *Doña* Pilar here now. She'll turn things around for the town. You wait and see."

What people refused to grasp was that *Doña* Pilar only did what was good for *Doña* Pilar and her estates. If Fuentespina happened to benefit, fine by her; if not, equally fine, maybe better. If she should decide a ghost town was more to her liking, what was to stop her from administering the coup de grâce, bulldoze the village and seed sugar beets on our graves?

"Fuentespina will be fine," *Señora* Rosario reassured him.

"If she can vanquish it," he said.

"Vanquish what, *Don* Adelfo?"

Instead of answering, he said. "I remember the very moment I decided to sign up."

"Do you?"

"Can you believe that? After all these years? But it was more than a decision, it was a calling. Remember Father Ezequiel?"

"Yes, of course. Father Ezequiel, he could talk up a storm."

"It was that Sunday when he warned about the ruin the Republicans were bringing to Spain.

"*That* Sunday? You mean every Sunday, from 1931 on, every single Sunday the man had one topic. Every occasion—funerals, weddings! Even my father, and you know how stalwart he was, even he tired of his tirades."

"Did he?" Adelfo frowned in disapproval. "I only remember a Sunday in late July of 1936. After the *Generalísimo* rose up in Canarias. *Arriba España*!"

"*Arriba*!" she echoed automatically.

"I'll never forget it. It was as if until that moment I'd been dreaming. One minute I was in church, staring at the back of the frayed collar on old Paco Serrano's jacket..."

"The old shepherd! I haven't thought of him in years. He used to hum, all the time, even during Mass."

"That's the one. I was staring at the back of his neck, wishing I'd snuck off with my friends, when Father Ezequiel's voice cut through my childish fog— anarchists burning objects of veneration, boarding up churches, raping nuns. How communists had forced a crucifix down a priest's throat. How the Holy Father Pope Pius warned of the Republicans' satanic hatred of God. 'We did not drive out the Moslem infidels,' Father Ezequiel thundered, 'to end up cursed and bedeviled by this atheistic republic!'"

Señora Rosario shook her head. "You would have thought Father Ezequiel had fought in the Holy Wars right next to Isabel and Fernando."

"But he was right, Charo. Nearly twenty centuries of Christian civilization. How could we not give our all to defend it? He was speaking the word of God. I felt it in my blood—it was a righteous call to Crusade. Saint James the Moor-killer would again descend from the heavens on his white stallion to come to our aid. It was our duty, our privilege, to defend our women, our country and our faith, to fight for love and honor and Christ. That Sunday in July, one moment I was staring at the back of Paco Serrano's jacket, smelling the sheep on him, his humming low and relentless. The next, I was all at once truly awake, truly alive, truly a man." He raised his hand in the fascist salute. "*Viva la muerte!*" he shouted. He lowered his arm and pushed it out again. "*España: una, grande y libre!*"

"Spain: one, great and free!" *Señora* Rosario echoed, much less fervently than the old bastard. She was concerned about him getting overexcited. "But you were fifteen, Adelfo," she said.

"Fifteen and a man. I was called. Nothing could stand in my way. Nobody could stand in my way."

Señora Rosario remembered with nostalgia the thrilling sensation of succumbing—as a mystic surrendered to God—to the hurricane wind that was the fascist revolt. The war carried them along, exalted them, blotted out their meagerness, their individuality. It made them one with the primordial storm gales of history.

"Nobody," the old bastard repeated.

"No," she agreed, "nobody could."

23

That morning I'd left the door open to the service patio. It was chilly in the shadows but the light shone strong and new. I liked the way it flirted into the kitchen, coming in at a slant, teasing the floor tile. It would have been the perfect spot for a cat to sit. I miss having a cat about—*Doña* Pilar can't stand them—and I hate messing with mouse traps. I pulled my cardie tight about me and found reasons to go in and out, out and in. Feeling almost jolly, wasn't I—what with the crisp morning air, the kitchen smelling of cleanser and hot coffee, and the afternoon's novelty ahead: fresh conversation with a fresh-faced girl—Esmi would be coming to tutor the *señorito.*

But at the moment it was still morning. I'd shut the door against the coolness outside, and I was facing Reina across the old workhorse of a table. She sat there, poor thing, hunkered over her coffee cup as if someone were about to rip it from her hands. A slight sour smell hung about her. She didn't look me in the eye, and she didn't say anything. The thick pine planks of the table were stained and scarred, and once in a while she rubbed her finger over a hollow in the wood next to her cup. There was nothing new in any of this, but at that moment I didn't know how much longer I could sit there, connected as we were by only silence and a table from somebody else's century.

I was thinking about cooking something special to offer

Esmi that afternoon, like the town specialty, an almond carrot cake. Her mother probably used to make it and so that might please her. On the other hand, her grandmother might have already made one. Maybe some *floretas*—egg batter, deep-fat fried and drizzled with honey—messy to make, but pretty, like big crispy flowers and served up with hot chocolate. I'd need some old newspapers to lay out on the floor. Had I used them all up?

I stood to freshen my coffee, deep in thought, weighing alternatives. As I passed Reina I placed a hand on her shoulder. It might have been a crow lighting there, the way she jumped.

"Reina, *mi reina. Tranquilo*," I said. "You're going to wear yourself out."

I pulled a bottle of sherry from the cupboard, and poured a shot into her cup to help soothe her, and into mine to celebrate a change in this musty old house. A change, I thought, that could only be for the better.

Reina looked at me as if she were going to confide in me, then she shook her head and took a sip. She gave a sly smile and sipped again.

Just then there were two raps on the outside kitchen door. As I looked up, it swung open and *Señora* Rosario called out, "Morning, Narda. It's me."

As if there were any doubt.

Reina leaped to her feet, knocking her cup over as she did so. She let out a little moan of regret. Then she muttered a "Goodbye, Nardita," and a "Thank you, Nardita," as she scurried past *Señora* Rosario and out the door.

Señora Rosario looked down her nose at the departing

Reina with an even uglier sneer than usual. "Good riddance to bad rubbish," she said.

"*Señora* Rosario!" I said. "This is my house."

"Actually, Narda, it's *Doña* Pilar's."

"Well, it's my kitchen," I said in a tone that said contradict me at your own risk. I mopped up the spilt coffee with a dish rag. "Would it kill you to be civil to her?"

Señora Rosario simply raised an eyebrow and cocked her head.

"How many times do I have to say this? You are welcome, and Reina is welcome. Neutral territory. In this kitchen we're all Swiss cheese."

"Ah, Nardita, you're a saint, putting up with that crazy old..."

"See the Matterhorn in that corner there?" I interrupted. "And where you're standing—Lake Geneva."

Señora Rosario raised her hands palms toward me and gave a little shrug.

"The way you two act. After all these years, it's crazy."

I was no longer in such a good mood. I placed Reina's cup in the basin and placed a mug on the table with a bang. "Coffee?"

Señora Rosario thanked me and sat down, making a point of not sitting in the same chair as Reina. I slid the cup toward her and poured.

My cup was still upright, steam rising and carrying with it the aroma of sherry. *Señora* Rosario sniffed the air. She patted her permed hair. "Are you playing favorites, Narda?"

I took the bottle of sherry from the cupboard and poured a shot into her cup.

"Satisfied?" I said.

"Yes, Nardita, quite."

I sat down and took a sip myself.

"I just had the oddest conversation with *Don* Adelfo," she said, all eager to tell her news. "He didn't seem well, not well at all, quite agitated, in fact."

I couldn't have cared less about the health of the old coot, or his mood, and I hoped my silence would change the subject, but *Señora* Rosario acted as if I'd said, "Good heavens, do tell."

"He was reminiscing about when we were kids, before the war, actually about the start of the war." Her own eyes took on an unnatural gleam. "Sometimes, after all these decades, one forgets what it was like."

"I'd think that would be a good thing," I said, but she didn't seem to hear me.

"You should have seen him back then, Narda. He was all boy that one. Handsome, dashing. Even after the war, if you didn't look at that one side of his face, if you saw him from the other side, or from the back..." She shook her head, took a sip from her cup as consolation.

"He said some peculiar things. He was talking one foot in the grave this and one foot in the grave that, and when I tried to reassure him, he said, 'If she can vanquish it.'"

"Vanquish?" I said. "That's not a word you hear every day. Vanquish what? And who's 'she?'"

"*Doña* Pilar."

The image of *Doña* Pilar as crusader put a wry smile on my face.

"But vanquish what, I don't know. He tried to hide it, but

he was clearly quite unnerved. I don't know that I've ever seen him like that. I thought maybe you could, you know, tell me what's going on?"

I harrumphed. "*Don* Adelfo and I don't talk," I said.

"But you talk to his wife."

It was true. Because of Lourdes, I knew more about the old bastard than I ever cared to, but I didn't know what bee he had in his *boina* now, nor did I want to. Besides, I took my promise seriously to Nuestra Señora de Soledad, I vowed to Our Lady, that I would keep a person's unspoken truths to myself.

"More coffee?" I asked.

She wagged her finger at me in answer.

"I haven't told this to anyone, Narda, but I, too, have been feeling an odd sense of foreboding. I keep telling myself, 'Everything is fine, Rosario, everything is fine,' but..." She pursed her lips and shook her head.

Imagine that. *Señora* Rosario talks to the old bastard about some sinister danger, and just like that, she too reports a sense of foreboding.

"*Vaya coincidencia!*" I said.

Señora Rosario drew herself up. "Don't mock me, Narda. You're not the only one who's...sensitive."

"Pardon me," I said. "So, when did you start having these premonitions?"

She took a sip and licked her lips. "I didn't say I had premonitions."

"OK, when did you start having these non-premonitions?"

She gave me a mild little scowl, but took the question

seriously, her eyes searching the ceiling for an answer. "I'd say it was two, no, three days ago. I remember because it was the day before Adelfo's granddaughter came to town." She said it innocently enough, but when she heard herself say it, her eyebrows went up and her eyes widened. "Do think there's a connection?"

"A connection to what?"

She lowered her voice. "Do you think it's Teresa's daughter that's the problem?"

"Esmi?"

She nodded fervently.

"Of course not."

She shrugged in a way that said, maybe yes, maybe no.

We sipped in silence a few moments. My mind starting to drift back to the afternoon ahead and to what I would bake once *Señora* Rosario left.

"Nardita, I know it's none of my business..."

Oh, boy, I thought, here we go.

"But," she lowered her voice conspiratorially, "I know about a certain stranger, a certain someone's gentleman caller, who I must say is awfully young for you."

Oh dear Mother of God, I thought. Here we go again.

But despite my alarm, I had trouble keeping a straight face—*Señora* Rosario thought I was having an affair with *Señor* Iban! *Ojalá!*

My mind raced to the grateful conclusion that my having a nameless lover in the house was far less threatening to my job than the truth. As long as *Señora* Rosario didn't find out *Señor* Iban's name, and as long as *Doña* Pilar didn't find out the identity of my supposed paramour...

"I suppose," *Señora* Rosario blathered on, "it's in your blood." She whispered, "You know, that dalliance your mother had with the Gypsy... But, Narda, really, is it wise? A stranger like that—I mean, what do you actually know about him?"

The unspoken question, "What does he want with you?" was loud and clear.

She reached out and placed her hand on mine. "What if he is *Don* Adelfo's evil and my foreboding? Have you thought of that? It would be terrible, Nardita, terrible if something were to happen to you. Who would I have left to talk to?"

I did not blink, or acknowledge in anyway what she'd said. Instead I raised the bottle of sherry and as I poured another shot into her cup, hoping to distract her, I said, "What brought *Don* Adelfo out of his house, anyway?"

She heaved her well-meaning bosom, not put off the scent for a moment.

"Narda! This is serious."

I stared her down, my face impassive as a rock—you might have thought I really had been sired by a Gypsy. She looked away first—I had more at stake. She muttered something under her breath, and tasted her refreshed coffee. It was a minor victory and a fleeting one—it was impossible that she drop such a juicy topic for long. I was going to have to convince *Señor* Iban to get out of town right away.

"What brought the old goat out?" I repeated.

Another heave of the bosom. "Narda, you should be more respectful. ...I think he needed to check in, so to speak —set foot in the plaza, put a hand on the fountain," she said thoughtfully. "Sometimes, when you're old, it's like you're caught in a maze of the past and other times the present makes all that's past seem impossible. It's good then to talk to other people who knew you when, or who experienced some of the same things. Don't look at me like that. Just you wait. You'll see."

Her voice brightened. "And he asked to borrow my whitewash brush," she said as if it were the most amazing request she'd heard for years, and maybe it was. "He said that when Lourdes tried to pull theirs from a pile of old implements, it hung up on something, and when she tugged, the handle cracked. He said it would be hard to repair, and the bristles were in bad shape anyway."

"Why are they whitewashing now all of a sudden, after all these years?" I didn't care. I just wanted to encourage the change of subject.

"Maybe the big house being spruced up has inspired him. There's life in the old town yet. We just need to apply some elbow grease. In fact, when he's done with my brush, I think I'll whitewash my house as well. If *Don* Adelfo sets a good example, we should follow it."

"By all means," I said sarcastically.

"Do you think *Doña* Pilar has an extra bag of lime lying around?"

24

I settled on making an almond-carrot cake. I cracked the nuts, blanched them and cranked them through the grinder, all the while trying to put *Señora* Rosario's curiosity out of my mind.

Meanwhile at the Tena house on the edge of town, Lourdes, aglow with purpose, informed Esmi the house had to be whitewashed. She led her across the patio, past the old bastard and his radio, to the shed by the back wall. The door creaked open and she pointed out an old, wobbly, homemade ladder.

"Now while I get organized I want you to pull that ladder out of there and haul it to the front of the house," Lourdes said.

"Grandma, that looks like a broken hip waiting to happen."

"Nonsense," Lourdes said.

But Esmi was right—whitewashing is no job for an old woman. If you aren't perched up there balancing a bucket of water, you're climbing up and down the ladder—up and down, up and down.

[And remember, that's just the prep. Then there's the whitewash to mix and apply.]

Lourdes, explaining these steps, tugged on a bag of lime, but the bag got the better of her. She stood up—not any too straight—with her hand on the small of her back.

"Be useful," sounded a sharp voice inside Esmi's head. Her father's voice! From what forgotten corner of her brain had that moldy, old bubble surfaced? He'd left when Esmi was five to go back to his hometown on the Mediterranean, and Esmi hadn't seen him since. Of all the things he and her mother used to fight about, Esmi had been high on the list—he thought Teresa spoiled her.

But Esmi didn't feel spoiled. Her mother pushed her hard, always on her about her future. "Study," Teresa would say. "One drudge in the family's enough. School, *hija*—that's your job."

One time, when Esmi was nervous about upcoming exams, she rebelled.

"*Mamá*, why do I even need to be an engineer?" Somewhere along the line Teresa had got it into her head that that was the career for Esmi. "I'm tired of studying all the time."

"You know why," Teresa said.

Esmi rolled her eyes. "Money."

"That's right, baby. Scads of it."

"But you despise people with money."

"Ay, *mi amor*."

"You always say they're smug and stuck up."

"That's OK," she said, waving her cigarette, holding it between outstretched fingers as Esmi herself did. "Make me proud. Make me despise you."

"There's no arguing with you!" Esmi wailed.

Her mother had smiled. "That's right."

She reached to the back of Esmi's head and pulled it down to her so she could kiss Esmi on the top of her head.

Esmi wrangled the ladder across the patio—the most direct route to the front of the house was back through the house. As she passed the old *hijo de puta*, he leaned toward his radio, hands clasped between his knees and scowled at the possibility of an interruption.

The skin on her neck felt sticky and sore under the starched cotton kerchief that Lourdes had given her to use instead of her red one.

"You can't do proper work wearing that silky thing," she'd said.

At the kitchen door Esmi heard clanking and water sloshing—Lourdes was pumping water into a bucket.

Be useful, the voice said again.

"Easier said than done, Dad," Esmi said under her breath. To her grandmother's way of thinking, she was hopeless at anything that mattered. Her kind of skills— knowing how to negotiate the subway, get money from an ATM, zap her dinner in a microwave and, of course, write software for computers—were all useless here.

Lourdes called out directions and warnings every step of the way as Esmi carried the ladder into the kitchen, maneuvered it down the corridor that divided the house in two—every room hidden behind its own closed door—and on out the front door. In front of the house, Esmi jiggled and rocked the ladder in the dirt lane until she found a somewhat even footing and then leaned it against the wall.

She stepped back from the ladder and eyed it leerily. At least whitewashing was better than tiptoeing around inside that stuffy house. Several strands of hair had come loose and coiled about her eyes. While she re-twisted her hair up and re-clamped it in place, Lourdes started brushing the wall with the broom. When Esmi took it from her, Lourdes brought a chair out from the kitchen and sat down. As Esmi reached the broom up to the top of the wall, Lourdes explained the finer points of whitewashing, because, "It's important to know these things, *hija*."

Esmi did not argue. Instead she pictured her dream apartment, the one she'd buy when she owned her own start-up: marble floor in the lobby, uniformed doorman, brass doors on the elevator, parquet floors—a four-hundred-million-peseta price tag, and not a whitewash brush in sight. The corners of her small mouth pulled straight down—her mother would never see it.

After she finished with the broom, she was informed that step two was to wash and moisten the wall.

[That's so the whitewash adheres better.]

Lourdes steadied the ladder while Esmi climbed it as if it were made of egg shells, a pail of sudsy water in one hand.

"Be careful, *mi amor*." Lourdes said.

Esmi pulled the hog-bristle brush out of the water and started scrubbing along the top of the wall.

"It doesn't have to be spotless," Lourdes said. "Just get the dust off."

[Otherwise it will muddy the whitewash.]

When Esmi had finished the upper part of the wall,

Lourdes retrieved a second worn brush from the kitchen and they worked side by side.

"I was going to send you to Narda to borrow a whitewashing brush," Lourdes said, "but your grandfather went for a walk and came back with one! If you can imagine, your grandfather out strolling! He said he wanted to see the plaza. He wanted to see the fountain. Heaven knows why. I've never seen a more miserable town square. It's not even square."

"No, it's more of a trapezium."

"What?"

"The shape of the plaza—a quadrilateral with no parallel sides. That's what it's called."

"*Madre Purísima*! There's a name for that?"

Esmi shrugged.

"And then that old pock-marked fountain! What a disgrace. I keep telling Narda to drop hints to *Doña* Pilar to replace it with something pretty, or at least with something that would hold water."

She stopped scrubbing, and pointed out some spots Esmi had missed.

"Well, he grew up here," Esmi said, "I suppose it has sentimental meaning. Old people get that way, right? Nostalgic?"

Lourdes raised an eyebrow. The old bastard was enough older than her that she did not appreciate being lumped into the same category.

"There's being nostalgic and then there's just being daft—that plaza has absolutely nothing to recommend it."

"That's not the point, is it? Something doesn't have to be pretty for you to be fond of it."

"But he acted as if they might have moved it on him or hidden it from him."

She rubbed a drop of water off the wooden cross around her neck with the cuff of her sleeve, and dropped in inside her neckline—next to her heart for safekeeping.

"And then not only does he go out for a walk, but he runs into *Señora* Rosario and comes back with her brush. I don't like the idea of borrowing from that woman."

"I met a Rosario," Esmi said, water dripping down her wrists and along her arms.

"Well, there's only one of her, *gracias a Dios*. I hope she was civil to you." Lourdes sank her brush into the pail, and scrubbed at the wall. "She refuses to give me the time of day."

"Why?"

"They all think I stole your grandfather away from them. They think, what business did I, a snip of a girl, have snapping up the most eligible bachelor in the village? Me, an outsider, and my family being..." She broke off. "They've never made it easy on me."

"What's *abuelo* say?"

"Oh, they're always peach sweet to me anytime your grandfather's around. But that's my cross to bear. Small price, no? A good husband, a good house, children. Who needs the rest of them?"

Lourdes dipped her brush back in the pail. Dipped her fingers in, too, and dribbled a few drops of water down Esmi's back.

"Hey!" Esmi squealed, scrunching her shoulders up to her ears. Lourdes smiled and turned back to work on the wall. They worked in silence for a few minutes.

"Thank heavens for Narda. Bless her heart," Lourdes muttered, more to herself than to Esmi.

"I like Narda," Esmi said, surprising herself with the statement, with the bluntness of it. She shrugged it away.

Lourdes nodded. Their brushes made scratching sounds against the wall. The old whitewash, damp now, gave off an acrid smell mixed with the odor of wet earth.

"What did you mean about your family?" Esmi asked.

Lourdes didn't answer. After a few moments she said, "We'll need that whitewash brush soon."

"I think your *Señora* Rosario is a bit *loca*," Esmi said. "She was spewing a bunch of nonsense about wild beasts— lynx and wolves and I don't know what all."

"You should respect your elders, *m'ija*," Lourdes said dutifully, "Even her." Then she added, "They do happen, you know, attacks by wild animals. Maybe she thought you being a city girl, you might not know. Probably thought I wouldn't think to warn you."

"You didn't."

"Well, maybe I should have."

"I think she was just trying to scare me."

"Why would she do that?"

"I don't know. For the fun of it?"

"No. If she'd wanted to scare you, she would have told you about The Black Hand."

"What's that?"

"It's a disembodied hand, very big. In the night it taps

you on the shoulder, and when you turn around it rips out your eyes."

"Grandma!"

"Or there's the *Coco*..."

"I know about that one."

[How about The Fatcutter, the People of Death ghosts, Lanú the goat-man, the demon Gruñu, the hag Jáncanas, The Sharpener, The Wolfman...?]

"And there's the old vampire story."

"Vampires!" Esmi protested.

"The vampire and the Visigoths. In the seventh century? Or the... I don't know when, but the Visigoth king Leovigild is still famous around here for running a vampire out of town."

"You can't be serious."

"Out here, a cow dies or a sheep dies, sometimes even a person, and the why and wherefore are not always so clear."

[You city people don't know everything.]

"Beasts, monsters. Who's to know? You can usually tell a wolf attack—they always go for the throat. But then so do lynx. And vampires... Who knows?"

"Really, Grandma!"

"The city newspapers aren't going to care if a cow is found out here in the middle of nowhere with a ripped neck. Nor are they going to believe us, a bunch of yokels from the same middle of nowhere, when we say someone has died under mysterious circumstances."

"And have they? Died under mysterious circumstances?"

Lourdes dropped the brush in the pail and stood back, hands on hips, to admire their work. "Ay, *mi amor*, the house is going to look very nice. It's needed this for a long time now."

25

I opened the door to Esmi at 5:00 p.m. on the dot—she was punctual, you have to grant her that, but without an ounce of eagerness. She winced when I opened the door, actually winced. She met my gaze for half a second and then turned her attention to the door frame as if she were going to buy it but didn't want to pay the asking price.

"I'm here," she said.

"So I see."

The girl was barefaced under her makeup—she hadn't been trained like the rest of us in putting on a false, shielding kind of face, so it took no gift at all to tell what she was thinking. It was splashed across her face plain as day—she'd given in. Now giving in to her grandmother was one thing, but giving in to *Doña* Pilar was a whole 'nother kettle of fish. Giving in to *Doña* Pilar rankled, and rankled deep.

Still, she'd made an effort, bless her heart—skirt instead of jeans, although it was a very short and very tight skirt, that silky red scarf and those blue, blue shoes. In some ways the shoes were more shocking than the red scarf or the tight mini-skirt, screaming as they did of fashion holding sway over practicality, of blatant sexiness and of, well, whimsey—all things in short supply in Fuentespina, all weeds in the village's well-tended vegetable patch.

[She strutted around in those high heels like they were real shoes.]

Down dirt streets she'd walk, and across the uneven stones of the plaza, as casually as sashaying across a plush carpet in some penthouse, a gin and tonic in hand. Those shoes of hers were that exotic.

Esmi hugged one of Lourdes crocheted shawls close to herself—Lourdes had declared the girl's jacket too mannish. I recognized the shawl right off because most women around here favor triangle shawls in neutral colors and fringe, but this was a green half-circle with a pineapple design and scalloped edges—a pattern that Lourdes told me her mother had taught her. Needless to say, it looked different on Esmi than on Lourdes. Esmi looked like a butterfly in it. Or a rainbow.

I can imagine how happy it made Lourdes—except for the shoes, the scarf and the tight mini-skirt—to bless her granddaughter with the sign of the cross and send her off to the big house looking scrubbed and ready for church. Well, as ready as Esmi was going to look. No doubt, at that very moment Lourdes was beaming across the kitchen table at that old *hijo de puta* Adelfo's ugly mug.

Esmi met my eyes again and begrudged me a crooked smile. Still, the smile was for me, and deep inside I accepted it, with gratitude. I told her *Doña* Pilar had already gone out, and the girl's tight-lipped smile relaxed a little. She let go of her grip on the shawl and tossed one end of it over her shoulder, the green lace overlaying the red silk of the scarf.

"I'll take you up to meet the *señorito*," I said briskly, "and then, when you finish teaching him, come down to the kitchen. I made us a cake."

"So I see," she said. She reached out and brushed at my cheek.

Her touch was cool, and light as the wings of a moth grazing my face.

"Flour," she explained.

I covered my cheek with one hand—I felt caught out, girlish—and with the tips of the fingers of my other hand I covered my lips. A smile escaped through them.

"My mother's specialty," I said. "Almond carrot cake. Well, the specialty of most of the women in Fuentespina, but hers was the most special of all."

"I've never had it."

"Your mother never made you almond carrot cake?"

"She wasn't much of a cook."

As we went upstairs, I pointed out the stone steps worn by footfall, the patina on the walnut handrail—hundreds of years of Fernán-Iñíquez hands sliding over the carved wood—and the piece of wall from a Roman villa on display at the head of the stairs—a fresco of a tiger in the act of bringing down a wild boar.

"Ugh!" she said about the painting.

"It's very old and very rare—about the only frescos that survive were ones buried in ash, like at Pompei."

She screwed up her face. "It's still ugly. I wouldn't want to see that every night as I went to bed."

I stopped then and looked at it, as I often did while I caught my breath after climbing the stairs. The artist had caught the boar—bristly, with long curving tusks—in the instant when it realized all was lost. You could see it in its eyes, and the boar writhed in panic—the cat's deadly jaws poised at its throat. Esmi was right; you couldn't call it pretty. But it was skillful, and faithful to fact, and the cat had to eat, didn't it.

"That's *Doña* Pilar's room," I said nodding to one of the doors we passed. "If she's at home, that's where she holes up. She keeps it locked. Of course I have a key, but she doesn't know that." I saw Esmi raise her eyebrows just a tad. "Not that I make use of it," I added quickly, "But I am the housekeeper—the keeper of the keys. What if there were an emergency?"

I stopped two doors down. "Here we are," I said. I knocked once and opened the door to the boy's room. "*Señorito*," I called. "Looky here. Your tutor's arrived."

Señorito Roberto had a sensitive nose, and the room smelled of the vanilla-scented candle he was burning. When I'd collected his tray after lunch he'd been propped up on pillows, doodling ornate swords and weird monsters in a school notebook, but now he was slumped to one side, eyes closed.

Esmi gasped.

I turned to see what the matter was, but she'd already ducked into the hall. I found her bending forward, holding her arms over her stomach, her face pale as sheets drying on a line.

"What's wrong?"

She pointed to the room.

"It's OK. I'll wake him. He can nap later."

"Wake him?"

"He wouldn't want to miss you."

"You mean he's not dead?" she whispered.

"Of course he's not dead. Come in." I said, jerking my head toward the room.

She took a step away from me.

"I saw..." Her voice was quiet and urgent, and I went close to hear her. "A couple days ago I was in the emergency room at the hospital—with a friend, a broken wrist. There was this old woman on a gurney, and I saw her before they covered her up. That's..." She pointed toward Roberto's room. "That's what that she looked like. Like him."

I shook my head at her, thinking, what a silly girl.

"He can't very well be dead, can he, if I can wake him up?" I said.

I went back into the room. Esmi stood outside.

"*Señorito*, rise and shine. *Señorita* Esmi is here to teach you."

His pale brown eyes opened into a squint. He was a thin boy, still many inches away from an adult height—lanky, slack-shouldered, with dishwater blond hair and an ashen complexion.

"You can't learn if you're asleep—*camarón que se duerme, se lo lleva la corriente*," I said, and cast a knowing look over my shoulder at Esmi.

Señorito Roberto pulled himself upright. "Ask the *señorita* to wait outside a moment, Narda. I want to get up and put my robe on before I meet her."

Although I was telling myself, "See, the girl is overreacting," for the briefest of moments I saw the boy through Esmi's eyes—his eyes were darkly rimmed and feverish, glazed; his skin was a bleached white; and he was thin, too thin.

"Of course, *señorito*," I said. I turned to Esmi and pinched an inch of air in front of my face to tell her to wait, and closed the door between us. I placed *Señorito* Roberto's leather slippers on his feet, his skin was cool to the touch, too cool, and he tottered to standing. I held the fine-wool robe for him to slip on. He adjusted the silk, navy-blue print ascot he wore because he always felt cold—the stone walls of his room seemed to spawn drafts and chills. The only kid in Fuentespina, and he looked like a little old man from another century.

He wanted to sit at the table in his room. I held his arm the short, slow distance across the room.

I'd seen the boy every day. Was it that his deterioration had happened in baby steps, almost invisible, for me not to have noticed?

"What's the matter, Narda?" he said.

I shook my head and opened the door to invite Esmi in, but she wasn't there. I told the boy that the *señorita* seemed to have stepped away for a moment.

"Go find her, Narda."

I found her sitting on the bottom step, gripping the handrail.

I called to her in an upbeat voice, "*Señorito* Roberto is ready for you."

She looked up at me with disgust.

Why didn't I say to her, right then, "He's very sick, isn't he?" Why didn't I explain that I hadn't realized before, but I could see now that she was right? Instead, under her gaze, I felt my lungs seize up, as if trying to cushion my heart.

If only. If only this, if only that. My mother had taught

me that if-only was no way to live a life. But if only I'd been willing to stand up to *Doña* Pilar. If only I'd been willing to lose my job instead of my soul.

"Don't look at me like that," I said.

"Narda, what are we going to do?"

"Do? I'm going to go scrub the kitchen floor. And you're going up there and tutor *Señorito* Roberto."

"You can't be serious."

"And after, we'll all have a nice piece of cake."

"Narda, we have to find *Doña* Pilar right away. We have to get that boy to a hospital."

I remembered this girl standing up to *Doña* High-and-Mighty in the plaza, and how that had been what tickled me about her in the first place. But this! I squeezed out a laugh that sounded like someone choking.

"*Doña* Pilar's not going to drop everything just because..."

"Because her stepson is dying?"

"Don't talk foolishness. Why, he's up there now, isn't he, sitting at his table waiting for his lesson." I didn't sound all that convincing even to myself, and I suddenly felt very prickly—in truth a lot more than prickly—towards the boy, and myself, but mostly towards Esmi for making me feel so dull-witted and lily-livered. "Besides, the boy is her responsibility," I said. "Not mine. Not yours." I could feel the heat building in my face and my blood fighting the walls of my blood vessels.

"But Narda..."

I went to the front door and opened it. "Fine," I said, my heart all tight-fisted. "Go, if you feel that way. Go. Find

Doña Pilar. But mark my words, she'll fire you. Except that will suit you just fine. That's what you want, isn't it? You'll go back to Madrid and your fancy job and I'll be left here to get the blame. It will all end up on my shoulders." I held my arms over my chest to hide the trembling.

"This isn't about you," she said.

"No, it's about you."

"I can't pretend that boy up there is perfectly all right." she said.

"Kids get sick, don't they. It's no big deal." I shoved my hands in my apron pockets. "I have my own problems. I don't need you making me new ones." I snapped my head in the direction of the outside air. "Why don't you go back to Madrid and leave us in peace."

And so she left.

If only this, if only that. If only.

Sacrifice

*S*omeone's pounding on the front door. Sledge-hammer loud. The boy clambers out of a dream and into the dark hallway. It's summer and the house is hot, stuffy—his neck is damp, his nightshirt sticks to his skin. His eyes fix on the candle flame that comes floating from his older brother's room, the room that had been their parents'. His brother's finger is crooked through the curled handle of the tin candle holder—his feet are bare, his white shirt unbuttoned, his belt hangs down from the waist of his trousers like a long tongue. He clasps the boy by the shoulder.

"Go back to bed," he orders.

Fito jerks free. He isn't a kid anymore—he's 14. Almost 15.

His brother turns the knob and the door bursts inward, knocking him back into the hallway. The candlestick flies from his hand and the metal clatters on the floor tiles. Men in green uniforms wield electric torches. The beams bounce about the hallway, one catching Fito's wide eyes. Another trains on his brother as he scrambles to right himself—he tries to fend off the glare with the raised palm of his hand.

"That's him," a voice says. "That's the one."

One of the soldiers reaches in and grabs the older brother's arm, reeling him in as if a big fish. Before he can protest, a second soldier grips his other arm. He struggles and manages to pull away from the first soldier, but only for a moment. A third strikes him in the stomach with the butt of *his rifle, and Justino doubles into the blow. He's hit again, and Fito sees blood pouring down his face.*

"Justino!" Fito screams.

All three soldiers are crammed into the narrow hallway, and Fito can't see what happens next. He hears thuds, grunts, his own cries.

And then the hall is empty. The soldiers are hauling his brother into the street towards a waiting truck—his feet drag in the dust.

Fito rushes to the door but a fourth man, standing just outside, stops him. Fito looks up into a pale face shiny with sweat. It's someone he knows: Don *Pablo Salgado, the father of his friend Charo. He's wearing a uniform, too.*

"Please, Don *Pablo. Stop them."*

Fito's vision blurs and he rubs his sleeve across his face. Snot mixes with his tears. Don *Pablo lays a hand on the boy's shoulder. His aftershave cloys in the boy's throat.*

"No, son." It's the voice that identified his brother to the soldiers: That's him; that's the one.

"It's a mistake, sir. Bring him back. Please."

"Hush now. What you did was very brave."

"I never meant for this... Sir, please, Justino hasn't done anything."

"Our country is in grave danger, hijo. *Unwholesome, diseased elements jeopardize our way of life, threaten our very survival and must be eradicated, must be cut out. It's no time for halfway measures. You turned your brother in as antagonistic to the* Generalísimo. *Very patriotic, a very patriotic act indeed. And most necessary,* hijo. *You remember that. Most necessary.* La patria *is in your debt."*

"He wouldn't let me join the army," Fito sniffles. "I just wanted you to make him let me,"

"Pull yourself together. You're the man of the house now. Or will be soon enough."

"What do you mean?"

"Hijo, we are all called upon to make sacrifices for the fatherland. What you need to keep in mind is this: you did the right thing."

"Please, Don Pablo. Where are they taking him?"

"Leave that to us. You go back to bed." He pats Fito on the back, he gives him a wink and a wan smile, then he raises his arm in the fascist salute.

From the doorway Fito listens to another door being pounded on. He hears shouting. Two gunshots. Screams. He slips inside and shuts the door.

The house is dark. It smells of dirt and leather, gun oil, sweat-soaked wool, fear. It smells like someplace he's never been before.

His toe touches something hot and soft—wax. He reaches down and his hand brushes against the candleholder. He sweeps his palm across the floor, feels something wet and wipes his hand on his nightshirt. Then his hand finds the snuffed candle. He feels his way to the kitchen to find a match.

Don Pablo is an important man, and he's told Fito he's done the right thing.

And he has.

He has.

He has done the right thing, a noble thing.

In the light of the candle Fito sees the reddish smear on

his chest and the traces of a stigmata on his hand. He works
the pump handle at the basin. He washes Justino's blood
from his hand, the tears from his face, and then daubs at his
nightshirt with a kitchen rag.

26

When Esmi got home, she slammed the front door
—probably cursing me and *Doña* Pilar in equal measures.
Lourdes winced at the door banging, but it was good to hear
noise in the house that wasn't of her own making. Esmi's
steps pounded down the corridor.

"You're back early," Lourdes called from the kitchen and
turned smiling just as Esmi burst into the room, her face a
confusion of emotions. Lourdes couldn't tell if she was
angry or hurt. Or was she seeing fear? Contempt? "What's
wrong? What's happened?"

"I need to talk to you and Grandfather."

Esmi brushed past Lourdes, calling to her grandfather as
she charged out the kitchen door to the patio. It took the old
bastard by surprise. He furrowed his brow at the ruckus and
turned off his radio.

"What's all this about?" he grumbled.

"I don't know," Lourdes said. She hurried past Esmi to
stand by the old fart's chair.

"It's the boy I'm supposed to tutor," Esmi said. "I think
he's dying."

"Dying!" Lourdes made the sign of the cross. "Oh,
Adelfo."

"Isn't there anyone in town with any medical training?"
she demanded.

Lourdes shook her head, and Adelfo's face became stony.

"Is there any way to get him to a hospital? Maybe

someone with a farm lorry who could take him into Badajoz?"

Adelfo turned aside. "This is not our business." He switched the radio back on. An announcer shouted football scores with lifeless urgency.

"But, Grandfather..."

Lourdes shushed her, and then turned to Adelfo, "*Viejo*," she said. She clutched her cross necklace. "If the boy is ill..."

"It's not our concern."

"Then how do I find *Doña* Pilar," Esmi said.

"I don't know, *mi amor*," Lourdes said. "You'd have to ask Narda."

"*Basta!*" the old son of a bitch growled and pulled himself to his feet. He turned on Esmi, all coiled and menacing, "Did you not hear what I said?"

Esmi was mystified by the old bastard's reaction.

"But Roberto..."

"*Señorito* Roberto, to you."

Her amber eyes sparked at the correction. "Oh, it's OK to let him die as long as we're polite about it?" Her jaw set just like her mother's.

He spat back, "You think tinkering with computer machines qualifies you to be a doctor?"

"I never said..."

"*Desgraciada*, I will not have you show me such disrespect."

"I'm not, but why won't you do anything? Or maybe you think *Doña* Pilar wants her stepson to die. Is that it?"

"Esmi!" Lourdes warned, eyeing the old bastard

nervously. She tried to take Esmi's hand but the girl pulled away. "Esmi," she mouthed, pleadingly.

She didn't know about her grandfather's nightly battling with Evil, or the buttons she'd pushed so expertly by talking back to him—she didn't even realize she'd talked back. Nor did she take into account his sense of honor—not a resigned sigh, not some sterile code of "it's not cricket," but a sparking in the blood, an explosion in the gut. And then again there were her eyes, her mouth, her brow, her facial expressions...

"That's enough," Adelfo snarled. "Get out! You don't belong here."

Esmi went cold all over.

Lourdes gasped, the radio announcer kept shouting, the chickens still scratched and clucked, but Esmi heard none of it. She heard only her grandfather's words and saw only his face twisted in outrage. And then blood—Tena blood, no doubt—rushed back into her face, burning hot, and she struck back.

"Are you so afraid of that woman? You bootlicking old..."

Adelfo's hand raised, like a concert pianist ready to nail a dramatic chord. Except the only thing in its path was Esmi's face.

Lourdes cried out and stepped in front of Esmi, grabbing Adelfo's arm.

"No, *viejo*, no!"

He pushed Lourdes aside. "*Puta!*" he yelled at Esmi. "Get out! Get out of my house!"

Esmi wanted nothing more than to get away from him.

She reeled toward the gate in the back wall of the patio. Lourdes followed, and as Esmi reached the gate, Lourdes caught up with her and grabbed her arm.

"Whore!" the old bastard spit. "Damned be the day you were born. *Mala... Maldita...*" he cursed, all the while advancing, fists clenched.

Esmi struggled to disentangle herself from Lourdes.

"Damned be your mother!"

"*Hijo de mil putas!*" she screamed back at him. She loosened Lourdes' grip on her arm and tore open the gate in the wall. Her eyes stung. Her throat felt raw. "Don't you dare talk about my mother."

"Rosa, don't go," Lourdes pleaded. She latched onto Esmi's hands. "He doesn't mean it, not really. I'll talk to him. It will be all right. You'll see." She tugged on Esmi, pulling her back into the patio, back toward Adelfo.

The old bastard kept his one working eye trained on Esmi. "Evil... *Puta...* Whore..." He didn't seem to see or even hear Lourdes.

"Let me go!" Esmi shouted, and she wrenched her hands free from Lourdes'.

Lourdes stumbled back, falling into Adelfo; and Esmi ran from the yard.

"The blessing, Esmi," Lourdes shouted after her, frantic. "The blessing!" As if Esmi leaving the house without Lourdes making the sign of the cross on her forehead were the real problem. Lourdes crossed herself hurriedly and she flung her hand out, reaching after the fleeing Esmi—blowing her a blessing instead of a kiss.

Adelfo stood gazing with grim satisfaction toward the

empty sweep of land beyond the wall. "Your blessings are lost on that one, old woman. Look how she ran—fast, brazen, like a coward, like a demon."

Lourdes made her way to Adelfo's chair and dropped onto it, heavy and aching. Wisps of her hair had escaped from her neatly pinned French roll.

"What have you done?" she said, bewildered.

The old bastard didn't answer. He was too busy with his own twisted, muddled thoughts.

She repeated herself. This time it was an accusation. "What have you done?"

Adelfo looked at her as if he'd forgotten she was there. "I've preserved the honor of this house."

"Honor?"

"Disrespectful tart. *Nadie me falta al respeto*. Nobody, do you hear? Not in my house. Never again. Causing uproars. *La sinvergüenza*. Just like her mother." His voice pitched higher. "And trying to drag *Doña* Pilar into her scheming. I won't have her shame us in front of the whole village. A Tena must be able to hold his head high."

"She's just trying to help the *Señorito* Roberto, *viejo*. There's no shame in that."

"And sneaking out in the middle of the night? What about that? Ah, you thought I didn't know. Well, it means only one thing, *mujer*, and you know it. A man."

"A man? In Fuentespina? Think, Adelfo! What man in Fuentespina could possibly be of interest to a beautiful young girl like Esmi?"

He shrugged. "If a female's in heat, she's not so picky— the males will sniff her out."

Lourdes lowered her head to one side and closed her eyes, her brows a tight knot over her nose. "Don't speak so crudely, Adelfo. Not about our Esmi."

"Our Esmi," he sneered. He turned his head and spit. "Men will sniff her out. They'll come in from the farms, from the highway. Don't think they won't." He stood directly in front of Lourdes. "That's the way things work," he said. "And the bitch is waiting for them with her legs open."

Lourdes blanched. She clutched the wooden cross that hung around her neck and looked aside. Her chest tightened so, she found it hard to breath. She stood and moved away from him.

"Well," he said in a low menacing voice, "I'll not have whoredom—not in my house and not in my town."

He sat back down in his chair. He looked at his radio—the horn section of a pre-war recording of "The Good Ship Lollipop" bounced through thick static as if the broadcast were time traveling.

"None of that's true," Lourdes said. "Not about our Esmi. She's a good girl."

Adelfo turned the radio off. "Are you defying me?" His voice was an icy blade.

"Of course not. But you can't run our granddaughter off, not when she needs us the most. Where is she to go?"

"I don't give a damn. As long as it's far from here. She doesn't belong in this house and she doesn't belong in Fuentespina. *Doña* Pilar knows. I discussed it with her the other night. She sees through her. Or she will. She will."

"What are you talking about?"

And so he explained how after his nightmare the night the girl arrived, he'd never got back to sleep. Lourdes, snoring to beat the band, didn't hear him get up before dawn. He'd dressed and gone to sit in his chair in the patio, but with that bee of a dream in his bonnet, he couldn't settle. He took his rifle from where it stood with the shotgun in the corner of the kitchen and headed out the back gate. He had no plan in mind, he just started walking and ended up skirting the town—a bit of reconnoitering, as he put it. When his path crossed the road into town, he stopped to catch his breath.

That's when the old sod saw the Land Rover approaching. He decided then and there that he was meant to warn *Doña* Pilar about his dream. So he planted himself in the middle of the road and waved his arms.

"Oh, Adelfo!" Lourdes exclaimed.

Not being the good Samaritan type, *Doña* Pilar—her running lights rocking wildly—drove off the road to bypass him.

"She thought she was going to go around me," he told Lourdes.

So, what did the crazy old coot do but run off the road into the path of the veering car. He was darned lucky *Doña* Pilar bothered to slam on the brakes. The car raised a cloud of dust and old Adelfo coughed and rubbed his good eye.

"You could have been killed!" Lourdes said.

He shook his head and continued, "*Doña* Pilar leaned her head out of the window of the Land Rover. 'Idiot!' she said—you see, I'd taken her by surprise. 'What do you think you're doing?'

"I approached the car, took off my *boina* out of respect. 'Good morning, *señora*, a very good morning,' I said, very correct, very firm. 'Adelfo Luis Tena Prieto, at your service.' I said.

"'Yes, yes, *Don* Adelfo,' she said, 'I know who you are.'"

He nodded proudly at Lourdes.

"'What is it you want?' *Doña* Pilar said.

"'I've had a dream, *señora*, a dream that concerns Fuentespina de Vico, so it is only right that you should know.'

"She started to protest. '*Don* Adelfo,' she said, but I raised my hand to interrupt her.

"'Evil, *señora*, that's what I have to tell you. Evil with a capital E.'

"'Evil?' she said.

"I nodded that that was indeed the case.

"'Get in, *Don* Adelfo.' she said to me."

I'm surprised she invited him in. Not least of all because she was funny about old people. She didn't like to be around them—I think they gave her the heebie-jeebies—and she didn't bother to hide her distaste.

The old bastard rubbed his hands up and down his pants legs. Lourdes listened horrified, but he smiled at her, all pleased with himself. He told her that after he'd said his piece, he climbed down from the car. He raised his hand in farewell and *Doña* Pilar sped off toward town.

As it happened, that was the same morning *Señor* Iban left Esmi by the fountain, and *Doña* Pilar drove up to the big house right after that, breaking up the little chinwag Reina and Esmi were having.

When Lourdes got up—none the wiser to Adelfo's gallivanting—she'd found him in his usual spot, with the radio turned relatively low.

"How could you speak to *Doña* Pilar that way about Esmi?" Lourdes said.

"I never mentioned the girl outright. I wasn't sure yet."

"Sure of what?"

"I told *Doña* Pilar that we should be on the look out for anything unusual, for any strangers, say. *Doña* Pilar agreed we would have to keep an eye out."

"But sure of what?"

He clenched his fists. "How that girl is linked to the evil. If she's a harbinger, or something more."

"You can't believe that."

Adelfo forced his fists open and stood. Then, as if to keep them from clenching again, he grasped Lourdes by the shoulders.

"Listen to yourself, woman," he said. "Don't you see? This is just like before with Teresa. You all upset. Everything wrong. Just like before."

"It's not the same, *viejo*. Esmi is not Teresa, and she's not to blame. Not for anything. Isn't it time, Fito, time you finally admitted the real reason you never got along with Teresa? At least to yourself? At least to me?"

"I don't know what you're yammering on about."

"It might help end your nightmares." Her voice turned into a squeak. "It might help a lot of things. Esmi..."

Even the old bastard could not doubt that Lourdes had

anything but his best interests at heart. He changed tack. In a gentle tone he said, "Old woman, you're soft-hearted about the girl, just like you were with Teresa."

"I never interfered between you two, Mother of Heaven, forgive me. Maybe if I had, Teresa wouldn't have left. Maybe we wouldn't have lost her."

His irritation returned. "That one," he sneered, "She would have left no matter what. She had the itch."

"Adelfo. I will not listen to you talk like that about our daughter, may she rest in peace." She crossed herself again and then covered her eyes with one hand. Her mouth twisted and she slid her hand down to cover her mouth.

"*Vieja*, don't deceive yourself. She was no good. And her daughter—not a whit better. A good deal worse, I'd say."

"No, Fito."

"Open your eyes, woman. Look at the way things are all turned on their head. If she's not evil, then evil has followed her here."

"Listen to yourself. You hated Teresa. Your own daughter. You hated her and you were hateful to her. And now poor Esmi."

The old *hijo de puta* shrugged off her words. "Teresa shamed us, Milú. It's all well and good for you to be tender-hearted about her. You're her mother. But it falls to me to protect the honor of our family. It's my duty. I have to be clear-headed. I have to uphold the principles of..."

"Adelfo, stop it!"

It was probably the first time Lourdes had ever raised her voice to the old bastard, and I wish I'd been there to see his face. To his way of thinking, it was bad enough for Lourdes to put up the protest she had, however weak it might be, but raising her voice, practically telling him to shut up, well, up was down and down was up. He was speechless.

"Can't you admit for once why you really hated Teresa?" Lourdes insisted. "Why everything she said and did ate at you? For just one reason, Adelfo. She was the spitting image of your brother, may he rest in peace." She crossed herself again.

"You don't know what you're talking about."

"Oh, I know I never met him. I've never even seen a photo of him. But when you weren't around, there were plenty of people to comment on the resemblance between Justino and Teresa."

"That means nothing." he sulked.

"It means everything, you stubborn old man. Don't you see? And now you've turned against Esmi, God love and protect her. You're doing it all over again. You have to listen to reason."

His words came out slow and frosty. "I said it means nothing."

"Our granddaughter needs us and I'm going to go find her."

"Stay where you are," he commanded.

"But, Adelfo."

"She's not welcome in this house, Lourdes. That's final. Now go. Lock the doors and shutter the windows." He went into the kitchen.

"We can't turn her out," Lourdes said, following him. "I won't do it."

He grabbed the rifle from its place in the corner.

"You've never defied me before, Lourdes. Never. Don't you see? That's the proof—the bitch is evil. Deep down I suspected it all along. Now I know it." He placed a box of ammunition in his trouser pocket.

"What are you doing?"

"Lock up as I told you."

Adelfo turned to leave through the back gate. Lourdes grabbed his arm to stop him. In reflex, he lifted the butt of the gun. Lourdes cried out and covered her face with her hands. Adelfo stopped himself in time.

Lourdes sobbed into her apron as he cursed her and stormed out the gate.

"Lock the house, *mujer*," he shouted over his shoulder. "Lock it up good. You hear me?"

27

Lourdes' love for Esmi may have peppered the air like lead shot at her end of town, but you'd have been hard pressed to find kind thoughts for the girl anywhere else—not in Madrid and certainly not in most of Fuentespina. I myself was feeling pretty huffy about our clash that afternoon—I had to deal with *Señorito* Roberto's disappointment and await *Doña* Pilar's displeasure. It wasn't fair—life as usual—and I'd built up quite a case in my mind against Esmi.

After Lourdes had cried herself to a dry husk, she did as the old bastard had ordered and locked the house up good and proper. Then she sat at the kitchen table to wait for the old bastard. What would happen when Esmi came back? She would come back, wouldn't she? Tears welled up again. She opened the back gate and scanned the horizon. Then she relocked it. In the kitchen she picked up a knife and set an onion on the cutting board, but she stared at the empty corner.

She couldn't stand the silence, or the worry about Esmi. And Adelfo, well...

She tidied her hair and came looking for me at the big house. She knocked on the kitchen door, puffy-eyed, but acting all nonchalant. She asked after *Señorito* Roberto and fished for information about Esmi. As soon as the first sentences came out of her mouth, I knew Lourdes was AWOL and anxious to get home before Adelfo missed her. I also saw why—the nightmares, the arguments, the old *hijo de puta* chasing Esmi off—but I was in no mood to hold Lourdes' hand.

"God help me, Lourdes, why come bothering me? Why ask me about Esmi? What do I have to do with it? She's your granddaughter."

"But, Nardita..." she wheedled.

"I've got my own troubles. Your husband's unhappy with the girl, right?"

She turned red.

"Well maybe he has a point," I snapped. "Have you thought about that? Because as far as I can tell, she's caused nothing but trouble since the moment she stepped into that plaza out there."

Lourdes was nonplussed at my lack of feeling. I was known to be tetchy on occasion, but this was something else. While she was off balance, I ushered her out the door without ceremony—almost a bum's rush.

As for Esmi, after she'd skedaddled out of the old bastard's reach, she stomped through the empty fields outside the village. The ground was rough and uneven. She was wearing her heels, the tight little skirt and the camisole top—no pockets, so no cigarettes. The wind stabbed through the crocheted shawl and lashed her bare legs.

Finally she slowed to a halt and took a gander at her whereabouts—the scrubland lying about her and, a ways off, the dusty shape of Fuentespina curled in on itself like a sleeping dog. Other than a lizard skittering for safety under a scrawny rosemary bush, she was the only living being in sight—with nothing between her and the dome of sky, nothing between her and the lizard's co-critters and not a thing between her and any of those creatures that *Señora* Rosario had warned her of.

She didn't want to be out there come nightfall.

She doubled back to the outer edge of Fuentespina—the backside of houses and adobe-enclosed yards, one wall crowding into the next, propping each other up like drunken soldiers on leave, and forming an unbroken, mud-baked fortification to the outside world. In this case her.

She trudged along, her stomach empty and growling, until she came to a crumbled breach in one of the walls. She picked her way over the little mound of rubble into an abandoned patio with a grandfather of a chestnut tree in the center, its big gnarled roots undermining the wall.

Leaning against the trunk, she slid down to the ground— the tree bark scraping her back—and covered her head with her arms. She'd arrived at the end of the world—that's how it felt. The pain was starting to thud, not just in her throat but throughout her body. She was due for another pill, not to mention a cigarette.

It had only been the night before that she'd turned her back on *Señor* Iban and hiked back from the ruins, the night before that that she'd arrived in Fuentespina and gone wandering through the village and met you-know-who by the fountain, and the night before that... Less than seventy-two hours since Lucho had attacked her, since the emergency room, since she'd fled the city.

A led to B led to C, or it should, but she couldn't keep any of it in a straight line. Everything swirled into a muddle of images: Lucho's face bloated with rage. The sheet covering the frail body of that old woman. Me, Narda, pointing out the fresco of the dying boar. She and her grandmother facing each other—her mother's bed and a sheet taut between them. *Doña* Pilar driving in the night and the fear that flickered in the Ice Queen's eyes when she stopped. The blur of landscape outside the train window. Her mother prying Lucho's hands from her neck. The wind whipping through the Roman ruins. The stark moonlight. Her standing alone by the side of the road as the roar of the bus faded away. The boy white as marble and just as still. *Señor* Iban sitting on the edge of the fountain, content as a cat in its patch of sunlight. Her grandfather's raised hand. His words. It all overwhelmed any timeline. It all pulled her down. What was happening to her?

A dog started barking in a nearby house, the sharp yapping like little slaps in the face. She pulled herself up. It was time she focused on practical matters.

How could she get to Madrid? She'd left everything in her room: clothes, pain pills, cigarettes, ID, money. And what about Roberto? Once she made her way to a town, should she go to a hospital? To the police? Would they even listen to her? Roberto was a stranger to her, a boy she'd only gotten a glimpse of. And right off they would ask for ID. She was tempted to chuck it all and leave Roberto to his fate. After all, didn't everyone keep saying it was none of her business? Didn't she have enough problems of her own?

But Roberto was just a kid.

What if Tony hadn't stepped in, as he insisted he had, and broken Lucho's stranglehold on her? Whether it was her mother or Tony, she'd been saved. Wasn't it her turn now to do the saving? What kind of person would it make her if she didn't? Her plate already held heaping servings of guilt and shame. She didn't need any more.

Maybe she could wait where she was—a tree trunk for her only friend and support. Then when her grandparents went to bed, she could sneak back and grab her things. But then what?

It would be dark soon, the temperature dropping, and she would have to hike out to the highway. Even if a bus did pass—and there was no guarantee that it would—it might not stop for her.

No. Humiliating as it was, she had to go face her grandparents straight away. She had to claim her things. She shuddered remembering her grandfather's open hatred of her; but her pain medication might help her think more clearly; jeans, trainers and a jacket might give her more confidence to hike to the highway...

[It wasn't confidence that hussy lacked.]

And money and ID would give her more options. It would be best to take the pain pills with food, but that wasn't going to happen.

It would still be dark by the time she reached the highway. But first things first.

The deserted house across the yard from the chestnut was not in much better shape than the patio wall. The back door was off its hinges but propped against the doorframe. Esmi lifted it out of the way and entered the shadowy house. Dirt and dust covered the tile floor and softened her footfall. She yanked on the front door. It gave just enough for her to slip through and back into the dubious arms of the village.

She wandered until she got her bearings, and then, stomach churning, she made her way to her grandparents' house. The fresh whitewash on the house smelled sharp and earthy. It would need more coats before it would gleam white, but she wouldn't be the one doing it.

She tried the front door. It was locked. She took a deep breath and knocked. Nothing. No one answered. She knocked louder. Were her grandparents refusing to open? She kicked the door. Twice.

Of course neither Lourdes or the old goat were home. He'd gone out with the gun to who knows where, and about then Lourdes was at the big house trying to pump me for information about Esmi.

Giving up, Esmi went around the side to her bedroom. There, out of sight from the street, the wall was even dingier—dirty and patchy. She would climb in the window as she had the two previous nights and snatch her things without being caught. But the window was shuttered. She grabbed the edge with her fingertips and pulled. It didn't budge—it was barred from the inside.

"Am I so dangerous?" she yelled. "Am I such a monster?"

Refusing to answer the door, locking even the windows, it meant no return, period. She lurched from the house. Tears blurred her vision and her thoughts and emotions spun and flung and came back in a knot.

Out of the tangle came only one clear thought: Iban. He was the only one who could help her now, the only one free of *Doña* Pilar's influence. He might even be glad to see her. But how to find him? Stake out the fountain that night and see if he showed up? Gamble on finding him at the ruins, that is if she could find them again?

She felt a skittering on her arm, like a mouse running along it. She cried out and jumped, brushing at her arm. She looked down to find Reina at her side. Hard to say who was more startled, but Reina latched onto Esmi's arm again, this time more firmly, and pulled on it.

"This way," she whispered. "This way."

"Not now, *señora*," Esmi said.

Reina looked down at the cobbled street and murmured, "Call me Reina, *señorita*. Everyone calls me Reina."

She tugged on Esmi's arm again.

"Leave me alone. I have to find someone." Esmi sighed. "Somehow."

"Your beau, you mean. That outsider. I can help you. Come, *Señorita* Esmi. Come with me."

Esmi let herself be led to a small, run-down dwelling made of adobe brick. It was wedged in a corner and bridged the walls of two larger houses. Esmi doubted it had ever seen plaster or whitewash. Reina opened the door to the house's one room. Esmi did not like the looks of it—it was like a cave, with only one tiny window that had bars on the outside and wooden shutters on the inside. She stopped Reina before they went inside.

"Reina, what do you know about Roberto?"

"The *señorito*? He stays up in that room of his. He's no concern of mine."

"I think he's very ill."

Reina shrugged.

"But you know Narda?"

"Oh yes," Reina said.

"I don't understand why she isn't doing anything to help him."

Reina's shoulders bobbed again. "I have no love for that family. But Narda, *señorita*... Narda, I'd trust with my life."

A scruffy cat dashed inside with them and rubbed against Reina's leg. She reached down and gave the skinny thing a few fluttering pats. It neither meowed nor purred, as silent as her owner. Reina opened one of the shutters a few inches so there'd be light to see. An unlit kerosene lamp sat on a rough-hewn wooden table. On the wall hung an old calendar, apparently kept for the faded photograph of children playing by the sea. Reina made Esmi sit down next to the table on the one narrow, rickety chair. Reina perched on the edge of the bed, the coverlet worn and shabby. She popped up again.

"That fellow. The one you're looking for. Our Narda lets him into the big house. Every day. As soon as it's dark."

"The big house? What does he do there?"

"You don't know?"

"No."

Reina frowned. She'd hoped for some inside information, and Esmi had disappointed her.

Reina said, "*Señora* Rosario thinks your beau's having a fling with Narda. I overheard her."

"Narda?"

Reina touched her fingertips to her mouth. "Do you know what I think?" Her voice was high-pitched and whispery. "I think he..." She stopped herself, raised a curved finger near her lips, "*Señorita* Esmi, please, what's his name?"

Esmi hesitated. "Iban. Iban Velasco."

"And his mother's family?"

"Ylla-Gual. Iban Velasco Ylla-Gual. Why?"

"Oh," Reina said, again disappointed. She studied the floor.

"What's the matter?"

Reina, *mi reina,* did not fill Esmi in on the gossip, but this is how it goes: that time I got fired when I worked in England—and it was just the once, mind you, in all those years—the general consensus back home was that I'd lost the job because I got pregnant. Depending on who told the story and the time of day, either an employer had forced himself on me, or because I was young and naive he'd deceived me, or I'd had an affair with a son of the family—that Gypsy blood again, you know. The hitch was that the next time I came home to Fuentespina for a visit, I was alone—no baby. So then it was decided that I must have left the child on the steps of an orphanage—did Protestant countries have such charitable institutions?—or I'd given the child up for adoption, probably to a wealthy British family.

So Reina, with her romantic turn of mind, reasoned that the mysterious stranger I let into the big house each night must be my long-lost—and I might add non-existent—son, who had tracked me down to Fuentespina.

But what she said to Esmi was, "Iban Velasco Ylla-Gual, that name's not English, is it? Not a bit." She shook her head, a bit sad, a bit confused—apparently the stranger was not my love child after all.

The room reeked of dried cod, stale linen, urine, ointment and kerosine. Esmi saw no reason to stay any longer—Reina didn't seem to be making much sense or getting her any nearer to finding *Señor* Iban.

"*Señora* Reina, I have to go," she said and stood to leave.

Reina pulled down on Esmi's arm to get her to sit again. Her eyes were moist with affection, and this was not lost on Esmi.

"I'll get you to him, *señorita.*"

"How?"

"He sneaks into town during the siesta, when everyone is indoors. He hides in the church and waits there until the coast is clear."

"But the church door has big chains on it."

She held up a finger to her lips for secrecy. "Not the side door."

28

Esmi sized up the side door to the church. Long before she was born, its boards and skeleton-key lock had been painted a slapdash green and a modern-keyed brass lock cobbled into the wood above the iron knob. Her heart sped up. Would Iban be on the other side?

He'd taken up residence in her thoughts from day one, but now that she'd decided to ask for his help, his image loomed ever larger—more handsome, more mysterious, more promising—filling the space of all the people who'd turned their backs on her. But after leaving him in the lurch the night before, would he even be glad to see her?

She took hold of the iron knob and braced herself for the noise of door hinges tearing the air with creaking groans, but the door swung smoothly inward—the hinges having been recently greased. I know because I'd given *Señor* Iban the tin of oil myself. In fact, I was the one who told him about the side door in the first place, how it was sheltered from view and the lock broken.

The door did not lead directly into the sanctuary as Esmi had expected but into a small, unlit, windowless room of empty cupboards. She carefully closed the door behind her and lingered with one palm against the rough wood. With the door closed, there was no light whatsoever. Her hand automatically fumbled for the switch and flicked it, but the electricity had been cut long ago.

The stale air in the sacristy smelled of dust and candle

wax, and the closeness in the room thickened in the darkness. It made her head feel wrapped in cotton wool, and she could think only to be free of it. But if she bolted back outside, her only ally would be a batty old woman. If she crossed through the suffocating dark toward the church proper, she might find *Señor* Iban.

She reached her arms out and felt her way over to the inner door and through it to the main part of the church. A very little twilight—seeping in through the few small windows set high in the walls—made pools of gray in the wide sweep of blackness below. Esmi could see she was near the altar and that the nave stretching before her disappeared at the far end—it and the main doors hidden in deep shadow. She took in more details: our one-time Church of Our Lady of Loneliness was narrow, its ceiling high and vaulted, and the altar and walls stripped bare.

The panic she'd felt in the sacristy had passed now, but if possible, her heart thudded and thumped even harder.

"Iban," she whispered. "Iban? It's me, Esmi. Are you here?"

A figure stepped into the nave from the darkened area of the front doors, hidden behind the light of a torch aimed in her direction. The beam of light found her face and stayed there, blinding her. She shaded her eyes. Leather-soled shoes ticked against the stone floor toward her, sparking little echoes.

Should she call to him again? Was it even him? She stood frozen, her heart punching at her rib cage.

When he came within reach—that is, if both of them had

stretched out their arms to each other, their fingertips might have just touched—he stopped, dropped the torch to his side and clicked it off.

It was *Señor* Iban all right. She couldn't make out his face yet—her eyes were still getting used to the dark after the bright light he'd flashed in her face—but his mere silhouette aroused hope in her. Hope and something more.

When his features took shape it was as if she were willing them into existence. They remained dim. His silence and his face, barren of emotion, stunned her. Her heart stopped its pounding and caved into an ache so deep she had to lift her hand to cover it.

He took a step closer into a patch of feeble twilight, and she saw that although his face was stony, his eyes were not—they were wary. He must have listened to her bumbling about the sacristy, and then heard her stumble into the sanctuary, all the while straining to understand what might be happening, alarmed that his hiding place had been discovered.

But why did he need a hiding place?

"Hi," she said.

"Hello." His voice was as unyielding as his face.

It was not the reception she'd hoped for, and she took a step back. She might have even turned tail and fled, but *Señor* Iban lunged and grabbed her forearm. She gasped and he placed a finger on her mouth, his face softening. Heat spread across her lips. She decided right then and there that she'd done the right thing coming to him for help—his touch couldn't possibly feel like this if it were a mistake. From the strain of the last few hours, of the last few days, really, she started to tremble head to foot, and *Señor* Iban took her in his arms.

This time, looking up at the high arching ceiling, she did not pull away from him. She leaned her face against his, and he held her and stroked the back of her head as if she were an upset child, which in a way she was. She closed her eyes, felt the roughness of his cheek, smelled his scent up close, and instead of feeling suffocated, she sensed the walls retreating. She felt almost afloat. When she stopped trembling, he moved his hands to her shoulders, held her away from him and studied her face.

"What's happened?" he said.

She shook her head slightly. She felt warm and safe and didn't want to think about how she came to be there. She felt, here finally was someone on her side, no matter what. She smiled a little.

[What nonsense. Young people and their foolish ideas. Love at first sight and whatnot. When she didn't know a thing about him or his family.]

What can I say? *Señor* Iban had a way about him. When you were around him, you felt he was the answer, never mind the question.

His lower eyelids tightened and his voice turned stern, "How did you find me?"

Esmi didn't answer. She didn't know where to start— every first word concealed a knife that would lay her innards out like a gutted trout on newspaper.

Señor Iban led her to the nearest pew to sit down. The legs of the simple open-backed bench scraped against the stone floor and the sound echoed in the bare sanctuary. He held both her hands and she stared down at them.

"Esmi, say something."

"Last night..." She shook her head and stopped. No reason to get bogged down in truths and confessions—he certainly didn't, did he. She looked up at him. "I need your help," she said.

"My help?"

She nodded, made herself hold his gaze, keep a space open between them for an offer, a promise of aid however conditional. It didn't come, but his hands still held hers, and that seemed more important than any words.

She was ashamed to admit to him that her grandparents had locked her out. How had her life become so sordid?

"Let's just say it's time I went back to Madrid, but everything I brought with me is in my grandparents' house. And I can't go back there."

"Why?" he said, wary again.

She shook her head, the smallest of lies out of reach.

"If you need money," he said. He relaxed slightly, ready to be magnanimous. Money was a simple problem.

"I'm afraid I do, but there's something else, and you're the only one who can help."

"Why me?" He sounded cautious.

Because, she thought, I'm asking you. Isn't that enough?

"Because you're an outsider. You're the only person I know who's not under *Doña* Pilar's thumb."

He paled visibly, even in the scant light. His hands actually cooled.

"You're not, are you?" she asked, alert.

"Of course not." He smiled, but his hands were still cold. "How can I be of service?"

"I don't know exactly. It's *Doña* Pilar's stepson, Roberto." She found it was a relief to talk about the boy instead of herself. "I met him today and... Iban, you should see him." She shook her head and squeezed his hands. "He's very sick. And no one will listen to me. No one seems to care. Somebody has to help him, and I don't know how."

"Have you spoken to the boy's stepmother?" he said.

"I don't know how to find her. And I'm not sure what good it would do." She shuddered. "He's emaciated, Iban, wasted away. I mean, he didn't get in the state he's in overnight, and so far she's done nothing about it."

"Maybe you're over..."

She cut him off. "I know I'm not a doctor. And I know I don't know anything about kids. But, and I know it's crazy, but I could see it, feel it—his death. It's like very little of him is in this world. It's like... I don't know."

Iban looked away. He stood and turned his back to her.

"You think I'm imagining it," she said.

He shook his head no, but he did not look at her. He ran a hand through his hair. When he turned back, he looked grief-stricken.

"You must know how this affects me," he said.

"What do you mean?" she said, bewildered.

"Narda must have told you. Why else would you be here?"

"Narda? Told me what?"

"I misled you. I'm sorry, but I had my reasons. Obviously, I do know *Doña* Pilar. And Roberto. He's my nephew."

"Your nephew?" It took her only a moment to rethink the situation. Relief spread across her face. "Then you can..."

He shook his head. "Pilar won't let me near him. Years ago, when I found out that Manuel Felipe, that is, my brother-in-law, planned to remarry so soon after my sister's death, I was outraged. A number of very public rows ensued. I'm afraid I was less than gentlemanly and often less than sober. I've tried to make it up with her since, for Roberto's sake, but she won't have it. She possesses a long memory and an unforgiving nature.

"But Roberto is my only family, and before my sister died, I promised her that I'd keep an eye on him. So, I came here on the sly to see him. And yes, Esmi, I too fear for Roberto."

Esmi stood and touched his arm. "But, if you're his uncle..."

"There's nothing I can do. Narda lets me in to visit the boy in secret. But she'd never let me remove him from the house. In any case, Roberto's in awe of his stepmother. He would never leave without her permission."

"Pick him up and carry him out. From what I saw he's too weak to put up a struggle. Surely Narda wouldn't stop you."

He pulled away from her. "I can't do anything for Roberto if I'm in jail."

"Jail!"

"Pilar is quite capable of having me arrested."

"For what?"

"Kidnapping. She's threatened me with as much in the past."

"You think she was serious?"

"Deadly so."

Not only had Esmi forgotten about the old bastard throwing her out, but her concern for *Señor* Iban's well-being was busy at work crowding out her concern for *Señorito* Roberto.

"What about getting a doctor and bringing him here."

"You think I haven't gone over every possibility a hundred times? Pilar would refuse him entry. You may have noticed, she can't tolerate her authority being challenged. And if she found out I'd been in the house... Pilar is a vindictive woman. Who knows what charges she might drum up against me? Or how she might make Roberto pay for his disloyalty? Or Narda, for that matter. I can't risk it."

He sat down on the pew again. He leaned forward, resting his elbows on his knees, and stared down at his clasped hands in a gesture that in no way resembled prayer.

"Then what?" Esmi said. "I go back to Madrid? And you stay here and watch him die?"

"Of course not. I have to do something."

He sat up and pulled a pack of cigarettes from his pocket. Esmi came and sat next to him.

"It's what I've been struggling with."

He lit their cigarettes, the brief flame made the interior of the church seem all the blacker.

"What if I make an anonymous complaint to the Guardia

Civil about Roberto being neglected, or abused?" Esmi said. "It's the truth after all. Wouldn't an officer have to come investigate?"

"We're talking about the highly respected and influential *Doña* Pilar Sepúlveda-Villanova Bendiscana de Fernán-Iñíquez, mistress of Fuentespina de Vico and of the land for miles around. She can call on important contacts in Badajoz: lawyers, judges, bankers, politicians... The Guardia would make a polite telephone call, 'Excuse me for bothering you, madam, but we've had an anonymous and no doubt crank call...' 'Yes, officer. I appreciate your concern, but I assure you my son is quite well.' Click. End of investigation."

"Then go to the Guardia in person.You are the boy's uncle, after all."

He didn't answer. He just shook his head with an unpleasant little smile that said she was incredibly naive. But he took her hand, and she thrilled just a tad at this sign of tenderness and solidarity.

"Look," he said, "according to Narda, Pilar is always back at the big house at midday. I'll go tomorrow, hat in hand. Catch her off guard. I'll say that I just came to town, that I regret our past differences. I'll beg her to start over. Somehow I'll win her over."

"You'd already have done that if you thought it would work," Esmi said.

"Well," he smiled ruefully, "I don't relish a face-to-face confrontation, but if I can't charm her, there's always blackmail."

"Are you serious?"

He searched her face. He was taking her measure again.

She could feel it, as well as the click of a decision that followed.

"You may have heard the gossip—that my brother-in-law deserted his family, that he's living with his young lover on the Riviera. Well, however convenient it may be for Pilar to play the martyred wife, it's not true."

"How do you know?"

"It would be totally out of character for Manuel Felipe."

Now Esmi thought that *Señor* Iban was the one being naive. "Isn't that the thing about mid-life crises, that they come out of the blue?"

"Not Manuel Felipe. He was always a great believer in marriage. An occasional fling, that would be one thing. Desert his family, his only son and heir? Never. Moreover, I haven't been able to locate him. Not in France or anywhere else."

"Maybe he doesn't want to be found."

"Private detectives haven't been able to find him either."

"You hired detectives?"

"I was concerned. He is Roberto's father."

"OK. Then what do you think happened?"

Iban shook his head. "Now you'll think I'm crazy."

He caged her hand in both of his, and stared at it.

"Iban?"

"She killed him."

"What?"

He met her eyes. "I'm convinced Pilar killed Manuel Felipe."

Esmi was dumbstruck. Just a few days ago detectives and murderers were merely characters on the TV shows

Tony watched. One mean-spirited phone call on her part and somehow she'd slipped into a treacherous netherworld—first in Madrid and now here in Fuentespina—as if the fragile boat that had been her life had capsized and she was trapped below the water, unable to break through to the surface.

"I'll go to Pilar tomorrow," he said, "and try to convince her that the detectives have come up with evidence. There isn't any, nothing hard, nothing I can take to the police, but If I can get her to believe that there is, maybe she'll trade Roberto for my keeping quiet about his father."

"I don't know, Iban. That sounds very iffy, and dangerous. I mean if she has killed before..."

"Yes, well," he said, rather forlornly, "we know Pilar will be back in the big house around noon tomorrow. We have until then to come up with a better plan."

For the moment Esmi had forgotten about her own predicament. She wanted to comfort him, but it was *Señor* Iban who put his arm around her.

"How did you find out about me being here?" he asked. There was a false calm to his voice. "It was Narda, wasn't it?"

Esmi shook her head. "One of the old ladies in town told me."

"What? What old lady?"

She heard panic in his voice, and then anger.

"The little, odd one. Reina," she said.

Señor Iban looked trapped. He leapt to his feet.

"She was just trying to help me find you. I don't think she'll say anything to anyone else."

"We don't know that. Don't you see the danger? I have to take Pilar by surprise."

Esmi reached for him, but he paced, looking about the church as if for an escape.

"I can't stay here," he said. "I'll meet you tomorrow. Back here after I talk to her."

"Tomorrow?" she said.

What, she wondered, was she supposed to do in the meantime? She didn't fancy the prospect of spending the night alone in this ex-church. She was about to remind him that she'd come to ask for his help. But he gave her that sad smile of his, and she hesitated—what with Reina discovering his hiding place and *Señorito* Roberto sick and the prospect of *Doña* Pilar breathing down his neck, now did not seem the time to burden him with her family squabbles.

He pulled her to him, and again she felt the slight disorientation whenever he drew near.

"Trust me," he said.

She closed her eyes, breathed in his scent, heavy and intriguing beneath the subtle odors of soap and shaving cream. She felt light-headed, until they kissed. In her mind's eye, she seemed to step into his silhouette, the one that had approached her out of the darkness at the end of the nave—black and opening and familiar, adventuresome and safe all at once. She felt something so elemental, a desire more primal than anything she'd ever experienced before—blood calling to blood, to bone, to flesh, and all aswirl, all lifting in a spiral.

He pulled her to him harder. His mouth on hers, he said again, his breath penetrating hers, "Trust me."

How could she not?

29

Señor Iban slid out the side door of the church, and even though it was barely dark he made a beeline for the big house. Tap, tap, tap went the door knocker, not much louder than if he were a cat scratching to get in, as if no one would see him if they didn't hear him.

It was a bit early, but I'd gone to sit in the entryway to wait and fret and give my courage a final squeeze—*Señora* Rosario's visit that morning had made it clear that I could not risk any more visits from *Señor* Iban. So I heard the sound, and knew it was him.

Besides worrying about *Doña* Pilar discovering *Señor* Iban's visits, I'd been flustered ever since Esmi had come and said those terrible things about *Señorito* Roberto. I swear, until then he'd looked fine to me. But then, with Esmi standing outside his room, for just a moment I saw him as Esmi described him, and it was as if ice water trickled down my neck. When I turned my back to him to close the door before helping him out of bed, the sickly scent of fake vanilla tingling in my nose, I furtively crossed myself and tried to order my emotions before facing him.

Later I would understand my blindness to Roberto's plight, but at that moment I was frightened and ashamed that *Doña* Pilar had hoodwinked or just plain bullied me into going along with her. So when Esmi challenged me on the stair, I lashed out. I defended myself—out of fear, out of shame, out of habit.

After she left, that is to say after I kicked her out, I dreaded going back up to *Señorito* Roberto's room, but I couldn't leave him waiting for her—I had to tell him she wasn't coming back. I opened the door, full of dread, but there sat a normal boy at the table, in his dove-grey robe and navy-blue ascot—a bit pale as was to be expected, but that's all. I swear. Just a little pale.

What a relief! In zero seconds flat, I went from despising myself to doubting Esmi's motives—a much more comfortable state of affairs, let me tell you. Maybe, I told myself, she was more like her mother than I'd first believed, just an upstart, a spoiled city girl sowing discord wherever she went. From there it was the tiniest leap to indignation—imagine making up such a terrible story just to get out of tutoring the boy, and putting me on the spot like that. And now I was the one who was going to have to break the news to *Doña* Pilar.

I went into the kitchen and surveyed the nicely set table with the golden cake glistening in the center. "Ah well," I sighed. The girl who'd made such a scene was not the one I'd made the cake for. That's all there was to it.

I put water on for tea and cut into the cake. I took a piece up to *Señorito* Roberto. He was even more sullen than usual—not a word of thanks. Later I saw he never even touched it.

"Everything around here is my fault," I muttered as I left his room. Back in the kitchen I poured hot water on a teabag and sat at the table. I cut myself a nice slice of cake, but ended up pushing it away.

Of course the *Señorito* felt let down. The promised break

in his loneliness had evaporated, as do so many hopes in this dried-up, old town. Worse, I knew he had more disappointment in store—no more visits from *Señor* Iban. And the fault for that would be squarely mine, but there was no help for it. I had to turn *Señor* Iban away.

Tap. Tap. Tap. There he was.

I tiptoed to the door and stood stock-still, my hand flat over the crack between the wood and the doorjamb, listening.

Tap. Tap.

If only he would give up and leave.

"Narda," came a gruff whisper. "Let me in."

I placed my foot almost against the door and opened it an inch.

"Please, *Señor* Iban, go away," I whispered, my face near the crack. "I can't let you in anymore."

"Narda, you must."

I withdrew my face from the narrow opening to close the door.

"Wait," he said. "Do you want more money? Is that it?"

"No."

"Narda. Let me in. Let's talk about it."

A narrow sliver of his face was inches from mine. Even that narrow sliver was a handsome one—his voice, like whispered strokes, tempting.

I shook my head.

"You must at least let me say goodbye to Roberto."

Guilt twanged inside me like an untuned guitar. "I'll say goodbye for you," I said.

"Narda, I'll raise my voice. I'll cause a scene."

That scared me, even though I knew he was bluffing.

He pushed hard on the door, but I was ready for that and already leaning against it.

Then, feeling an idiot, I said loudly, "Go away... Jorge." Jorge was the first name that came to mind. "I can't see you anymore... Jorge." In Fuentespina there were always ears to hear, especially if it were me giving my erstwhile lover his marching orders. "It's wrong. Never return."

"Are you insane, woman?" *Señor* Iban growled, and he did the natural thing—he looked over his shoulder.

I took the opportunity to push the door closed and bolt it. I leaned with my back against the heavy wood. I was scared, I'll tell you. I'd been daft to put myself between *Señor* Iban and *Doña* Pilar. I waited for him to bang on the door, to shout. Nothing. Moments passed. It was still quiet—as if we didn't already have enough silence around here.

I felt heavy all over, inside and out. Just my forehead alone felt like a slab of meat troweled over with concrete. No more of the handsome *Señor* Iban—*Señor* Iban of the Sad Countenance—slipping me euros and compliments. No more Esmi, either, with her freshness, her flash of style, and that hunger hanging on her for anyone to see. There would be just me and *Señorito* Roberto, day after day. Visits from *Señora* Rosario. Visits from Reina, *mi reina*. Buying eggs from Lourdes. And every two weeks, something to look forward to—whoop-de-do—the arrival of the grocery-mobile. I foresaw my future—the life I would lead, and it would be a small one, droughty and dismal.

Oh, what I wouldn't give for that life now.

30

While I'd been waiting by the door, dreading *Señor* Iban's arrival, Esmi was doing some dreading of her own, only about his leaving.

She watched him melt into the darkness of the sacristy, while she held a hand over her mouth as if to hold his kiss close. And then she was alone.

His absence felt tangled with the gloom in the church. She thought that he must have been exaggerating about *Doña* Pilar. It was easy to dislike the woman, but would she stoop so low as to having him put in jail? Was she really purposely standing by as Roberto died? Could she have murdered her husband? It all seemed outlandish. But, then again, she knew things like that happened. It was just that before now, they hadn't happened to anyone she knew.

She longed for the clean simplicity of binary code. Her fingers itched for the rhythmic clicking of computer keys. She missed the glow of her computer screen, the ticking of the fluorescent lights in her cubicle and the straightforwardness of her solitude there.

She chose a pew and sat. Reaching out to take hold of the edge of the seat, her hand brushed against coarse burlap— the cloth's tiny barbs prickled. It was a roll, more than a foot long. When she slid it towards her, it weighed more than she expected and metal clanged against metal. Was it Iban's? The increasing chill distracted her from the bundle. She rubbed her legs for warmth. Dusk was giving way to night, and the thickening shadows swallowed first the vaulted ceiling, then the side aisles and the altar.

When darkness swallowed up the last crumbs of light in the nave, the blackness flattened into a wave that bore down on her, making it hard to breathe. Without warning the church pitched into a void without top or bottom, only to have the drowning wave of darkness slam back into her. Back and forth they swung—void-wave-void-wave. She gripped the edge of the pew and concentrated on her breathing—made the air go in and out. Her lungs ached from the effort.

She shot to her feet, bolt upright—she couldn't stay here, not like this, not all night. The pew screeched against the floor, its sharp echo setting off a second echo thudding in her heart. She told herself that she could get her bearings if she got back to the sacristy with its closet-lined walls and normal ceiling. Feeling her way—half expecting at any moment to trip into a chasm or collide with something unspeakable—she found the door off the altar.

Inside the sacristy her relief soared, but only for a second. The room was small, human-sized for sure, but stuffy, very stuffy and even darker than the sanctuary—no windows at all. She groped her way to the outer door and, as if she expected someone outside would be holding on tight to the knob to keep her from leaving, she yanked hard to open it. The door flew open, knocking her off balance. She stumbled into the narrow passage along the side of the church and breathed in the cool night air, laced as usual with Fuentespina's dust.

She didn't have to wait in the church for Iban all night, she told herself, just be back to meet him the next day after noon. Where would he be spending the night, she wondered. Back at the ruins? She was cold in her mini-skirt and crocheted shawl. She adjusted her red scarf and pondered where to go.

She supposed Reina would take her in. Calling to mind the one-room hidey-hole of a house, she sighed. The only place to sleep would be in a rickety chair or on the floor. She doubted Reina would even have a spare blanket, and it was creepy the way the old woman never took her eyes off her. Still, where else could she go?

She would ask to stay with Reina, just not yet.

She wandered out to the fountain. In the big house, lights glowed through two gauze-curtained windows—one upstairs, maybe in Roberto's room, and another downstairs. They threw two patches of weak light into the plaza. Esmi perched on the edge of the bone-dry fountain, arms crossed, legs crossed, and studied the two lighted windows. She yearned to tell someone how hurt she was by what her grandfather had said and done, and by what her grandmother had not said and had not done. She longed to talk about Iban, and about her and Iban. And the person she wanted to confide in wasn't Reina. It was me, Narda, of all people, only I had kicked her out.

Someone carrying an electric torch entered the square, and Esmi's spirits lifted. Iban must have come back for her. She stood to greet him.

"Mother of Heaven!"

Esmi recognized the voice. It was her grandmother's.

She plopped back down on the edge of the fountain.

"*Niña*, I'm so relieved to find you," Lourdes said. She switched off the light and sat down next to Esmi. "You'll catch your death of cold out here."

Esmi said nothing, thinking only: And who's fault is that?

"Say something, *mi amor*. Are you all right?"

Esmi pulled the shawl tight about her.

"I've been so worried about you," Lourdes said. "Look, I've brought your things."

She set Teresa's old suitcase down at Esmi's feet. Esmi should have been relieved to have her things hand-delivered to her, but she wasn't. The suitcase reeked of failure. It felt more like a curse she couldn't shake.

"I came to talk to Nardita about putting you up. I'm sure she'll do it." She reached to push the hair away from Esmi's forehead.

Esmi jerked away. "Don't touch me." She took off the shawl and tossed it at Lourdes.

"Rosa Esmeralda! I'm your grandmother!" Lourdes protested.

"What good is that to me?" She opened the suitcase and took out her jacket. "All those vile things Grandfather said. And you, what did you say? Nothing. He threw me out of the house, Grandmother! And you let him."

Poor Lourdes—to Esmi it was so simple.

"I came back later," Esmi said, "to get my things."

Lourdes tried to take Esmi's hands, but Esmi shook her off.

"Was it you who locked the door? That's how you were

with my mother, wasn't it?" Esmi was bluffing but she wanted to hurt her. "No wonder she hated you."

Lourdes gasped. "She hated me?"

"What do you think?"

"I tried..." She stammered. Clutching her cross, she started again in hopes of better controlling her voice. "I did what I thought was best. Your grandfather... I was a good wife, Rosa Esmeralda. I am a good wife."

"Bully for you. Where did that leave my mother? Or me? Where does that leave me?"

"But Esmi..."

"You've picked your side."

"What side? We're a family. There are no sides."

"Go home, Grandmother."

"You hate me, too." Lourdes' voice broke with emotion.

Esmi wanted her gone, but Lourdes sat, like dead weight, gripping the wooden cross around her neck. Esmi saw that she would have to be the one to leave. She made to stand, but Lourdes threw her arm across Esmi's waist.

"Wait," Lourdes pleaded.

She yanked the cross off over her head. She grabbed Esmi's hand and wouldn't let her pull it away. She placed the cross in her palm and held it there.

"I don't want your necklace," Esmi said. "I don't want anything from you."

"I may never see you again, and it's all I have to give you. I want you to have it. My father, your great-grandfather, made it."

"For your wedding to my grandfather, I know. My mother told me. I don't want anything to do with it."

"Well, your mother was wrong."

Esmi gave her a warning glare.

"Oh, I told her and your *Tío* Ramón that other story because I didn't want them to know the truth. But my father made it before I ever met your grandfather."

Esmi was annoyed. Her grandmother had always worn the large cross and Esmi had always known it was a wedding present.

"The truth was too painful, and dangerous." She shined the light on the necklace in Esmi's hand. It was a dark reddish brown with lighter streaks. "That's olive wood. The color is dark like that because the tree was very old." She switched the light off.

Esmi felt Lourdes' warmth next to her, smelled the lilac eau de cologne sent by Ramón every January for Epiphany. She wanted her grandmother gone, but she calculated that that would happen sooner if she listened to her for a minute.

"In 1820, my great-great-grandfather planted an olive tree in the patio behind his house to celebrate their new home and the birth of their first son. That son, my great-grandfather grew to maturity along with that tree. And all the generations that followed, we all grew up playing under that tree." Lourdes took the shawl and tucked it over Esmi's bare legs.

"After the Civil War..." Lourdes looked away a moment. Her voice became that of a plaintive child. "They took the farm away from us. It was a very little farm. Our home. Our only means of support. And It was terrible, Esmi, so terrible to be thrown into exile from our home."

Lourdes choked back a sob. Her face was wet with tears.

Esmi had had a taste of what losing a home was like, and she did feel sorry for her, but she still felt like swatting her away like an annoying fly.

"The day we left, my father cut a branch from the tree and hacked it into chunks. It was my job to carry the pieces to our mule-drawn cart. Later he carved each of us a cross from the wood so we could keep our home close to our hearts."

"Where's the danger in that?" Esmi asked, impatient. "You said the truth was dangerous."

"Losing the farm that way meant our whole family was politically suspect. It wasn't long before they came for my father. They put him in a concentration camp. So many years. Decades. Every day people all around him were being shot or dying of terrible diseases, but he survived.

"Thanks be to God, my mother was never arrested, and a miracle that was. But the confiscation of our home and *Papá* being in prison made the rest of us pariahs. It was near impossible to get work, and when we did, we got paid next to nothing. It was a terrible time, terrible. Our two little brothers... Their stomachs ballooned—it was malnutrition. They both died.

"My mother decided to send my little sister and me to live in Zafra with relatives, cousins on her side—it would mean fewer mouths to feed, and would put us some distance from our shame. And for me, there was a high school there —there'd only been a grammar school in our little town. The cousins were an older couple, and didn't want to take on the care of a young child—my sister was only ten—but they agreed to take me for one year, as long as there was no scandal or threat of political retaliation. I tried my best to be a model citizen and student. It was in the early fall toward the end of my allotted time that I met your grandfather—he'd come to town for the San Miguel livestock fair.

Esmi had been feeling some sympathy for Lourdes, until she went and brought up her grandfather.

"Your grandfather married me despite our family's taint. He was very good to me and to my family. Without him, I don't know what would have happened to us."

Esmi didn't care about her explanations, but Lourdes persisted. She wanted to make the girl understand.

"I was taught that being a good wife was the highest calling for a woman. I also have a debt of gratitude, Esmi. Your grandfather saved us. I can never forget that."

"OK, you were grateful," she said.

"But that's not why I married him, Esmi. Your grandfather's a good man and I married him because I loved him. I can't stop you from passing judgement on me or on your grandfather anymore than I could ever reason with your mother. But please, Esmi, keep this cross, and someday, for me, pass it on to a daughter of your own. It's home."

Esmi looked at the necklace in her hand. This was home?

Esmi nodded and thrust the cross into her jacket pocket. As far as she was concerned, nothing Lourdes had said changed anything. Esmi was just eager to be rid of her.

Lourdes stood to leave. She rested her hand a moment on the top of Esmi's head and made the sign of the cross on her forehead in blessing, as if that could put things to right.

"May God bless you," Lourdes said, her voice breaking. She took a few steps away but she turned back, tears rolling down her face. "Esmi, I don't want to lose you."

Esmi was about to say, "Too late," but a scream sounded inside the big house. And then another.

31

The odd thing was, I was the one doing all the hollering, and here I thought I'd been struck dumb.

The sound was so wrenching that Esmi grabbed Lourdes' hand. And Reina and *Señora* Rosario, as if conjured up, appeared at opposite corners of the plaza. Both of them knew the worst of life from up close, and they stood, eyes fixed on the big house as if to say, "Here it is again, as expected—and if anything, long overdue."

I tore down the stairs and out into the square, as if I could outrun the horror of it all, as if it would be that easy to get rid of. Esmi, Reina, *Señora* Rosario and Lourdes all rushed to me. They tried to calm me so that they could find out what had happened.

"He's dead!" I said, frantic. "He's dead!"

Esmi paled and stepped away. The older women still faced me. The expressions on their faces were stoic. As for me, my eyes must have been rolling around like those of a spooked horse, because *Señora* Rosario placed her hands on either side of my face and pressed like a vise.

"Narda," she said, "look at me."

"He's dead," I said, my voice pleading now—I guess I was pleading with them to make it untrue.

Señora Rosario ordered Reina to go into the big house and get the bottle of sherry from the kitchen. Reina balked but she did move toward the house.

"Who, Narda?" *Señora* Rosario said. "Tell us."

I clenched my eyes closed. Who did she think? My imaginary lover?

Adelfo, rifle in hand, appeared behind *Señora* Rosario. Since he'd gone through the back gate that afternoon, he'd been haunting the streets, patrolling the perimeter, reconnoitering. He'd yet to return home. When Esmi saw him she backed into the shadows.

"Who's dead?" he barked.

Señora Rosario shushed him. "Narda, tell me."

But if I said his name, wouldn't that call his ghost to me?

She gripped my shoulders and gave me a shake. "Narda!"

"The *señorito*," I whispered.

Señora Rosario and Lourdes gasped and crossed themselves. Adelfo, scowling, took off his *boina* and held it to his heart. *Don* Anselmo and others had showed up and clustered by the fountain. *Señora* Rosario's brother Valentín came forward and placed his hand on his sister's shoulder. Lourdes looked about trying to locate Esmi.

Reina, who'd been hovering near the open front door, too fearful to go in for the sherry, gave out a startled shriek.

We all turned to see a figure framed in the doorway. Because it was backlit, it was dark and featureless, a mere silhouette, but as erect as a soldier standing at attention, and clearly female.

Doña Pilar.

It was a surprise to see her because her Land Rover was missing from the front of the house—when she was home it crowded the small plaza like a big cockroach.

She said, her voice slow and solemn, "I am grieved to announce that my stepson, *Don* Roberto Inocencio Fernán-Iñiquez Seco has passed away in his sleep. May he rest in peace."

"May God have mercy on his soul," said *Señora* Rosario, and made the sign of the cross.

"Amen," muttered Adelfo and the others.

"His neck," I mumbled. "Dear Virgin protect me. I saw his neck."

Lourdes heard me and stared at me, her face a confusion of fear and regret. *Señora* Rosario jostled her as she eased herself down on one knee.

Adelfo leaned in to steady *Señora* Rosario and help her all the way down.

"Let us pray for poor *Señorito* Roberto's soul," she said.

Adelfo nodded approval. He tossed a stern look at Lourdes and motioned sharply with his chin toward *Señora* Rosario. Lourdes followed his gaze. He expected her to get down there next to that woman?

"What about my soul?" I cried. I dropped down in front of *Señora* Rosario and reached out to her. "What about me. It's my fault. It's all my fault."

"Narda!" *Doña* Pilar snapped.

I shriveled inside. I hauled myself to my feet, but could not force myself to go to her. Instead I reeled over to where Esmi stood hanging back from the others. Everyone's attention followed me to her, except for Adelfo who kept his eye on *Doña* Pilar.

I grabbed Esmi's arm. "Esmi," I said, "I should have listened to you."

One eye on her grandfather, Esmi stepped further away from the light pouring from the door.

"Please, forgive me," I cried. "Please. Somebody has to forgive me."

"Narda," Esmi said, as if not hearing my plea. "Pilar just gave Seco as the family name of Roberto's mother. That can't be."

"Don't you understand?" I said. "It's my fault."

"Iban's last name..."

It wasn't until that moment that I realized Esmi knew *Señor* Iban, and I thought, of course she did. That was what the picnic basket was about. A man like that's not likely to be satisfied with the company of a sick boy and a bunch of dead Romans out at those ruins he liked so much—not when there was someone like Esmi around.

"Shhh!" I turned her sharply from the others. "Don't let anyone hear *Señor* Iban's name," I whispered. "Esmi, stay away from him. He's..."

"Narda!" *Doña* Pilar ordered, "Come here. Come into the house."

I wanted to hide behind Esmi. I took a few steps toward the house, but faltered. I couldn't make myself go any further.

I started blubbering, "I can't, *señora*. I can't."

Now everyone was gaping at me, pelting me with their stares—Adelfo with disapproval; Lourdes and Esmi with curiosity; Reina, sympathy; *Doña* Pilar, fury.

"Narda!" *Señora* Rosario said, scandalized. She came up alongside me and said quietly, "This is no time to shirk your duty."

Someone by the fountain said, "*Doña* Pilar shouldn't face the next hours alone."

"Go on," came another voice. "A lady like that, she might not even know what to do."

I covered my face with my hands. "I can't," I stammered.

There was silence. I had just defied *Doña* Pilar publicly, very publicly. And she, on top of everything else, in mourning.

Adelfo barked at me, "Pull yourself together, woman."

I knew everyone was right, even the old *hijo de puta*, but I couldn't face *Señorito* Roberto—not his poor mutilated body and not his ghost. His spirit had to be trapped in that house—his soul couldn't possibly be at peace after such a dreadful death. And I was to blame. I was the one who let *Señor* Iban into the house and the one who kept his secret. I was the one who refused to see the danger the *señorito* was in. It was all too horrible.

I had to get away.

I tried to bolt but hands restrained me. In that moment, I saw Esmi's pale face. She had not moved and stood apart from the scuffle. I feared seeing hatred in her eyes, or disdain, but no. I saw only questions. That was my sole comfort, my only talisman: Esmi didn't despise me.

I tore free. And before anyone could stop me, I fled into the night.

32

Every blasted time I climbed those stairs at the big house, I had to stop and catch my breath. And here—for the first time since God knows when—I was running? It may be all the rage in the city, but around here, running is for children, animals and criminals. I didn't get far before I was too winded to go on. I leaned over with my hands on my knees—the wind snapping my skirt and pulling at my hair—and panted like an old hound. As I got control of my breathing, I wanted to kick myself. There I was, out in the night, all alone, exposed to every kind of danger, except—Virgen Santísima, make it so—for the ghost of *Señorito* Roberto.

Overhead, the sky was a mass of stars—all that emptiness, and the wind tearing about in it. A whole new kind of dread grabbed hold and shook me, like it was the dog and I was the rabbit in its mouth. I felt woozy, felt like I might fall off the face of the earth. I got down on my hands and knees, gripped the ground as best I could and hung on.

I found that if I kept my eyes open and fixed on the dirt between my hands, things stopped spinning. OK, but I couldn't very well stay like that all night.

The big dark shadow that was Fuentespina hunkered on the plain behind me. I could crawl back there—a much-deserved penance, for sure—never getting off my knees. But, as scary as it was out there away from the village, I was more afraid to go back.

"Now what?" I asked myself. I hadn't a clue what to do. I'd run off like a maniac, and now I had to go somewhere. If not to the big house, then where? Feeling my fingers in the dark dirt, feeling it grind into my knees and palms, I wished there were light enough to see its familiar reddish-brown color. Would I ever see it or sunrise again?

Then it came to me. I knew just the place. I forced myself to my feet, and even though each step felt like I was skirting a precipice, I made my way there.

Back in the village, people were almost as shook up by my leaving as I was. Lourdes wanted to follow me, but Adelfo forbade it. *Señora* Rosario tried to get her brother to follow, but *Señor* Valentín told her to mind her own business for once and leave me be.

Without speaking, people drew into a line to pay their respects to *Doña* Pilar. Esmi still stood apart and Lourdes didn't want to call Adelfo's attention to her. The old goat seemed unaware of her—he didn't see very well even in daylight, plus he was all but gawking at *Doña* Pilar, who was lit by the light from the open door. Lourdes managed to pass the electric torch to *Señora* Rosario and whisper to her to please give it to Esmi when she could. *Señora* Rosario looked at her with a raised eyebrow, but she took it.

As the villagers filed past *Doña* Pilar, she nodded to each in turn. One by one, as if released, they fell aside and drifted from the square.

Lourdes tried to catch Esmi's eye as she and Adelfo left, but Esmi avoided looking at her. After they'd gone, she queued up, too, the last in line. She would offer her condolences to *Doña* Pilar, but mostly she wanted to look the woman in the eye, see if there was any grief there, any remorse or guilt.

If Esmi wanted to see guilt and remorse, all she had to do was find me, look at me.

When it was Esmi's turn and she stood in front of the Ice Queen, she looked down into *Doña* Pilar's wide blue-grey eyes. She didn't see a speck of sorrow there, or any other emotion for that matter. Unlike the villagers, who had muttered, with a bow of the head, the expected phrases of sympathy, Esmi extended her hand. I, for one, had never seen *Doña* Pilar shake hands with anybody. The great lady hesitated, but took Esmi's hand, flinching when they touched. Esmi thought maybe it was the sudden warmth of her hand because *Doña* Pilar's was icy cold. Shock, Esmi supposed. *Doña* Pilar turned from Esmi without a word and disappeared into the big house.

As soon as the door closed, Esmi found herself flanked by *Señora* Rosario and Reina. Reina held the suitcase and Lourdes' shawl that Esmi had left by the fountain. She stood by and listened as *Señora* Rosario, begging and bullying in turn, laid out all the reasons why Esmi should go search for me and why she and Reina should stay put: the danger of overexertion and heart attacks, of falls and broken hips.

"Besides," *Señora* Rosario said, "it would hardly be seemly for us to leave the village at night, unaccompanied, as it were," She glanced down at Reina. "I mean a lady like myself, of a certain standing."

Esmi's eyebrows raised. She'd been in Fuentespina too

long—she not only caught *Señora* Rosario's insinuation, but found it insulting.

"You're not from here, are you?" *Señora* Rosario reasoned. "I mean, you haven't shown yourself overly concerned with proper standards of decency.

"And we need to be here in case Narda comes back. I think that would be best. Besides," *Señora* Rosario added, a bit miffed, "everyone saw how, of all the people in the plaza, you were the one Narda sought out. Maybe, to you, she'll listen."

Reina nodded vigorously.

Esmi didn't let on that she'd already decided to follow me for her own reasons, and every reason on her list started with *Señor* Iban.

"All right," Esmi said. "I'll try."

Señora Rosario jutted out her jaw and smiled with satisfaction. Reina covered her mouth with her hands and closed her eyes in a sign of gratitude.

"But, how can I possibly find her out there?" Esmi said.

"She may be acting like a chicken with its head cut off," *Señora* Rosario said, "but at some point she's going to calm down enough to realize that she has to come back here and face the music, or find some shelter out there for the night, in which case I can think of only one possible place for her to go."

It seems like most kids build forts—out of scraps of wood or cardboard, by draping blankets over chairs, by flattening tall grass into hidden nests—but we kids in Fuentespina had always had the real thing. It stood a mile or so away. An abandoned fortress—well, one remaining, crumbling wall of it, at any rate.

St. Julian's Wall predated the town—hard to imagine that: Fuentespina not existing. Nonetheless, there was a time when Fuentespina de Vico simply was not. Way back then all this area around here was Moslem-held, but for only a mere five hundred years. In the early 1200s the Knights of Alcántara—modeled after the Templars, but figuring that fighting Moors here in Spain was no less a Crusade than the wars in the Holy Land—brought the fighting to our neck of the woods, got a toehold against the Moors and pushed the infidels back long enough to build a stronghold against their return. A small frontier boomtown appeared like a mushroom in the shadow of the fortress. Once it proved that the battleground had indeed shifted for good, the Knights of Alcántara abandoned the fortress to follow the fighting, and most of the people in the town drifted away. After a respectable century of relative peace in the area, the Count of Vico, with the blessing of King Alfonso—I forget which number—built a country house nearby and a church, and named it all Fuente de la Sagrada Corona de Espinas de Nuestro Santísimo Señor de Vico. The few people still hanging on in the ghost town by the fortress eventually gravitated to Fuentespina, and the Alcántaras' abandoned fortress was all but forgotten.

Like every generation of Fuentespina children, we were convinced that The Wall was our find, our secret—secret because we didn't want to give our mums, who worried about things like wild animals, snakes, scorpions and falling rock, a chance to forbid it. In our time, it was our leader,

Ramón, Lourde's son, who got the credit for finding The Wall for us. We played tag there. We dug with our hands for buried treasure. We played *Cristianos* and Moors, or cops and robbers, or cowboys and Indians. For a time it was magical.

But then more and more frequently, Lourdes' darling boy would insist we play *Ejército Salvador* (Franco's Liberation Army) and Reds. This was always a problem, because although some kids—Ramón was not one of them—could be talked into playing the part of the Moor or the robber or the Indian, nobody, but nobody, wanted to play the communist. So then there would be arguing, and then sniggering, and then, "Hey Mateo and Lolo, you be the Reds—like father like sons," or "Narda should be a Red—she's a natural," and some git would say, "Huh?" and then there'd be comments, some whispered and some not, about my mum.

When Ramón got on that high horse, I got so I'd just walk away. One time, though, I shoved him. It caught him unawares and he fell down on his bum. I turned on my heel, a wave of laughter behind me, Ramón laughing too. And me? I fumed and cried all the way home.

Sometimes Ramón's buddy Toño would suggest a new game and occasionally he got Ramón to go along, but mostly Ramón jeered at his ideas. Sometimes that bloody-mindedness of his—a chip off the old block he was—caused a scuffle. But, even if it didn't come to blows, it always broke up the play, kids wandering off in groups, leaving Ramón and Toño and a few others on their own to fight imaginary Reds. In the end, we all stopped going out there.

Señora Rosario told Esmi about St. Julian's Wall and handed her the torch from Lourdes and a bottle of her brother's home-brewed aguardiente that she'd sent him to fetch for her—for the shock, she said, and the cold. She pointed out her house, at the far edge of the plaza; she would keep a light on in case either of us showed up, and she would pray.

Esmi went with Reina to her house. There the old woman busied herself and avoided looking at Esmi—the only privacy she could afford her—while Esmi changed into her jeans and trainers. She shoved her wallet in her pocket and left her suitcase by the bed. Reina pressed a frayed blanket—the thicker of the two she owned—into Esmi's arms.

"I'll bring it back," Esmi said.

Reina shook her head. "Bring Narda back," she murmured, looking at the floor.

There was nothing left for Esmi to do now but find St. Julian's Wall.

Now, as I crouched at the base of the Wall, shivering and praying and trying not to think beyond getting through the night, I saw a light jouncing toward me. Roberto's ghost? Or maybe *Señor* Iban? I didn't know which to dread more and thought my heart would stop from terror. I tried to pray an "Our Father," but my voice refused to cooperate, making little animal sounds instead of words. Then the light shone straight into my face—if I hadn't had my eyes clenched shut, it would have blinded me.

"Narda?" called a smooth, young voice, "It's me, Esmi."

Terror to relief in a heartbeat—and more than relief, a

tiny bit of elation even, because despite everything I'd said and done and not done, Esmi had come looking for me.

She lowered the light and I opened my eyes. She'd changed clothes since the plaza, and wore jeans and her tweed jacket, her hair down now. She carried the crocheted shawl from earlier, a rag of a blanket and a bottle of liquor. She wrapped the blanket around my shoulders and tucked the shawl over my legs. She uncorked the bottle and insisted I drink. She explained that Reina had sent the blanket, and *Señora* Rosario, the aguardiente. In between the first swigs, Esmi rubbed her hands up and down my arms. She sat next to me, her arm around me, and pulled the blanket so it covered us both. I couldn't remember the last time someone had taken care of me like that.

She waited until I quit shivering to speak.

"Why did you run off like that?"

"I can't go back in that house. I just can't."

"Why not?"

"How can I face *Señorito* Roberto's ghost? It's my fault he died."

Esmi argued with me that ghosts were pure superstition. I stubbornly shook my head no. I wish she'd tried instead to convince me that *Señorito* Roberto's death wasn't my fault. I don't think I could have believed her, but I would have liked to have tried.

"I want to ask you something," she said. "About Roberto."

I looked away and crossed myself.

"According to what *Doña* Pilar said tonight, the family name of Roberto's mother was Seco."

I nodded. "His father's surname is Fernán-Iñiquez and his mother's was Seco—Roberto Inocencio Fernán-Iñiquez Seco."

"But Iban told me that Roberto's mother was his sister. So, Iban and she should have the same last name, but he told me his surname was Velasco. Iban Velasco. Not Iban Seco."

"*Señor* Iban told me his name was Seco. Iban Seco Velasco. You must have got the order mixed up. Velasco was just the family name of his mother, that's all," I said.

"No, he told me his mother's surname was Ylla-Gual. Nothing at all about Seco."

"So, he lied to one of us." I shrugged my shoulders, not particularly surprised, but once again puzzled that with him I could never see what he left unsaid. "But Esmi, none of that's important. *Señor* Iban killed the *señorito*."

"Narda! How can you say that?"

"It had to be him. I was stupid to believe him, stupid to let him into the house. Everything that's happened is all my fault." Something sprung to mind, a glimmer to maybe ease the terrible guilt I felt. I grabbed Esmi's arm. "I think *Señor* Iban had me under some kind of spell," I said.

"A spell?" she said, as if such a thing were preposterous.

"Esmi, please believe me, the *señorito* did not look sick to me."

"Narda, really!"

"Well, for a moment when you said he was going to die, I looked at him and I think maybe I saw what you saw. But then when I looked back at him, I swear he looked OK, just a little pale. But Esmi, *Señorito* Roberto didn't die of an illness."

Esmi looked at me askance as I described the red puncture marks on his neck.

"Only a vampire makes wounds like that," I said. "And who else could be a vampire but *Señor* Iban? He's the only stranger here."

Esmi protested that she was a stranger too.

"You didn't visit the *señorito*. *Señor* Iban did." I said. "Vampires can't tolerate sunlight, you know, and I've never seen *Señor* Iban except at night. Esmi, you must stay away from him."

I had to warn her, but I'd just betrayed the vampire's secret. Who knew what he might do to me? Who knew if Esmi was trustworthy when it came to him?

"I must get away from here," I exclaimed. I struggled to my feet, but she stopped me from running away.

"You can't go wandering about in the dark. You'll break your neck."

I crossed myself. "If only that were all that happened to me!"

Esmi stood with her hands on my arms, afraid I'd dash off. "Tell me what you're so afraid of."

She listened impatiently while I explained that vampires were the dead who stayed alive by drinking the blood of the living—a filthy, unholy existence—and that if you were killed by a vampire, your eternal soul was in danger of damnation. I covered my mouth in horror and said several more heartfelt prayers for *Señorito* Roberto's soul.

Of course Esmi didn't believe a word of it. She convinced me to sit back down. "Nobody's going to get to you tonight, not way out here and not with me here." She passed me the bottle. "Drink."

What she said made me feel only the tiniest bit safer, but the panic had passed for the moment. I took a swallow.

"Everyone's worried about you," Esmi said. "Everybody wants you to come back."

I shook my head. "I doubt that. As soon as the sun comes up, I'm off to the highway. I'll hitchhike to Badajoz." I shuddered. I had never wanted to set foot in another city, but there was no help for it. "I'll get a job. I'll get swallowed up in some household and be invisible. No one will find me there. No one."

I begged her to stay with me until morning. It wasn't a hard sell as it happened. She had no more place to go than I did.

We passed the bottle back and forth. The night was quiet, too quiet. And empty. We started to talk. She'd been holding so much in, the words gushed and spurted. Whenever she stopped, I asked her for more. For the first time, someone told me everything. She told me about Teresa and Lucho and Lourdes and Adelfo and *Señor* Iban. The air was cold on our faces, but we were sheltered from the wind by the stone wall. It was almost cozy, snuggled together for warmth and no longer feeling the bite of aguardiente, just its warmth in our stomachs. Her stories, her life, filled the night, filled me, and sometimes I forgot for a moment or two how miserable I felt. But when those moments passed, I'd shudder, and Esmi, thinking it was the cold night at work, would rub my arms to warm me.

Then, maybe her throat was tired from so much talking, she said, "Narda, you listen to everyone, don't you?"

I let out a bitter little laugh. "I don't listen to *Doña* Pilar if I can help it. And I certainly don't listen to that old *hijo de puta* of a grandpa of yours."

"Who listens to you? What are your secrets?"

And to my surprise, I told her. I told her about my mother and the Gypsy lover everyone said she had, about her going to prison before I was born, and how she would never talk about it, about my neighbor who came home from prison when I was a teenager and the stories she told before my mother advised her to keep her troubles to herself. I told her about *Don* Niceto and the Widow Ugalde's pigs, and about going to work in London. About the one good job and a string of bad ones. About getting fired because the wife saw her husband make a pass at me.

And I told her about my beau Zaki—a big secret I'd kept from my brother and his wife because Zaki was Pakistani. I talked to him in Spanish—he didn't understand a word. He'd talk to me in his language—worse. Sometimes we tried to speak in English. Me, just to take care of business, "Tuesday, no," or "Movie, yes." He mostly took me to the movies or for ice cream. He loved ice cream—spumoni was his favorite. Zaki was a sweet man, but it turned out he had a wife. And not a wife in faraway Pakistan either, which would have been bad enough, but this one was right there in London. What a terrible day, a terrible scene when he told me. I was crying. He was crying. He even said he would divorce her, but I said no. He said why, and I said, "I Spanish. Catholic. No *divorcio*. Bye." I felt very noble, for all of about twenty minutes. Then I was miserable for a very long time. Poor

Zaki, my only sweetheart. I wondered who he took for ice cream after me.

"He probably didn't," Esmi said. "You were probably the love of his life."

"Ha! I say 'poor Zaki,' not because I broke his heart, but because he was destined to have his heart broken, over and over and over, and to break the heart of too many others along the way. Mine included."

And I didn't stop there. I told her about coming home, about nursing my mother until she died, about I don't know what all. Once I started, I couldn't seem to stop. I was still spilling my guts when the blackness of the night thinned to a dark blue.

33

If you've ever been outside at sunrise and away from your town walls, you'll know that moment just before the sun lumbers above the horizon, that hushed moment when the world seems to hold its breath. Esmi and I had crossed the long night hours and reached that moment, huddling together for warmth.

We were talked out. My poor voice box felt as raw as my heart—a bundle of regret wrapped in fear, that was me. Still, I had to marvel at Esmi, at all us human beings—each soul a pulsing universe, infinite and unknowable even to ourselves. Me, a universe rubbing shoulders with Esmi, another universe.

How is it that we so easily forget that and treat the people around us as if they were cardboard cutouts and, worse, act as if that's all we were ourselves? Look at me, I'm the cardboard cutout you talk at. And as for those who talk, well, in my head I play with their stories like paper dolls I've snipped from a magazine—she said, he said, she felt, he didn't say... But people are not dolls and they're not characters in a *radionovela*, these are my neighbors, the witnesses to my life, galaxies of flesh and bones. *Virgen Purísima*! How had I presumed to know them?

We sat together in that short-lived, in-between-time silence, Esmi and I feeling at peace, at least with each other. Can you understand what a rare gift that was for me? I hope not. There may be more familiarity in Fuentespina than you can shake a stick at, but friendship? Loneliness is part of the air here, and the air's thick with it.

In some ways it was less lonely in London. I would come home to my brother and sister-in-law, and all those millions of people, all that astounding strangeness and friendlessness stayed outside. We nestled in our damp little space pod with our own language and our family jokes, a calendar from a restaurant in Badajoz on the kitchen wall, and our air supply pungent with the odor of smoked paprika, cod, fried onion and sausage; and for a few hours, outside didn't matter so much.

Esmi had grumbled she had nothing anywhere near as cozy as that. She saw plenty of familiar faces on the subway and in the shops and takeout places near her apartment, and she'd say hello to the *portera* and other tenants in her building. At work she knew everyone, but only in the most superficial of ways. She had nothing more than that—no family, no one she belonged to. Lucho had come and gone, and Tony, well, their friendship had turned out to be more brittle than she'd realized.

I sympathized and soothed, thinking, knowing, she wasn't as alone as she thought. What I didn't understand then was that neither was I.

Esmi leaned her head on my shoulder, I leaned my cheek against her hair and smelled her shampoo, something tangy and sharp—exotic for not being the one brand sold in the grocery-mobile. Birds began to chitter and whistle. Then the sun eased into the sky, and the plain breathed its sunrise sigh.

I didn't say anything to Esmi about it, but several times

since that dream about Teresa, I'd had the sensation of her presence, a kind of annoying buzzing in my ear that gave me the same irritation I'd felt with her when we were girls. I'd dismissed it as pure fancy—with Esmi about, of course I'd think about her mother. But now, with ghosts on my mind, Teresa's presence returned—stronger, more insistent, clearer than before, as if she were tugging at my elbow, giving me little jabs.

At least it wasn't the ghost of *Señorito* Roberto—please, *Diosito,* let his soul rest in peace. I made a cross with my thumb and index finger and kissed it. But if this were Teresa, what was she doing way out here where I thought I'd be safe from village ghosts? The humming in my head nudged me again, pushed up on my arm. I lifted it and put it around Esmi's shoulders. Peace.

OK, I thought. Teresa, pushy as always, seemed to want me to look after Esmi. Personally I wouldn't have picked me for the job. She needed someone braver, more capable and connected, who could pull strings, but I understood. She was trusting me with her daughter because she had no other choice.

And I did want Esmi to be safe. I wanted me to be safe too. As far as I could see, the best thing for both of us was to get away from Fuentespina.

"You don't have to hitchhike," she said, knowing I was waiting for daybreak to hightail it to the highway. "I've got some money with me. You can use it for bus fare."

"I wouldn't feel right about that. Unless you come too. Fuentespina is over for us, for both of us. Time to move on, don't you think? I really want you to come with me."

"I can't, Narda. I have to go back to Fuentespina and try again with my grandparents."

Only I knew the real reason was that she wasn't ready to give up on *Señor* Iban—she wanted him to explain himself. The thought of her going anywhere near him made my blood run cold.

"I know, you don't believe in vampires. Or in ghosts," I said, giving her shoulder a squeeze. "And if you think I'm crazy, fine, but humor me." I smoothed the hair by her face. "Come with me. Please. If you stay behind, I'll worry something terrible."

I had to settle for her saying she'd walk to the highway with me and stay until I got on a bus. She would agree to no more, but I hoped once I got her as far as the highway, I could convince her to take the next step and leave with me. Then together we would break free of the village's pull. I grew very quiet thinking of getting on that bus.

"Narda, what's wrong?"

"I'll never come back here again," I said—the enormity of it all had just hit home. So little tethered me to this earth, and I was leaving it all behind.

"You don't know that. I bet before long you'll feel differently about everything."

I shook my head. "I have no right to, but I have another favor to ask."

"What is it?"

"I can't go back to the house..."

"You won't go back."

I'd been wringing my hands I realized, and now I dug my chin into them.

"There are some things... I can't bear thinking of leaving without them: an album of saint prayer cards I've collected, some family photos, and the silver crucifix from my mother's coffin. You understand, don't you? I don't want to leave without them. It's all I have. And there's money, too. All my savings. I earned that money, and I'll need it when I get to Badajoz. I feel terrible asking this, but if you insist on going back to Fuentespina, would you maybe collect them for me?"

"Well, I suppose. If you're dead set against setting foot in Fuentespina."

"You'd really go to my room for me and get my things?"

She shrugged. "I don't see why not. What about you? You won't mind waiting for me out here all alone?"

I shivered and looked up at the watery-blue sky.

"At least the sun's up now."

I'd never heard of ghosts or vampires out and about in daylight. I explained to her what I wanted and where to find it. I thanked her, and thanked her again. By any standards, it was kind of her to go to the big house in my place. Even if she did have unfinished business in town, I knew the last thing she wanted was to run into *Doña* Pilar.

Esmi promised to return as soon as possible. I felt such gratitude to her, I felt almost happy. Soon I would have my nest egg in hand and a few personal things to cling to. I loaded her up with don'ts. "Don't go anywhere near *Señor* Iban, Promise me. Don't tell anyone where I am, no matter what, no matter who."

I insisted and repeated, and she nodded, more and more impatient.

"I got it, Narda."

She lifted her arms, so graceful, so unselfconscious and pinned her hair up, as if to show me she meant business. She gave me a little "buck up" hug.

"Stop fussing. I'll be back before you know it."

I crossed my arms over my chest, trapping her quick embrace in my memory and holding Lourdes' green shawl close. I watched her leave, feeling a new twinge of guilt—I almost stopped her. So many warnings, so many fears. I was sending her where I should have gone.

I paced a bit, and then, dry-mouthed and queasy-stomached, I went back to sit against the Wall. I pulled Reina's blanket over me and felt dismal. And there was that gnat-like Teresa buzzing in my head.

I told myself I should catch up with Esmi. Yes, that would be the thing to do—catch up to her and turn her away from the village, abandon my meager belongings and drag her, if need be, out to the highway.

But I didn't move. I rubbed my stiff back against the stone of the wall—I guess hoping that some of that grit would work its way into my spine.

Crossings

A middle-aged woman clutches a tattered blanket and huddles at the base of a lone stone wall. The edge of the morning sun has slit the horizon and slipped into the sky. The wind rises to meet the day and the colorless dawn sky will soon give way to a stark blue. A nest of twigs three feet across crowns the highest section of the wall. In it stands one of a pair of storks. The bird stretches its wings and clatters its bill. The odd noise startles the woman. She crosses herself and looks up to see the stork raise its wings and lift away.

A shiver runs through her. During her childhood, the silhouette of a stork standing stilt-legged in its nest atop the bell wall of the church was as commonplace a sight as that of a dog dozing in the shade.

When had the gangly birds abandoned the town?

She gains her feet with much less grace than the stork and peers into the distance. What was she thinking, sending Esmi to Fuentespina in her place? The wind ruffles Narda's short hair and tugs at her clothes.

She touches the stone wall but rejects the protection it offers. She must follow Esmi.

She looks at the sun and tries to gauge how much time has passed since they said goodbye. Can she possibly catch up? No matter. If she has to, she'll knock bold as brass on the door of the big house to find her. She sets off.

The expanse she is crossing is vast. In the distance sand

grouse saunter across the scrubland. Dark-winged scavengers soar high above. To keep her fear at bay, she fixes her eyes on her feet and the little patch of earth traveling between them.

Her heart pounds with dread and exertion. She must catch up with Esmi. It was wrong to send the girl back alone. With each step she becomes more convinced of it. The butterflies in her stomach die in a pit of black nausea. Her heart stings, singed by cowardice and fear and regret.

And after the sweetness of the night! Companionship. Shoulder to shoulder, hip to hip under the frayed blanket, warmth and ice—warmth where their bodies met, ice where they were exposed to the night air. For the first time in a very long time, her soul had glimpsed a lightness she'd forgotten existed.

Her mouth and lips are parched—all that alcohol the night before. The wind makes her skin feel like cracked clay. She keeps her thoughts on Esmi. The girl has her mother's lovely amber eyes but none of Teresa's jangled nerviness. Deep within Esmi is a pocket of quiet that's hers alone.

Narda stumbles. The sole of her shoe—after months of threatening—has finally split from the upper and flaps free from toe to heel. Cursing, she searches her mind and apron pockets for a temporary remedy. She finds no solution—no piece of string or rubber band. She refuses to let an old shoe stop her—she will go barefoot if need be, as in a pilgrimage, and is this not a kind of pilgrimage, with the cross and love and salvation at its end? She feels the edge of her skirt where she's been meaning to repair the hem and unpins a large safety pin. She pokes the point through the edge of the worn leather, but cannot force it through the sole. She grabs hold of the droopy hem, leaving her sun-bleached slip to cover her legs, and uses her teeth to start a rend in the cloth of the skirt. It makes her teeth ache. She rips a strip of the dark material from along the hem and leans over to tie the cloth around sole and upper.

Did she see something move from the corner of her eye? She glances in that direction.

A hundred feet away Doña Pilar stands still as a stone. Narda blinks, not quite believing her eyes. Doña Pilar stretches out her arms as if taking in the horizon, and her form begins to blur.

Narda thinks, am I seeing things? She rubs her eyes and squints. Doña Pilar's body contracts, condenses, reshapes. For Narda there is no possibility of understanding. And no time.

A hundred feet away, something muscular and feline takes shape. A lynx, alert and frozen in place, gazes at her.

The shame and fright that overwhelmed Narda when she ran from the big house the night before seem as a light dusting of snow compared to the glacial fear, the primal terror that now seizes her. She turns and runs, straining every muscle, gasping, propelling herself forward, half stumbling, half falling.

The tufts of hair on the lynx's pointed ears stand erect, her whiskers point forward, her yellow eyes blacken. She takes a few steps, head jutted forward. She lowers her belly. A moment of calculation, anticipation. Then she pushes off with powerful hind legs. She reaches the human just as it falls.

A normal lynx might be deterred by prey that fights back, might give up to search out a deer or a rabbit, maybe a lost sheep. But this lynx bites and rips at the flailing limbs, and when the human's eyes meet hers, the human freezes in a moment of recognition, realizing that all is lost. The lynx sinks her fangs into her prey's neck. She holds tight, more amused than impatient, until the thrashing ceases.

The lynx lies down next to the body. The wind ruffles her fur, blows distracting scents her way. The sun is climbing, the sky turning an ever deeper blue. She stands, rests her front paws on the torso. After a few moments, she lopes away.

34

I had assured Esmi that she would be able to slip in and out of the big house unseen because I figured *Doña* Pilar would be upstairs sitting with *Señorito* Roberto's body. So Esmi goes around to the kitchen entrance and lets herself in with my keys.

I want to stop her, but all I can do is watch.

There are stories about spirits who don't know they're dead. Well, that's not me—when you die like I did, it's hard not to face facts. That's not to say it's not a shock—if I could down a glass or two of sherry to calm myself, I would—but I'm dead. And even though no one seems to be able to see or hear me, that doesn't mean I'm not here. I am. I'm just missing a corporeal presence and the clothes to hang on it.

If you must know, I never had a body you'd write home about. It and I were often at odds, but now that it's gone... Well, it's a strange thing to come to terms with. Also it's unnerving how one second I'm floating by what's left of my body, and then presto, here I am next to Esmi. I feel like a leaf tossed about on the whims of some psychic or spiritual wind, blown to and fro by some force as invisible as I am.

I do feel a warm glow or its non-body equivalent, anyway, to be with Esmi, but I'm not happy to be back at the big house, not happy at all.

Esmi stands just inside the door, listening. The quiet is absolute. She hurries to my room off the kitchen.

The room is long and narrow, with a tile floor and a high

ceiling. One small window way up high lets in a bit of light, so at the far end of the room Esmi can see the single bed with its iron frame and sagging mattress. My night gown is folded under the pillow—I can see the edge of the faded pink flannel. On the wall over the head of my bed hangs my mum's casket cross—dark walnut with silver tips and silver Christ. Below the little drawer in the nightstand, looking forlorn, sit the rosy-pink satin album I've had since I was a teenager and a biscuit tin in which I keep a few family photos and postcards. *Virgen Purísima*! Did the room look this dreary when I still lived here?

In the middle of the room, a bare bulb dangles on a long cord from the ceramic fixture on the ceiling. The braided cord is cloth-covered and furry with dust. From the fixture another braid of cord snakes across the ceiling and down the wall, ending in a round switch by the door. The room is big enough that it could have been partitioned to add a small bathroom, but I was expected to use the privy in the back and a shower that had been jerry-built into an old outbuilding.

On a narrow table against the wall, sit a pitcher, washbowl, hairbrush, toothbrush, nail scissors and a little plastic container that holds bobby pins. The only other piece of furniture in the room is an old, scarred wardrobe. It has a couple drawers where I kept underwear and stockings, and on the inside of the door is a mirror in need of silvering.

How was it I'd never noticed how dismal it all looks? It has the air of an emptied storeroom, which it probably was—clean but in need of a coat of paint, a comfortable chair and a proper rug instead of the blue bath mat I'd placed by the bed so I didn't step on cold tile when I got out of bed.

Esmi goes first to my bed. She pushes aside the chamber pot and finds my money where I told her it would be: beneath a loose tile under the bed. Her eyebrows raise at the substantial amount I'd squirreled away. *"Puta madre,"* she mutters, and puts the roll of bills in the tin with the photographs. She places it and the album with its pink, padded covers on the bed. She looks in the wardrobe and shakes her head at the one change of clothes almost identical to what I was wearing—dark skirt, pale-blue top and a dark cardigan in a much heavier knit than the one I was wearing. She turns up her nose at my Sunday clothes—a dark polyester dress, with a small print and a pair of black patent-leather pumps to match the belt on the dress—last worn to my mother's funeral. On the floor of the wardrobe sits my worn leather handbag.

I hadn't asked her to bring my clothes because I hadn't thought of it. I'd even forgotten about my rosary on the nightstand, but she casts a glance around the room for a suitcase and seeing none goes into the kitchen and finds a woven plastic shopping bag. In it she puts my clothes, my nightgown retrieved from under my pillow, my brushes and my handbag. My cardie, she puts on.

I'm afraid she will forget the cross. Of course at this point it no longer matters to me, but it looks so forlorn there. She kicks off her shoes—her mother trained her well—and climbs onto the bed, the springs squeaking each time she shifts her weight. I am nearby, looking up at her.

Does she hears something? She stands stock still and listens.

All is quiet. She goes back to her task and lifts the crucifix off the wall.

Pilar appears in the doorway.

"What do you think you're doing?" she says.

35

E smi, standing on the bed in her bare feet, crucifix in hand, looks like a cross between a sneak thief and a kid caught jumping on the bed.

"Get down from there," *Doña* Pilar says. The threatening edge to her voice makes clear she does not view this intrusion as anything so innocent as a prank.

It's hard for me to look at her, even though I know she can't see me. I want to run away, but I'm compelled to stay near Esmi.

Esmi turns beet red. She climbs down and stands on the fuzzy, blue mat.

I'm frantic. I have no way to warn her, no way to shout, "Run!"

"Narda asked me to pick up a few of her things," she says.

She sits on the edge of the bed to put her shoes back on. Up close, I can see she is not nearly as calm as she is trying to seem. She takes sideways glances at Pilar as she ties her shoelaces, and not just because she's nervous. Like me she's sizing up what Pilar is wearing—a white nightgown, full-length and flowing, with bloused sleeves ending in long, tight cuffs. It's a far cry from her usual tweeds, and she's not exactly dressed in mourning, either. The deep V-neckline disappears into a high, broad waistband and the white silk spotlights the pallor of her skin and the lack of warmth in her ash-blond hair.

Still, she wears the familiar brass chain around her neck. I've never seen her without it. Brass might seem an odd choice of jewelry for the likes of her, but now and then I've glimpsed the amulet that hangs from it—all gold and silver. There's no buttoned jacket to hide it now.

Her hair is down and loose about her face. It makes her chin look even smaller and her wide-set, grey-blue eyes even paler. Strange emotions range across her face: indignation, of course—that I'm familiar with—but there's something else, something new. Is it fear?

"I'm sorry for disturbing you," Esmi says.

Whatever suspicions she harbors about *Doña* Pilar, I know the idea of holding vigil alone over Roberto's corpse all night gives her the willies.

Shoes on, Esmi picks up the album with the tin resting on top, and with one arm she cradles it against her body. In the other hand she grips the cross.

"Put it down," *Doña* Pilar says.

"It's Narda's." Esmi says.

"Put it down." Pilar lets each word drop in turn, cold and clear. "All of it."

Esmi holds the crucifix toward her. "You think I want to steal this?"

Pilar turns aside and covers half her face with her hand. Esmi must think she's going to faint, because she drops the crucifix on the bed and rushes to her side.

Let her fall, I want to scream. Let her fall and get out of here.

Esmi grasps *Doña* Pilar's forearm. "Are you all right?"

"I'll be fine," she says.

But she sways. Esmi holds on to her and guides her the few steps into the kitchen and the nearest chair. She seems taken aback by Pilar's apparent weakness.

"Can I get you a cup of tea?" she says.

Doña Pilar nods.

Esmi glances about. She lifts the kettle on the stove. It's heavy with water, so she lights the burner.

"Please join me," Pilar says.

Her sudden good manners scare me to... you know what.

"Please," *Doña* Pilar repeats, a note of pleading in her voice, something I certainly have never heard before.

Esmi nods, and sets about locating cups, a teapot, tea.

"Narda's not coming back?" Pilar asks with a masterful blend of disbelief and hurt feelings.

Esmi shakes her head no. *Doña* Pilar looks at her questioningly.

"She feels very..." Esmi stops mid sentence.

I don't want her to explain anything to that monster. Esmi knows I feel guilt—thick, undiluted, suffocating guilt—but she doesn't have to betray me to Pilar.

"Guilty," Esmi finishes.

"Don't we all?" *Doña* Pilar says.

Esmi's face lightens. Maybe she's thinking Pilar's human after all.

Esmi pours hot water into the teapot and sets the tea on the table to steep. She sits across from *Doña* Pilar. "You don't have to go through this alone," she says.

"Are you offering to take Narda's place?" Pilar asks.

"No," she says a bit too strongly. "But I'm sure my grandmother would help out for a while, and *Señora*

Rosario, and surely others. Or an agency in Badjoz could send someone."

A shiver passes through *Doña* Pilar's body. "I can't abide strangers in my house," she says.

"You've invited me to have tea, and I'm a stranger."

Doña Pilar reaches out and places her hand on Esmi's wrist. I cringe. She searches Esmi's face as if for some kind of clue, then she withdraws her hand.

"Sometimes it seems we've met before," she says.

"What? In another life?" Esmi laughs.

"Something like that." Pilar sighs. "Or maybe it's that this moment is fated to be."

"I don't believe in any of that."

"Of course not, you're very young. The longer one lives, the less clear things become."

"You're not all that much older than me," Esmi says, irritated.

"You flatter me. Now, if you could convince me you're just a girl who's come to Fuentespina for no purpose other than to visit her grandparents, I would be very happy."

"Well then, be happy," Esmi said. She flushes. "I'm sorry. That sounded very flippant, under the circumstances." She wrinkles her brow. "But why else would I be here?"

Doña Pilar shakes her head. She has a very piercing gaze, and it makes Esmi as uncomfortable as it always did me—Esmi keeps looking away, which makes her look like she has something to hide. She pours tea into their cups.

"I'm glad for your company," Pilar says.

"It must have been a long night." Esmi casts her eyes upward.

"Yes, of course, there is that. But, I'm glad for your company because you're an intelligent young woman, and full of surprises. Pleasant surprises."

"You're being very nice," Esmi says, suspicion in her voice.

Pilar smiles wanly, "Death strips away hardness. Hardness and many pretenses."

"I didn't realize you would be so affected by Roberto's... by..."

"His death," *Doña* Pilar supplies. "Death is the word you're looking for."

"Yes. I know you're supposed to say it more politely, but I find it hard to say things like 'he passed.' It sounds so..."

"Insipid? Insincere? Yes. There is no adequate synonym for death. And euphemisms are an insult." She looks vacantly into her still-full teacup. "My earliest memory is of people screaming, falling, dying about me, of corpses..." She looks up and locks onto Esmi's eyes. "Your generation has been spared war and plague. What, I wonder, must that be like?"

Esmi looks shocked. "Where did that happen? When?"

Doña Pilar shakes her head dismissively. "The point is, Beto is dead and I will miss him."

Beto! I haven't heard anyone call the *señorito* by that nickname since his father left. The Ice Queen seldom said the boy's name in any form, much less *Beto*.

"He may not have been a particularly charming child," she continues, "but I'd raised him since he was quite small, and that creates a bond. I was, indeed..." she looks at Esmi as if daring her to challenge her, "quite fond of the boy."

Esmi shrugs. "I guess I've misjudged you."

"Most likely, my dear, most likely. But I'm used to it. It comes with my position."

She picks up the teapot and refills Esmi's cup.

"If you've come to Fuentespina to visit your grandparents, as you say, why have I not seen you here before?"

I expect Esmi to gloss over the truth, to tell *Doña* Pilar it's hard to get away because of her work or something, but you can't underestimate Pilar—the power of her gaze, the intensity of it. And, she's being nice. I for one have never seen her act like this—calling Esmi, "dear," and pouring her tea! It makes my blood run cold. All the more so because I can see it's having an effect on Esmi—she's letting her guard down.

"I've been having problems with an ex-boyfriend. It seemed a good idea to get away for awhile."

"How sordid," *Doña* Pilar says.

Esmi smiles.

To both of our surprise, *Doña* Pilar smiles back. And for a moment a thick sense of equilibrium descends on the room. In the silence Esmi sips her tea. *Doña* Pilar lifts the cup to her lips, but does not drink. Over the top of the cup, she scrutinizes Esmi. After a moment, her attention becomes unbearable, and Esmi squirms, fishes for a change of topic.

She says, "That's a very striking necklace."

Pilar lifts the amulet. "I'm pleased you noticed it," she says.

It's a four-inch-long rod so richly worked in silver and

gold that you cannot tell if the silver is decorating the gold or the gold, the silver. The bottom ends in a ball, and the upper end, in a somewhat larger ball. Clearly the rod is hollow, and you can see that the upper ball is a separate piece, a lid of some sort. The whole thing hangs suspended by double brass chains so long that the amulet rests not on her breast, but below her heart.

"It was a gift from my husband. It's very very old. Very rare. Dacian in origin."

"What's that?"

"Dacia was an ancient country in the Carpathian Mountains of Eastern Europe, bounded by the Black Sea in the east and extending to the Danube in the south. It was conquered and became a Roman province."

"I've never heard of it, but I've never paid much attention to history."

"It's now Romania and Moldova, with parts of Hungary, Bulgaria, Serbia and Ukraine."

"I'm not much better at geography."

"Do you see a vulture on the amulet?"

Esmi leans forward and shakes her head.

"Precisely. If there were a vulture holding a fish in its beak and a rabbit in its claws it would indicate that the piece had something to do with Gebeleizis, the supreme Dacian divinity and alter ego of the great Goddess Bendis. But, as you see, there is no representation, no figure, animal or symbol—meaning it was most likely made to evoke Zamolxis, the God of immortality, worshipped by the young warriors called Dacian Wolves."

Esmi smiles politely.

"Look closely, the interlacing design has interesting qualities," Pilar says.

The words feel familiar. I want to scream, but I can do nothing. I can only watch as Pilar dangles the foul amulet in front of Esmi's eyes. Within moments, Esmi falls into a trance.

Pilar leans back and smiles.

36

Pilar strokes Esmi's cheek. "Esmi, Esmi," she says, like someone's just given her a present, one that's unexpected and spot-on.

She might as well be touching me—I cringe till I feel turned inside out, but Esmi does not pull away. Her hypnotized face shines with peace. Soft warmth radiates from her skin, whilst the chill from Pilar's hand is as smooth and dense as marble.

She gazes at Esmi and grins—it's an ice pick of a smile that shows her sharp, little teeth. It seems her face will crack and shatter, but instead, the smile ends, full stop, and her face twists in distaste.

"Have you any idea what it's like in this village, sustaining oneself amidst decrepit, shriveled, old mummies? Water, water everywhere and not a drop to drink, isn't that the saying? And now you, my Esmi. After months of that anemic, insipid, inbred child, you will be a banquet."

She reaches out, wavers, then removes the clip from Esmi's hair. She smiles when Esmi's hair falls about her shoulders. She touches it here and there as if arranging it just so. "That's better," she muses. "Not the Implacable One. Not great Nemesis. Simply a girl come to visit her grandmother. Just that and nothing more."

But a shadow crosses her face, a fleeting doubt. She gives her head a shake and smiles that horrid smile again.

"Now then, to business. Listen well. There is danger out there, Esmi, it lurks just beyond my door. Danger and death."

Esmi's body grows rigid; her expression, troubled; her breathing, raspy. The words ring familiar to me. I feel cold, as cold as a block of ice and as useless.

"You can't trust anyone out there, Esmi. Do you understand? No one but me. I won't let anyone or anything hurt you. I am a powerful protectress and you will be perfectly safe as long as you are here with me. Do you understand? Answer me."

"Yes."

"Fine. You are at home now. Relax."

Esmi does not comply. Her face is pale and trembles on the verge of tears. Pilar looks annoyed.

"You are safe, I said. Completely safe. Safe and sound and..." She searches for the right words. "And loved, protected, peaceful." She looks exasperated. "Safe as a babe asleep in its mother's arms."

Esmi's body slackens and her face grows blank—not innocent and serene like before, but expressionless, lifeless. How I want to dig my fingers into Pilar's neck.

Pilar is pleased to see Esmi yield on cue, and her tone changes. She croons in a silky voice, an accent almost Castilian, but not quite, "You are safe here with me, Esmi. I will always take care of you. I will never desert you. When I awaken you, you will remember that, and only that, that you feel safe with me and that you want to stay with me and please me. With each of these encounters of ours, you will feel increasingly safe with me, and only with me, and so you will long for these meetings of ours. With each one you will feel ever more indebted and bound to me. Do you understand?"

Esmi nods.

"Now then, let's get rid of this tawdry scarf so we can see your lovely neck."

Pilar runs a finger from the point of Esmi's chin, along her jaw and down her neck. She unknots the red scarf.

I am a sob no one can hear. I can't look, can't leave, can't not look.

Pilar removes the scarf.

Dear Mother of God! Esmi told me about Lucho attacking her, but she hadn't shown me her neck. Settled in next to her as I am, I can see it's a mass of scratches and inch-round bruises—much worse than I imagined. She can downplay the attack all she wants, but now that I see the wounds, I can guess how deeply shaken she must be.

Pilar winces. "What in the name of eternity is this?" she growls. A look of disgust crosses her face. She looks away, but she's agitated. Her nostrils flare in anger. She licks her teeth. They've grown. I can see points of her canines against her lower lip.

"You idiot girl," she says.

Her hands shake as she ties the scarf back around Esmi's neck. She sits collecting herself a moment. Then she grabs Esmi's wrist. "This will have to do for now," she says, and brings Esmi's wrist to her mouth.

No, no, no! *Virgen Purísima*, Holy Mother, protect her!

Pilar bares her fangs, grazes Esmi's skin with them—a

gruesome caress. Then she stops, drops Esmi's arm, stands and turns her back. Her shoulders rise and fall with her labored breaths. When she turns back to Esmi, her face is composed, her closed lips betray no deadly teeth.

"All in good time," she says. "No need to rush. No need at all."

She reaches over, as if to prove to herself her self-control, and straightens Esmi's scarf, pats the ends where they lie against her collar bone.

"There. So, where were we?" Her voice has an edge to it. "Esmi, let's say I tell you you must leave immediately, go out through that door and never return."

Esmi's smooth, empty face contracts—her forehead, the muscles about her eyes, her mouth, every nerve.

"How do you feel?"

Esmi's ragged breath breaks her words, "I'm afraid... I want to stay with you. I... I could help you."

Pilar places her hand on top of Esmi's on the table.

"Please, let me stay."

"Shh, child. You may come here whenever you like and stay as long as you like."

Esmi's face resumes a bland smoothness.

"Remember, it is I who wants you to be safe and happy," Pilar says. "We will have more of these little chats, just you and I, and with each one you will feel safer and happier. Would you like that?"

Esmi gives a hesitant nod.

"Good. It's a start, a very good start." She withdraws her hand. "Now, you've just said, 'That's a very striking necklace.' Awaken."

Esmi opens her eyes. Her face regains its usual look, focused and intent.

"Forgive me, my dear," Pilar says. "So much on my mind. I drifted off for a moment. What did you say?"

"I said, that's a very striking necklace."

"Yes, isn't it. It was a gift from my husband."

"It looks very old."

"An interest in antiquities is the one thing *Don* Manuel Felipe and I had in common. This piece is quite unique, from Dacia, modern-day Romania."

"Oh? I think I've heard of that."

"I've grown very attached to it. I never take it off."

"Is there something inside?"

"Yes. Water from the River Jordan. It was a most thoughtful gift. But what about that pesky ex-boyfriend of yours?"

Esmi's hand flies to her neck, a knee-jerk reaction. Her fingers land on the knot. It's tied differently and more tightly. A look of confusion crosses her face. I want to jump up and down, get her attention.

"What did you two have in common?" Pilar asks. "Not antiques, I'd hazard."

"I'd rather not talk about it," she says, and looks down at the table.

She sees her hair clip there and her hand shoots to her hair—she doesn't recall taking the clip out. Her brow crinkles for just an instant.

Yes, Esmi, pay attention, I want to scream. The clip! It's a warning, if you'll just see it.

She moves both hands to grab her hair, to twist it back and replace the clip.

"Why don't you leave it down, Esmi? Wearing your hair up is too severe for your face and age."

Esmi, a bit confused, nods and places the clip in her pocket.

Pilar urges her to talk, "Won't you confide in me a little? It would take my mind off my worries."

Esmi shrugs. "It turns out we didn't have a thing in common. His family was Opus Dei in a very big way."

"An estimable organization, don't you think?"

"No, I don't." She pauses. "I could tell you about this, but it would be a waste of time. You wouldn't understand."

"Perhaps not. But time's not an issue. Where did you meet him?"

Esmi sighs, forces herself to go on. "At a discotheque. We hit it off, he needed a place to stay, so... See, you don't approve."

"No, I do not." Her voice goes all silky again. "You see, my way of life may be conventional but it offers safety, security."

Esmi seems to shrink within her body. She lowers her head.

"And this house, don't you sense that it's a kind of haven?"

Esmi nods.

"I'm glad. What happened between you and this boy?"

"When we met he said he needed a new start. His family had disowned him. He had nothing. Even his job at a bank was iffy because he'd gotten it through family connections. He'd been sleeping on a colleague's couch in a tiny apartment—a married colleague with a wife and two little kids. So, I took him home. But my kind of life didn't take, I didn't take. In the end he went back to his family, and back to the girl they wanted him to marry."

"And has he?"

"What?"

"Married. Has he married the girl?"

Esmi shrugs, and then shakes her head. "Not yet."

"Why Esmi," Pilar purrs, "You're afraid of him."

Esmi blanches and sits up straighter.

Pilar reaches out and touches Esmi's wrist. "I do have connections, my dear. For instance, there's a certain Lieutenant Colonel Fusi in the Civil Guard in Badajoz. He could be very helpful. I'm sure he'd know the right people in Madrid."

I shudder even though I'll no longer be going to Badajoz or anyplace else.

"I don't want to cause you any trouble," Esmi says. "Besides, Lucho doesn't know I'm here. No one does."

Pilar smiles. "Lucho. So that's the villain's name."

Esmi looks startled, suddenly aware that she's said more than she meant to. She pulls back, sits up primly. She changes the subject, wanting to be smooth, but it's like shifting down from third to first.

"I'm surprised you're still here in Fuentespina," Esmi says. "I mean, your husband's left. You could have gone anywhere, right? But you stayed on here in this house."

"Yes, but the house is insignificant. Fuentespina is insignificant. People come. People go. People die. But the land lives on. What matters, truly matters is the land. That's why I stay on. The land is perpetual, eternal. You can love it, embrace it, count on it."

Pilar pulls back. Has she said more than she meant to? She clutches the amulet.

"I've enjoyed our chat, Esmi, but I have a busy day ahead."

"You're going to work?"

"Mourning is work, Esmi. There's much to do when someone dies. And that fool Narda, taking off like a spooked mare, and at a time like this. I could wring her neck. These peasants and their foolish superstitions."

"Narda!" Esmi exclaims and stands. I think she'd forgotten why she'd come—Pilar has managed to distract her totally from the business at hand. Maybe now Esmi will get the hell out of here and take me with her.

"Perhaps you could stay and help in her place for a few days," Pilar says.

No, I scream. But not a bug hears me, not a mote of dust is disturbed.

"I'm sorry," Esmi says, "I can't."

Good girl! I cheer her on.

"I understand. No doubt Narda's waiting for you. But, Esmi, I must insist you leave her things here."

Without thinking, Esmi thrusts her hands into the pockets of my cardigan, but at least she does not let the ring of keys jangle and betray itself. She starts to protest, but Pilar stops her.

"Narda will have to come retrieve her belongings herself," Pilar says, "and I suppose collect her final pay, though she doesn't deserve it. I don't mean to be harsh, my dear, but this is between Narda and me. Unfinished business."

Seems to me our business is about as finished as it can be.

Esmi seems to snap out of the spell Pilar has been casting. Tension returns to her posture—tension and reserve and her usual suspicion of Pilar. "I have to leave," she says and moves toward the back door.

"I'm glad we talked, Esmi. Our conversation has soothed me."

Esmi smiles with irony and takes hold of the door. She freezes a moment.

"Is everything all right, dear?" Pilar says.

Esmi gives a firm nod of her head and slips out the door.

Litany of Our Lady

<table>
<tr><td>Leader:</td><td>Response:</td></tr>
<tr><td>Holy Mary, Mother of God,</td><td>pray for us.</td></tr>
<tr><td>Holy Virgin of virgins,</td><td>pray for us.</td></tr>
<tr><td>Sorrowful Mother,</td><td>pray for us.</td></tr>
<tr><td>Mournful Mother,</td><td>pray for us.</td></tr>
<tr><td>Sighing Mother,</td><td>pray for us.</td></tr>
<tr><td>Afflicted Mother,</td><td>pray for us.</td></tr>
<tr><td>Forsaken Mother,</td><td>pray for us.</td></tr>
<tr><td>Desolate Mother,</td><td>pray for us.</td></tr>
<tr><td>Mother most sad,</td><td>pray for us.</td></tr>
<tr><td>Mother engulfed in anguish,</td><td>pray for us.</td></tr>
<tr><td>Mother overwhelmed by grief,</td><td>pray for us.</td></tr>
<tr><td>Mother crucified in thy heart,</td><td>pray for us.</td></tr>
<tr><td>Sighing Dove,</td><td>pray for us.</td></tr>
<tr><td>Fount of tears,</td><td>pray for us.</td></tr>
<tr><td>Sea of bitterness,</td><td>pray for us.</td></tr>
<tr><td>Field of tribulation,</td><td>pray for us.</td></tr>
<tr><td>Mirror of patience,</td><td>pray for us.</td></tr>
<tr><td>Rock of constancy,</td><td>pray for us.</td></tr>
<tr><td>Remedy in perplexity,</td><td>pray for us.</td></tr>
<tr><td>Joy of the afflicted,</td><td>pray for us.</td></tr>
<tr><td>Ark of the desolate,</td><td>pray for us.</td></tr>
<tr><td>Refuge of the abandoned,</td><td>pray for us.</td></tr>
<tr><td>Shield of the oppressed,</td><td>pray for us.</td></tr>
<tr><td>Solace of the wretched,</td><td>pray for us.</td></tr>
<tr><td>Medicine of the sick,</td><td>pray for us.</td></tr>
</table>

Help of the faint-hearted,	*pray for us.*
Strength of the weak,	*pray for us.*
Companion of the sorrowful,	*pray for us.*
Terror of the treacherous,	*pray for us.*
Treasure of the faithful,	*pray for us.*
Pearl of Virgins,	*pray for us.*
Queen of thy servants,	*pray for us.*
Holy Mary, who alone art unexampled,	*pray for us.*

Pray for us, most sweet soul, most Sorrowful Virgin,

Amen.

From the "Litany of Our Lady Of Seven Sorrows"
by Pope Pius VII

37

I hope Esmi will take off running as soon as she's out the door, but no. She just stands there, her back pressed against the outside of the kitchen door. Maybe *Doña* Pilar has gotten to her and shaken her confidence; or maybe she's trying to think how to break the bad news to me that Pilar is holding my belongings hostage; or maybe she's listening to see if the coast is clear, thinking she might yet go back in, get the album, tin box, bag of clothes, and the crucifix she's left on my bed.

Finally, she peels herself from the door and peers into the square from the corner of the house. At the far edge of the plaza, *Señora* Rosario sits crocheting on a wooden chair in front of her house. Two wrought-iron birdcages, long-empty—flat on the back and rounded in front—are bolted flush against the wall, one on each side of her.

Esmi swears under her breath. She's not in the mood for the old busybody or her third degree, but soon *Señora* Rosario hauls herself up and toddles inside. She's left the yarn and hook on the chair—she'll be back soon. Esmi sprints across the square to the deeply shadowed pathway next to the church. Has anyone seen her? She checks out the square from the shadows, and for a second her shoulders drop in relief.

Virgen Purísima! A hand clamps over her mouth. A strong arm circles her waist. It pulls her backward and off balance.

Vampires everywhere! Out of the frying pan, and right into hell.

Iban's whispers in her ear, "I've been waiting for you."

I warned Esmi to stay away from him!

Iban has her halfway through the side door to the sacristy before she starts struggling, flailing with her arms, grabbing at the door jamb.

He's startled at how fiercely she's fighting. "Esmi, it's me!"

He manages to pull her inside and lets go of her so he can close the door behind them. Esmi twists and dives, but he's got good reflexes. They both land at the same time, with shoulders against the inside of the closed door. Esmi recoils from his touch and runs to a corner of the room.

"What the hell's wrong with you?" he says.

Esmi doesn't answer. She darts from the small room into the nave of the church of Our Lady and without thinking dashes to the front doors. She pulls on the big iron rings, but to no avail. In her panic she's forgotten they're locked, chained from the outside. She turns, her back to the door.

Iban has followed her into the nave. He sinks on the raised platform where the altar used to be. He buries his head in his hands.

"What kind of nightmare is this?" he says.

"You killed Roberto," she says.

"What?"

"Narda told me."

"That's crazy—he was very sick, as you well know."

"So, his death, it's not news to you—you already knew."

"Yes, because I went back to the church last night to find

you. But you were gone. Then I heard all the commotion in the plaza. I slipped out to see what was going on. I heard it all."

"Or you were the one who killed him."

"What are you saying? Why would I kill my nephew?"

"He's not your nephew."

Iban stares at her with suspicion, but he does not contradict her.

"The names don't match, Iban. You said your name was Iban Velasco. If Velasco was your father's name then your sister would be a Velasco, too. But Roberto's mother's name was Seco. She couldn't have been your sister."

Iban shakes his head. "That's why you think I've..." his voice catches nicely. He looks hurt to the quick. "My name is, as I told you when we met, Iban Velasco Ylla-Gual. My sister, Susana, was Susana Seco Ylla-Gual. Our mother was Beatreu Ylla-Gual. Same mother, different fathers," he says as if exhausted. He puts his head in his hands again.

Esmi doesn't move.

He looks up. "Is there anything else you think I'm guilty of?"

Esmi answers, less sure, "Narda says you're a vampire."

Iban looks at her and shakes his head again. Then he laughs, dry and bitter. "And how am I to prove to you I am not a vampire? Let's see, we're not supposed to have reflections. Do you have a mirror handy? Maybe some garlic?"

Esmi crosses her arms, but she looks sheepish.

"It does sound silly when I say it out loud," she says. She grins a little.

OK, so now that I know only too well the truth about Pilar, I suppose I was wrong about Iban killing Roberto. But she shouldn't forget a vampire killed Roberto—I told her about the marks on his neck.

"Roberto's dead, Esmi." Even in the dim light, his face is ashen, the shadows there deep and marked. "He's dead, and I couldn't save him. I've failed him. I've failed my sister."

Esmi approaches him, slowly, and he makes no sudden moves to startle her. She sits down next to him. After a moment sitting together in silence, she leans into his shoulder.

"You scared me half to death, grabbing me like that."

"I'm sorry."

"I'm sorry about Roberto."

She puts her arm around him and he leans his head on her shoulder.

"And I'm sorry I called you a vampire." She smiles.

Iban runs his hand up and down her leg. She closes her eyes. He reaches over with his other hand and plays with the lapel of her jacket. She sighs and leans her head against his a moment.

If it were me in her place, I'd be remembering our parting kiss. I'd be thinking, forget about Pilar's poisoned promises, here's a harbor that's much safer, with broader shoulders and eyes to get lost in to boot. If it were me in his place, I'd be imagining that here in this alluring young woman is solace from my grief, and I'd want to embrace life in the face of death. If it were me...

He sits up and puts his arm around her shoulders and brings his face close to hers. Her lips part, but he moves away. Gently, he leans her back so she's lying on the dusty platform. He nuzzles her scarf-wrapped neck. She flinches only a little.

He whispers in her ear, "I need you."

Esmi opens her eyes. His hand rests on her hip bone. He again moves his face toward hers, almost touching. Esmi parts her lips again and raises to kiss him, but Iban turns his head so that her lips land on his neck. Taking deep, uneven breaths, she pulls him on top of her, but he supports himself above her, his back rigid. She caresses his back. He kisses her forehead.

His lips move back to her ear. "I need you, Esmi," he says again. "*Para siempre.*"

She gives a little moan.

"Forever."

Her hands move up his back and she pulls down on his shoulders, but he does not move. Her mouth seeks his but he turns his head so her lips can only play about his neck. She reaches for the fly of his trousers and he repositions himself so that for a moment it seems he will lower himself, embrace her, but instead he shifts his arms beneath hers so hers are caught over her head. She wraps them about his neck, with one hand in his hair. As he finally lets himself down on her, his hand reaches down and grabs her between the legs. Esmi gasps.

That's when I turn away.

38

I turn my back on Esmi, and find myself in front of the Tena house, just as Adelfo comes out the door—somewhere else I don't want to be and with someone I don't want to see. He's followed by Lourdes, who hesitates by the door. She carries her egg basket in one hand and, reaching out, she runs her free hand over the wall. The house's one thin coat of new whitewash somehow makes it look worse than before, and Lourdes asks if, with *Señorito* Roberto awaiting burial, it would be disrespectful to put another coat of wash on that afternoon. The old *hijo de puta* does not bother to answer. She reaches for the cross around her neck, and in the instant before she remembers that she's given it to Esmi, she looks stricken. Then the hand being at loose ends and Lourdes probably not wanting to draw the old bastard's attention to the missing cross, she uses it to straighten her cardie.

Adelfo fumbles with an iron skeleton key, like a sixth bony finger in his hand. He is taking great pains to lock the front door, and Lourdes looks fixedly away. His white shirt is starched and his black trousers, pressed; but I see there on top of his head a little hole in the felt near the center of his *boina*. He gives the door a shake, checking to make sure it stays locked. Other than yesterday, God knows when that key was last used, or when they last ventured out together. It's certainly clear they lack the knack of walking in concert, and even though the streets are uneven, the old bastard does not offer Lourdes his arm. I know because I am drawn after them, an unwilling escort, all the way to the big house.

Lourdes fidgets on the stone threshold before the great door. The old *hijo de puta* looks at her with disapproval, waiting for her to stand still. He looks up at the stone coat of arms over the door before he lifts the life-sized bronze hand and raps the bronze apple on the door—one, two, three times.

"If Narda's back. I know she'll want these eggs," Lourdes says for no purpose other than to fill the empty moment.

Adelfo harrumphs. "Damn fool woman."

"She was upset, *viejo*, and for good reason."

"No excuse for leaving one's post."

I notice the old bastard is standing very soldier-like, as if at attention.

"Of course, you're right, *viejo*. She shouldn't have left *Doña* Pilar like that.

"No one's answering," she observes.

She takes a few steps back and shades her eyes, looks for any movement in the upstairs windows. She returns to Adelfo's side.

"Narda must not have come back last night. Mother of Heaven, I hope she's all right."

Adelfo snorts. He knocks again.

"She won't answer," a voice behind them says.

It's Rosario.

Lourdes lets out a startled yelp and the old bastard glares at her. Her free hand again grabs at the cross.

"*Buenos días, Señora* Rosario," Adelfo says.

"*Buenos días, señora,*" Lourdes echoes.

"*Buenos días. Don* Adelfo," she says and nods vaguely in Lourdes' direction. "*Doña* Pilar won't answer. I've already tried."

"The wife was just saying that no one answering the door, maybe Narda didn't return last night."

"I'm afraid that's so," Rosario says. "I'm so very worried about her."

"Yes," Lourdes pipes in. "Me, too. I do hope she's all right."

"She acted so strangely, don't you think?" Rosario asks Adelfo.

Adelfo harrumphs, so Rosario turns from him and looks right at Lourdes. Lourdes freezes for a second, not sure what is expected from her.

"She's not normally one to panic, is she?" Rosario says to Lourdes.

Lourdes shakes her head. "I wouldn't think so."

"All that talk about it being her fault! As if Narda could in any way be responsible for..." Rosario crosses herself. "*El pobrecito.* May he rest in peace."

"What if she doesn't come back?" Lourdes says. Tears come to her eyes, and she looks away. "I can't imagine..."

"I can't either," Rosario says.

I'm taken aback. They seem so upset.

"Aren't you forgetting why we're here?" Adelfo scolds. "A child has died."

Rosario looks properly admonished.

"And not just any child. *Don* Manuel Felipe's only son, *Doña* Pilar's stepson, dead; and you two are carrying on about that Gypsy bastard. Gypsy bastard of a red whore!"

Rosario blanches—she's obviously appalled at Adelfo's language. Sometimes she'll act all shocked when she's not really, but it's no act this time—such coarse language and in front of ladies, in broad daylight, in front of the big house, a house of mourning at that. Maybe she even wishes she could defend my mother's honor, and mine.

"Adelfo!" Lourdes says with distress, glancing at Rosario, but her voice is faded and unconvincing.

Adelfo grasps the bronze knocker again. Lourdes places her hand on his arm.

"Fito," she says, "maybe we should leave *Doña* Pilar in peace."

"*Buenos días*," Rosario intones, as if leaving them to it, but slow to leave in case there's something to be seen or heard.

The old bastard clangs the metal apple against the door five times.

"*Viejo*, we should go," Lourdes whispers.

The door opens. Lourdes, again taken by surprise, gives another little cry and steps behind Adelfo.

Adelfo says under his breath, "For Christ's sake, woman. Get a grip."

Doña Pilar stands several feet back from the threshold.

"Ah, *Don* Adelfo," she says.

Adelfo whips off his *boina*.

"How timely. Come in. I need to speak to you." She steps further away from the door.

Adelfo pulls on Lourdes' arm and they shuffle inside, coming to a stop barely across the threshold.

"All the way in," Pilar snaps. "And close the door behind you. No need for the whole village to gape at me."

Lourdes has only seen Pilar at a distance and wearing her usual tweeds, but here she is, the great lady herself, looking like something out of a fashion plate and close enough that Lourdes could reach out and touch her, touch her and the luscious black silk of her dress—the row of little silk-covered buttons from wrist to elbow on the slender sleeves, the thickly embroidered bolero vest. Poor Lourdes. She's trying not to gawk, trying to keep her eyes on her own shoes, but she's drawn to the point where the deep V of the neckline of Pilar's dress meets the upside down V of the broad waistband. A large, ornate silver and gold amulet glitters there and above it Pilar's skin gleams an unearthly white next to the black cloth.

Lourdes' eyes dart about like a scared rabbit. She looks past Pilar, glances up the stairway where the *señorito*'s body must be, takes in the details of the fine entryway—the Roman mosaic underfoot, the bronze urn on a parquet table, the wrought iron chandelier overhead—and again sneaks a peak at Pilar.

Adelfo says, "*Señora,* we've come to offer our condolences..."

Doña Pilar cuts him off. "Yes, yes. You did that last night. We have other matters to discuss."

"*Señora?*"

"It pains me to tell you this, *Don* Adelfo. We all admire the sacrifices you've made for our country in time of war."

She says this as she studiously avoids looking at his scars. I realize now that she finds any kind of disfigurement repulsive. And old people, in general, I already know, repel her. It's truly astonishing how squeamish she can be, considering.

"Also," she continues, "I'm well aware of the position of respect you hold in the village, and deservedly so. Because you came to me the other night and made clear how seriously you intend to safeguard your honor and the well-being of our beloved Fuentespina, I will be frank. It's a despicable act to take advantage of someone at a time like this, at a time of mourning."

Adelfo assumes a somewhat military stance. "*Señora*, I hold your honor as sacred as my own. If someone has offended you, I am at your service."

"I appreciate your consideration, *Don* Adelfo. The fact is, I caught your granddaughter today in this house, stealing."

Adelfo turns white, his jaw clenches.

It's Lourdes who bursts out, "No, *señora*, it can't be! Not our Esmi."

Pilar turns to her as if she'd not noticed her in the entryway until then. Her eyes burn with indignation. Her whole body is rigid with threat and I pull back, wishing I could pull Lourdes with me.

"Lourdes!" Adelfo snaps. "Hold your tongue."

Lourdes quivers with anger and fear.

"I believe," *Doña* Pilar explains, "that your granddaughter is in league with my housekeeper. I don't know precisely what they are up to, but it's very difficult for me, as you must appreciate—two people whom I trusted, whom I brought into my household, who knew *Señorito*

Roberto, betraying me under my own roof while my stepson's body lies barely cold."

"Unthinkable, *Doña* Pilar," Adelfo fumes. "The ingrates, *las sinvergüenzas, las desalmadas!*"

Hah! If anyone around here is without shame, without a soul, it's certainly not me or Esmi.

"Adelfo!" Lourdes protests.

"I don't think Rosa Esmeralda got away with much, but I felt it my duty to advise you. I have no desire to bring public shame upon your good name. What I ask is that you bring her to me, *Don* Adelfo. There's no need for the authorities, no need for anyone to know your granddaughter is a thief. You and I can take care of this matter."

"No!" Lourdes exclaims. "*Doña* Pilar, Esmi's a good girl. You must be mistaken."

Don Adelfo glares at her, and opens his mouth to reprimand her, but Pilar places a hand on his arm to stop him.

"I understand your loyalty, *señora*," she says in frigid tones, "but it is misplaced. How well, truly, do you know the girl?"

"Of course I know her, *señora*. She's my granddaughter, my own flesh and bone."

"But she left Madrid very abruptly, you must admit. How do we know she's not here hiding from the police?"

"No, *señora*!" Lourdes says. "Adelfo, say something," she pleads. "Tell her."

"I will bring her to you, *señora*. Her and the Gypsy mongrel."

39

I shoot out of the big house like a proverbial bat out of hell, a soul catapulted by fury. Fury and outrage. The old bastard *hijo de puta* in cahoots with that monster, and against my Esmi!

And then for a heartbeat I am nowhere, adrift in a void. No sound, no scent, no sight. But before I can panic, I am boomeranged back to the fountain—yanked there, I suspect, by someone thinking about me, maybe even praying for me. The church is right there, like a big dusty tombstone, but considering what Esmi and Iban are up to inside, I doubt they're the ones who called me.

Then I see Rosario trundle back to the chair in front of her house and pick up her crocheting. Ankles crossed and lips pursed, she flicks the wooden hook through the yarn, a gaudy acrylic doomed through no fault of its own to end up in afghan limbo—the stockpile of afghans spread several feet deep on the bed in her sons' old room. It's Rosario's stash of presents awaiting an occasion that never arrives. It grows higher and higher, and yet she's not moved to find a home for a single one of them. Still... flick, flick goes her hook.

If only Rosario knew what was going on inside the church! She doesn't, of course, but she shakes her head, as if in disapproval of the goings on, and drops her work in her lap.

Just as she gives out a deep sigh, Reina scurries into the

square from around the corner of a building, stopping cold when she hits the sunlight and sees Rosario.

Startled out of her doldrums, Rosario's hand flies to her chest.

"Holy Mother of God!" she exclaims and scowls at Reina.

Reina does not hurry away as you would expect. Instead she looks lost, like she's forgotten where she is.

Rosario picks up her work again. Flick, flick. She watches Reina from the corner of her eye.

"It doesn't seem right, does it?" Rosario says finally.

Reina stares at the stones at her feet.

"About Narda, I mean."

Reina turns toward Rosario, her head still bent.

"Her running off like that," Rosario says, as if to the afghan. "I can't imagine..."

Reina, head still bowed, raises her eyes to Rosario, defiantly.

Rosario keeps her eyes on her work. "I pray she's all right. May the Blessed Virgin protect her."

Reina's eyes soften and she raises her head.

"She will come back, of course. She has to come back," Rosario says.

Reina scuttles toward Rosario. She stops a number of feet away and nods once.

For Reina this tiny action amounts to grand bravura; and I, for one, am amazed. Rosario, too, because she gives a start, and then in an effort to hide her ruffled feathers, she holds up the future coverlet as if measuring her progress. She lays it back down and smoothes it over her legs.

"What will we do if she doesn't?" Rosario says, looking straight at Reina.

Reina covers her mouth with her hand, and shakes her head.

I want to hug her. I want to hug them both.

I've let them down—Reina and Rosario—and there's not a blessed thing I can do about it. I might as well add them to the ever-growing list: Roberto, Esmi, even Teresa. I've let them all down, and there's nothing I can do about it. I spent most of my life as a fly on the wall, a bystander, a looker-on, and now I have no choice in the matter.

Reina hurries off in the direction she came. The plaza is empty again except for whatever it is I am. And Rosario. Her black shape against the dull wall is like a shadow, only with a variegated pink, green and yellow puddle in her lap.

If this is purgatory, it's not what I expected.

40

Adelfo trudges along—with me in tow, for my sins —his rifle slung over his shoulder.

I look out over the scrubland and I find I feel barely a twinge of unease at the wild, unhinged openness of it all. I look up, too—the sky is blue and relentless, with not a cloud to soften it. And up ahead is an olive tree. Its silvery leaves flicker in the wind and draw me to it. But Adelfo stops a good 30 feet short of it. He readjusts the leather strap of his rifle and mops the back of his neck with his handkerchief.

Lourdes comes to the same halt but 15 feet behind him. Half of her face sags with weariness and sadness, and the other half—thin lipped and squinty eyed—is set in determination. She looks like my aunt Abila after she had her stroke, only Lourdes hasn't suffered any stroke—Adelfo is her only affliction.

For now, he's given up shouting and threatening her.

After they left the big house—with me trapped in their wake—the *hijo de puta* went home and grabbed his gun. He told Lourdes to stay put in the house, but she refused—she didn't trust what might happen if he found Esmi. So she (and I) followed him at a distance. Whenever he turned and took a step toward her, she'd match his step backward, and he would curse her in a way that made her brace herself.

Finally she said, "Go ahead, shoot me," and he gestured roughly as if backhanding her with all his strength. Now he continues on as if she weren't there.

For her part she's given up pleading with him—a waste of breath at any rate. He was more than primed to believe Esmi a stain on his honor. And now that *Doña* Pilar has declared that Esmi and I are no more than common thieves, there's no way the old *hijo de puta* is going to give either of us the benefit of any doubt. Even in the best of times, doubt's not an easy bedfellow for Adelfo, and as for pity and compassion, he kicked them out from between the sheets long ago.

We've just come from St. Julian's Wall where Esmi and I spent the night. With its ragged arch and tumble of rocks, it seemed more solitary and lonely than ever. Adelfo kicked at the old blanket and empty bottle of aguardiente and grunted with distaste.

"What is this place?" Lourdes asked, but Adelfo did not answer.

Now they stand apart from the meager shade of the olive tree, and Adelfo stuffs his handkerchief back in his trouser pocket.

"Adelfo!" Lourdes cries out. "Look!" She points up at the sky.

The old coot ignores her and, out of pure stubbornness, keeps his eye on the ground.

"Adelfo, look!" she insists.

Several vultures, wings stretched wide, float on air currents. They are almost directly overhead, circling a dark spot on the earth below.

The moment I've been dreading is upon me.

Lourdes groans and covers her mouth. Then she crosses herself and pleads, "Dear Mother of God, protect our Esmi."

"Don't go getting hysterical," the old bastard says, neck stretched, looking up. "They're just after roadkill."

She doesn't argue that the road is miles away. It could be an animal. But that flash of white cloth... Adelfo motions to Lourdes to stay put, and she does.

He troops to the spot.

Lourdes is crying now, "No, no, no..."

He waves at her to hush and looks down at my body as if studying my situation. Damn the old bastard. Why does it have to be him who finds me? He ambles back toward Lourdes. Her cries take on a higher and higher pitch the closer he comes.

"Shh," he says. "It's not her. It's not Rosa."

Lourdes collapses to the dirt, still crying, "Thank you, Virgencita, thank you, thank you."

I don't blame her. I understand. I'm glad it isn't Esmi, too.

Adelfo rests his hand on Lourdes' shoulder. She smiles up at him—a painful little grimace-like smile.

"It's that Narda," he says.

41

According to Adelfo, the thing to do is for the two of them to go back to town. Then they can enlist Valentín and old Anselmo—Anselmo has a cart—to come pick up my body. But Lourdes won't budge. He tries to bully her—he swears at her and argues that bodies on a battlefield are left unattended—but Lourdes insists on staying. She points out that this is no battlefield, and asks him to leave the rifle so she can keep the carrion away.

It is something to see, Lourdes standing up to Adelfo. First the old bastard couldn't get her to stay, and now he can't get her to move. It warms my heart, and downright nonplusses him. But she has propriety on her side, and he well knows it.

So he decides he will stay and Lourdes will go back to Fuentespina. He says it's not seemly for her to be out here all alone. And it's true, but I think Adelfo may in fact want to save her the woeful task of watching over my body. After all it's not like I died peacefully in my sleep. As far as he's concerned, he's the war-hardened expert on death; and Lourdes, to be protected from such bloodshed—in this case the frightful spectacle that is me.

Lourdes voices her reservations because she knows what Adelfo thinks of me, but her courage wanes and she lets herself be swayed.

He stands at attention as he watches her walk away. She

stops once and turns to wave. Adelfo raises his arm in something closer to the fascist salute than a wave.

So, now we're alone. Just me and the old *hijo de la puta madre*.

When Lourdes is an indistinct speck in the distance, Adelfo walks back to my body. My skirt is hitched up—I wish I could right it. A bit of my white slip is showing, somehow unstained with blood. I try not to look above that spot, because I know what I'll see.

He grimaces. The eyes in my body stare, unseeing, frozen open in terror. My neck gapes, ripped open, a red and yellow yawn. And the blood... It has soaked into my hair, my clothes and into the earth.

Seeing one's body like that, as meat, as a ripening carcass—I wouldn't wish it on anyone.

Adelfo, not willing to let me get the better of him even in death, pulls his features into a flattened, ironed-smooth poker face.

"You think I haven't seen worse?" the old bastard says to me.

He snorts, transfers his tobacco, papers and matches from his jacket to his trouser pocket and then covers my head with the jacket. Nice touch, but I have no illusions that he's covering my body out of respect. He just doesn't want to have to look at me. He steps some twenty feet away, and urinates with his back to me. Such delicacy! Before he zips up he looks back at me over his shoulder as if he suspects I might peek, as if his shriveled little pecker ever held any interest for me.

He comes back, not too close, and uses his rifle as a prop

to ease himself to the ground. He sprinkles some tobacco on a paper, rolls it back and forth, back and forth, until it's good and tight, and he brings it up to his mouth, his ugly tongue darting the length of it to seal it. He lights it, shaking the match hard three times, and he pinches the cigarette as he holds it to his mouth. The smell of tobacco smoke mixes with the smell of dust, sage, and blood.

What has the world come to, I wonder—the body of Roberto, son of *Don* Manuel Felipe Fernán Iñíquez, lies alone and uncared for in the big house, and here I am the housekeeper with *Don* Adelfo Luis Tena Prieto, the old bastard himself, holding vigil over me.

"I remember your mother," he says.

Now he's going to talk to me. Just what I need.

"That Marigraviela was a looker."

I do not like the turn this one-sided conversation is taking.

"Even before her body became so splendid, there were those black eyes of hers. She was a couple years older than me. Even so, I noticed when she started getting breasts. Oh ho, I thought, look at that. Look at that.

"You, on the other hand, you took after your father. A looker like Marigraviela marrying old Gordo Vilaplana." He shakes his head, bewildered. "But then, funny things happened during the war, and that one, she'd picked up some foul politics. Strange what people become. I have this memory of her as a little girl, a dress too big for her, head high, proud of the rag doll in her arms. Sweet. To think of her corrupted, a communist, *puta madre!*" He shakes his head again.

For the record, my mum was not a communist, she was an anarchist, and proud of it.

"They say she came to her senses later in life. Well, if she repented before she died, I'm glad of it. Not many did. That's why they needed to be stamped out.

"People like to tell that story about her and the Gypsy. Personally I don't buy it. Not that she wouldn't go off with a Gypsy, that I do believe, but not that you were the fruit of her sin. You, I freely admit, were no bastard. Definitely old Gordo's daughter—you have his same intense little pig eyes for one thing. Shaped like him, too."

He chuckles, inhales on his cigarette and still pinching it, points it in my direction. "You know, it's true what they say about you. You are easy to talk to.

"Your mother sure took a wrong turn when it came to politics. Marigraviela, a fucking communist. Those breasts, those black eyes. What a waste. Sweet Marigraviela a Red! That's how twisted things had gotten. Your generation, you don't understand what it was like. We needed the war, welcomed it. Evil showed itself in a hundred different guises, a thousand. The world had gone wrong, turned upside down, and we had to put it right."

I don't want to hear this. I want to be far away.

"We all made sacrifices, some willingly, some not so willingly. Either way they are sacrifices in the eyes of God. I should know.

"I don't talk about it—water under the bridge, *a lo hecho pecho*—but I sacrificed a brother. Oh, I know what people say, but it's a lie. Why would I turn him in to get the house and land, the tiny bit that it was? I wasn't quite fifteen. What did I know of land and property? Nothing. Nothing.

"You know what a fifteen-year-old does know? He knows right from wrong, and my brother was wrong. What happened, he brought on himself. Oh, he wasn't a card-carrying communist like your mum, but he supported the Republic, didn't he? Much the same thing in the end." He stubs his cigarette out in the dirt.

"People will say that the reason he wouldn't let me join the army was because of my age, that he was trying to protect me." He shakes his head and flicks the cigarette butt in my direction.

"No, it was the Republic he was trying to protect. People say I could have run away, joined up and left him out of it. No. If the enemy is in your home, what's the point of traveling across the country to fight? That's pure foolishness. If you are going to eradicate a cancer, if you're going to save the body, you must be ruthless.

"Mind you, I did not expect them to shoot him. I did not." He rubs his mouth hard. "A few nights in jail, I thought, a warning."

His eyes stare at the horizon.

"But they dragged him out of the house, took him to the plaza with the others." He clears his throat. "I do not regret what I did. I do not. And I don't give a damn what you think, you filthy corpse, filthy *hija de puta, hija de roja.*"

The sigh that comes from him is more of a groan.

"I'm tired. Not getting much sleep."

His voice rises again, "Franco—people forget what we owe to him—he kept the forces of darkness and chaos at bay for as long as he lived. Long decades of peace and righteousness. Now it's all gone wrong again. He was hardly cold in his grave before the country leaped headlong into ruin. Socialists running the country." He spits in disgust. "People's Party! That's the problem with democracy, the evil of it. Franco had it right, you can't argue with that."

He lowers his voice, "And now, Lourdes talking back to me, can you believe that?" He gives a dry laugh. "Look who I'm talking to. And don't think I don't blame you. Putting ideas in her head. I forbade her to be friends with you. My wife fraternizing with the daughter of a Red whore? Not bloody likely. You encouraging her to do God knows what. But did she heed me? It's all part and parcel of the same thing. That's what these damn nightmares are all about—a warning. The time of sacrifice is at hand. I'm old, but I'm not dead.

"Rosa Esmeralda," he snarls. "Lourdes changed when that girl came here, everything changed when she came." His voice drips with hatred. "Rosa Esmeralda with that red rag around her neck, whoring, stealing, pissing on my honor. Pissing on it.

"I'm old, but I'm not dead," he repeats. "I'm not dead yet."

42

Here I am—I've been whisked back inside the church of Our Lady—and much relieved to get away from that dirty bastard.

But, so much for warning Esmi to stay away from *Señor* Iban. They lie entangled on the floor by the altar. Nestled in his arms, her head resting on his chest, she looks so peaceful, so content—that's what she gets for not listening to me. Now that I know Pilar is the villain, why do I still mistrust him?

After all, you can't say he's not appealing. When he showed up the first time at the big house, even though he was a perfect stranger, I could have swallowed him whole, what with those sad, dark eyes watching me so intently, that soft voice so cajoling, and all that attention focused on me, Narda, of all people. He wore some kind of cologne, light and intriguing, that made me want to stick my face up close and inhale, run my nose along his neck and snort him up, like they do in the movies with cocaine. I thought about warning him against wearing it because I worried Pilar would pick up on the scent and know a stranger had been in the house. But I didn't. It seemed too intimate to talk to him about his toiletries. Besides I liked the way it tickled my nose. I made a bit of a game of it, seeing how long I could detect it after he left. Even without the cologne or aftershave or whatever it was, the air tingled about him. I was convinced that if I covered my nose and my eyes I would still be able to tell when he was within reach—an experiment I would've liked to have tried.

He insisted on secrecy with both Roberto and me, and the *señorito* and I never acknowledged his visits, never once mentioned his name to each other. It was like an adventure—delicious and dangerous, and all in all, I was glad *Señor* Iban had come to Fuentespina. He broke up the monotony, provided endless fodder for idle thoughts and fattened the nest egg I kept hidden under my bed. And I liked helping him. He made me feel like I was his friend in need, his co-conspirator, and Roberto even perked up a bit, so all around it was a bit less gloomy around here.

So, I know full well his appeal, even though he never turned his attention on me full blast like he does with Esmi. It makes me shiver to think of it. I always avoided meeting his eyes for long because I felt like they about swallowed me up.

So why don't I trust him with Esmi? For one thing, lying there, he does not look peaceful or content. His eyes are narrowed, his mouth set. It scares me. How can he hold her so tenderly and yet look like that?

Esmi is dozing. Iban squeezes her and whispers, "Esmi, wake up."

Let the poor girl sleep, I want to tell him. Don't you know we had a long, cold night?

Esmi startles awake. She looks up at him. He smiles gently and kisses her.

"I have to go," she says, but she snuggles deeper into his embrace.

"Why?"

"I have to meet Narda." She pulls away from him with effort. "You know, Pilar's housekeeper." She shakes off her contentment, bless her heart, and grabs her jeans. "She'll think I'm dead or something—I'm so late. First *Doña* Pilar and now this." She smiles, leans over and kisses him lightly.

"What do you mean, first Pilar?" His voice is icy, his brow furrowed. He props himself up on one elbow.

"It's a long story." She stops dressing and looks at Iban thoughtfully. "But Narda's afraid to come back to Fuentespina. I told her I'd help her leave today."

"You mean you're leaving, too?"

"I can't stay here either."

"Back to Madrid?"

"It's where my job is. Narda's talking about Badajoz, but maybe she'd come with me to Madrid."

"How about Barcelona?"

Esmi smiles slyly. "Barcelona?"

"You and me."

"Seriously?"

He nods.

Esmi considers. "No one knows me there," she says.

I can tell she likes the idea—not just of Iban, but of starting over.

"Only me," he says.

"Only you."

They kiss again.

"What about Narda?" she says.

He hesitates, and then nods.

"Let's go right now," Esmi says.

"She's at the big house?"

"God, no. Wait. She's convinced you killed Roberto."

"Why would she think that?"

Esmi winces. "She thinks you're a vampire, remember?"

Iban drops back onto his back and runs his hands through his hair. He expels a big breath of air.

"Where is she?"

"At the old wall outside of town."

Iban sits up. "The Alcántara fortress?"

Esmi nods. "I'll have to go by myself."

"But Narda's not there."

"What do you mean?"

"I go there sometimes. I was upset about Roberto, and this morning I went there to think."

"She probably hid from you."

"She wasn't there, Esmi. I would have seen her."

"Then where is she?" she demands.

He shrugs. "Probably back at the big house, so there's no hurry for you to leave." He pulls her to him.

"No, she'd never go back there."

It's obvious Iban does not share Esmi's worry about me. He plays with a strand of her hair.

"Maybe Reina will know," she says. "She seems to know everything else." She locates her shoes. "Anyway, once we find Narda, we can leave."

"*Mi vida*, I can't leave yet."

She looks down at him "Why not?".

"You just said, Narda thinks I killed Roberto. By now the whole of Fuentespina will think so too—that's the way villages work."

His voice does not sound as worried as his words, but they alarm Esmi.

"And once Pilar knows I'm here..." He shakes his head. "She'll be glad to blame me for Roberto's death."

Did Esmi tell him about the vampire wounds on Roberto's neck? Maybe while I was stuck listening to the old bastard?

"Then let's find Narda and get out of here."

"Whether I'm here or in Barcelona, Pilar will send the police after me."

"But Pilar won't find out. Narda certainly won't tell her—she's afraid to go anywhere near her or the big house."

"Believe me, Pilar will find out. And then, no Barcelona, no us, no anything."

Esmi clings to him. "But Narda can tell everyone you're innocent. They'll believe her."

"But you said that she thinks I'm guilty. Besides, we don't even know where she is. She could be halfway to who knows where. But Esmi, you can help me." He caresses her face. "In fact, you're the only one who can."

"What are you talking about?"

"I need you to help me prove Pilar killed Roberto."

"What? How could I do that?"

"Roberto confided in me. Pilar gave him special medicine from an amulet she wore around her neck. I think that medicine must have been poison."

I feel a tingle of fear. What is he up to?

"Poison? You said yourself he was ill."

So, now she thinks he died of an illness? Did Esmi never believe me about Roberto being killed by a vampire?

"I'm sure of it," he says. "Something slow-working, accumulative. Maybe arsenic."

"Iban, that's crazy. "

Now I regret holding back from Esmi exactly what I saw in Roberto's room—his white body tossed on the bed like a rag doll, his blood-smeared neck, dribbles of blood dried like ghastly beads. I hadn't wanted to say any of that out loud. I couldn't rid myself of the image and I didn't want to burden her with the horror of it. Poison? Poison doesn't leave holes in your neck.

"I wish it were crazy, Esmi. I wish Roberto were still alive. My only hope, *our* only hope is for you get hold of that amulet. Once we have it, we'll have power over her."

"Power? You mean blackmail again?"

"No, evidence."

"Evidence we turn over to the police," Esmi says.

"Of course."

Esmi's quiet, sorting things out.

"Well?" he says.

His eyes are alert—no longer sad and plaintive. Does Iban really believe what he's saying, that Roberto died of poisoning? But if he doesn't, if he's deceiving Esmi, what can he gain from it?

"You want me to steal *Doña* Pilar's amulet," she says, as if testing the words.

"Is that a problem?"

"Yes."

Iban pushes her away. "Ah, you have qualms. How nice for you."

Esmi recoils from his anger.

"She's a murderess, Esmi! She's killed my nephew! We're talking about evidence."

"It's still stealing. I've seen that necklace and..."

"You've seen it?" Iban says, his voice excited and wary all at once.

"Yes. And she never takes it off."

"So, she gets away with murder?"

"I don't know."

"You're just like everyone else in this bloody town, kowtowing to her, covering up for her."

"That's not true."

"You'll have to choose between her and me."

"There's no choosing. We can leave, together, right now."

"And let Pilar get away with killing Roberto? Let her frame me for his death? Because I guarantee you, that is what will happen."

Iban gets up, sweeps his trousers off the floor and turns his back to her in one angry movement.

Esmi sits on the altar platform, shoulders slumped. She fidgets with her scarf, which I see has stayed tied around her neck during their lovemaking.

Iban stands, head bowed a moment. He lets out a big sigh that catches like a sob, and he pulls his trousers on and straps his belt.

"I want to help you..." Esmi stammers.

"Help *us*."

"But I don't think I could get away with it."

Of course you can't, I want to scream. How dare Iban try to get her to take such a risk.

He turns to face her. "I thought you and I..." He breaks off. He shrugs and his face turns hard. "But then, I don't really know you, do I? And you don't know me."

From her expression, he might as well have slapped her in the face.

"After all, you lie to your grandparents, sneak about in the night to meet men."

"To meet you," Esmi protests.

"You act like someone who's running away, someone who has something to hide. If there's a vampire in Fuentespina, maybe you're it." He shrugs theatrically. Then all the sarcasm and anger seem to drain from him.

Esmi tries to put her arms around him, but he steps back, holding both hands in front of him, palms out.

"I thought..." he says, "I thought you were the one. That first night you found me by the fountain, I had just come to the decision that I'd best leave Fuentespina that very night, leave before Pilar discovered I was here, get out before it was too late." He shakes his head bitterly.

"Iban," Esmi pleads.

"But I stayed, because of you. And now my life is to be ruined because you don't want to do this one thing."

"But we can go away."

"You mean run away."

Esmi shakes her head. "Everything will be fine. We'll be together."

"Until the police find me. You don't know Pilar like I do. My life is on the line." He holds up an admonishing finger. "This is where I find out what I can expect from you. If I can't count on you now..."

Esmi is fighting back tears. If there's one thing she's been in her life, it's dependable.

He comes to her and places his hands on her shoulders. "I need to know," he says, "if we have a future together. If I have any future at all."

I can see that sometime this morning Esmi has made up her mind, as she puts it, "to invest" in Iban. I think it's a lousy decision—that is, if one actually makes a decision when it comes to loving someone. I pray I'm wrong, but it seems to me she's made a leap of blindness instead of a leap of faith. So now, when she appears to hold back, it's not very convincing.

"If you think you don't know me...," she says with deep hurt in her voice. She stops and starts over. "If you think I'm hiding something, if you think I'm a sneak and a liar, why do you want to have anything to do with me?"

"Esmi, *mi vida*. Everybody has something to hide. Everybody lies. You must know that. Everybody."

"I don't want to believe that."

"It's not a matter of belief. People lie to each other. Worse, they lie to themselves. But that's not you, Esmi. That's not us. Let's not have any false scruples. Without that amulet, there's no more fairy tale, no happy ending. There's no more you and me. I was telling you the truth earlier. More than anything I want our story to come true. Don't you?"

He lets her embrace him in answer.

"You do want me to be free of Pilar so we can be together?" Iban says. He holds his arms loosely about her.

Esmi squeezes her eyes closed. "Of course."

Iban holds her tight, a reward. He kisses her fiercely. His

hands grip her upper arms. One tear slides from the outer corner of Esmi's eye. Iban pulls back. He kisses her again lightly, and pulls away again, leaving Esmi off balance as she leans toward him.

"You understand, we need that amulet," he says.

"Don't."

"Don't what? Kiss you?" He pulls her into his arms and kisses her passionately.

This time she pulls away. "It feels like you're threatening me."

"It's not a threat, Esmi. It's fact. Without that amulet..." He looks away a moment and then turns that intense, sad gaze back on her. "Without the amulet, it all gets very ugly."

She goes back to the platform, picks up the shoes she left there and sits in a pew. He watches, not breathing.

"All right," she says.

I can't believe she's agreed.

Iban sighs a healthy sigh of relief, and grins. "That's my girl."

My heart is breaking.

"It shouldn't be hard," he says. "Pilar has no reason to suspect you of anything. But how will you get in?"

Esmi shakes her head. "It's not a problem."

"But..."

"I'll take care of it. Trust me." She smiles wryly, which makes Iban study her face. She puts on her shoes.

"What will you do if she's wearing it?"

"I don't know."

"You know it has to be you—Pilar wouldn't let me anywhere near her."

Esmi nods.

She smiles weakly. He sits next to her on the pew. She leans her head on his shoulder, and he kisses the top of her head.

"About Roberto's body..." he says.

Esmi shudders. Her brow furrows. Is he going to ask her to do something else?

"Don't look at it, *mi vida*."

She's clearly relieved. "I don't plan to. I don't want to."

"It's best to remember people as they were. And, getting the amulet and getting out of there safely is the best way to pay your respects."

She nods.

"You better go now. It's midday, and that's the best time. It's Pilar's habit to take an early siesta before going out in the afternoon."

"OK."

She twists her hair up and clips it in place.

"Esmi, this means so much to me, so much to us."

Esmi kisses him as if she were going to work.

43

When Esmi leaves Iban in the church, she does not, bless her heart, go straight to the big house as he wants. Instead, winding through the back streets and avoiding the square, she seeks out Reina to see if maybe she knows where I am.

Esmi doesn't know that Reina would never answer a knock on her door, but she comes across her by chance in a street near her house. Reina, of course, knows nothing of my whereabouts, and she gets all flustered that Esmi has lost me.

"You must find her, *Señorita* Esmi."

Esmi jumps down her throat. "And how am I supposed to do that?"

Reina cringes. Esmi sighs. She turns and strides toward the big house. Reina hesitates only a moment before she follows on Esmi's heels like a lost puppy. She is so intent on keeping up, that when Esmi comes to a corner and stops short, Reina almost barrels into her.

"Look, Reina, I have an errand to do at the big house. Why don't you go home? That way Narda will be able to find you if she needs you."

Reina keeps following, but she slows until her steps dribble to an uncertain stop. She stands in the narrowest of streets, wringing her hands.

At the big house, Esmi squeezes in through the back door and hurries to my room. From my bed—still where she left them—she retrieves the shopping bag with my clothes and the little pile of my belongings. Maybe she hasn't let Iban bamboozle her after all.

She sets the shopping bag outside the kitchen door. The pathway there is a slipshod arrangement of broken pieces of slate roofing. She hears the sound of a pebble rolling on the stone and just about jumps out of her skin. Reina sheepishly shows herself.

"*Puta madre*, Reina!" Esmi whispers fiercely. "I thought you were going to go home."

Reina stares at the path, but does not retreat.

"Fine. Make yourself useful." Esmi piles the album and tin in Reina's arms and tucks the crucifix under her arm. Then she forces a smile. "Take these back to your house, will you, and keep them safe for Narda?"

I don't like this—Esmi being here, maybe still planning on carrying out Iban's plan; and Reina leaving her all alone, not that she would be much help against that monster Pilar.

Reina nods and disappears with her load. Once she is out of sight, Esmi slaps a hand to her chest and heaves a sigh. Back inside, the house is unnaturally silent. Using both hands, one on the knob and one spanning the door and the jamb, she quietly shuts the door behind her.

I'd be lying if I said I'm not scared being back in the house, but at least I don't fear the *Señorito*'s ghost anymore. I realize now that it was a very flimsy thread that tied him to us here in Fuentespina, and once it was cut, he must have left this place as quickly and freely as an escaped balloon. If anyone's haunting me now, it's myself.

I shouldn't even have anything to fear from *Doña* Pilar—

after all, what more can she do to me? But she can hurt Esmi, so fear still clings to me: fear for the living.

Esmi creeps from the kitchen into the main part of the house. At the foot of the stairway, she pauses and listens.

Absolute silence.

She tiptoes up the stairs. At the top, she stops again and listens.

I am fuming, furious with Iban for sending her here alone. And for what? A wild-goose chase.

Esmi must pass Roberto's room to get to Pilar's. The door is ajar. Is she thinking Pilar might be sitting with Roberto's body? She edges up to it and peeks in. Of course Pilar is not there, but Esmi sees something else, something clearly not right—maybe the disorder of the room, or a flash of color where it shouldn't be, Roberto's navy-blue ascot with the silver flecks lying in the middle of the floor. Whatever it is she steels herself and opens the door wider.

Poor boy. He lies on the bed, but not, as you would expect, laid out with arms crossed over his chest and a rosary entwined in his fingers. He's not even a straight figure under a white sheet. Instead he lies just as I last saw him, as if flung across the bed, limbs akimbo. The blood on his neck has dried to a dark color, brown and rusty against the white bed clothes.

Esmi stifles a gasp. She drops to a squat and holds her head in her hands.

I would have saved her that grisly sight, but maybe it will serve some purpose. Now that she has seen with her own eyes that Roberto did not die either sick or poisoned, she can forget about the damn necklace and get out of here.

After a moment she stands. She's pale but she's got that dogged look about her—doubtless she's inherited some inflexible genes from Teresa and the old bastard. She leaves the door ajar as it had been and continues on.

She stops in front of the door I'd pointed out as Pilar's room. She's told Iban she would get him the amulet and apparently that's what she's going to do. But she doesn't open the door, she just stares at it as if willing it to fork over its secrets. Holding her elbow close to her body, she rubs the side of her thumb back and forth over her lower lip.

I still hope against hope that Esmi will come to her senses and leave.

But, no. She screws up her courage. She shakes out her arms and runs her hands through her hair as if imitating Iban. It dislodges the clip, and she smoothes her hair and re-twists it into place. She puts her ear to the door.

Not a breath to be heard, but the wood is thick. She tries the door latch, squeezing her eyes shut as she does. The door is locked, of course. She takes the keys from my cardie, tries them until she finds the one that fits, and unlocks the door.

Does she have a story ready in case she comes face to face with Pilar?

She opens the door a crack. Inside it's utterly soundless, and thick damask curtains clothe the room in darkness. She opens the door a few inches more. A shaft of dim light shoots across the bed, and across Pilar's legs—the white silk of her nightgown one with the white linen of the bed.

Esmi freezes.

It's hard to say which of the two, Esmi or Pilar, is stiller, except Esmi's heart is pounding. Even if I didn't feel its beat as if it were my own, I can see the tremor of pulse on her skin. After a long moment, seeing no movement from Pilar, she moves cautiously to the dressing table in search of the amulet—after all, with its sharp metal edges and cumbersome chain it's not something any normal person would wear to bed, and Esmi still thinks Pilar is more or less normal. A thick cloud of dust motes swims in the beam of muted light coming from the hall.

Esmi quickly searches the dressing table. No luck. She turns toward Pilar. Reluctantly, and gingerly, she crosses the intricate, red pattern of the oriental carpet. The room smells musky, earthen. She approaches the bed and gazes down at Pilar. Her face is in shadow, but the precious metals of the amulet glitter between Pilar's breasts. The chain is slack, but her hands lie crossed over her chest, trapping the amulet.

Surely Esmi will give up now and get out. But no. Wincing, she reaches behind Pilar's neck, and as if a practiced pickpocket, she undoes the clasp on the slackened chain. Is she so scared or so single-minded that she doesn't notice Pilar is not breathing? Does she not notice that the stillness in this room is the same as that looms in Roberto's?

The chain in hand, she tries to slide the amulet from its nest. It doesn't budge. A single tendril of Esmi's hair has come loose and tickles the corner of her eye, but she ignores it. Delicately, she lifts the shield of Pilar's hands with three of her fingers, just slightly, and draws the chain smoothly with her other hand.

Pilar's breast rises with a breath. Her eyes flutter. Esmi freezes. Pilar's eyes open, fix on Esmi's face, which is surprisingly stony. Burning through the darkness, I see in Pilar's eyes something I never thought to see—terror.

"Nemesis," she whispers.

Esmi yanks on the chain she still holds in her hand, but Pilar, although physically sluggish and groggy, locks her hands about the amulet.

Esmi drops the chain and darts for the door.

Just as she reaches it, Pilar calls out in a weak voice, "Esmi, stop."

Esmi has one hand on the edge of the door and the other on the jamb, ready to propel herself into the hall and down the stairs.

"Run, Esmi, run," I shout with my whole being, but she can't hear me—I am part and parcel of the silence in this house.

To my dismay, Esmi hears Pilar and obeys. She stops in the doorway and slowly turns towards her.

"Come here," Pilar croaks. She struggles to support herself on one elbow.

Esmi's face is twisted with fear, but I can't tell if it's fear of obeying Pilar or of disobeying. The monster reaches out a hand as if to bless her.

Esmi takes a step toward the bed.

To my enormous relief, she stops there and goes no closer. It seems Iban's pull on her may be a match for Pilar's powers.

"I'm sorry," Esmi says, her voice thick with emotion. "I'm sorry."

She reels to the door and runs down the stairs.

Pilar's hand drops. She topples forward. Her face sinks

sideways into the pillows. I can see one of her eyes. It glazes over and then all light goes out of it.

44

Esmi rushes headlong down the stairs. In the kitchen she lunges at the back door and tears it open. The path outside is not empty—Reina's come back for a second load and has just picked up the shopping bag of my clothes left outside the door. Esmi charges through the door but does not crash into her. The old woman's timid, self-effacing ways serve her well—she never stands squarely in front of anyone or anything, much less a door.

Reina stifles a cry and drops the bag. Esmi lets fly an oath and throws a worried glance over her shoulder. Since Esmi did not see Pilar collapse back into death, she doesn't know that no one, at least no one in the big house, is coming after her. As Reina leans over to pick up the bag, Esmi grabs her by the arm and pulls her away from the house. Reina asks no questions and hightails it with Esmi as best she can.

When Esmi hesitates at a corner of the plaza, Reina takes the lead and guides Esmi through a warren of back lanes to her house. Once inside, Esmi leans her back against the door and slides down to a crouch on the floor. Reina throws the heavy iron bolt on the door.

Reina tugs and pulls on Esmi until she's standing again, then she leads her to the bed and lays her down. Esmi folds into herself and trembles. Reina takes her own cardigan off and lays it over Esmi's legs. She stands back and waits.

"I have to find Iban," Esmi says.

Reina answers by going to the tin pitcher on the table.

She pours some water from the dented relic into a jelly glass and brings it to Esmi. Esmi shakes her head. Reina sits on the chair and takes a tiny sip.

"I have to find him," Esmi says, struggling now to sit up.

She moves as if in pain, as if she's been pummeled. Reina pops to her feet.

"Stay still, *Señorita* Esmi. I'll bring your gentleman to you."

Esmi lies back down, a bundle of misery.

Reina stares down at her, her face so pure in its commiseration, it calls to mind our very own Virgen de la Soledad, if the Virgin were a shriveled up old woman. Then Reina leaves the house, looking furtively about her.

I've always had a soft spot for Reina, but for the first time I realize how courageous she is and my admiration for her grows large. She's not paralyzed by fear as I'd always thought— twisted and stunted, yes, but not paralyzed. The world shuns her, and yet most days she pulls back the bolt on her door and ventures forth from her hidey-hole of a house. Why? Desperation for human contact? A burning need to keep an eye on her enemies? Whatever the reason, each day is an act of bravery.

Even though I long to stay near Esmi, I find myself drawn along with Reina to the alleyway by the church. There she falters—inching toward the side door to the sacristy, then shying away. Finally she raises her hand to touch the wood and makes a mouse-tapping on the door. But it's too much for her, too bold and reckless; and she scurries back to the plaza, shoulders hunched, miserable under the weight of her failure. She stalls on the far side of the fountain, making little moaning sounds. She must be torn between going home to Esmi empty-handed and returning to the church to complete her mission.

Even though it's April, and spring, for weeks now there's been no softness to the days—the sky glaring a merciless blue and the afternoon sun baking the stones in the plaza and the black metal of Pilar's Land Rover. But now clouds are crowding in from the west.

Lourdes staggers into the plaza, her face raw with grief.

I imagine she's been framing and reframing my death into words—and repeating them like a kind of chant—as she walked back here all alone. Reina is the first person she comes across, and the bad news about me bursts from her. She breaks into tears and slumps on the bench of the fountain. Reina covers her mouth with both hands and rocks back and forth.

"What in the world is the matter?"

Lourdes looks up to see Rosario in her doorway. Reina turns aside, and Rosario crosses to investigate. Lourdes tells her. More tears. I am astounded.

Rosario makes the sign of the cross. She wants to pray for my soul.

"*Señora*," Lourdes says, "please, let's bring Narda's body home first."

Reina nods fervently. Rosario agrees reluctantly. She crosses herself again for good measure and starts for the big house.

"Where are you going?" Lourdes says.

"*Doña* Pilar must be notified, and she'll arrange for the body to be brought back."

"No," Lourdes states.

I do believe she's getting the hang of being contrary, but Rosario is not used to being contradicted.

"What do you mean, no? *Doña* Pilar has every right to know what has happened, after all Narda was her employee. It's the correct action to take. And it's how things are done here."

Lourdes does not reveal that Pilar has accused me of thieving. Instead she says, "*Señora* Rosario, take pity on her. Remember she is already in mourning for her stepson. Certainly we can take care of this ourselves."

Reina nods in agreement. "She's our Narda."

Lourdes again urges haste. "Is your brother at home, *señora*?"

Rosario sticks her head in her door and calls for Valentín to come out, and after Lourdes tells her story again, he and the three women go together to find old Anselmo, stranding me at the fountain. But from my perch there, I see Anselmo and Valentín drag the cart out into the street and I see and Rosario and Reina walk a short ways with them and Lourdes. Then Rosario and Reina fall back and take up posts of vigil at the edge of town.

The squeak and clatter of the cart fades away, and a dismal quiet returns to Fuentespina.

Rosario's lips move as she prays, rosary in hand. But what's on Reina's mind as she stands staring out into the scrubland? Has she forgotten all about Esmi in the excitement, or is she ashamed she's failed to fetch Iban? Or maybe she thinks Esmi's better off without the handsome and mysterious stranger. Does she suspect him of the same crimes that I did this morning—ages ago that seems now, the far side of a mountain range ago—when I still lived, still breathed fear and suspicion?

Before, I would have filled in the blanks and said, "Well, Reina does such and such because she feels x, y and z." But now I find people are deeper and more mysterious than I ever believed. Frankly, I haven't a clue what is going on under Reina's tired, grey bob.

Meanwhile Esmi, I imagine, dozes undisturbed in Reina's house; and I suppose Iban has been in the church all this time, listening at the door and trying to make out the hubbub in the plaza. Now that it's quiet, he comes out of the narrow passageway alongside the church with a bundle under his arm.

He walks right towards me, and I feel a flutter of jitters. Of all people is he the one who will see me? But no, he's simply walking to the fountain where, after looking through me and over both his shoulders, he plants the roll of burlap in the dust of the basin. He lingers there a moment, tugs on his shirt cuffs, paces, yanks on the cuffs again. Is he hoping to see Esmi or hoping to let himself be seen by her? Either way he's running a risk, and as it turns out, he loses.

The front door of the big house opens and he's caught out. Pilar steps into the plaza, and Iban stiffens. She raises her eyebrows when she sees him. They stare at each other.

Iban speaks first. "Stepmother. *Buenas tardes.*"

Stepmother wears mourning weeds, of a sort—the sleek, black dress with the thickly embroidered, black bolero jacket, the one that took Lourdes' breath away. Now she's added a mantilla worthy of the Queen—yards of black silk lace draped over a *peineta,* the comb high and curved at the back of her head. One end of the cloth lies tossed over the opposite shoulder. Plus she's donned her usual mirrored sunglasses. All in all, not a get-up one sees every day.

Pilar comes forward.

"Iban! You, here in Fuentespina? What a miracle!" The irony in her tone does not mask the brightness of recognition and something akin to warmth in her voice.

Iban shrugs and a corner of his mouth tugs upward.

"You look well, *querido,*" she coos. "Very well. I think of you often."

"And I of you," he says with a curl of the lip.

"Let me look at you, *mi amor*. How long has it been?"

"Fifteen years."

"Ah, a mere heartbeat." She takes a step forward.

Even though he's a good 20 feet away from her and the house, he takes a step back. It's reflex and he reaches behind him as if feeling for a wall or for a weapon at hand. Finding nothing there, his open hand clenches into a fist behind his back. He's shown fear and he winces in self reproach.

Pilar advances no further and pretends not to notice his retreat. She speaks as if coaxing a feral cat. "You've grown more handsome, *mi cielo*, but you've lost something, too."

"Have I?"

She nods. "That eager-to-please, puppy-like quality is gone. What's happened to the man-child I once..." she pauses, seemingly searching for the right word, "...knew?" she says, finessing the final word.

Iban holds his face impassive, but I hear him gulp, see sweat bead on his forehead.

"Time passes, for some of us," he says.

She tilts her head and nods once in regal acceptance.

"And things happen that change one," he says. "Driving the stake through my father's heart, the... decapitation..."

"A rite of passage, you might say," she says lightly.

"A... singular... rite of passage," he agrees. "But I can't regret that part, because I saved his soul. I saved him from you."

"Good for you, *mi alma*."

She adjusts the black drape of mantilla across her chest. Her ash-blonde hair shows through the lace, along with a bit of the reddish brown filigree of the tortoiseshell *peineta*.

"If it lessens your guilt for sleeping with your father's wife, all the better for you."

"And then the long years of searching. But again, I can't regret that either because I've finally tracked you down."

"*Ay, mi rey*. Determined as ever. It's that great strength of will that sets you apart from most mortals and makes your heartbeat so memorable." She clasps her hands together. "I suppose you still think it's you or me."

Iban doesn't bother to nod.

Pilar smiles. "Guess who'll win."

"You're not infallible."

"Aren't I?"

"You didn't know I was here."

Her smile fades.

"And, you killed Roberto. That was a mistake."

"So, you know about Roberto." She parts her hands, palms up. "Yes, a regrettable... miscalculation. As you can see, I'm in mourning. But it makes your sudden arrival, *mi corazón*, most fortuitous."

"You're slipping, Pilar. I've been here over a week."

She looks shaken—her mouth flattens into a hard line, and she looks down and adjusts her sunglasses.

"That's even better," she says, looking up at him again, her slight smile returning. "More people will have seen you. If there's anything the people of this town are more suspicious of than each other, it's a stranger."

Iban says nothing.

"Yes, you'll do very nicely indeed: as the culprit, as Roberto's deranged killer."

"It won't work," Iban bluffs.

"Maybe not, but then again, maybe yes. You know my powers of persuasion. If I'm in need of witnesses, I shall have them. Besides, there's that other murder you committed." She shakes her head and clicks her tongue in mock dismay. "So senseless, so bloody."

It's Iban's turn to be taken aback. "What other...?" he asks, unable to hide his confusion.

"What a despicable animal you are, *querido*, first killing a defenseless child and then a defenseless woman. The villagers are right. You can never trust an outsider."

He squints at her, trying to figure out this new ploy of hers. Then panic flashes across his face. "Esmi? Dear God!" he exclaims. "Not Esmi!"

Pilar smiles a surprised but self-satisfied smile. "Esmi! My, the situation's more intriguing than I thought."

"I'll kill you."

"I believe we've already established that's why you're here, *amorcito*. Relax. Esmi's fine, as far as I know. No, it was my housekeeper whom you killed." She speaks as if working out the details of the scheme aloud, "Narda was a witness to Roberto's murder, so... you had to kill her... or she stood in the way of your next victim... Yes, Esmi. You had to kill the old girl to get to dear Esmi, or perhaps you simply stalked her like a wolf and ripped open her neck for the pure pleasure of killing. Yes, I like that."

She redirects herself to Iban. "So, that's settled. They'll hunt you down in due course. They might even take you alive, *cariño*, but it will all work out in the end."

"Don't you have the nerve to kill me yourself?"

"Results, *guapo*, results are what matter. Speaking of which, tell me about my latest protégé, my pretty little Esmi."

"Protégé? I'll kill her first!"

"You disappoint me, *cielito*. You're missing the irony— first you shared me with your father, now you share Esmi with me. I think it's a generous offer, considering our history."

Iban stutters, "Have you...?" He stops, considers and continues more calmly. "No, you haven't initiated her yet." But then a doubt crosses his face. Is he remembering the scarf hiding Esmi's neck? His voice falters, "You couldn't have."

"No," she sighs. "She's not tasted my blood. Yet. But she will, *mi alma*, and soon."

"Over my dead body."

"Exactly, *guapo*, exactly. And there's nothing you can do about it. You *and* Esmi—things really are looking up. I didn't mean for Roberto to die yet, but good riddance. And good riddance to that busybody Narda. Irritating woman."

"So Roberto and Narda are vampires now?" Iban said, as if trying to sort things out.

"Please, give me some credit for taste. They were tiresome in life. Why would I want them around for eternity? But Esmi's a different story. I will transform Esmi. She should prove to be a superior companion in the centuries ahead."

Iban bristles. "I'll kill..."

Pilar holds up a hand to stop him. "I know, you'll kill me. Really, *mi cielo*, I don't remember you being so single-minded. I do hope you won't be a bore.

"I had such plans for you, my man-child, but then you turned against me. Well, we can put all that behind us, don't you think? Once they kill you, we can kiss and make up. Once you've joined me in immortal life, there will be plenty of time to talk about our future, and Esmi's, more rationally."

"Never."

"Iban, we have drunk of each other's blood. You can't change that. Immortal life awaits you. I await you. You just have to die."

"Not if I kill you first."

"That would let you off the hook, wouldn't it?" Pilar says. "But I can't allow it. You don't seem to appreciate the commitment I made to you by initiating you—much more binding than any marriage. Think about it, Iban. We could be content here.

"Did you know this is where my Roman centurion brought me after the fall of Dacia? Is that how you found me?

"I held on to this land for 400 years, until the Visigoths overran it. I was very satisfied here—I made it my home. And I missed it when I left, yearned for it for more than a millennium. Now I've finally reclaimed it. I'm back, *mi vida*, and I'm here to stay. I will not leave again."

"I am just as determined," Iban warns, "to destroy you and thus purge my blood of yours and purify my soul."

"My sweet Iban, so dramatic. I do enjoy how your eyes flash, but this discussion is pointless. Soon you will succumb to your fate, and we shall embrace again."

45

Old Anselmo's cart bumps along the rough road back to Fuentespina. He cobbled it together many a decade ago—attaching a pair of old tractor wheels to a box he made out of splintery planks. It was meant to be pulled by a donkey, but the donkey is no more. Instead, Anselmo and Valentín pull the cart, each taking a shaft.

And without warning, I find myself with them, as good as chained to the cart. Believe me I'd much rather be back at the fountain.

Valentín limps slightly—not from a war injury but from a boyhood tumble down the bell wall steps. His face is red, but Anselmo's is grey, and he huffs—his breathing shallow but regular.

And me? My body bounces about in the back.

I'm bound for Fuentespina, whether I want to be or not. How could I have ever thought I could just traipse off, leaving my shame behind?

Clouds spread across the sky and the air is muggy. Adelfo walks by my side as if in escort and Lourdes follows, crying—sometimes sniffling, sometimes sobbing.

I see Rosario ahead. She's waiting in the road where it enters Fuentespina. Her nose is red and the skin about her eyes, puffy. When we get a few cart lengths away she rushes forward and the men stop. Lourdes catches up and rests a hand on the side of the cart.

Rosario takes Valentín's place and Reina—standing in

the shadow of the outermost building, dry-eyed and pale—darts forth and takes the shaft from Anselmo. Rosario dismisses the men, saying the women will take it from here. The three men nod. They sigh and press their fists into the small of their backs. They stretch their arms, self-satisfied as if coming home after a day in the fields, work which none of them has done for many years.

"Thirsty work," old Anselmo says. He suggests the three of them pay a visit to the bottle of aguardiente in his kitchen. "In memory of the *difuntita.*"—the little dead one.

Virgen Purísima! That would be me.

Rosario and Reina heave the shafts and drag the cart into the shade where Reina had been standing. The three women come around to the back and stare where old Adelfo's jacket covers my head. Rosario shakes her head. Reina lets out a strangled moan.

"I can't believe it," Rosario says. "She was like the daughter I never had."

Lourdes raises her eyebrows.

"What does it matter?" Reina whispers.

Rosario flashes an angry look at her, thinking she's criticizing her, but when she sees Reina's bleak face, she softens.

"She was our Narda, our own," Reina adds, earnestly.

Rosario looks at Reina and nods. Lourdes sniffs and wipes her eyes with a limp handkerchief.

"Let us pray," Rosario says.

Reina shakes her head sadly.

"Later," Lourdes says. "There will be plenty of time later."

Rosario starts to protest, but falls silent. Then she cries. "Later, and later, and later. Lord, I didn't think time could become any more..." She searches for an adequate word.

"Empty," Reina says.

Lourdes reaches out and touches Reina's shoulder. Reina shies, but does not entirely pull away.

"Look at us sniveling away. Narda would be plain disgusted with us," Lourdes says, trying to buck them up.

Rosario responds with a reflex sneer aimed at Lourdes, but she reins it in and nods in agreement.

Lourdes is wrong—I'm not disgusted. Not with them. But I am kicking myself, ashamed of all the times I've sniped at Rosario and snapped at Reina. And Lourdes, well her deference to all things Adelfo drove me to distraction. More often than not, I've seen them as yet another chore, when I should have cherished them.

I mean, take Lourdes. Who else would have had the strength to tolerate that old *hijo de puta* of a husband of hers? And Rosario, however misguided, she knows who she is. Then there's Reina, poor broken soul. She brought out a tenderness in me that was all but dried up.

Each of them a fragment of my life, but not of each other's, at least not in the normal sense. I loved them all— they'd known it and I hadn't.

Well, that's Fuentespina, isn't it—our lives grains of silt, tiny bits and pieces of ignorance and stupidity, drifting in the never-ending hard luck of the town—hard luck that comes bubbling from the earth like spring water.

"We can take her to my house," Rosario says. "The three of us can take care of her there."

Lourdes nods. She helps Reina with her shaft of the cart, and slowly they maneuver the cart toward the square.

46

Who knew you could still have so many questions after death?

Having been swooped off to watch my body trundled back to town—a disheartening sight if ever there was one—I now find myself back in the plaza, the same old place as a moment before, only now it's as if I'm seeing it from a different angle, as if I were perched on the top bowl of the fountain. Yet, I can see Iban's face and Pilar's perfectly well, as if I were standing right in front of them.

Now if I can just stay put, because I don't want to let Pilar out of my sight.

Pilar lording it over everyone as lady of the big house made my blood run cold, but as a vampire... *ni hablar*. And knowing that she might at any moment turn back into the beast that attacked me makes me want to curl into a quivering ball, and I'm already dead. But Esmi's not. Esmi is at her mercy, and Pilar has no mercy. She can attack her, kill her, turn her into a vile creature, damn her very soul, and there is nothing I can do about it. Nothing.

And what about Iban? Is he a threat to Esmi as well? He may not be a vampire, but he's apparently some kind of vampire cadet, vampire-in-waiting, and if you ask me, that's too close to the real thing.

The wash of clouds covering the sky softens the afternoon light, and the plaza is free of shadows. Iban still stands by the fountain—his white shirt gleams against the dull, pocked stone; and the wind lifts his collar and ruffles his hair. Pilar, all in black, stands sheltered by the big house. The air between the two of them hums with tension. It's a standoff. They've made their pronouncements, their promises of death, and now they stare each other down.

For the moment, Iban's bluff holds, but it can be only that, a moment—Pilar can attack at whim. She watches him, all wary and cunning, toying with him. And Iban, trying to look unshakeable—never mind the sweat beading on his forehead, the stink of fear coming off him—meets her gaze. He dares not blink.

And me? Breathless—truly breathless—I eye them both, and wonder who will break the deadlock, and how.

As it happens, it's a wild card that sets the earth spinning again and, unfortunately, that wild card is Esmi. She must have pulled herself together and then gotten tired of waiting for Reina to return, because she emerges from one of the side streets. She sees Iban and rushes towards him.

"Iban, thank God," she says.

He thrusts out a hand, palm up, never taking his eyes off Pilar. "Give me the amulet," he says to Esmi. "Quickly. Now!"

Esmi stops, taken aback. She stares at his empty hand. It's trembling.

Pilar steps forward. "Hello, Esmi."

Esmi gasps. She was so fixated on Iban, she hadn't noticed Pilar standing there. Esmi sidles next to Iban and does not meet her eyes.

"Give me the amulet," Iban snaps.

Pilar swallows a triumphant little smile. The black lace of her mantilla frames her face. Because she's tossed one end of the mantilla over the opposite shoulder, her bolero jacket is shrouded by folds of fine lace. She slips her fingers beneath the edge of it and lifts so that the web of cloth falls free from her shoulder, unveiling the amulet hanging on its bronze chain around her neck, its silver and gold shining against the black silk of her dress. Pilar, smiling like the cat that's got the cream, touches the pendant and cradles in her fingertips.

"Is this what you're looking for, *querido*?"

I can see Iban start to crumble, like a building falling in on itself. He is bolstered only by anger. He shoves Esmi.

"You useless..."

"I tried," Esmi stammers, stunned.

"What do I care if you tried?" he shouts. "Years I tracked her, years for Christ's sake—Italy, Romania, Turkey. Finally I find her. Finally I corner her. And for what?"

"Don't mind him, *mi amor*," Pilar says to Esmi. "He gets petulant like this now and then."

Esmi looks from Pilar to Iban. She's not so upset she doesn't notice Pilar's tone and the familiarity that she's claiming, like a cat marking its territory.

"Come here," Pilar orders.

There's something in her voice that Esmi seems to respond to. She hangs her head, and Iban emits something like a growl, something like a groan.

"I'm sorry about the necklace," Esmi says, but she's not talking to Iban, she's talking to Pilar. "I've never done anything like that before, I swear."

"Don't worry, my dear. I can see that Iban put you up to it—he can be most persuasive. Come."

She says the last word sharply and Esmi flinches.

"I forgive you your transgression," Pilar insists. "Did I not promise to protect you? Now, come here."

Esmi takes a step towards her.

"Don't do it, Esmi," Iban says.

Esmi glances angrily in his direction. Then, shamefaced, she goes to Pilar and stands before her—head tilted, humble like in my stamp of St. Francis looking down at a lamb.

"I won't do anything like that again," she says.

"Of course you won't, *mi linda*," Pilar coos.

I am incensed, fuming. She's standing directly between Iban and Pilar—damn them both. How could Esmi let herself get into this predicament? Iban moves a tad to keep Pilar in view and Pilar shifts slightly in response. If Iban fired a gun at Pilar, or Pilar at Iban, Esmi would take the bullet. Without knowing it, she's's serving as weapon and shield to them both.

Pilar smiles at her and Esmi pivots to face Iban. With her back to Pilar, she stands straighter. I groan at the anger and pleading I see on her face. It's bad enough she's gone over to Pilar, but she hasn't given up yet on Iban, and I don't trust him any farther than I can throw Pilar.

"Don't you see?" Esmi snaps at Iban, "You were wrong about her. She could help us straighten out this mess with Roberto."

"You idiot," Iban says in utter frustration. "She has no reason to straighten out anything. She's trying to destroy me."

Esmi may be furious with Iban, but she knows fear when she sees it—it's something she's especially sensitive to these days. Maybe that's why she cuts him some slack. She turns back to Pilar and pleads for him. "We're afraid people will think Iban had something to do with Roberto's death, but he didn't, I swear."

"I'd like to believe you, Esmi, but when it comes to men, I don't think your judgement is to be trusted."

"Please, *Doña* Pilar," Esmi says.

"Esmi, don't," Iban says. "She's trying to use you to get to me."

Pilar laughs. "Really, Iban."

"She can control your mind, cloud your thoughts."

Esmi stiffens. Maybe he's hit a chord.

"She's dangerous," Iban says, "more dangerous than you can know."

He's got good reason to steer clear of Pilar—she could kill him in the blink of an eye. But why doesn't he rush forward anyway, grab Esmi—overpower her if that's what it takes—and carry her to safety?

"Remember, Esmi, she killed Roberto," he says.

"Pay no attention to him, *mi vida*," Pilar says. "My stepson has always had a deep-seated hatred of me."

"Stepson?" Esmi says.

47

The clouds have thickened, clotted, and give off the scent of possible rain; but Esmi, Iban and Pilar don't notice, locked as they are in a nasty triangle, deadly and airless.

Poor Esmi. She looks as if she's been struck. And Iban, is he blinking back tears?

"Iban, what does she mean?" Esmi says.

Pilar smiles sadly and puts an arm around Esmi's shoulder, but she addresses Iban. "Lying again, Iban, and to our Esmi?"

"He told me that his connection to you and Roberto was through Susana Seco, his sister and your husband's first wife."

"Nonsense," Pilar says. "First of all, *Don* Manuel Felipe's first wife was Beatriz—Beatriz Carmela, an only child. Anyone in town can tell you that. And before I married him, I was married to Iban's father. A brief and unhappy marriage—Iban saw to that."

Esmi speaks accusingly to Iban. "Susana? Beatriz? Whoever she was, she wasn't your sister, was she. And you weren't Roberto's uncle."

"Esmi, you don't understand what's at stake here," he says, anguish in his voice.

Doubt and dread cloud Esmi's face. "Why were you visiting Roberto?" she asks.

"I hate to think," Pilar smirks.

"I can explain," he says to Esmi. His anger returns, "But first come away from her."

"You sent me to her," Esmi snaps.

"You do have unerring bad taste in men, don't you, my dear?" Pilar says. "It's fortunate for you that you failed to steal the amulet—it's very valuable. Its theft would be grand larceny."

"He said it contained the poison you used to kill Roberto," Esmi says in way of explanation. She turns on Iban. "But I saw the body."

Her having seen the body surprises Pilar, and she doesn't look pleased. Her arm around Esmi's shoulders becomes a grip on her arm.

"Roberto wasn't poisoned, Iban. There was blood on his neck. I don't know why I still tried to steal the necklace, but I wanted us to be together and your words kept going round and round in my brain—the amulet, the amulet, the amulet."

"As I said, Iban's very persuasive," Pilar says. "Unfortunately he's a pathological liar, always has been."

"That's not true," Iban says. He looks like he might cry.

"His father used to worry terribly about what would become of him."

"Don't talk about my father," Iban says.

"When he was still a teenager, he tried to seduce me—his own stepmother. When that failed, he used his lies to break up my marriage with his father."

"She's lying, Esmi."

"And then, one day his father was dead, and the circumstances, quite mysterious."

"Because you killed him!" Iban shouts.

"You see, Esmi," Pilar says, "There's something not quite right in his head. Just as you and I are starting to understand each other, he tries to drive a wedge between us, just like he did with his father and me."

Iban runs a hand through his hair and shakes his head. He emits a dry, hollow laugh. His face is sweaty; his voice, shaky. He reeks of desperation. If he'd come to the big house like this that first time, I'd have slammed the door in his face.

"Esmi, *mi vida*," he says, "remember this morning, the church, our plans for the future."

"Did he tell you pretty stories?" Pilar says. "He's an expert at pretty stories."

"Shut up!" Iban yells. "Esmi, we still have a chance. If you'll listen to me, trust me. It's true Pilar was married to my father. Esmi, don't turn away from me. But, it was she who seduced me. I was just a kid. *She* seduced *me*. She was using him, using me."

"I don't have to listen to any more of this slander," Pilar says. She guides Esmi toward the open door.

"Esmi, wait," Iban says. "You have to listen!"

Esmi stops, more from anger and exasperation than interest in what he has to say.

"Vampires..." his voice is earnest. "Vampires exist."

Esmi shakes her head, as if pitying him is all that's left.

"Pilar is one of them," he insists. "You said yourself, you saw Roberto's body. You said there was blood on his neck?"

Esmi shudders. "Yes."

Iban takes a few steps towards her, keeping his eyes on Esmi, even though Pilar is next to her grasping Esmi's shoulders with both hands. I think it may be the most courageous thing I've seen him do. It takes nerve to sneak into Pilar's house night after night, but facing her, walking up to her when you know what she's capable of... I can't imagine.

He's still a good ten feet away when he reaches out to Esmi. In spite of the distance, Esmi shies away, withdrawing into Pilar's embrace. Pilar looks smug.

Iban presses on. "Pilar lived..." He stops as if gagging on the words that should follow.

Esmi lets Pilar pull her into the doorway.

He forces himself to continue. "She lived off my blood, Esmi. Pilar drank my blood. She did the same to Roberto. Roberto's blood has been keeping her alive. And now that Roberto's dead, she needs you."

She tightens her grip on Esmi. Esmi flinches and looks at her, startled.

"Amazing," Pilar says. "Time has made you only more inventive."

"She twists everything, Esmi. She makes you think she's doing you a favor, makes you feel grateful to her," Iban says.

"Come Esmi," Pilar says.

For the first time Pilar takes her eyes off of the two of them. She looks about the square and up at the sky—I feel her gaze slither over me and I shiver.

"I think it may rain. Let's go into the house where it is dry and *safe*."

"Stop!" Iban pleads. He follows them to the threshold. "For God's sake, listen." His voice drops, as if speaking in confidence, as if Pilar were not right there. "There's one big difference between Roberto and me. It's true we were both Pilar's stepsons, but..."

"He's dead," Esmi says, flatly.

"Yes, he's dead, and he'll stay dead," Iban says. "But with me... She..."

"Go ahead," Pilar says. "You're only digging your own grave, so to speak."

Iban grasps Esmi's hand, and Esmi reluctantly lets him. Pilar's so cocksure of herself and of Esmi now that, except for one hand resting on Esmi's shoulder, she lets loose of her.

"Damn it, it's hard to say." He speaks staring down at her hand. He's almost whispering. "You can't understand... The shame. The anger." He glances up at her. "How wretched you feel when you fall victim to, well, to someone you love."

He has her attention. The misery on her face matches his, because she knows firsthand what he's saying.

"And, God help me, I did love her," he whispers. His face is close to hers now. He takes her other hand in his. "Esmi, she made me drink her blood."

Esmi pulls back, looks at him as if he's a madman, and I have to admit he doesn't look any too sane.

Pilar laughs.

But Iban doesn't give up. He can't. He plunges on, speaking quickly. "Because of that, we—Pilar and I—are united for eternity. And she's right, I do hate her, because of what she did to my father and what she did to me. When I die, I, too, will become a vampire. That is my curse, my fate, unless I can destroy her first."

"This is no longer entertaining," Pilar says. She pulls on Esmi's shoulder.

Esmi tries to free her hands, but Iban holds tight.

"If she dies before I do, then I'm free, and countless others will be saved, and you and I, Esmi, we'll have a future together."

"Come away, Esmi," Pilar hisses. "He's obviously deranged."

"I lied about the amulet," he admits—a calculated risk. "I knew there was no poison."

"That's the first sensible thing he's said," Pilar purrs in Esmi's ear. Esmi leans her head toward the sound.

Iban pulls himself together and speaks as forcefully as he can. "At least not poison in the usual sense. You see, she used to have to return to her tomb each sunrise—that's the way with vampires—but over the centuries she's evolved. Now all she needs is that amulet—it contains earth from her tomb. She cannot endure without it."

"This is crazy, Iban," Esmi says. "Even if vampires existed, look it's daylight, and *Doña* Pilar isn't crumbling to dust. Isn't that what's supposed to happen to vampires?"

"She's more than 2,000 years old. With each generation, each century, she's become stronger, more unassailable. It took her a thousand years to free herself from returning daily to her sarcophagus, where inside she would lie in a thick layer of earth from her original tomb. At the same time, she was striving to adapt to sunlight, so she could be less conspicuous and less vulnerable."

"What a fairy tale," Pilar laughs.

"Over the centuries, she's come to tolerate the weak,

slanted light during the hours after sunrise and before sunset. Anything stronger weakens her, and during the day when the sun is highest in the sky and night is at its most remote, she's nearly helpless. Like a lizard in the cold, she moves more and more lethargically, until she must seek refuge and retreat to the dark, and become dead again."

"Esmi, I must insist..." Pilar says.

"If there's no truth to what I say, Pilar, then let Esmi see what's in the amulet."

"Esmi knows what it contains. Tell him."

"Water," Esmi says, her voice faltering.

"From the River Jordan," Pilar adds.

"Have you seen it?" Iban says, in a soft, urgent voice, pulling Esmi toward him. "Take the amulet and look. If it really contains water, why should she stop you?"

Esmi searches his face for reasons to believe or disbelieve. Those sorrowful eyes of his are as compelling as ever. The corner of Iban's mouth and the corner of his eye twitch together in an abbreviated smile and wink of encouragement.

She turns toward Pilar. Tentatively she reaches for the amulet.

Pilar wrenches Esmi's hand by the wrist to stay it and snarls, actually snarls—her upper lip drawing back over her teeth which are suddenly much too long and much too pointed.

Iban backs away. If only I could kick Pilar in the gut or smash her head with a rock.

"You killed Roberto!" Esmi cries, and twists her arm free.

She runs to him.

"No, Esmi," he shouts, pushing her back toward Pilar. "The amulet. Get the amulet."

48

Culpability. Even in death it's a sticky, murky, hulking thing. It's lead cotton in the lungs, sludge in the eyes, bile in the throat, clay in the mouth. It's a soggy towel hanging heavy from your heart, and it's the belt that cuts into the flesh.

I think back on Iban showing up at the big house. I turned him away the first time. I did. If only I'd kept saying no. And Pilar. If only I'd been stronger and not let her blind me to what was going on. And if only I hadn't run away, Pilar wouldn't have had reason to come after me. I'd be alive now, wouldn't I. I could pull Esmi away from both of them. I could shout to her, "Come to me, Esmi, to me," and because I'd still be alive, she would hear me.

I wring my silent hands, alone in my desperation. And yet not alone. I feel a bristling energy about me—since it sets my teeth on edge, so to speak, I take it to be Teresa, raging alongside me, as helpless as I am.

At least now, with Pilar showing those teeth of hers, Esmi sees her for the animal she truly is. I hope she also sees Iban for the conniving, treacherous bastard he is.

Imagine! Pushing my Esmi toward that monster!

Esmi gawks at him. And the shock on her face shifts to hurt and then to anger. Her voice is a hoarse whisper. "Go to hell!"

Iban stiffens and his face turns ashen. He's lost Esmi as an ally, and without her or some other miracle, hell's as good a description as any for the fate that awaits him.

Esmi turns her back on him, but that brings her face to face with Pilar. She sidesteps and pulls away from both of them—she's about to bolt but the rumbling of Anselmo's cart distracts her as Reina, Rosario and Lourdes haul it into the plaza.

"*Ay, m'ijita!*" Lourdes cries out when she sees Esmi. Fresh tears flow and she rushes toward her, that is until she sees Iban and Pilar.

Reina drops the shaft of the cart and shrinks back, averting her eyes from them, but Rosario recognizes Iban as my secret visitor at the big house.

"That's him!" she shouts. "That's Jorge."

I never had a chance to tell anyone but Esmi that I thought Iban killed Roberto. But no matter. Rosario has jumped to the conclusion all by her lonesome. She points a finger at Iban.

"Murderer!"

She brings her hand behind her ear and points at him again, throwing her accusation as if it were a rock, again and again, as if stoning him.

"Murderer, murderer!"

I spot Valentín and Anselmo at the edge of the plaza, and then a few others drawn by the shouting. Adelfo, too. Only the old bastard doesn't hang back. He carries his Mauser at the ready—he's got the bayonet attached to it now—and he creeps toward the center of the square.

Rosario calls to her brother and he ambles forward.

"Valentín, that's the man I told you about! That's Jorge! If he hadn't killed Roberto, Narda would never have run away from us." She stifles a sob, and turns her attention back to Iban. "Poor Narda. All alone out there at the mercy of any wild animal. You're to blame. You as good as killed her, too."

With Rosario commanding center stage, as she is wont to do, nobody takes note of the old *hijo de puta*. All grim and wary, he advances in a soldier's semi-crouch. He and the gun are right chummy; it's like a fifth limb—the center of gravity of his body dancing with its weight.

Still, it's an odd stance for an old man—as if his emaciated body were the same one that marched across Spain in Franco's army 60 years ago. The old bastard can't summon up anything like the fluid movements of a young man. And he has one less eye than in his military days—half his face like the surface of the moon, white and pocked and criss-crossed with scars. So while his body proceeds like a stiff old cat, his head whips about like a nervous robin, trying to keep everyone in sight.

He comes to a stop near the fountain and trains his gun on Iban.

"Hands up," Adelfo orders. "On your head."

I find myself almost liking the old goat.

"What the hell do you think you're doing?" Iban says. "Who are you?"

Adelfo pulls back the bolt. The metallic sound reverberates off the stone in the plaza and sets off a surge of gasps, oaths and prayers from those present in the square.

Iban struggles to hang on to his indignation—it's a way to keep panic at bay.

"Hands on your head, *coño*," Adelfo growls.

Iban obeys.

Lourdes hurries forward to embrace Esmi; and Esmi, half in shock, lets her.

"Are you all right, *mi amor*? That terrible man. Terrible." She pats Esmi's hair, her shoulder, her face.

A few more people have drifted into the square—pretty much everyone in town now present and accounted for.

"*Señora*," Adelfo says, nodding his head to Pilar. "As you requested, I searched for the girl and the housekeeper." He looks with disapproval in the direction of Esmi. "I see you have found the girl. And I," he jerks his head toward the cart, "have found your housekeeper."

Esmi looks around for me. She doesn't understand.

"*M'ija*," Lourdes says softly. "*Mi amor*, Nardita has passed."

Esmi pulls away from her.

"What?"

"It's true," Rosario chimes in.

"You mean she's dead?" Esmi says. "Narda can't be dead."

"She was killed by a wild animal—we think a wolf or a lynx," Rosario says and crosses herself.

"That doesn't make any sense," Esmi protests.

She heads for the cart. Lourdes tries to stop her, but Esmi pulls away.

Adelfo's voice thunders, "Halt."

She stops. I can see she's irritated with herself for obeying her grandfather, as well as furious with him for, on top of everything else, giving her an order. She glares daggers at him and continues toward the cart.

Maybe Reina and Rosario want to spare Esmi the sight

of my body or maybe they know Adelfo means business, or maybe for both reasons they close ranks in front of the cart. Rosario crosses herself, and Reina closes her eyes and shakes her head. It's seeing those two old crows that makes Esmi stop and lets the truth seep in. She covers her eyes with one hand and when she draws it away, she smears tears across her face.

Oh that telltale wetness on her face! If only I could comfort her. If only I could comfort me.

And then—maybe because my girl's no fool and doesn't buy the wild animal story, or maybe because she's ready to blame Pilar for anything and everything—Esmi leaps to the truth of the matter and turns on Pilar.

"Why?" she accuses. "Why Narda?"

"Shut your trap!" Adelfo bellows.

Esmi gapes at her grandfather.

"Have some respect," he orders.

"Respect? Narda was my friend, and she..." Esmi juts her chin in Pilar's direction. "She killed her."

"Esmi!" Lourdes cries out in dismay.

A couple of the people along the edge of the square exclaim, but most keep their comments under their breath. Others cross themselves. Some do both. Reina mutters something to the stones at her feet.

"You'll keep a civil tongue in your mouth, if you know what's good for you," Adelfo says.

"It's quite all right, *Don* Adelfo," Pilar says. "Your granddaughter is understandably distraught. She doesn't know what she's saying."

"I know you're a murderer, a monster," Esmi says.

That's my girl, I want to shout.

More gasping and murmuring and hands fluttering to make the sign of the cross.

It's not the truth or falseness of Esmi's words that shocks but the brazenness of saying them aloud, and right to the Ice Queen's face. After all, the big house may look proper and sedate, but here in Fuentespina we have no illusions about its occupants—we need only remember Pilar's predecessor. When old *Don* Cayetano died, the usual Masses were said for the repose of his soul. They were all well attended, of course—it would have been foolhardy to stay away—but at home many a glass was raised and many hopes whispered that he suffer in hell for the torments he'd inflicted here on earth.

But now the villagers ask themselves, wasn't it a wild beast that killed the housekeeper? Surely this upstart of a girl doesn't think Pilar can command wild beasts to do her bidding—no one believes her to be as powerful as all that. Except, perhaps, Anselmo. He once told Valentín, who mentioned it to his sister, that he suspected Pilar of being a witch, and that he didn't give a hoot how out of fashion his beliefs were, because he knew what he knew.

"A wild animal killed our Narda," Lourdes says. "It's terrible, *mi amor*, but sometimes these things happen."

All attention is aimed at Esmi, so Iban lowers his hands.

Adelfo raises the gunsight close to his face. "Keep your hands on your head."

Iban replaces his hands with every show of frustration.

"Look, granddad, none of this has anything to do with me. Those women just said Narda was killed by a wild animal."

"And *Señorito* Roberto?" Adelfo growls.

"Iban hasn't killed anyone," Esmi says.

She may be hopping mad at how Iban's treated her, but fair's fair.

"You," Adelfo orders Esmi, "over there with him where I can keep an eye on you." He motions with the barrel and bayonet of the Mauser towards Iban.

Even though she's never faced a gun before in her life, she hesitates.

"You can't be serious."

"Please, Esmi," Lourdes whispers.

Reluctantly, Esmi obeys.

"I knew you had a man hidden somewhere." He raises his voice, "Didn't I, Milú? I had her pegged."

"Adelfo, you can't..." Lourdes can't seem to find words for what he should not do.

I want to hit her along side the head. She's lived with the old bastard for half a century—how dare she be dumbstruck when, as far as I can see, Adelfo is being exactly and precisely himself?

In any case Adelfo ignores her.

"*Doña* Pilar," he says, "*mi señora.*" With a mean little smile, triumphant, he indicates Iban with the barrel of the rifle. "I give you *Señorito* Roberto's killer." His weaselly smile turns to a grimace. "And the thief."

He means Esmi—Pilar having accused her and me of stealing (stealing my own things) from her so that Adelfo would bring Esmi to her.

"No!" Lourdes cries out.

Pilar casts a fierce look at Lourdes to quiet her. "Thank

you, *Don* Adelfo," Pilar says. "Fuentespina, once again, owes you a great debt."

"*A sus órdenes, señora*," Adelfo nods.

"*Señora*, please. There must be a mistake." Lourdes pleads. "Please don't call the Guardia Civil. Esmi's a good girl. She's not a thief."

"*Abuela*, don't," Esmi says impatiently.

"Do not be concerned, *Señora* Lourdes," Pilar says. "This is a matter between Esmi and me, and she and I have come to an understanding. She knows all she has to do is come to me, and all will be forgiven."

Lourdes' face beams with relief.

"*Perdóneme, señora*," Adelfo says. "If you want to forgive my granddaughter, that's your business, but with all due respect, I cannot." He rubs his mouth against his shoulder. "This is a family matter. Rosa stays where she is." He snaps his head about looking for complaints. "My honor is at stake."

"*Don* Adelfo," Pilar says icily, "I order you..."

"Forgive me, *señora*, but there's more here than meets the eye. The village must be kept safe and... unpolluted." He nods in Esmi's direction without losing his aim. "The harlot's not what she seems—she's taken you in, just as she has my wife."

"Adelfo..." Lourdes approaches on his blind side.

Startled, he swings the rifle barrel in her direction. Lourdes freezes. Several people cry out. Adelfo pays them no mind.

He sees it's Lourdes. "Good God, woman," he barks.

Immediately he swings the barrel back, re-aiming at Iban.

Iban cries out. "Don't shoot, please, don't shoot!"

His hands are still on his head. Esmi slips her arm around his back, as if to reassure him. Maybe she feels responsible, since it's her crazy grandfather behind the rifle. Maybe she still thinks her grandfather won't shoot with her so close.

"Please, Esmi, don't let him shoot me. I can't die, not before Pilar."

"Quiet!" Adelfo booms. "Down. On the ground!"

Esmi helps Iban down—his hands are still on his head. He sits cross-legged, leaning against Esmi's legs. Her hand lights on his shoulder.

Overhead the clouds have thickened and darkened—the light, strained to an unnatural hue.

"None of you understand," Adelfo says. "There's evil here in Fuentespina. It's been lying in wait a long time, biding its time, but it's back. The *guapo* there, he's a common murderer, but her... That one." He spits on the ground. "Am I the only one who sees through her?"

Esmi blanches. She finally realizes she's no safer from the old bastard than Iban is.

49

"Grandfather," Esmi's voice quavers, "I'm not the threat here, I swear."

"Ha!" Adelfo says.

"When I saw Roberto's body, I didn't understand what I saw. But I do now. Go and look for yourself and you'll see. Iban didn't kill him. And no common animal killed Narda, either. The same creature murdered them both. A vampire."

Many in the plaza cross themselves. No one smirks or laughs. After all, evil is more than a mere notion in Fuentespina. Just this lot alone, in their one shared lifetime, has survived hunger, epidemics, war and executions. It's suffered and inflicted prison and concentration camps. It's been brought to its knees and forced other to theirs. It's beat and been beaten, raped and been raped, tortured and been tortured. Why not a vampire? If evil isn't in our immediate family circle, then it's that shirt-tail relative who keeps showing up on our doorstep, invited or not.

Esmi points at Pilar, "And she's it. Pilar is the vampire."

Rosario and Lourdes cross themselves multiple times. Reina folds her hands over her mouth.

"Grandfather, you've got to believe me. Go and look at Roberto's body. She's the evil here; she's your culprit. Not me and not Iban."

Rosario, clearly curious, takes a step forward; and several people who've been hanging back venture further into the plaza. Are they thinking they'll go take a gander at Roberto?

Pilar draws herself up to her most imposing. "This is my house," she proclaims.

Everyone stops cold.

"Forgive us, *Doña* Pilar," Rosario says. "The girl's story is nonsense, of course, but there's no harm in looking, is there?"

There's a murmur of agreement—no harm in looking, not at all—and people move forward again. Rosario starts to approach Pilar. Lourdes is right behind her. Even Reina. She follows the other two women, peering around them.

Pilar quivers with fury. "No one enters my house."

None of you riffraff, she means. But how to keep them out?

Adelfo lifts his rifle and a shot cracks the air. Everyone comes to halt.

When the echo of the shot dies, Adelfo says, "Who are you, any of you, to question the *señora*? All that is good and holy demands that we respect her and give her her due."

"Surely, *Don* Adelfo, nowadays..." Valentín says.

Anselmo cuts in, "For Christ's sake, Fito. Two people are dead. If there's a killer on the loose, we have a right to know what we're up against."

"Have you forgotten that *Doña* Pilar is in mourning?" Adelfo says, indignant.

Rosario protests that he's the one who brought up the issue of evil. "Doesn't that bear investigating?"

"We must respect the *señora's* privacy. Anyhow, I told you who the problem is," the old bastard says, "and it has nothing to do with *Doña* Pilar. "

"Thank you, *Don* Adelfo," Pilar announces so that all can hear. "You are a true gentleman." Then she addresses the villagers as a whole, "People of Fuentespina, it's true my stepson did not die of illness. It was foul play, but I kept his murder quiet because I did not want to alarm you or create a panic. I trusted in *Don* Adelfo to capture the killer, which he has. This man here." She gestures to Iban. "He's the one responsible for *Señorito* Roberto's death." She turns to Adelfo and speaks to him so that everyone can hear. "Be ever vigilant, *Don* Adelfo. The brute is sure to try to escape."

"If he does, *señora*, I swear he won't live to tell about it."

"I didn't kill him." The pleading in Iban's voice scrapes away its usual smoothness.

The tail of his shirt has worked loose and the fine linen cloth sticks to his chest and back. It's hard to look or sound innocent in such a state, what with your hands on your head, a rifle pointed at you and everyone looking down at you in the dust.

He says it anyway, how can he not? "I'm innocent. I didn't do it."

This poor devil's a far cry from the one who sweet-talked me into helping him.

"Pilar's the killer," he says. His face looks like something melted and then hardened back into shape. "She's a vampire. See that amulet around her neck? She won't let anyone near it because she can't survive without it—she's a monster. She keeps dirt from her tomb in it."

"What nonsense!" Pilar says, attempting a laugh.

"If you have nothing to hide, show us what's inside it," Esmi says.

People are nodding.

Old Anselmo says, "Yes, show us."

Others echo him.

"No!" Pilar says, her voice like ice and her bearing rigid as iron. "I will not pander to anyone's idle curiosity. The man's merely stalling for time. And the girl, too, because she's in love with him and desperate to save him. But he's a criminal, a killer, and their inventing absurd stories about me will not change anything."

"How are we to know they're lying, if you don't show us?" Anselmo calls out.

"How dare you question me, you worthless, shriveled old relic! How dare any of you! Go to your homes, all of you, and leave me in peace."

"If it's just a necklace, then show them the contents," Esmi reasons.

A murmur of agreement ripples through the plaza.

"Ingrates," Pilar hisses. "Don't you know there would be no Fuentespina without me? It would serve you right if I were to go away and leave you all to your own devices."

There's quiet, and more than a few bowed heads. To my surprise, it's Rosario who persists.

"*Doña* Pilar, with all due respect, we ask you to show us the contents of your necklace."

Reina stands close to her and nods.

Lourdes pipes in, "Yes, *señora*, with all due respect."

"Stop this," Pilar says, "or you will regret it."

She glares at Lourdes, at Rosario, even at Reina, and

they each fall back a step. Then she sweeps the whole plaza with her scorn.

"Every one of you—you'll all regret this."

Rosario nudges Lourdes, and Lourdes advances in small halting steps towards Pilar, as if walking a tightrope.

She has to pass by Iban and Esmi to get to Pilar. She casts nervous glances, first at Esmi, then at Pilar. And Adelfo? Adelfo she avoids all together.

" Milú, keep back," Adelfo says. "He's dangerous."

Lourdes is swayed, but for only a moment.

"Lourdes!" Adelfo snaps.

Lourdes shrinks into herself but, eyes downward, she continues forward.

Adelfo shouts at her, "Do you hear me?"

He starts to shift his grip on the rifle—he wants to grab her, pull her aside, but that would mean taking his eye off Iban, so he curbs the impulse. He halts, realigns his aim on Iban and tenses behind the rifle.

"Fool woman," Adelfo grumbles. "Danger everywhere..."

He shifts the walnut stock, holds it firmly against his right side to better use the bayonet. He braces it there with his left arm outstretched, his hand near the barrel. He tests his balance and points the blade at Iban's throat.

Iban closes his eyes and lowers his head, bringing his elbows onto his knees.

"Don't move. Don't even twitch," Adelfo says to Iban.

The people in the plaza have been moving in from the edges, like an incoming tide lapping at the shore—back and forth, back and forth, but ever closer. The *hijo de puta* can no longer ignore them. He swings his glance between them and Iban.

Lourdes soldiers on, closing the gap between her and Pilar.

"I won't tolerate this impudence." Pilar loses control of her voice—its pitch rises and she's almost shouting. But she does not draw back, either too proud or too scared to dash into the house and bolt the door. "This lack of respect is intolerable!"

Lourdes is quite close now. Everyone is watching her; everyone but Adelfo, who keeps his eye glued on Iban; and Iban, whose eyes are squeezed shut. Lourdes keeps her head down, her shoulders hunch forwards as if she had wings to fold in.

Pilar's jaw is clenched so tight it contorts her face. "Stop her," she commands. "*Don* Adelfo, have you no control over your wife?"

Adelfo glances in the direction of Pilar and Lourdes, but not as if he sees either of them. With the strain of the day, and the weight of the rifle, he's mumbling and his breathing is uneven.

Pilar huffs in disgust. She turns all her displeasure onto Lourdes. "What kind of woman are you—disgracing your husband, with the whole town as witness? Have you no shame? "

"I believe my Esmi," Lourdes says, and she stands a little straighter.

Esmi, watching her grandmother close in on Pilar, has been rubbing the side of her thumb over her lower lip, her brow wrinkled as a dried fig; but now her face softens in marvel as sees Lourdes stand up to Pilar, stand up for her; and Esmi's eyes shine.

Lourdes takes the final step that places her squarely in front of Pilar. She holds out her hand, palm up.

Everyone in Fuentespina holds their breath—the only movement in the square is the tremble in Lourdes' hand.

50

Well, I never thought I'd see the Ice Queen challenged, much less cornered.

Pilar stares at Lourdes' outstretched hand. The insolence of it, the threat of her secret being laid bare, it's all too much for her. She snaps. Baring her teeth, she hisses at Lourdes like a cat and drops into a semi-crouch. The border of her mantilla brushes the dust. She hisses again.

People let out startled cries and draw back. Lourdes freezes in place, too dumbstruck to flee, while Rosario and Reina duck behind Anselmo's cart. Esmi digs her fingers into Iban's shoulder and calls to her grandmother.

Then something happens to Pilar—she starts to blur at the edges. It's as if we're looking at her through smeared glasses or eyes bleary with tears. We all see it, but I'm the only one who knows what's happening—what's going to happen—and I want to run away screaming.

Adelfo doesn't see anything—not with his attention, locked as it is, on Iban. But when he hears the panic on every side of him, he swings his head and gun about trying to make sense of what is going on.

Iban puts a hand flat on a paving stone and plants one foot to stand. "See, you old fool, see!"

Adelfo's good eye narrows to a slit. In one smooth movement he throws himself forward and expertly brings the butt of the Mauser down on the side of Iban's head. Since everyone's staring at Pilar, nobody notices what's happening to Iban until he cries out and sinks back to the earth. The old *hijo de puta* swings his bayonet back into play, bringing the point of the blade to bear on Iban's chest. I am seized with horror. Some people shriek. Others cover their eyes. While Esmi, gripped by astonishment, is rooted in place, hands up as if caught in the instant before hiding her face.

The *hijo de la gran puta* grins. "Old fool am I?" Then his expression turns flat and menacing. "*Nadie me falta al respeto.*"

We await the lunge, all of us, as one—those who are appalled and those who want blood—all held together by the dull steel blade pinning white cloth to flesh.

A moment passes, and Iban is still alive.

Without thrusting the bayonet, Adelfo springs back. It would seem he wants to hang on to his trophy. It seems he's satisfied, for the moment, with having made his point.

"No one disrespects me or Fuentespina, least of all, *coño*, a degenerate like you."

Iban is alive, but not unscathed. Besides the blow to the head, Adelfo has slashed his shirt, scoring a thin line of red across his chest. Esmi cries out, and the suspense that's held everyone silent snaps. People draw sharp breaths all around. They curse, murmur, spur Adelfo on or cry out to God and the Virgin.

Adelfo sweeps the barrel of his gun back and forth in search of attackers. While Iban, doubled over, groans and holds his head. Esmi drops to her knees to aid him.

Esmi says Iban's name over and over, asking him if he's all right. He grabs her arm, brings her face close to his, his voice low and rasping. She shushes him and lifts him to sitting. Blood pours from his brow down the side of his head. He looks at it on his hands, stunned, bewildered.

"*Hijo de puta, viejo loco!*" Esmi yells at Adelfo.

Adelfo snarls back, muttering unintelligibly, his rifle trained once again on Iban.

Lourdes, Rosario and Reina all rush forward, surrounding Esmi and pulling her up and away from Iban. Iban's blood is on her hands, her shoes, her jeans and shirt.

And Pilar? Well, during Adelfo's attack, she's pulled herself together. She stands in front of the big house, like a ship's figurehead—good and solid—erect and haughty as ever.

But, then she sees Iban's blood on Esmi. Her wooden face twitches. Still, she raises her arms. She calls for quiet and pulls everyone's attention to her. We all look away from Iban, away from Adelfo. There she is, the great lady, as she should be. Many are already doubting that they've just seen her spitting and hissing. They must have imagined it. And the way she looked all blurry—well, their eyes aren't what they used to be.

"Once again," Pilar says, "we have *Don* Adelfo to thank for saving us."

"Saved you, you mean," one of the villagers calls out from the edge of the plaza. A few voices mutter their support, others their disapproval.

The old bastard does not seem to hear Pilar's praise. The attack has taken a toll. He's hunched over the gun, as if the weight of it will topple him.

"This is our Fuentespina, our Fuente de la Sagrada

Corona de Espinas de Nuestro Santísimo Señor de Vico," Pilar continues. "This ancient place is our cradle, our hallowed earth, our grave. Are we to allow the likes of him..." She points at Iban. "Are we to allow him to defile it? Are we to put ourselves at the mercy of outsiders?"

People fall silent—she's managed to cow them again. The old bastard's attack on Iban has frightened them, stirred memories. They've seen upheaval and turmoil from close up, they've lived with it and through it—they'll tell you it's best avoided. Besides, Pilar has spoken a truth about outsiders: you can't trust them.

I always knew Reina for a timid soul, but for the first time I see how fearful we all are.

"This man, this outlander," she gestures to Iban huddled on the ground, "is a murderer. And he will pay for his crime. But Rosa Esmeralda will stay with us. After all, she is *Don* Adelfo's granddaughter. She's one of us."

"No!" Esmi looks at the women who surround her, as if they are her jailers instead of her protectors.

Pilar catches sight of her, of her face resolute and stony. And then her eyes are drawn to Iban's blood on Esmi's white camisole. It shakes her concentration.

"We will bury my beloved stepson, and I...."

Blood seeps through the cloth of the sleeve that Iban's holding to the gash on his head and blood dribbles from the cut on his chest. Pilar can't keep her eyes off him. Her voice grows shaky, distracted.

"...I will go on. Life... That is, Fuentespina de Vico..."

Esmi has had enough. She pulls away from her watchdogs and launches herself at Pilar, who is caught unawares. Esmi makes a grab for the amulet. She yanks on the chain so hard that the links break, throwing both her and Pilar off balance. Pilar grabs at the doorway for support. Esmi staggers backward and the necklace flies from her hand as she lands on her rear end on the stones of the plaza. Pilar does not see Esmi lose hold of the treasure and she scrambles to reach her.

Meanwhile, the amulet has fallen at Reina's feet. She stares at it as if it's a mouse that's come to curl up and rest there, then she snatches it up.

Rosario shrieks. "Reina's got it!"

Pilar turns her attention to Reina, but too late. Reina opens the amulet and tips it upside down. Dirt the color of cocoa and ash falls on the stones.

Pilar's unearthly screech shivers in the air as she pushes Reina aside and clambers to recover what dirt she can. Clenching it tight, she raises her fists towards the dark clouds.

She turns on Esmi and bares her teeth.

Lourdes has rushed to Esmi where she fell and kneels next to her. She puts her arms around Esmi to protect her and Esmi clings to her.

"Implacable Goddess," Pilar hisses, "Nemesis." She brings her fists together and looks daggers at Esmi. "I'm not through yet."

The whole town watches as her body becomes hazy, a smudge that turns into a swirling vapor, but her twisted features, her burning eyes, continue to glare at Esmi. Esmi buries her face in Lourdes' arm.

Iban shouts, "No! Stop her!"

Adelfo sees the little tatter of fog that Pilar has become and starts panting in the strangest way—the air moves through his vocal cords creating an eerie keening noise. Shaking, he aims into the vapor.

The mist becomes smaller, denser, darker. There in midair it hardens and takes on edges. It's not the lynx I feared. It's something quite different. I can make out sharp talons, fierce eyes and brownish-black feathers. The murk that was Pilar becomes a very dark, very large vulture.

Everyone stares, dumbfounded, not believing what they are seeing.

The creature hangs in the air for a breath, then pulls back her powerful wings. With a jerky motion, the great scavenger flies off.

As if released from a spell, people cry out, turn to each other, fall on their knees in prayer.

"Stop her!" Iban screams. "For the love of God, somebody stop her!"

Adelfo, still pointing the Mauser vaguely upward, pulls the trigger. The noise of the blast is bone-chilling, but the bullet misses the monster vulture.

"Long live death!" the old man shouts. He fires again. "*Viva la muerte!*" It doesn't seem like he sees who or what he's shooting at anymore. "*Viva!*"

Reina, Rosario and Lourdes crowd around Esmi again, shielding her. Iban crawls toward them, but stops before reaching them.

Adelfo relaxes his rifle arm and the gun hangs by his side, level with the ground. He holds it now, it seems, with as much intent as a piece of firewood. He wipes his brow.

He may look spent, but beware. Nothing will pry his bony fingers off his duty as he sees it. Reina, Rosario and Lourdes know it. That's why they cluster around Esmi.

"Old woman," he calls to Lourdes, "step aside." His voice is tired, but there's menace in it.

"No, *viejo*," she says.

She hunkers over Esmi with more determination.

Adelfo takes a deep breath. He brings the Mauser back up into position and aims it at Iban. Iban rolls into a ball, covering his head with his arms and whimpering. Reina stands up. Lourdes and Rosario squeeze closer about Esmi.

Reina steps between Adelfo and Iban.

"Reina, what are you doing?" Rosario says.

Reina, *mi reina*, stares down at the stones of the plaza and speaks softly, "You're a bully, Adelfo. You always were."

"Get out of my way," Adelfo orders.

"I told Justino that," Reina says. "I said, 'That boy's going to cause you nothing but grief.'"

"Enough!"

"But Justino wouldn't listen to me. 'Fito's my kid brother,' he'd say, 'What do you want me to do?' Or he'd say, 'The kid's OK. He'll grow out of it.'" She glances up at Adelfo and then returns her eyes to the earth. Her hands are shaking—she clasps them together to make them still. "But you didn't grow out of it. And I'm the one who grieved. I'm the one who grieves still. You stole my life, Adelfo.

"No one will even let me say his name." She juts out her jaw. "Justino," she says.

"Shut up!"

"Justino." Her voice gains a bit of volume, but not much. Still, in the dead silence in the plaza, it's enough. "Justino," she repeats.

"Shut up!" Adelfo shouts again.

As if it were a planned distraction, as if they could hear my pleas, Rosario and Lourdes stand with Esmi to move her very slowly toward safety.

"*Hijo de puta.*" Reina's eyes meet Adelfo's. " My Justino existed. Justino's blood, your brother's blood, is right here." Reina points at her feet.

Adelfo trains the Mauser on Reina.

"I'll shoot you, you red hag."

Rosario leaves Esmi to Lourdes and goes to stand, if not at Reina's side, a few feet away.

"Shoot me, then," Reina says. Her hands are still clasped together against their trembling.

"*Don* Adelfo," Rosario cajoles. "Fito. Pay her no mind. She doesn't know what she's saying."

Don Adelfo turns his attention, and the gun, to Rosario.

Rosario's hands flutter to her breast. "Adelfo. It's me, Charo, your old friend."

Lourdes is still trying to ease Esmi, a step at a time, toward the edge of the square, but Esmi stops near Iban. He sits alone on the stones, in a daze. She glances between him and Adelfo. She wants him to grab the chance to find cover.

I concentrate with all my might, trying to put words in her mind, "Leave him—save yourself!" but it does no good.

She reaches out and touches him lightly on the shoulder. She gets his attention, but not in the way she expects. Iban doesn't look up, instead he cries out in terror.

The old bastard, damn him, swivels and lifts the gunsight to his eye. He shoots.

Iban's body jolts. Then it slackens into a heap.

"Iban!" Esmi screams. She drops to her knees next to him. Her face next to his, he murmurs to her. Then he's dead.

Esmi pulls back—her face contorted, her arms outstretched, fingers spread wide as if trying to rein in her horror.

"That's one," Adelfo says.

He turns the gun onto Esmi and pulls back the bolt.

Reina, Rosario, Lourdes and I all roar, "No!"

Everything is happening at once.

Yelling, Reina and Rosario charge Adelfo from the side, jarring the barrel of the old Mauser off target, just as Lourdes throws herself in front of Esmi and the *hijo de la gran puta* pulls the trigger.

Lourdes cries out and falls.

Rosario grabs the rifle from Adelfo while he's still off balance. Reina tries to yank it from Rosario's hands, but Rosario holds on tight.

Esmi throws her arms around her grandmother. Lourdes winces and clutches her wounded shoulder.

51

“That day”—the voice drops an octave—“*el día ese.*” That's how the people of Fuentespina refer to what happened. But only if they absolutely have to. Heaven forbid they talk out loud and straight on—it might bring more calamity down on their grey and balding heads.

After all, things are bad enough as it is, what with the big house lying vacant and the village having lost a few more of its breathing citizens. To the handful who remain, the truth must be as plain to see as the bullet holes in the fountain: the Fates are through with Fuentespina de Vico. No more stays of execution.

Time for a last meal, confession, maybe a cigarette.

Fuentespina, dead. *Dios mío.* What will that mean to them? To me? Where does the mesh and mishmash of the village end and the lone soul begin?

I keep thinking back on something my mum used to say, devout anarchist that she was.

“That's the thing, Nardita,” she'd say, “with institutions, and movements, too, whether it's the Church or prisons or Communists. They're all like the wolf *Tío Juan*—they want you body and soul, but unlike *El Amigo*, they claim it's for a greater good.”

Whenever she'd tell me these things—even when she

was old and flat-out delighted she'd out-lived Franco—she'd first look carefully to see we were alone, and then she'd speak in a low voice, like a lullaby,

"But, I ask you this, *hija,* how could there be a greater good in trampling any human being? Each carries the divine spark, each as unique as the whorl on his fingertip, like a snowflake in flesh and bones."

So now I wonder, can a single snowflake be lifted from the drift? And what about the snowflake that lands in the ocean, or on the warm cheek of a child?

Like slow clockwork, the grocery-mobile pulls up by the fountain, just as it has every 15 days for several years now. The man honks his horn three times to announce he's open for business. He lumbers out of the cab, his belly hanging over his belt, and with the help of a pole, he lifts the side flaps to reveal the stores inside. It's the first time he's come since *"el día ese,"* and people wander out of their houses as if in a trance, stunned by this normal thing come back into their lives. They straggle into the plaza with their baskets and plastic shopping bags to buy the usual: bread, olive oil, dried cod, onions. The grocery man peers down at his customers, the familiar faces. He's always taken their reserve as a personal challenge, determined to win them over with his good humor. Today he finds them even more standoffish than usual, which is saying a lot.

"Where's my number-one customer?" he asks. "Where's *Señorita* Narda?"

I'm surprised, and pleased, he's thought to ask about me.

Old Anselmo is the first to meet the man's gaze. He shakes his head sadly, tells him I moved to the city.

"What about the big house, then? Who's taking care of it?"

"The family's gone to their villa on the Costa del Sol for the season," Anselmo says.

The grocery man nods. I can see concern flit across his face, the calculations of loss of business. "What about *Señora...* You know. What's-her-name?"

Anselmo feigns puzzlement.

"You know, the lady with the green shawl and the big cross necklace. Where's she today? Not under the weather, I hope."

"Ah," Anselmo nods, "she's visiting relatives for a few weeks."

The man smiles, "Well, that's nice for her then."

Rosario, listening at a distance, frets to Valentín, wondering how much sales can fall off before the man crosses Fuentespina off his list of stops.

The grocery man checks his watch with a sigh. He lowers the side boards and latches them, climbs into the cab and drives away.

With the grocery-mobile gone again, the village seems more desolate than ever. I find myself looking for a flash of red silk, listening for the click of blue stilettos on stone—but though I miss Esmi, the love I feel for the survivors here keeps me good company.

That snap to the air about me—that prickliness on the skin that I took to be Teresa—seems to be gone now. She and her vexation and anger are off my back. Just like that. Can't say I miss her.

About now Esmi and Lourdes will be on the train racing toward Madrid, not that they are in any hurry—the train goes the speed it goes. The bruises on Esmi's neck have faded, and the red scarf is stuffed in Lourdes' pocket. Any wounds Esmi carries now are on the inside. As for Lourdes, I imagine her with her arm in its navy-blue denim sling. One moment she stares out the train window with blank eyes and sagging shoulders, and the next she smoothes her skirt with her good hand. When she reaches over to pat Esmi on the knee, Esmi takes her hand and gives it a squeeze and tells her everything will be OK.

They'll be silent most of the trip, but as they draw closer to Madrid they'll get more talkative. Esmi will suggest places in the city to show Lourdes. Lourdes will ask what her days will be like. Where will she shop for food? What time will Esmi leave for work in the morning? Esmi reminds her that they'll call *Tío* Ramón in Australia, maybe arrange a visit—she'll be able to meet her grandkids. A smile will tug at the corner of Lourdes mouth. Australia, she mouthes and raises her eyebrows. She wonders, what if the children don't speak Spanish? Then she'll tell Esmi again everything she knows about her exotic Australian grandchildren.

"*El día ese,*" Anselmo had remembered enough battlefield first aid to tend to Lourdes—the bullet had torn through her upper arm. He still had an emergency field dressing kit from the war. and a bottle of aguardiente. He cleaned the wound and staunched the bleeding, but Esmi wanted her taken care of properly. At first Lourdes said no—wouldn't the doctor have to report a bullet wound?—but then she gave in. So Anselmo borrowed Pilar's Land Rover. "If you can drive a tractor, you can drive anything," he said, and he chauffeured Esmi and Lourdes to a hospital in Badajoz.

Esmi had warned Lourdes to say as little as possible to the doctor, so she was a bit taken aback when her grandmother launched into a story about a fox getting into her chicken coop, about her grabbing the rifle from its corner in the kitchen to scare it off, and her slipping and the gun going off. The doctor looked doubtful. Then tears came to Lourdes' eyes as she told him the fox got every single hen, every one, blood and feathers everywhere. The doctor nodded sympathetically, then shot a wry smile over her head at Esmi and patted Lourdes' good shoulder.

Esmi called Tony from the hospital waiting room in Badajoz. He launched into a litany of grouses about the flat—the rent was due; the newspaper snatched two days in a row; the *portera,* insolent—and Esmi broke in to ask if he'd seen Lucho or heard anything about him.

Tony reported that, out of curiosity, he'd had a girlfriend check on him at the bank. She was told he'd quit suddenly, and rumor had it he'd left the capital.

"But, where is he? What's happened to him?" Esmi said.

"I don't care," he said. "And by the way, my wrist is not fine, thanks for not asking. It hurts like hell."

Of course, he had not asked after her injuries, either.

"Look, one of the reasons I'm calling is to tell you that I'm bringing my grandmother home with me."

"Your grandmother! There's not really room for visitors."

"To tell the truth, I'm bringing her back to live with me. That's why I'm calling, to give you a heads up."

Tony said, "You're kicking me out? Over the phone? This is the thanks I get for saving your life?"

I think Esmi still gave her mother the credit for saving her. And of course Lourdes had saved her life too, but she wasn't about to get into all that.

"You never know," Tony said, "Maybe the old girl and I will hit it off."

In the background, the tv in the flat blared: gunshots and squealing tires.

Esmi smiled. "You mean you think you can charm her. Well, I know my *abuela*. She'd make you pick up after yourself and keep regular hours. And you'd have to bring your girlfriends home for approval."

He made a shuddering sound.

Esmi wasn't entirely sure any of this was true—she knew from her mum that Lourdes had treated *Tío* Ramón like a princeling, and Esmi wouldn't put it past her to cater to Tony as well.

"She wouldn't rest until you were properly engaged."

"Is that what's going to happen to you?" he said.

Lourdes was sitting, waiting at a distance. Esmi caught her eye and they smiled at each other.

"Look, Tony, I need to make a fresh start. I want to take care of her."

"Fine," he said, doing his darnedest to sound hurt.

"She needs me right now," she said, but really it was she who needed her grandmother.

Outside a siren sounded. An announcement in some kind of hospital code crackled over the intercom. The elevator chimed loudly.

"Where are you?" Tony said.

"It's a long story, and this is a long distance call."

"It's a pain in the ass to move."

"I know. I'm sorry. Look, we'll be home in a couple days."

They had a funeral to attend before they left Fuentespina for good.

"I can't wait."

"And Tony, could you clean up the apartment a little? I don't want my poor grandma to have a heart attack."

Tony grunted.

"By the way, do I still have a job?" she asked.

"As far as I know."

In the village these days, an endless topic of conversation is whether Lourdes will stay in Madrid or come home to Fuentespina. Valentín says that she won't come back until old Adelfo keels over, and then just for the funeral. Rosario's money is on her coming back soon, and for good. "Habits of a lifetime die hard," she says.

You can say that again. Look at me. I'm still here.

For some people, like the boy, Roberto, they die and "poof," they're gone—no hanging about for them. For others of us, letting go of all that weighs us down is a slower process. And letting go of our own importance? Trickier yet.

The afterlife, it turns out, is not the same unendingness one is led to believe. Little shifts take place—revamps and nuances. Like at first I was bouncing all over the place. Then mostly I hovered about the plaza, looking down into every corner of the village —I was beginning to feel as if the plaza were my new body. But that's changed, too. Now it's more like Fuentespina is my new skin—like a membrane between me and the universe. But there's a worry. If Fuentespina is doomed, and it clearly is, what will happen to me when it is no more?

"*El día ese.*"

"That day", as soon as Anselmo announced that Lourdes would be OK, a town meeting flared into being on the spot, the first since before the war. But since decisions had to be made, and no one in the big house was giving orders, they figured out how to do it. First order of business: my burial, and the burial of Roberto and Iban.

But how to explain Roberto's death? They would need to come up with a story that side-stepped the issue of vampires—nobody wanted outsiders snooping around, sneering at them, telling the world they were a bunch of hicks, and batty to boot.

"We all thought that dead fellow was the killer," Rosario said. "Let's stick with that."

Old Anselmo said, "I suppose we could."

"Sure," some one said. "A psychopathic killer who

fancied himself a vampire. Why not?"

Someone pointed out that that might spark the imagination of reporters in the city, and who knew where that would end?

Valentín said, "What if the bodies were put in the big house?"

"What good would that do?" Rosario huffed.

"Well, if the house burned down..."

"*Válgame Dios*!" Rosario was horrified.

"A fire like that, it could get out of hand," Anselmo said. "Could burn down half the village."

"Why does anyone have to know anything?"

"Yes, what business is it of anyone's?" several people agreed.

Wasn't the best thing to keep quiet, keep the authorities out of it—no *guardia civil* snooping around, thank you very much?

"Because even if they believed us..." Rosario said.

"Which they wouldn't," Reina said softly.

"They would never be able to bring *Doña* Pilar to justice."

"Mum's the word, then," Anselmo said.

"What about *Doña* Pilar? What if someone comes looking for her?"

"If anyone asks," old Anselmo said, "Pilar and her stepson are on an extended trip."

Everyone nodded in agreement: no outsiders. When it comes to secrets, Fuentespina knows what it's about.

So about the burial. After a brief theological discussion,

everyone agreed that even though the church had been deconsecrated, the graveyard must still be holy ground—their dead were buried there. Rosario got her knickers in a knot at the idea that there would be no priest to preside over the service. So Valentín drove her to Mérida in Pilar's Land Rover. They found the rest home where old Father Patricio resided and invited him out for the day. Father Patricio had been our last priest—a genial, slovenly man, already past retirement age when he first arrived in Fuentespina and sent to us because he'd been out of favor with his bishop. Father Patricio was delighted to be sprung from the home, happy—head bobbing—to speed down the highway and bounce over the familiar dirt road to the village.

Meanwhile, others had cut through the chains on the door of the church and cleaned the sanctuary. Reina hung my mother's crucifix behind the altar, and Rosario, before she' left for Mérida, handed over her family Bible, since it was large and showy and gilt-edged. She'd also produced some communion wafers she'd confiscated when the church was closed—it hadn't seemed right to her that the village be left with nothing. Old Anselmo went to the big house and brought back a candelabra (silver from Mexico), an antique goblet (gold from Peru) and a fine white cloth (lace from Belgium) for the altar—the relics of Empire, he called them. He also went out and picked some wild flowers and plopped them in a jar. Others with trees in their patios brought in lemon and cherry blossoms.

I know I wasn't the only one being buried, but my heart still bubbled and bloomed at their efforts.

I've come to see my guilt for the parasite it is—a thing feeding on me, a tapeworm in my body and spirit. And in a way, hateful though it is, I see I coveted it, whispering to me as it seemed to do, "You, only you." Well, no more. My guilt, always so ample and sticky, now seems to be breaking down and seeping away. Good riddance is all I can say.

And with it, so goes the aloneness. Even though I might as well be bound and gagged in a floating straight jacket for all the effect I have on my living ones, I feel a connectedness, a downright chumminess with them like never before. It's a new and wonderful feeling. It's like coming home after a long day in the groves, all grimy, muscles in knots, and slipping into a hot bath—one I didn't have to haul and heat the water for first and one I didn't have to wait in line to share. It's that good, like soaking in steaming, clean water on a cold night.

Don't get me wrong, fear and guilt and loneliness still trail after me—this is Fuentespina after all, not heaven—but less and less like hungry beasts and more like my own shadow. And shadows shrink as the sun gets higher in the sky.

The bullet had pierced Iban's lung "*el día ese.*" In his final plea to Esmi—fighting for breath and driven by his terror of becoming a vampire—he'd sketched what she should do.

"Fountain..." he'd managed to whisper. "I beg you." Then his last words, "Save me from Pilar..."

Esmi was determined. Iban had died in her arms, hadn't he. Shot by her own grandfather. And how could she leave him, or anyone, to Pilar's mercy? The thought turned her stomach—she could at least deliver him from that fate.

"*El día ese,*" no one else was much interested in Iban's fate. Esmi had to harangue them until they listened. There was no time to waste unless they wanted another vampire in their midst—nightfall would soon be upon them.

Finally old Anselmo spoke up. The girl was right. They should act without delay. Not for the outsider's sake, but for their own.

"But we don't have any holy water," Rosario said. "Don't you need holy water?"

Anselmo said no, and explained what needed to be done. Rosario blanched, and she wasn't the only one.

"Is that right, miss?" he said to Esmi. And Esmi nodded.

She went to the fountain and brought back the canvas-wrapped bundle Iban had left there. Inside were a silver-tipped stake and a mallet. No one volunteered, so my poor Esmi took the stake and knelt next to Iban. She looked about her and saw she was the only one present who had known him. She took a deep breath and placed the point next to his wound and over his heart. She closed her eyes and didn't move. I don't imagine knowing that someone you've loved was a rat makes mutilating his body any easier. People waited, shifted their weight and shuffled their feet. It was when Rosario started to mutter the rosary in Latin that Esmi dropped her hand to her side, the one grasping the mallet. She hung her head, her face wet with tears.

Reina came and placed a hand on Esmi's shoulder and nodded encouragement. Esmi set down the stake and the mallet. She rubbed her hands dry on her jeans and placed the stake once more on Iban's chest. Her eyes scanned the sky for the sun but it had already sunk below the rooflines. She pounded the stake with the mallet. Blood sprayed her face, and Iban's body spasmed and emitted a heart-wrenching scream of pain. Esmi clambered away in recoil and dropped the mallet in horror.

Anselmo stepped forward and picked up the mallet. Reina put her arms around Esmi. They huddled together on the ground and Esmi covered her ears and buried her face in Reina's shoulder as Anselmo finished the job.

Iban's body lay lifeless at last. And not a minute too soon—the sun was already sagging into the horizon. Soon they would have only twilight left. Reina wiped Esmi's face with the sleeve of her ragged sweater and petted her arm.

"His head," Esmi said, her voice hoarse, hardly more than a whisper.

Esmi couldn't have done the decapitation. And Anselmo and the others, who had finally taken pity on her, wouldn't have let her. When it came to butchering animals, they had the the tools for it, and the experience, although they didn't come out and say it like that.

Rosario told Esmi that the men would take care of it, that Lourdes needed her, and Esmi let herself be led away.

Coffin making: a skill not wasted in Fuentespina. The plain wooden boxes were lugged into the church of Our Lady before *Padre* Patricio arrived.

Three closed coffins. It probably wouldn't be the first secret burial he'd presided over, only this time he didn't know it was secret. He didn't even know what decade it was. Rosario gave him a sherry, or two or three, and Valentín told him the dead were victims of a communist landmine.

Valentín tolled the death knell on the church bells—the clanging reverberating, slow and doleful, through the silent streets. It was the first time the bells had been heard since the church was desanctified.

All of Fuentespina gathered in their usual pews. Except for the old bastard. Everyone had agreed it would be best to keep him in the dark about the service.

First the old priest listened to confessions, Anselmo stood near the confessional and as the confessants entered he urged them to be brief. *Padre* Patricio said the Mass with hardly a hitch. It took the fittest of them three trips to haul the coffins to the graveyard and lower them into the ground. It was awkward work for the old people, grueling really. The day was dark again—the clouds thick and the air heavy since "*el día ese.*" Rosario put my mother's crucifix on top of my coffin. *Padre* Patricio said the necessary words graveside. And Esmi cried. It truly hurt to see her so sad, but it did warm the innermost cockles of my heart to know that at least a few of her tears that day were for me. The wind rose. People pitched in and shoveled dirt into the graves.

There's something very cold and final about burial. I know that's stating the obvious, but it's always more of a blow than you expect, seeing your loved one tucked into the ground. So watching one's own body, nailed in its casket and lowered into a dirt hole... *Ni hablar*. It's chilling, isn't it—

the stuff of nightmares. Irrevocable. Not that I had any illusions before. But still, it's the final of the final.

Now what?

As they were filing out of the cemetery, rain started to fall in plops. Reina's quiet weeping gave way to body-shaking sobs, and she bolted from the line to go bear witness in the plaza. But Rosario caught her. She held her tight by both arms and talked quietly. Who knew Rosario could talk quietly?

"I've seen the blood, too, Reina, when it rains—Justino's and the others. But that was years ago. It's seeped in too deep now for mere rain to ever raise it. The dirt between the stones—it's Fuentespina, pure Fuentespina. If there's any blood now, it's that intruder's and Lourdes', and maybe a drop or two of Narda's."

Reina pointed towards the plaza.

Rosario shook her head. "Justino's at peace, Reina, if you'll let him.

"He was a good man, your Justino. When his parents died, even though he was not much more than a boy, he stepped up. He took on the house and the responsibility of his brother. So young. He didn't deserve to die, not like that. I'm sorry. I'm sorry I never told you that before."

Reina hung her head and whimpered, but she let Rosario sweep her along with the others to the big house.

Rosario is in front of her house, scolding Valentín for something as if he were still a little boy. Her eyes are magnified by her thick glasses. Old Anselmo walks by and Valentín lifts a hand in greeting—a gentle chop of the air. He looks back at his sister. He tilts his head and gives her a sweet smile. She huffs in exasperation and goes inside.

A spread of food had been organized and everyone had more than a few glasses of sherry and brandy from Pilar's *bodega*. Since nobody really knew Roberto, shut away as he was in the big house; and Iban was a stranger; I turned out to be the belle of the ball, so to speak. People—people unaccustomed to showing their emotion, people whose regard is not easily given, people I'd known all my life and thought of as strangers—said nice things about me, and things that made me realize that they really did know me. It makes you wonder. Here I'd fancied myself as leading a separate life—fenced off, free-standing and self-contained—when, as it happens, I was as entwining and entangled as any philodendron out of control.

After everyone went home, Esmi locked the house with my keys and gave them to Rosario.

The sun rises and the light glints on the iron cross atop the church. During the day each stone in the plaza absorbs its quota of radiance.

The sun sets behind the church.

At night the air sloughs off its heat, becomes crisp with stars. The stones pay back their borrowed heat a coin at a time until their pockets are empty. When the sun rises they will be cool to the touch.

"And the old bastard?" you might ask.

He sits in his patio. He no longer listens to the radio—the batteries are dead. He cocks his head and listens to the breeze, or he lifts his nose and sniffs the air. People take turns taking him food. He mutters a lot. Sometimes you can make out a word here and there. Sometimes that word is "Lourdes," sometimes it's "evil."

One day he asks Rosario if she's seen his wife.

"She's fine," Rosario says.

"I didn't ask if she was fine. I asked if you'd seen her. She should be here by now." He squints at the sun. "It's lunchtime isn't it? How long does it take to deliver eggs. Where is she?"

"Adelfo Luis Tena Prieto," Rosario scolds. "You shot her and she went to Madrid with your granddaughter."

"Madrid?"

"Madrid."

"Where'd she get a fool idea to go there? Place is cram-packed with commies and degenerates."

"You shot her. You can't expect her to overlook a thing like that."

"Hmph."

She shoves a bowl of stew at him.

"Did I mean to?" he asks.

"Just eat."

He shrugs and slurps a spoonful. "It is you, isn't it, Charo?"

She nods.

"I ask because you look so old."

Rosario scowls.

"What will I do without her?"

"I don't know, Fito. Pray? It wouldn't be a bad idea."

It's not a bad idea, but if you ask me, it would take a sledgehammer of a prayer to clean his black old soul.

A stork flies over the village, white and black against the blue sky. It circles back, glides and alights on the *campanario*. It looks about, then flies away.

Reina has taken over the care of the chickens. She carries the eggs home and hands them out to people who come to her door asking for them. They call her name gently, because knocks on the door still terrify her. One day Anselmo calls, "*Señorita*," and she corrects him.

"Just Reina, *Don* Anselmo, Reina dry and simple."

"That doesn't seem right."

"I'm used to it," she says softly.

"OK, *hermana*," he says. "See you next time."

Sister. She blushes a little, but she doesn't correct him.

And me?

Just when I'd been thinking this—Fuentespina de Vico —might be my eternity, things change. I change. Each day I feel more removed from these people, farther away. The sun ever higher in the sky, my shadow of guilt ever fading.

Is this what Pilar felt toward us? Distant? I can see now how she might feel superior to our fly speck of a life. But me? I don't feel superior. I feel immense love for each of them, and pity. Pity for their struggle. I long to lift their shame, their regrets, as I feel mine lifting from me, bit by bit, scale by scale. I'm even starting to feel a hint of a twinge of pity for the old *hijo de puta*.

At first, after I died, when I walked amongst them I felt their sighs on my face. Later it was as if I was looking down through their roofs, seeing into more than one house at a time. Now I can take in the whole village at a glance, watch the ebb and flow of its life. It breathes as one entity, only they don't know it.

My guilt feels lighter and lighter. I don't think I'll be here for long…

Epilogue

Extremadura, Spain

The wind teases the remains of a village in the flat expanse of steppeland. It thrums on the broken walls and skids over the stones of the toppled bell wall of a church. Pieces of masonry and other debris spiral out from the knob of the fountain in what was once a small plaza. Centuries of bodies rest underground, most buried properly, but some hastily under cover of night. One skeleton lies above the earth, in what was once the patio of a modest house, the bones scattered by scavengers and half-hidden by dirt, the dust mounded like snowdrifts. In the sky, waves of cranes fly a millennial route toward their winter homes.

A quarter mile away, a caterpillar track loader digs and scoops in a shallow pit, working the earth for the foundation of a house. The operator shakes his head at the future owner's choice—it's a lonely spot, a place that feels wrong, but once the house is built, no doubt others will follow.

His machine is old and simple—feeble headlights and no glass in the cabin to protect the man from the wind. Soon the horizon, like a band of sediment below a purple, cloudless sky, will turn reddish-orange with the sinking sun. He casts his eye across the empty plain and shudders. He has just made the machine bite into the earth and must finish moving the load before he quits for the day. He wants to be back in town before the sun goes down and the temperature drops.

And then there are the stories—strange, scrambled; rubbish, of course. He's not a superstitious man. But still...

He doesn't know how to put it into words, has never tried: he works with the earth—some is rich with promise and some is empty and lifeless, and then there is this other, like around here, where the earth makes your hair stand on end, makes you look over your shoulder.

Against his will he envisions a large beast—the one known in these parts as "Tío Juan", "The Other One", "El Amigo"—slinking through the ruins of the old village nearby. He doesn't name the animal, even in his thoughts—a foolish habit he's learned from his mother, because she warns, some wolves are more than wolves, and naming the beast will summon its presence. And with it its power, its evil.

He turns off the machine.

The man has spooked himself. His fingers are cold. As he climbs down from the machine he fumbles the key. It drops into the loose red-brown soil and he curses as the sun touches the earth.

Acknowledgements

Thank you to the members of my writing group who've read many iterations of this story. Karee Hall and Nancy Zaffaro come first to mind, being there at the beginning many years ago when the story started out as a play, and then later Karen Lewis, who always holds my feet to the fire of clarity. But as I write this, I am thinking of Susan Schnell who died in 2016. She was a poet to the marrow, a quiet, insistent force for truth and beauty. Besides helping me with medical questions, she was always encouraging, always reflective and kind, and I miss her.

I am grateful to many authors of books on the Spanish Civil War, and to the many generous souls who put their passions on the internet for the rest of us to learn from, enthusiasms that for me included everything from the birds of Extremadura to Spanish Civil War uniforms.

I've studied with many wonderful teachers over the years. I would like to thank my extraordinary high school writing and literature teachers in Centralia, WA, Noreen Higgins (d.2017) and Jean Bluhm, and especially Nancy Lester of Central Washington University. It makes me nervous naming them, because I still strive to measure up to their high standards.

Thank you, my first readers, editors and proofreaders, Molly Best Tinsley, Maggie Brown, Susannah White, Meg Hayertz and Brian Jelgerhuis. Hard-working Meg, who cultivates magic, is an inspiration, and Brian, besides being endlessly encouraging and supportive, as if that weren't enough, is a wonderful graphic designer and enormously generous with his time.

About the Author

Leslie Hayertz was born in Washington State. She earned a BA ed. at Central Washington University, and an MA in Spanish at Middlebury College. She teaches Spanish in the Portland Metro area.